Marrying Caroline

Marrying Caroline

SEAL of Protection
Book 3.5

By Susan Stoker

Table of Contents

Acknowledgements

Missy: Thank you for "making" me write Wolf and Caroline's story. You decided I'd cheated the readers out of the emotional satisfaction of seeing Caroline get married, and you were right. I hope I've done both Ice and Wolf justice.

Chapter One

C AROLINE OPENED THE door to *Aces Bar and Grill* and looked around for Matthew. Seeing him sitting at their usual table with his entire SEAL team as well as Fiona and Alabama, Caroline headed that way.

Waving at their usual waitress, Jess, as she passed, Caroline pushed her way through the crowd to her man. The bar seemed unusually crowded tonight, but as usual, Matthew didn't wait for her to get to him. Caroline smiled as Matthew made his way to her. It was almost annoying how the crowd seemed to part in front of him magically, but Caroline couldn't blame the patrons. Matthew was an imposing force.

Caroline analyzed her man as he came toward her. He was tall, around six foot three and had the look of a man that didn't take any shit. Matthew was wearing jeans and a short sleeve T-shirt that was just big enough to give him room to move, but didn't have any extra material either. Caroline could see his arms bulging as he moved. She stopped and let Matthew come to her.

She'd never get over how lucky she was that somehow this man, this wonderfully handsome, sexy, brave, intense man, was with *her*.

"Hey, Ice. Missed you."

Caroline smiled. "We saw each other two hours ago."

"I know, as I said. I missed you." Matthew "Wolf" Steel put his hand on the side of Caroline's face and leaned into her.

"I missed you too," Caroline admitted huskily. She loved Matthew's hands on her. He always made her feel so cherished.

Wolf captured Caroline's lips with his. Not caring they were standing in the middle of a bar and were being jostled by people passing them, Wolf showed Caroline just how much he'd missed her.

Caroline's arms came up to clasp Matthew at the back of his head and she lost herself in his kiss. She could feel her body softening and readying itself for his loving, but luckily, before she did something that would embarrass herself so much she'd never be able to step foot in *Aces* again, Matthew pulled his head back.

"God, Ice. You're amazing. Come on." Wolf let go of Caroline's face and grabbed one of her hands that had crept around to rest on his chest. "I ordered for you, everyone else is here."

"Hi guys!"

"Hey!"

"Hi, Caroline."

"Yo, Ice."

The greetings were heartfelt and sincere. Caroline had never felt so lucky. Not only had she gained a wonderful man when she moved in with Matthew, but she'd gained his teammates as brothers. Now that Christopher had found Alabama and Hunter had married Fiona, she also had some sisters and best friends too.

Matthew settled Caroline into a chair next to him, and they both sat.

"What took you so long?" Fiona complained to Caroline, smiling to take the sting out of her words.

"We were having a breakthrough at work. There was this compound that we've been testing for-freaking-ever and we finally figured out how to..."

Wolf put his hand over Caroline's mouth and stopped her words. "You're off the clock, Ice. No shop-talk tonight. We're here to relax, not to hear about your chemist stuff."

Everyone laughed.

Caroline mock glared at Matthew at the same time she stuck out her tongue and licked his palm sensuously. She watched as his eyes went molten and she suddenly wished they were anywhere but there.

Wolf leaned into her, took his hand away from Caroline's mouth and put it on her thigh. "You'll pay for that tonight, Ice."

Caroline could feel the goose bumps that rose on her flesh at the feel of his words against her ear. "I'm counting on it, Matthew."

Wolf kissed Caroline on the temple and straightened, not moving his hand from her leg. He was the luckiest son of a bitch in the world. He'd never forget how scared he'd been when he watched the video of Caroline being tortured. He'd never forget how he'd held his breath praying he wouldn't have to watch her execution. The terrorists had hoped sending the tape would make the SEAL team lose their cool, but they were too well trained for that. If anything, it had solidified their determination to get Caroline back alive and to take the terrorists down.

Wolf knew he owed Cookie a debt greater than the man would ever know. Cookie had tried to tell Wolf the debt was paid when they had to cut short a mission to get back to the States and to Cookie's woman, Fiona, when she was in trouble, but Wolf knew he'd never feel the debt would ever be paid in full.

Hunter "Cookie" Knox had been the one who kept Caroline alive when she'd been thrown overboard in the ocean. He'd been the one that had held the life-saving oxygen to her face and swam them away from the terrorist boat moments before it had blown up.

Wolf didn't begrudge Caroline the close friendship she had with Cookie. And the two were close. While Wolf was a possessive man, he couldn't bring himself to care in this case. In any other situation if a man dared to touch Caroline, Wolf would be all over him, but not Cookie.

There was only one thing about their relationship that bothered him, but Wolf knew he'd most likely never bring it up with her. It wasn't worth the angst it would bring either Caroline or Cookie. Wolf would just have to suck it up and deal with it.

Tonight was the night Wolf hoped would be the night he'd make the first step toward making Caroline his, officially. He'd asked all his friends here tonight because he was going to ask Caroline to marry him. Wolf knew how much Caroline's friends meant to her, and he meant to surround her with as much love as he could, before he asked her to wear his ring.

"How are you doing, Fiona?" Caroline asked gently, leaning toward her friend. She'd never forget how scared she'd been for her when Fiona had experienced a flashback of her kidnapping and had fled Riverton.

"I'm good, Caroline. I've progressed to seeing Dr. Hancock every other week now and honestly, I'm feeling pretty good about everything. I know I'll never truly forget what happened to me in Mexico, but anytime it gets...hard, Hunter's there."

Caroline reached over the table and squeezed Fiona's hand. "Good. Hunter'll take care of you. I have no doubt."

The two women shared a glance full of understanding. Fiona understood the relationship between her husband and Caroline, and supported it wholeheartedly.

"Hey, guys! You all ready for your food now?" Their waitress stood at the side of the table. Her long black hair was pulled back into a low ponytail that cascaded down her back.

"Thanks, Jess," Benny said, looking up at their pretty waitress. "We were just waiting on Caroline, but we're all here now."

Jess nodded and turned and headed back to the bar, obviously to tell the cook their food could be served up.

"So, what's the occasion?" Caroline asked, looking around the table.

"Can't we all just get together and hang out?" Sam "Mozart" Reed asked with a smirk.

"Well, yeah," Caroline said somewhat sarcastically, "but usually when we do, you guys," she motioned to the unattached SEALs around the table, "bring some skank with you and pretend you're dating her instead of just feeding her before you bring her home to..."

"Hey!" Faulkner "Dude" Cooper interrupted complaining. "That's not fair. We *are* dating the women we bring to dinner."

"Yeah, for the night."

The men turned in shock at the words. Alabama wasn't one to speak her mind, but every now and then she'd lay out a zinger, as she'd just done.

Christopher "Abe" Powers leaned into his girlfriend and chuckled. "That's my girl," he said with affection.

"Jesus, you women are lethal," Kason "Benny" Sawyer complained. "You bitch when we date someone, you bitch because you don't like her, then you bitch when we break up with her."

"It's because we care about you," Caroline said seriously. "You all deserve better than people like Michele and Adelaide. If you'd just listen to us you'd realize we can see through those skanks in a heartbeat."

"Just because you all," Mozart gestured around the table at his teammates with their women, "have found each other doesn't mean the rest of us are all fired up to do the same."

"Bullshit." Caroline said matter-of-factly. "I think you all want what we have, and that's okay because you all deserve it. But if you continue to only look at women you meet in this bar and who only want to spend a night with a Navy SEAL, you'll never find it. You have to open your eyes and see the other women around you. The good women. Take a look at the ones who you might never 'see' otherwise."

Just as Caroline finished her impassioned speech,

Jess came up to the table with a tray loaded down with food. "Hope I'm not interrupting…" she said hesitantly.

"Of course not," Benny told her gruffly, obviously glad for the break in the conversation.

Food was passed around the table and everyone dug in. After thirty minutes of good food and good conversation, everyone was relaxed against their chairs.

"So no one ever answered me. Is tonight a special occasion or what?" Caroline smiled at her friends. She didn't really care why they were there, she was happy being around her friends. She turned to look at Matthew as he stood up from the table. His hand had been on her leg throughout dinner. Of course he hadn't been still either. His thumb had caressed her thigh rhythmically and had Caroline squirming in her seat.

Caroline watched in surprise as Matthew went to his knees next to her chair.

"What the hell, Matthew? Get up."

Wolf swallowed hard. He shouldn't be as nervous as he was, but he couldn't help it. "I love you, Caroline Martin. More than anything in my life." He took both her hands in his and brought them up to his mouth. He kissed the back of both hands before putting them back in her lap. He didn't let go, and could feel Caroline trembling.

"I love you too, Matthew, but what…"

Wolf cut her off. "I've had great role models in my

life. You know my parents are still together after forty years of marriage. I've seen how important it is to find the right person to spend the rest of your life with."

Caroline gasped, suddenly realizing what was happening. "Matthew…"

Wolf powered on. "I've been in a lot of shitty places. I've seen horrible things. I've done some awful things. Deep in my heart, I know you're too good for me, but I don't give a shit. You make me a better person. Every day. Every single day I think to myself, 'Would this make Caroline proud of me?' If the answer is yes, I carry on, if it's no, I try to analyze how else to get through the situation."

Caroline was openly crying now. "Matthew, seriously…"

Wolf let go of Caroline's hands and brought his hands up to either side of her neck. He caressed her jawbone with his thumbs and lowered his voice, so he was talking just to Caroline. "I love you, Ice. I love you with everything I am. The best day of my life was being seated next to you on that plane. I can't imagine my life without you, and I don't want to. I brought you here tonight to ask you to be my wife. My partner. My everything. I wanted you to be surrounded by all your friends, and my friends. I want to see my ring on your finger so every other man knows you're taken. That you're *mine*. Will you marry me, Caroline?"

Sniffing, and holding on to Matthew with a death grip on his T-shirt at his side, Caroline said, "Can I talk now?"

Wolf chuckled and leaned in and kissed her once, briefly, then leaned back. "Yes, Ice, you can talk, but the only word I want to hear is, 'Yes.'"

"Yes." The word was soft, but everyone at the table could feel the emotion behind it.

Wolf tightened his hands and leaned in to seal the deal, but Caroline put a hand on his chest and stopped him.

"Yes, I'll marry you. I've dreamed of this moment for a long time, but I want you to know that I'm proud of you every damn day. You could sit on your ass all day, every day, and I'll still be proud of you. You haven't done awful things. *Other* people are the ones who do the awful things, you and your team prevent those awful things from continuing to happen to good people."

Caroline spared a glance at Fiona, and gave her a watery smile, when Fiona smiled back, Caroline turned back to Matthew.

"So yes, I'll marry you. I love you so much. I'll wear your ring with pride. I can't wait to become Mrs. Caroline Steel."

Wolf crushed Caroline to him as the table erupted with cheers and words of congratulations. Jess was suddenly there with champagne for the entire table. The rest of the patrons were also cheering for them.

Caroline pulled back and amidst the chaos, looked into Matthew's eyes and said, "I love you."

Wolf didn't say anything, but reached into the front pocket of his jeans and pulled out a ring. He took Caroline's left hand and kissed the base of her ring finger, before sliding his engagement ring down it.

Caroline looked down at her hand and gasped. The ring was beautiful. Her eyes immediately filled with tears again. Matthew had obviously paid attention to her taste in jewelry. She didn't wear a lot of it, and had often complained to Matthew about how most jewelry, rings, bracelets, and necklaces, got in the way when she was trying to work.

The platinum ring was inset with an emerald cut diamond in the middle. It was surrounded by two princess cut diamonds. All the stones were mounded so they didn't stick up at all. Caroline wouldn't snag the ring on her clothes, or anything at work. While the ring wasn't ostentatious, the diamonds were large. Caroline wasn't an expert, but the middle stone had to be at least a carat and the two side diamonds weren't too far behind it.

"Is it okay?"

Caroline could hear the worry in Matthew's voice, and she hurried to reassure him. "It's the most beautiful ring I've ever seen. If you wanted to get me something that I never wanted to take off, you certainly succeeded."

"I wanted to get you something huge, that would definitely tell anyone that saw it that you're taken, but I know you would've hated it."

"You know me so well, Matthew. Seriously. I fucking love you so much."

Wolf chuckled. "You can show me tonight how much."

Caroline loved the gleam in her man's eyes. "Oh, hell yeah."

They had a healthy sex life, but somehow Caroline knew tonight would be a night like no other.

"Come on, Matthew, let her up for air. I wanna see that rock!" Fiona exclaimed, making everyone laugh.

Wolf stood up and took his seat next to Caroline again. He kept his hand on the small of her back and dipped his pinky into the dip at her backside. He felt her wiggle and knew she was well aware of him and his hand. Wolf smiled. The first part of his plan had gone off without a hitch, he just hoped the rest did as well.

Chapter Two

TWO DAYS AFTER she'd gotten engaged, Caroline sat across from her fiancé and glared at him.

"Matthew, it's ridiculous to spend this much money on a wedding. Seriously, let's just do it at *Aces* and be done with it."

"Ice, I want to give you the biggest wedding I can. I want everyone in the county to know you're mine, and I want to have the biggest party I can arrange after it's done."

"But Matthew, seriously, that's crazy. I think everyone knows I'm 'yours' by the way you act. You grab me around the neck and kiss the hell out of me whenever anyone even glances my way. It was really embarrassing at the grocery store when the fifteen year old stock boy happened to catch my eye and you bent me over your arm! For God's sake, Matthew, you're acting crazy!"

Wolf took a deep breath. "I know I am, Ice, but I want to give this to you."

"But what if I don't want it?" Caroline watched as a

muscle ticked in Matthew's jaw. Suddenly she got it. "You need this, don't you?"

"If you don't want it, it's okay. We'll go down to the justice of the peace, or we'll go to Vegas like Cookie and Fiona did."

Caroline repeated her question, but didn't phrase it as a question this time. "You need this." Watching Matthew struggle with his thoughts made the decision for her. Matthew would do anything for her. All she had to say was "that's pretty" or "that's cool" and the next thing she knew, Matthew had bought it for her. Caroline had learned to be very careful what she said around him. She knew he'd give up the idea of a big wedding if she pushed. But it was apparent Matthew needed it. He wanted it. Caroline couldn't deny him.

"Okay. We'll do the big wedding thing." Caroline knew she'd made the right decision by the look of relief that crossed Matthew's face.

"Seriously, we can just…" He still tried to deny it.

"No. We'll do the big wedding, Matthew. But I need some help. I have no idea what I'm doing. I don't think Fiona or Alabama do either. Hell, Fiona went to Vegas and got married in a pair of jeans," Caroline's voice cracked, but she continued, "I always dreamed of planning my wedding with my mom, even though a part of me knew it would be a long shot. Since they were older, I knew there'd be a chance they wouldn't live long enough to see me get married, but I still hoped."

"Cookie."

"What?"

"Cookie can help you." Wolf put his hand on Caroline's cheek and brushed his thumb over her face tenderly.

Caroline looked at Matthew as if he'd lost his mind. "What the hell does Hunter know about weddings?"

Wolf took his hand off her cheek and ran it over his head. He was embarrassed, but needed to reassure Caroline. "Cookie held your life in his hands."

"What does that have to do with weddings?" Caroline's voice softened, knowing her kidnapping and rescue was still a very tough topic with Matthew.

"He held your life in his hands. I'd do anything for Cookie. After he met Fiona, we talked a lot about our weddings. How big they'd be. How they'd be a huge party, how beautiful you and Fiona would look in your wedding dresses as you walked down the aisle toward us..."

Caroline couldn't stand it anymore, she got out of the chair she'd been sitting in and came around to Matthew. She took his hand. "Come on, let's go sit on the couch."

They walked to the couch and Caroline pushed Matthew down and then climbed into his lap. "This is better. I love to feel your heat against me. The feel of your heartbeat against my cheek is comforting. Now, continue."

Wolf smiled. His Caroline was amazing. She knew this was hard for him, and did everything she could to make him feel more comfortable. "I was all ready to help him and Fiona plan their wedding, but Fiona told him that she couldn't handle a big wedding. That with everything that had happened to her, she simply felt uncomfortable in big crowds and would prefer a low-key wedding. Cookie agreed immediately. I owe him." Wolf's words faded out, and they both knew he was reliving the awful moments where he didn't know if Caroline was alive or not.

"I owe him, and this would be a way for him to experience a big wedding. I know he's a guy, and he's not your mom, and I sure as hell know it's not normal or traditional, but he'll do right by you, Ice. He loves you like a sister. Will you let him help you?"

"Of course." Caroline didn't make Matthew wait for her reassurance, but she continued, "I love that you want to look after your friend and I love Cookie as if he was my blood-brother, but seriously, Matthew, I'm not all into the wedding thing. If he plans something and it turns into a three ring circus, you can't blame me."

Wolf shifted until he could lay Caroline back on the couch and he was over her. He framed her face with his hands and leaned in close. "Ice, I couldn't care less if Cookie brought in lion tamers and tight rope walkers. As long as at the end of it you're mine, legally, I'll be the happiest man on earth."

"I love you."

"I love you too. Lift your arms. I think we need to seal this deal."

Caroline smiled up at Matthew and did as he asked. As he whipped her shirt over her head she said, "I love sealing the deal. Seal away my beautiful Navy SEAL."

She watched as Matthew rolled his eyes, but lost her train of thought when she felt Matthew's mouth at her breast. He pulled down the cup of her bra and immediately started sucking, with no preliminaries. Caroline pressed up into Matthew and felt how much he wanted her. Oh yeah. The last thought she had for quite a while was that she would enjoy negotiating with her man if this was how it ended.

Thoughts of a wedding and Cookie were soon lost as Matthew got busy making his woman feel loved and cherished.

"HOW ABOUT *GOD BLESS the Broken Road*, by Rascal Flatts?"

Caroline put her head in her hand and leaned her elbow on the kitchen table. Matthew had called Hunter and explained how he was now their official wedding planner. Caroline didn't think Hunter would be that thrilled, but Matthew had obviously not lied about how excited Hunter had been for his own wedding, because he was now over the moon about helping Caroline plan her wedding.

When Caroline had talked to Fiona about it, to make sure she was okay with the fact that her man would be planning Caroline's wedding, Fiona had just laughed and said, "Good luck." Caroline had smiled at the time, but now understood Fiona's implied warning.

That was three days ago. Hunter had wasted no time. He'd made appointments for them to taste different kinds of cake and to try to get the menu for the buffet locked down. Hunter had planned a day for them to go shopping for a dress and had even tortured her for hours showing her flowers.

Now they were talking about the first dance song. Hunter had a whole list of songs that he wanted to run by Caroline, and it was driving her crazy.

"I love that song, Hunter," Caroline told him honestly, "but I think it's been way overdone."

"Okay," Cookie immediately agreed, "what about *You Say it Best When You Say Nothing At All*, by Alison Kraus, or if you want something different you could go with Ozzy Osborne's *Here For You*."

"Seriously, Hunter, I don't know what I want to

dance to. I don't even know if Matthew can dance."

"Doesn't matter, Ice. You'll dance 'cos that's what you do at a wedding. Pictures have to be taken, traditions have to be followed."

"Do I have to decide right now?" Caroline continued to complain. "The wedding isn't for another two months."

"Two months isn't a lot of time," Cookie admonished. "The more decisions you can make now, the better off you'll be when the day comes."

Caroline put her head on the table and whined, "I can't decide today."

"What about, *To Make You Feel My Love*, by Garth Brooks?" Cookie persisted. "It's traditional, but since the song is older, it's not done as much anymore."

"Okay, that's it. I'm done with wedding crap for the day." Caroline stood up in exasperation.

"But we have to go over the quotes for the venue and talk about what shoes you're going to wear."

Caroline just gawked at Hunter. She didn't say anything, but picked up her phone and dialed.

"Hello?"

"Hey, Fiona?"

"Yeah."

"Come and get your husband." Caroline grimaced as she heard Fiona laugh.

"Had enough?"

"Yes. I can't believe he's this into everything. It's just not right." Glaring at Hunter as she spoke to his wife, Caroline continued, "I mean, seriously, he's a big bad Navy SEAL. He can kill people by looking at them…how is it possible he's *this* into weddings?"

"I'll come and get him."

"Thank you."

"See you soon."

"The sooner the better." Caroline hung up and crossed her arms over her chest. She watched as Hunter blushed and looked away.

"Okay, look. I admit I get carried away, but I want this to be perfect for you, Ice."

"I get that, Hunter, but you have to ease up. Seriously, if I don't pick the right flowers or whatever, it's not going to be the end of the world. Why are you trying to shove all of this planning into a week?"

"Because if we're called away in the middle of the planning, I don't want anything to fall through the cracks."

Caroline's irritation melted away at Hunter's words. Of course. They were SEALs, at any point they could be called away on a mission and there'd be no guarantee they'd even be back for a wedding. She could totally understand why he was so gung-ho on planning it. "Okay, I get that, I do. I'll let you keep planning, but you have to be more reasonable about it. Work is crazy for me right now, and I can't just blow it off to go dress shopping or look at invitation samples."

"Okay. Can we plan meetings over the weekends so we can make some of the decisions and get them done?"

"Yeah, that sounds fair. I'll give you the weekends, Hunter, but please, try to tone it down."

Cookie smiled. "Of course."

Caroline rolled her eyes, knowing he wouldn't be able to tone it down. She only had to get through the next two months, then it would all be over and she'd be married to Matthew.

Chapter Three

"TURN AROUND, CAROLINE, let us see the back," Fiona exclaimed excitedly.

Caroline obediently turned around to show her friends the back of the dress she was wearing. It was what seemed like the two thousandth dress she'd tried on that day, but her friends were relentless. It wasn't as if Caroline even felt like it was *her* dress anymore. She'd heard so many "nope, that's not it" and "not quite" remarks that she'd expected them to say the same thing about this dress.

But they hadn't. Fiona, Alabama, and Hunter had taken one look and agreed that it was the one. It was, of course, white and strapless. It hugged her waist and then flared out into a bell shape. There was a train, but it wasn't obnoxiously long, thank goodness. Caroline turned and showed her friends her back.

"Oh my God. Yeah, this is it," Alabama said breathily.

Caroline turned her head and looked at Hunter.

He'd done what she'd asked and backed off during the week. But the last few weekends had been crazy. He'd dragged her from one appointment to another and, even though Caroline had begged, Fiona had refused to come. She'd told Caroline, "I refused to do this for my own wedding, I love ya, but I'm not doing it for someone else's wedding either." They both laughed and Caroline wasn't upset at her friend. Fiona had been through hell, and Caroline would give her whatever she needed.

"Hunter? You've been quiet."

Cookie looked from the back of the dress Caroline was wearing to Fiona. Cookie had some long discussions with his wife about his role in Caroline's wedding, and Fiona had reassured him that she was okay with everything he was doing for their friend. He was so lucky to have Fiona in his life. Fiona understood that he and Caroline had a bond because of what happened to her in the ocean that day, and Fiona didn't begrudge him one second of wedding planning.

To answer Caroline's question, Cookie looked at his wife with an intense gaze. "The dress is perfect. The fact that there's no easy way to get you out of it will frustrate and turn Wolf on all day. But he'll know that all it'll take is one tug and the bow will come loose. He can slowly pull out each ribbon until the dress falls around your waist."

The air seemed to crackle and Caroline inhaled sharply, knowing Hunter wasn't really talking about her and Wolf, but instead seeing his own wife in her place.

"Time to go," Cookie said suddenly. He stood up and grabbed Fiona's hand. "Alabama, you can give Caroline a ride home, right? We've got things to do." He practically drug Fiona out of the small shop, but stopped to give his wife a deep kiss right outside the door.

Caroline looked at Alabama. "Holy shit. Guess he liked it."

They both laughed. The look Hunter had given Fiona was hot, and the kiss even hotter.

"Come on, get out of that thing and let's go before Hunter comes to his senses and rushes back to demand you do something else wedding related," Alabama told Caroline with a laugh. "Besides, I think I want to go home and see how Christopher is doing. I'm sure there's something I can help him with."

"Oh my God, you guys are nymphos!" Caroline griped good naturedly.

"As if you aren't!" Alabama groused right back.

Caroline just smiled. Yeah, Alabama had a point. Every time she made love to Matthew it just seemed to get better and better.

"Come to think about it, we *do* have some free time on our hands don't we?"

The two women got Caroline out of the dress as fast as they could. Caroline made sure to put a down payment on the beautiful dress and promised to call soon to make an appointment to get it altered, even though it didn't need too much done to it to make it perfect.

Alabama and Caroline left the shop arm in arm. "Thank you for coming with me today, Alabama," Caroline told her friend earnestly.

"I wouldn't have missed it."

"SERIOUSLY HUNTER, IT'S not my fault you got so turned on you had to go home and spend the rest of the day showing Fiona how much you love her."

"Be that as it may, Ice, we have to get this shit done."

Caroline didn't feel sorry for Hunter. "No, you promised me the weekends. It's not the weekend. It's Friday. I have to do this shit at work. I'll be done around four. We can do it then."

Cookie sighed. He knew he was being unreasonable, but he just wanted everything done. Once it was done, he could relax and then enjoy the wedding. "But we have to pick the food, the only time they can do it is today at one."

"Then *you* pick it, Hunter."

"Really?"

Caroline just shook her head in exasperation, knowing Hunter couldn't see it since she was talking to him on the phone. "Yeah, really. I don't care what we eat. Just make sure it's good. Make sure there's enough for everyone. Make sure there's a variety. There has to be something for the vegetarians, and the people who like meat, and then some chicken…whatever. Just don't go overboard."

"Would I do that?" Cookie asked, trying to sound innocent.

"Hell yeah you would. Seriously, just pick something, Hunter."

"Okay. What about *Inevitable* by Anberlin?"

"I'm still deciding, Hunter."

"But it's getting closer and you haven't picked a song yet. I'm helping."

"You aren't helping." Caroline could hear the smile in Hunter's voice.

"All right for now. Ice?"

"Yeah?" Caroline was ready for anything.

"Thank you."

"For what?"

"For letting me help you. For giving me this."

Caroline smiled. She loved that she *could* give this to Hunter. She might not have her parents around anymore, but Hunter was dead-set on making her wedding perfect. He wanted to make sure she wouldn't miss out on anything any other traditional wedding might have. She loved him for it. "You're welcome. Now, go and find us something good to eat at the reception."

"Yes, ma'am."

Caroline clicked her phone off and put her head on her desk. For the hundredth time she wished the wedding was over, but truth be told, she loved sharing the experience with Hunter. Even as crazy as he was acting. She would've had no idea what to do if it was left up to her.

"YOU REALLY DON'T care how much Hunter is taking over the planning of our wedding?" Caroline asked Matthew seriously that night. She'd thought about it a lot and Matthew hadn't really said much about the planning of the wedding or how much Hunter had been taking over it.

"I really don't care."

"But you said you wanted a big wedding," Caroline pressed.

"And I do."

"But…"

"I want the big wedding, but I don't give a fuck who plans it. I might have talked to Cookie about planning the wedding, but honestly, I wasn't all that into doing all the work for it. I'm happy as hell that he's getting to plan the wedding he always wanted."

"He's driving me crazy."

Wolf smiled and pulled Caroline closer. They were sprawled in their big bed after making love. She was snuggled into his side with one leg thrown over his thighs and was resting her head on his shoulder. One arm was curled up in front of her and the other was on his chest, idly playing with his nipple. He loved it.

"I know."

Caroline lifted her head and stared at Matthew. "You know?"

"Of course I know. You tell me every Sunday night how glad you are that the weekend is over. But Ice, you're gonna be beautiful, the wedding is gonna be beautiful, my parents are gonna cry. You're gonna cry, your friends are gonna cry, we're gonna party all night, then I'm gonna make love to my brand new wife all night. I think Cookie drivin' you crazy every weekend is gonna be worth it."

"You're a jerk," Caroline said with a laugh, obviously not meaning it. She put her head back on Matthew's shoulder.

Changing the subject a bit, she asked, "Do you have an opinion on a song for our first dance?" Caroline knew it was irritating Hunter that she hadn't picked a song yet, but she wasn't good at that stuff, but she knew *she* wanted to make the decision. At least in this one thing, *she* wanted to choose the song she and Matthew would dance to for the first time as man and wife.

"No."

"No?"

"No, I don't care what you choose."

"But it's our first dance."

Wolf rolled until Caroline was under him once again. He moved until his hips were in line with hers. He could feel against his hips how wet she was from their lovemaking, and Wolf immediately started getting hard again. He felt like a teenager around Caroline, and not a forty-something year old man that certainly shouldn't be able to get it up more than once a night.

"When the time comes for our first dance, I won't be hearing the music. I'll be reveling in the fact that I'm finally holding you in my arms as my wife. You'll be beautiful in your wedding dress and I'll most likely be trying to figure out the fastest way to get you out of it. We'll sway back and forth, you'll smile up at me, and I won't be able to think past the blood in my dick, trying not to get a woody in front of all our friends. So no, I don't care what song you choose for our first dance."

"Holy crap," Caroline breathed as she felt Matthew surge against her. "Okay." When Matthew didn't move or say anything further, she continued, "Glad we had that conversation...I want you."

Wolf smiled. Yeah, Caroline wanted him. He could feel how much. She shifted under him and ran her hands down his back until she cupped his backside and pressed him into her. "Anything else about the wedding you want to talk about?"

"Uh...huh? Oh...no. Matthew, please..." Caroline's back arched as Matthew slowly slipped into her wet heat.

"We could talk about something else if you wanted. The food? The decorations? The party favors?" Wolf teased as he eased back, then thrust into her harder than the first time.

"No, that's okay, I've got it."

Wolf stopped thinking about ways to tease Caroline about the upcoming wedding and instead got to work in pleasing her, not that it was hard. He loved that Caroline was always willing to do whatever he wanted. She never told him no, and was always willing to play. Wolf got to work playing with his woman.

Chapter Four

"ALABAMA, I HAVE no idea what song to pick for our first dance," Caroline complained to her friend. "I know Hunter would probably pick a great one, but I want to do this. But I have no idea what to choose." Caroline knew she was whining, but had no idea how to stop it. "Help me Alabama! Give me some suggestions!"

"Okay, let's see….you could go old school…*Only Fools Rush In* by Elvis?"

Caroline wrinkled her nose and shook her head. "I don't think I'll ever decide. How about this, just name some songs off real quick off the top of your head and I'll see if any of them strike me."

"*Amazed*, Lone Star; *Here and Now*, Luther Vandross; *Steady As We Go*, Dave Matthews; *You Won't Ever Be Lonely*, Andy Griggs; *Wonderful Tonight*, Eric Clapton; *From This Moment*, Shania Twain; *Your Arms Feel Like Home*, 3 Doors Down; *Grow Old With Me*, John Lennon; *Could I Have This Dance*, Anne Murray;

I'll Be There For You, Bon Jovi; *Evergreen*, Barbara Streisand; *Loving You Forever*, New Kids on the Block; *Because You Loved Me*, Celine Dion; or *Everything I Do, I Do For You* by Bryan Adams." Alabama took a deep breath.

"Hopeless," Caroline moaned. "I mean, every one of those songs are awesome. They're all romantic as hell and would make a great first dance song."

"But none are really what you want, are they?" Alabama commiserated.

"No. But that's the thing. I don't know *what* I want."

"I think you'll know it when you hear it, Caroline." Alabama tried to soothe her friend.

"But time is running out. Seriously!"

Fiona took Caroline by the shoulders and shook her a little. "Relax, Caroline. You. Will. Figure. It. Out."

"You're right. Fuck. I mean, I was held captive by terrorists, this should *not* be freaking me out. Right?"

"Right."

"It's not a big deal. Whatever. I'll just pick one. No, I'll just have Hunter pick one for me. That'll get everyone off my back about it." Caroline saw the look Alabama gave her and sighed. "Okay, I won't do that. I don't want to do that. I'll figure it out."

"Come on, let's go and get some ice cream or something. It'll help you relax."

"Any excuse for ice cream is okay with me." Caroline smiled at Alabama. "Thanks for being here for me."

"Of course, Caroline. I wouldn't want to be anywhere else. Come on."

CAROLINE PUTTERED AROUND the kitchen working on the salad she was making for dinner. She knew she had to bring up an uneasy topic with Matthew, and wasn't sure how to do it. She'd been thinking about it for a while now, and wasn't any closer to knowing how to approach Matthew. Finally she decided just to go for it. Maybe if they were both busy doing something, it'd be easier.

"Hey, Matthew, I need to tell you something about the wedding."

Wolf looked up from the steak he was grilling on the stovetop. "Shoot."

Caroline bit her lip and looked down at the green pepper she was slicing. It was now or never. She rushed through her words. "I'mgoingtowearHunter'stridentpinasmysomethingold." Caroline could feel the air in the room go still. She'd known Matthew wasn't going to like it. She didn't know exactly why Matthew wouldn't like for her to wear Hunter's pin, but there was something about it that Caroline knew was a big deal, but she didn't know what.

She rushed on, still not looking at Matthew. "I figured since he's had it for a long time and he gave it to me, so that it would qualify for something old. I mean, since he gave it to me it can't be something borrowed so…" The knife Caroline had been using to cut the vegetables was suddenly taken out of her hand and she found herself turned around.

Wolf turned Caroline until she was facing him. He knew he needed to take care of this before now, but he hadn't wanted to bring it up. "Ice, you know what our Budweisers mean to us, yes?" At her slow nod, but confused look on her face, Wolf knew she was lying. Caroline didn't know just what that pin meant to a SEAL. He continued, "I…" Wolf's words stuck in his throat.

Ever since he'd learned that Cookie had given his SEAL trident pin to Caroline when she was in the hospital, he'd been unhappy. It should have been *him* giving her his pin. He'd been an ass and had tried to give Caroline up. Abe had prodded and poked until he'd known he could never do it, that he needed Caroline in his life. But before he'd figured it out, Cookie had claimed her in his own way. It ate at Wolf, knowing Caroline had another man's pin.

Wolf loved Cookie as if they were related, but it didn't stop the feelings. Wolf loved Fiona as a sister and knew that she and Cookie were tight, that Caroline having Cookie's pin didn't mean anything as far as a relationship other than brother/sister went, but he still hated it. Wolf even knew deep down in his heart Caroline was his, and that Cookie knew Caroline was his. That Caroline considered herself his, but her having Cookie's pin still bothered him.

It wasn't rational, but it was what it was. Wolf cleared his throat and tried to continue, tried to get his feelings across to Caroline without looking like a jealous ass. "I fucked up that day." When Caroline shook her head, he put his finger over her lips. "Please, let me finish." She nodded and Wolf continued.

"I fucked up. I'd decided you were better off without me, and my friend and teammate did what I should've. I know you belong to me, I know you love me, but it eats at me that you have *his* pin."

There was so much more Wolf knew he should say, but he didn't know where to start or how to say it. He put one hand behind Caroline's neck and the other went to her waist. He pulled her into his embrace, resting his forehead against hers. "I love you, Ice. It scares the hell out of me how vulnerable you make me. Emotionally and physically. All it would take is one person threatening your life and I know I'd lay down every weapon I had and beg them to hurt me instead of you."

"Matthew…"

"Shhhh, let me get this out. Please." At her nod, he continued. "Our Budweiser's are a fucking important thing to every SEAL. We work our asses off for the pin and when we finally get it, it's a validation of all our hard work and it's also a validation that we're a part of the brotherhood that is a SEAL. You know the saying, 'A SEAL doesn't leave a SEAL behind, ever.'"

Caroline nodded again.

"I know I left you behind and it kills me. I'm trying to figure out how to explain it to you so you'll understand. I know on the surface it sounds as if I'm just being a caveman and I'm jealous, and no lie, that's a part of it, but it's more. You having Cookie's pin is like if I wore a ring another woman gave me on a chain around my neck."

At Caroline's sudden inhale of breath, Wolf tightened his hands and then relaxed them again. He hated to hurt her, but he had to make her understand. "Yeah, no one could see it, but you'd know it was there. Even if it was given in friendship, even if it meant nothing to me other than friendship, you'd still know it was there."

"I get it, Matthew. I do. I'll give it back to Hunter tomorrow."

"No. I don't want you to do that." At the look of confusion on Caroline's face, Wolf sighed and backed up a step. He leaned over and turned off the burner on the stove. If the steaks were ruined, so be it. Wolf took

Caroline's hand and led her to the couch. They seemed to talk best when they were in each other's arms.

Wolf sat, then waited as Caroline sat next to him, then turned into his arms. He curled his arm around her upper back and ran his free hand through her hair.

"I don't want you to give it back. That would hurt Cookie. He gave it to you because it meant something. The two of you went through some pretty emotional stuff in the waves. You have a connection as a result. I'd be an asshole if I tried to take that away from either of you. I'm gonna spell it out here, Caroline. I want you to wear *my* pin in our wedding. I want to give it to you and have you keep it close to your heart."

"Why didn't you tell me this before?"

"Because it makes me sound like an asshole."

"No. It doesn't."

"Well, then it makes me *feel* like an asshole. Like I'm in competition with my friend, but I know I'm not. I can't explain it, but it's like me putting my ring on your finger. That pin is the most important thing to me. Being a SEAL is a part of me, and giving you that pin is like giving you a piece of who I am."

"I won't wear Hunter's pin."

Wolf sighed. "Thank you, baby."

"I knew you weren't thrilled with me having it, but I didn't understand. I wish you would've said something earlier to me. I don't like you feeling that way and not letting me help you with it."

"I know, I should have. But the longer it got, the harder it was to bring it up. It wasn't like I could just bring it up out of the blue or anything. I love you, Ice. I'd be honored if you would wear my Trident on our wedding day as your 'something old.'"

"I will, Matthew. I promise."

"Hungry?"

Caroline laughed. "Yeah."

"Okay, then, up you go. Let's do this."

Wolf knew he'd gotten off easy, but that was Caroline. There was no way she'd make him wallow in his jealousy or guilt. She listened to him, heard how he felt, and immediately gave in. No drama. It was one of a million and one reasons he loved her.

Chapter Five

IT LOOKS LIKE everything is set, Ice."

Caroline nodded at Hunter. They'd both worked really hard over the last month or so to make sure everything for the wedding was planned and ready to go. Okay, well, Hunter had done most of the work, but he'd made Caroline agree to most of the arrangements. Caroline had only broken down once when they'd discussed who would walk her down the aisle. Her dad wasn't around to do it, and it hit Caroline really hard that he'd never see his little girl get married to the love of her life. They'd finally decided she'd make her way down the aisle by herself. Caroline didn't mind, she'd been independent a long time.

"We just have the first dance song and the arrangements the day of, to nail down." Cookie looked at Caroline expectantly. He'd been on her for the last month to figure out what song she wanted to dance to, and she still hadn't made a decision. It'd become somewhat of a joke between the two of them.

"Hunter, I'll figure out the song before the time actually comes, don't worry about it." Caroline tried to placate Hunter, but the truth was she was nervous as hell about that first dance, but didn't want Hunter to keep harping on her about it.

"But, what if the DJ doesn't have the song in his playlist? You have to tell him before the reception so he can be sure he's got it."

"I said, I'll figure it out." Caroline's voice was testy. She was quickly losing patience.

Knowing he was on thin ice, Cookie changed the subject. "Okay, then, so the day of. You and Alabama and Fiona will come here to the church and get ready. Yes?"

Caroline nodded, relaxing now that Hunter was dropping the subject of the song choice. She freaking loved the church they'd chosen. She wasn't terribly religious, but liked the thought of getting married in a House of God. Matthew didn't have a church of choice and had told her that he'd get married in any kind of church she wanted, as long as they got married.

Caroline and Hunter had looked at several churches in Riverton before deciding. The church they'd picked had a bright red door, and that had clenched it in Caroline's eyes. There was just something about a religious building that had the guts to paint the door bright red, that made it feel right to her. Knowing it wasn't usual to allow random people to get married in random churches, Caroline and Matthew had met with the pastor and she'd agreed to marry them.

Cookie continued with describing his schedule for Caroline's wedding day. "So while the girls get ready at the church, Wolf and the rest of us will get together at his house. Then we'll take the limo…"

Caroline rolled her eyes. She still couldn't believe the big bad SEALs were going to rent a limo. It all seemed so normal, but for her man and his team, it was anything but.

"…and we'll get to the church about thirty minutes before the wedding. I don't want to risk Wolf seeing you in your dress before the ceremony. Bad luck you know."

It was supposed to be bad luck, but Caroline had put her foot down on one tradition and refused to spend the night before her wedding away from Matthew. She'd declared it a stupid tradition and told Hunter that she spent enough nights away from Matthew when he was on missions, that she wasn't doing it the night before her own wedding. Luckily, Hunter had acquiesced without further cajoling needed. But he hadn't budged on Matthew seeing her in her gown before the ceremony. Caroline had relented on that, as long as she didn't have to spend a night away from Matthew when he was Stateside, she was okay with the other tradition.

"We'll take all the pictures after the wedding while the guests are making their way to the reception. There are lots of h'ordeuvres for them to eat while they wait for us. Not to mention the open-bar. You and Wolf will take the limo to the reception and the rest of us will follow in our cars."

"How will your cars get to the church?" Caroline asked, knowing the answer, but wanting to hear Hunter spit it all out.

"We'll drop them off the night before so they'll be there ready for us."

Caroline smiled. Hunter was so funny. He had no idea she was just teasing him.

"Then after the reception, you and Wolf will go on your honeymoon."

"Yeah, about that. How am I supposed to pack if I don't know where we're going?" Matthew had refused to tell her where he was talking her. Caroline hoped it was a warm beach, somewhere like Maui, but even when she'd begged, and even after one particularly energetic night in bed, he'd still refused to tell her.

"Fiona will pack for you."

Caroline groaned. She thought for sure she'd be able to use the "I have to pack" excuse to get someone to tell her where they were going.

"The Commander gave him the week off right?" Caroline wanted to be sure she and Matthew would be able to get away and not worry about having to rush back in case something came up.

"Yeah, Commander Hurt knows Wolf is getting married. He agreed that the rest of us could have a week off as well. I'm going to have a second honeymoon with Fiona, and Abe is doing the same with Alabama. I think Mozart is heading up to Big Bear Lake and who knows what the others are doing. But the bottom line is that you don't have to worry about being interrupted, you and Wolf will have the full week to yourselves."

Caroline smiled. Thank God.

Knowing Hunter was in a mellow mood, Caroline decided now was a good time to bring up the issue of his Budweiser pin. If it meant that much to Matthew, she had to discuss this with Hunter.

"Hunter, I want to talk to you about something."

"Okay, go for it, Ice."

"It's about the SEAL pin you gave me."

Cookie turned his full attention to Caroline. "Go on."

"You know it means a lot to me..." She didn't get anything else out before Hunter interrupted her.

"Wolf finally talked to you about it?"

Caroline looked askance at Hunter. "Yeahhhh." She drew out the word wondering where Hunter was going with his thoughts.

Cookie leaned over and took both of Caroline's

hands in his. "I knew this was going to happen sooner or later. Ice, Wolf was never happy you had my pin. Hell, he ordered me once to take it back, but I refused."

"I don't understand."

"Ice, me and you went through something I'll never forget in all my life. I'm a battle hardened Navy SEAL, but I've never been so touched by anything as I was with you while we were under the ocean. You didn't panic, you stayed strong, and the first thought when you came up out of the ocean was for Wolf."

Caroline nodded, waiting for Hunter to make his point.

"I gave you my pin because you proved yourself to me, and to the rest of the team. You deserved it and I was happy to give you something that meant so much to me."

"But?" Caroline could tell Hunter had something else to say.

"But now you're getting married. Wolf is your man, he isn't happy you have my pin."

Caroline got it. "Here's the thing, Hunter. Not to sound mean, but in regards to this, Matthew doesn't have a say." She held up her hand when it looked like Hunter wanted to speak. "I love the man more than life itself, but I don't think he has a right to tell you to take your pin back, or to tell me to give it back. Be that as it may, I think I need to give it back to you."

Cookie didn't say anything, just continued to look at Caroline.

"I didn't understand what it meant, or even how much it meant to the SEALs. But now that I do..." Caroline sucked in a breath. "I don't really know how to say this. And I know it's going to come out wrong."

"It's okay, Ice," Cookie soothed.

"So here's the thing. You have your own woman now. Even though I know Fiona doesn't really understand the pin thing either, now that I *do* know, it makes me uncomfortable to have your pin when Fiona doesn't. Does that make sense?"

Cookie reached over and pulled Caroline into his arms. "It makes sense." The words were spoken quietly, but with heartfelt emotion.

"I don't need your pin to know how you feel about me, Hunter. You'll always hold a special place in my heart. We don't need to give each other jewelry to solidify that," Caroline paused, and in order to lighten the mood, continued, "unless you want me to give you a friendship bracelet or something."

Her words did what she wanted them to do, lightened the atmosphere.

Cookie pulled back, kissed Caroline on the forehead and let go. "No exchange of jewelry necessary."

Caroline smiled at Hunter. "Thanks for understanding. Will you talk to Fiona and explain it to her? I can't…I don't want her to…"

"I'll explain."

Caroline sighed in relief. Hunter understood her fears without her having to say them out loud. She didn't want to lose her friendship with Fiona after all they'd been through together, especially after something that didn't mean anything to her, at least not in *that* way. "I'll return your pin the next time I see you."

"Which will be tomorrow. We still have to nail down the party favors."

Caroline rolled her eyes. "Right."

"And work on figuring out that first song tonight would ya?"

Caroline nibbled on her lip. "Okay." They both knew she wouldn't, but luckily Hunter let her off the hook.

Chapter Six

AFTER THE DRAMA with the Budweiser pin was resolved, the following weeks moved quickly for Caroline. Hunter had wrapped up the rest of the plans for the wedding and the day was finally here. Caroline was more than thankful for all of Hunter's hard work on her and Matthew's behalf. She knew she never would've had the patience to make her wedding day as beautiful as it would be because of Hunter.

Now Caroline was standing in the basement of the church getting ready with two of the best women she'd ever had the fortune to meet, to marry the love of her life.

"Turn around, Caroline, I'll lace you up," Fiona bossed.

Caroline held up the bodice of her wedding dress and turned so her back was to Fiona. "Thank you guys for being here with me today."

"We wouldn't have missed it for the world," Alabama told her seriously.

"I know we haven't known each other that long, but you're the best friends I've ever had and I'm so happy we all get along so well." Caroline knew she was gushing, but couldn't help it. "I just hope that when the rest of the guys find the woman they want to be with, she won't be a bitch. I mean, some of the chicks they've been with have been horrible. Can you imagine us trying to get along with them for the rest of our lives?"

"Stop, Caroline, seriously, you're completely freaking me out," Fiona told her tugging extra hard on one of the laces she was working on.

"Can we stop talking about bitches and start talking about how awesome this wedding is gonna be?" Alabama asked matter-of-factly.

"Fiona, I swear to God, you made the right decision in eloping to Vegas to get married," Caroline told her friend seriously. "I mean, I love your man like a brother, but he's been a giant pain in my ass for the last two months."

Fiona giggled as she tied the ribbons on Caroline's dress in a big bow. "I know. The way he's been about your wedding solidified my decision to run off and get married in Vegas."

Caroline turned to Fiona as she continued.

"But Caroline, I'll forever be in your debt for giving this to him. If I had known how much he really wanted all of this, I would've bitten the bullet and given it to him, no matter how uncomfortable it made me."

Without hesitating, Caroline leaned forward and pulled Fiona into an embrace. "Well, I'm glad you didn't have to. I needed the help, and Lord knows none of us would've been able to pull this off as well as he did." She didn't say the words to be mean, Caroline was just being honest.

"No kidding," Alabama chimed in. "Seriously, how women like us can be so clueless when it comes to the girly arts, I have no idea."

The three women laughed.

"But look at us now," Caroline said seriously. "You two are absolutely beautiful. Those dresses are the bomb. Hunter sure knows what looks good on women. The lilac color really works on both of you. And he somehow picked dresses that are sexy as hell but aren't slutty. It's actually pretty impressive. Come here you guys and let's take a selfie!"

The three women leaned into each other and Caroline held out her arm and took a picture of them with her cell phone. Alabama snatched the phone out of her friend's hand and started pushing buttons.

"What are you doing?" Caroline asked.

"Sending this to Christopher. You don't think you're the only one that'll be getting some tonight do you?"

"Oh you're evil...I love it!" Fiona said, then

snatched the phone out of Alabama's hand. "Give me that! I gotta send it to Hunter too."

"You guys are crazy. It's not like you won't get any tonight. Hell, if your men are like Matthew, you get it every night."

At the blushes that bloomed on both her friends' faces, Caroline laughed.

"Come on, let's finish this. The guys should be here soon. I know Hunter is keeping them on a tight schedule. I can't wait to see Matthew's face when I'm walking down the aisle."

WOLF GROWLED AND tugged at the bow tie around his neck. The medals on his breast pocket jangled as he shrugged on the white long sleeve jacket of his uniform. The full dress Navy uniform he was wearing had never felt so constricting. Wolf watched as the rest of his team, similarly attired, finished getting dressed as well. They were cutting it close, as Cookie kept reminding them.

Cookie had been a pain in the ass, but Wolf was thankful for his presence. He'd kept them all on track and had made all the arrangements. Wolf remembered Caroline making fun of them because they were taking a limo to the church, and he remembered agreeing with her that it was ridiculous, but now he was glad.

There was no way he could drive, at least safely. His

hands were fucking trembling for God's sake. He couldn't wait to make Caroline his wife. She was already his, but he couldn't wait for the moment when he slid the wedding band on her finger.

"You ready to go, man?"

The words had come from Abe, but Wolf turned to Cookie to answer. "Is the limo here yet?"

"Calm down, Wolf. Seriously. We're not late. I'm the one who is supposed to be freaking out, not you."

"Cookie, I left my woman in my bed this morning, soft and sated. The last thing she said to me as I left for PT was 'I'll see you at the altar.' So excuse me if I want to hurry the fuck up and get to the damn church and claim my woman already."

Wolf watched as all five of his teammates threw their heads back and laughed their asses off at him. He just scowled. They'd get theirs eventually.

"All right, sorry, Wolf. Yeah, the limo is here. It's out front. But we can't leave too early because then we might run into the girls. Besides, the last thing you want is to be standing at the altar for too long, and if we get there too early, that's what will happen."

Wolf ran his hand over his head and through his short hair. "Tell me again why we wanted big weddings, Cookie?"

Cookie came over to Wolf and put his hand on his friend's shoulder. "Because the moment you see your woman walking toward you, smiling, glowing because she's so happy she's about to tie herself to you, is the moment you realize that all the stress, all the crap you've put up with in the last two months, has been completely worth it."

"I'm sorry you didn't get that," Wolf told Cookie seriously.

"Oh I got it, Wolf. I might not have had the church and the dress and the trappings that come with a big wedding, but Fiona still walked toward me, she still smiled at me, and she sure as fuck glowed because she was happy she was about to tie herself to me."

"Fuck man." Wolf couldn't think of anything else to say. Military men weren't known as the most romantic men on the planet, and SEALs especially weren't known for it. But it was obvious that Cookie was one hundred percent all right with how his own wedding had gone down. He and Fiona had been through Hell, and their wedding was perfect for the two of them.

"Okay, enough mushy shit, let's get this shit done." Dude had spoken. He was brusquer than the others. It was obvious he was done with the bonding talk and was ready to go.

Wolf was more than ready to agree. "Hell, yeah, let's go."

The six men walked out of Wolf's house and headed for the limo. Abe and Cookie looked down as their phones trilled with the sound of an incoming text.

"Oh yeah, just wait until you see Ice, Wolf. She looks amazing." Abe rubbed in the fact that he'd just received a picture in a text from Alabama, and Wolf wasn't allowed to see his fiancé before the ceremony.

★   ★   ★

CAROLINE SAT ON the chair and couldn't stop the nervous twitching of her leg. It was ten minutes past the time when the ceremony was supposed to have started and the guys hadn't shown up yet. She clutched her cell phone in her hands and willed it to ring.

Fiona and Alabama sat on their own chairs, staring at their own phones.

"I'm sure they're okay," Alabama said nervously.

"Yeah, they're just running late," Fiona echoed.

Caroline took a deep breath. "Something's wrong."

"You don't know that," Fiona said in a not-too-convincing voice.

"I *do* know it," Caroline argued. "You know these guys. Hell, Fiona, you know Hunter, he had this thing planned down to the last second. There's no way they're just running late. Something happened."

"Matthew will be here," Alabama told her friend soothingly.

Caroline couldn't stay still any longer. She kicked off her high heels, which were killing her, why she'd let

Hunter talk her into wearing them, she had no idea, and started pacing the room. "Matthew is not standing me up. I know he's not. Hell, he fucked me so hard this morning before he left I can still feel him. He told me it had always been a dream of his to have sex with his girlfriend and his wife in the same day."

Caroline ignored the choking noise Fiona made as she tried to smother her laugh and continued on her tirade.

"Ergo, something happened. He wouldn't leave me standing at the altar. He'd know how much that would hurt me and he would never hurt me. So we need to figure out what the hell is going on. Pronto."

At her last word Caroline turned and glared at her bridesmaids. It wasn't their fault, and hell, their men were also late, but she couldn't get the sinking feeling out of her head that something dreadful had happened to their men. Caroline hated the feeling she had. It was worse than when they were on a mission, because this was *here*. In the states. In their hometown. When they were supposed to be here, on the most important day of her life.

Alabama's phone rang. The three women just stared at it for a moment, until Caroline screeched, "Answer it!"

"Hello?" Alabama's voice was low and wobbled a bit with her anxiety.

"Oh my God. Yeah. Okay. But he's all right? Yeah, okay. Where? Yeah, I'll take care of it." Alabama's voice softened and she took a deep breath. "Yeah, I did. Okay, thanks, Christopher. We'll be there as soon as we can. I love you too. Bye."

"What?" Caroline demanded as soon as Alabama clicked the phone off. "Oh my God, what?"

Instead of walking over to Caroline, as both Fiona and Caroline thought she would, Alabama walked over to Fiona. She put her hands on Fiona's shoulders and said evenly, "There's been an accident. Hunter was hurt, but he's going to be fine."

"What?" Fiona croaked. "Hunter?"

Forgetting she was supposed to be getting married, forgetting she was wearing a kick-ass wedding dress, forgetting everything but her friend, who at the moment looked like she was about to pass out, Caroline rushed across the room and put her arms around Fiona. She just made it in time to help Fiona to the ground as her legs gave out under her.

"Talk to us, Alabama. What did Christopher say?" Caroline kept her voice modulated and even, even though every part of her wanted to cry out and be hysterical. She cradled Fiona in her arms as they knelt on the ground and listened to Alabama.

"Christopher said they were in the limo and a car ran a stop light. It sideswiped the limo and hit the side where Hunter was sitting. They all have some scratches and stuff from the flying glass, but Hunter was unconscious. They took him to Riverton General to the emergency room to be safe. They're all there with him."

Caroline leaned over and looked into Fiona's eyes. "See? He's okay, Fiona. You hear me? He's fine."

Fiona could only nod, but she briefly put her head against Caroline's neck. Caroline could feel Fiona's hot breath against her skin as she did her best to pull herself together.

"Alabama, can you go and talk to the pastor and tell her what's going on and ask if she'll let everyone in the audience know? And I hate to do this to you, but can you also tell Matthew's parents? I know they'll be worried about what's going on. Just tell them I'll call them later and that Matthew is fine. Please also tell the pastor I'd like to talk to her after she explains to everyone. Then we'll be ready to head out and we'll go and see our men."

"But your wedding…"

Caroline interrupted Alabama. "Fuck it. It can wait. Nothing is more important than making sure Hunter and all the other guys are all right."

Alabama looked closely at her friend for signs she was faking it and she was more upset than she was letting on. Seeing nothing but concern for Fiona and the guys in Caroline's eyes, Alabama finally nodded and turned on her heel and left the room.

Caroline put her hand on the back of Fiona's head. "Christopher wouldn't lie to us, Fiona. If he said Hunter is okay, then he's okay."

Fiona took a deep breath and lifted her head. "I know. It's just...I don't know what I'd do without him."

"I know. Seriously, I *know*."

The women locked eyes and the sincerity and comradery Fiona saw in Caroline's eyes, strengthened her.

Fiona struggled to her feet while Caroline helped her stand. "But your wedding..."

"As I told Alabama, screw it. We need to get to the hospital."

"Should we change?"

"No, no time. We need to put real shoes on though. Grab your sneakers and I'll get my flip flops. We can't be walking around with these heels on. I'll get Alabama's shoes too. Grab our purses."

Caroline turned when the pastor walked in with Alabama.

"I'm so sorry, Caroline. I let everyone know what was going on. They're all very concerned about Matthew and the other men, but Alabama said they would be all right?" At Caroline's nod, the pastor continued, "Alabama says you wanted to talk to me?"

"Yes please. Alabama, you have the keys to Christopher's car right?" When Alabama nodded, Caroline ordered, "Okay, get Fiona to the car, I'll be right there."

Without a word, the two women gathered their purses and headed out the door. Caroline turned to the pastor to ask a huge favor.

Not too much later, Caroline hustled toward Christopher's car, holding the skirt of her wedding dress up so it wouldn't drag on the ground, her flip-flops thudding against the pavement as she walked briskly. At her arrival at the car, Alabama and Fiona's eyebrows lifted, but they didn't say a word. Caroline ignored the concerned looks of the guests who were now leaving the church, and settled herself into the back seat. She took a moment to lean forward and put her hand on Fiona's shoulder and squeeze reassuringly.

"Let's go, Alabama. Our men need us."

Chapter Seven

WOLF SAT IN the waiting room with his head in his hands. He looked down at his uniform, which was splattered with blood. This was the first time he'd really sat down and had time to think. The last hour had been horrifying, but his military training had kicked in and he'd been operating on auto-pilot.

He noticed briefly, that his hands were shaking. Wolf's team had been joking around one minute, and the next they'd been thrown around the back of the limousine as if they were popcorn kernels inside a microwave bag. After the glass had stopped flying, Wolf looked up and saw his teammates also groggily sitting up, except for Cookie.

Wolf would never forget the sight of his friend lying motionless on the floor of the limo. The side of the car where he'd been sitting was dented in and there was glass covering everything, including Cookie.

Wolf had seen dead bodies before. Hell, he'd seen way too many dead bodies, but most of the time they didn't really *mean* anything to him. But the sight of Cookie lying motionless, covered in blood, meant something to Wolf. He'd immediately crouched down in the wreck of the metal surrounding them, and breathed a sigh of relief when he felt Cookie's pulse.

They'd quickly extricated themselves from the twisted metal, checked on the driver of both the limousine and the car that hit them, and waited for emergency personnel to arrive. It hadn't taken long. A bystander had called 911 and the sirens had sounded quickly afterwards.

Wolf and Dude had ridden in the ambulance with Cookie and the cops had driven the rest of the guys to the hospital. They'd all refused medical treatment at the scene, knowing they were banged up, but not seriously injured. But Cookie had still been unconscious when he'd been loaded into the ambulance for the trip to the emergency room.

"I called Alabama," Wolf heard Abe say quietly. Wolf looked up at his friend.

"Fuck." Wolf knew he fucked up. He should've called Caroline way before now. "What time is it?"

"Calm down, Wolf, it's okay. The girls are on their way here."

"Fuck," Wolf repeated. He'd missed his wedding. Caroline would be so disappointed. She and Cookie had been planning this day for months.

"Don't even go there, Wolf," Dude warned, easing himself into the seat next to his friend. "Ice'll be cool."

Wolf couldn't get any words past the disappointment in his throat. He wasn't worried about Caroline being pissed about her wedding. He knew she'd be cool. But he'd been looking forward to this day. He wanted to make Caroline his for so long, now he'd have to wait even longer. Finally he answered Dude with a terse, "I know."

"You're disappointed," Mozart said suddenly from across the room.

Wolf didn't answer, it didn't matter if he admitted it or not, there wasn't much he could do about it now.

Benny stood up and paced the small room. "Maybe we can still make it. Mozart, call the Commander and get him over here with a car. We'll go to the church and…"

"It's fine, Benny," Wolf said with determination. "We need to stay here for Cookie. Caroline and I will get married, don't fucking doubt it, but not today."

The men fell silent. There wasn't anything they could say that would make their leader feel any better about missing his wedding.

The rest of the people in the waiting room gave the SEALs a wide berth. They were all big men and they were covered in bloodstains. Their white dress uniforms would never be the same again, they'd have to be thrown away. The flying glass, along with caring for Cookie at the scene, had ruined any chance of their uniforms being able to be saved.

The team was restless and took turns pacing the small room. Their jaws were tight and there was an aura of danger emanating from their corner of the waiting room.

"When the hell will we hear anything? What's taking so long?" Benny complained to no one in particular.

"They're waiting for Fiona. They won't talk to us, because we aren't related," Dude explained.

"The hell we aren't related!" Benny exclaimed, saying what they all were thinking.

"You know what I mean," Dude again tried to calm Benny down.

"This sucks."

Wolf could only laugh, and not in a ha-ha kind of way, but in a wow-is-that-an-understatement, kind of way.

Wolf looked up as the front door of the emergency room opened. Alabama and Fiona swept in, followed by Caroline. Everyone in the waiting room stared at the women. They looked as out of place in the hospital waiting room in their bridesmaid dresses and Caroline in her wedding gown, as a cowboy would look in a New York City dance club.

Wolf couldn't take his eyes off of Caroline. "Jesus,"

he muttered under his breath. She literally took his breath away. Wolf knew he'd be overwhelmed at how beautiful she'd look as she came toward him in the church, and he'd been right. It didn't matter that they weren't in a church. It didn't matter that they were in a county emergency room. It didn't matter that he was covered in bloodstains and scratches from flying glass.

It was as if he was watching Caroline walk toward him through a long tunnel. He couldn't get his mouth to form words, he couldn't get his feet to move. All Wolf could do was stare at his fiancée.

Wolf didn't hear the reunion between Abe and Alabama and he didn't hear Fiona's sobs as Mozart took her in his arms to reassure her.

Caroline finally stopped in front of him. Wolf lifted his hand and rested it on the side of Caroline's neck and he gripped her tightly. "Fuck, Ice." They weren't the words he'd dreamed of saying to his bride when he saw her in her wedding gown for the first time, but it didn't seem to matter to Caroline.

Her face crumpled and she took a step toward him, preparing to bury herself in her man's arms.

Wanting badly to take Caroline in his arms and whisk her away from the hospital, away from the pain he knew she was feeling about Cookie and about missing their wedding, but Wolf didn't want to muss her up. He put his hands on her shoulders and held her away from him. "Caroline, I'm covered in blood."

"I don't care."

"I'll get your dress dirty."

"I don't care."

"Ice…"

"I. Don't. Fucking. Care."

At her words, Wolf did what he'd wanted to do from the first time he'd seen her. He crushed Caroline to him. One hand went to her waist, and the other curled around to the back of her neck, where he held her to him. Wolf felt Caroline's arms snake around him and grab onto his white dress shirt at his back.

Neither spoke for long moments. They simply held on to each other as if they'd never let go.

"Thank God you're okay." Caroline finally broke the silence between them. Her words were spoken into his neck, and were soft and low, but Wolf heard them.

"I'm okay, Ice. I'm okay."

"I know. I'll be okay in a second. Just…don't let go yet. Please?"

"I'm not letting go. I'm not fucking letting go."

Caroline smiled at Matthew's words. He'd never win an award for sweet-talker of the year, but he was hers and she didn't care. He was here in her arms, whole, and mostly unharmed. She'd take it.

Chapter Eight

CAROLINE FINALLY PULLED back out of Matthew's arms when a nurse called out, "Is there a relative here for Hunter Knox?"

Mozart called out, "Here," as he guided Fiona toward the nurse. The rest of the group followed behind, making quite a spectacle of themselves. Five large men, covered in scratches and bloodstained white military dress uniforms, two women dressed in lilac bridesmaids' dresses, and one woman in a strapless wedding dress with a short train trailing behind her on the dirty waiting room floor, could never go unnoticed or uncommented on.

The nurse looked at the large group converging on her in consternation. "Uh, Mrs. Knox, if you'll follow me, we'll go into over here to speak in private."

"No."

"What?"

"I said no." Fiona had straightened away from Mozart and had her arms crossed in front of her chest. She was holding her elbows, so her position looked a bit more vulnerable than she probably wanted it to be, but no one said a word. She continued, "These men are as much his family as I am. They've fought next to him, they've suffered alongside him, they train with him. Whatever you say to me, you can say to them as well."

The nurse looked flustered, but didn't disagree with the obviously distraught woman standing in front of her. "Okay, well, let's still go over here to get out of the way, and I'll explain what's going on."

The nurse gestured toward an empty room to the side of the waiting room and everyone crowded in.

"Mr. Knox is conscious and doing fine. From what we can gather, he hit his head pretty hard on the window when the car was hit. That's why he lost consciousness for so long. He's got some superficial cuts and scratches, much as most of you do."

"When can I take him home?" Fiona asked. Dude was now standing behind her with his hands on her shoulders supporting her.

"He can go home later tonight, but the doctor wants to keep him here for observation for a while, just to be sure he'd okay. Because he was unconscious for so long we want to make sure he doesn't have a concussion."

"Wouldn't be the first," Mozart said under his breath.

Ignoring Sam, Fiona asked, "Can I see him?"

"Of course," the nurse said, looking glad the conversation was almost over. Obviously being in room with that much testosterone was too much for her. "Follow me, and I'll take you to him."

Caroline asked quickly, before the nurse could leave the room. "Can he have other visitors?"

"Well, I'm not sure…" the nurse hedged.

"Please? You said it wasn't serious. It'd mean a lot to all of us if we were able to go in there and see him." Caroline pulled out the big guns. "He was supposed to be in my wedding today. He's a groomsman and we'd all like to see that he's okay for ourselves." Caroline tried to put an innocent look on her face.

The nurse thought about it for a moment, then finally agreed. "Okay, but you'll have to make it quick. It's not fair to all the other patients to have a ruckus going on in one of the rooms."

Caroline beamed at the nurse. "Promise. No ruckus. Thank you."

Wolf turned to Caroline. "What are you up to?"

"What makes you think I'm up to anything?"

"I know you."

Caroline laughed. "I love you, Matthew."

"Now I *know* you're up to something."

Caroline snuggled back into Matthew's arms and sighed as she felt his arms go around her again. She hadn't been able to breathe right until she'd seen for herself that Matthew was all right.

"Do you trust me?"

"With my life," was Matthew's immediate response.

Caroline felt her insides melt even more. She looked up at Matthew, noticing the rest of the guys had left the room. They were alone. "I want to marry you."

Wolf felt his insides seize up. Fuck. "Ice, I'd move heaven and earth to become your husband today, but I'm afraid we'll have to do it later." Wolf looked at his watch. "It's been two hours since we were supposed to exchange our vows. I know members of the church are patient, but this might be pushing it a bit far."

"I kinda bribed the pastor to come to the hospital with me."

Wolf leaned back and put his hand under Caroline's chin and forced her to meet his eyes. "What?"

At the stern look in Matthew's eyes, Caroline stumbled over her words. "Uh, yeah, well, when I heard you guys were in an accident, but that you were okay, I kinda lost it and refused to believe that we wouldn't be able to get married today. We'd been looking forward to it for so long and Hunter put so much work into everything, I really wanted to do it for him. I didn't know if he'd be okay or not, but I hoped…so I told the pastor that if she came to the hospital with me and agreed to marry us here, you'd make a sizeable' donation to her church."

Wolf threw his head back and laughed. He felt lighter than he'd felt since he realized they'd been hit. "You can still be my woman today?"

"I'll always be your woman."

"I mean, you can still officially be my woman today in the eyes of the law?"

"Yeah."

"Fuck." Wolf couldn't get any other words out. His throat seemed to close and he squeezed his eyes shut. He felt, rather than saw, Caroline reach up and kiss his lips, then both closed eyelids.

"I'd marry you anytime, anywhere, Matthew, but I wanted to give this to Hunter. He's almost as invested in our marriage as we are."

"I love you, Ice. You're everything I ever wished for in my life. When I was little and saw how happy my parents were, I prayed that I'd find someone like my dad had. I didn't really understand it then, and as I grew older, I realized how lucky they were. It's fucking hard to find that kind of love. But at thirty six thousand feet, I found it. I found you."

"Matthew…"

"I know I haven't told you this yet today, but you are absolutely beautiful. You in this dress? Jesus, Ice. I'm so fucking glad you're mine. I can't wait to get my ring on your finger and get you home, and unwrap you from this dress. Then I'm going to spend the rest of the night showing you how glad I am you're officially, and legally, mine."

Now it was Caroline's turn to tear up. "It might not be a traditional wedding, but you'll never find anyone more in love with you than me."

Wolf leaned down and took Caroline's lips with his own. He didn't hold anything back, but devoured her. Caroline turned liquid in Matthew's arms as she let him take what he needed. She loved it when Matthew got all dominant on her. She wasn't usually submissive, but it was obvious he needed it right now. Besides, Caroline knew she'd reap the benefits when they got home.

Wolf finally lifted his head and ran his thumb over Caroline's kiss swollen lips, now devoid of any kind of lipstick. "Can we go and get hitched in the eyes of the law anytime soon yet?"

Caroline smiled up at the man who would soon be her husband. "Yeah, let me make sure the pastor hasn't been scared away and let me sweet talk the nurse some more. We'll go see Hunter and get this done."

Wolf leaned down and kissed Caroline one more time. "I love that you want to give this to Cookie. He's my brother in all ways other than by blood. You doing this for him means the world to me. *You* mean the world to me."

"I know. You can pay me back tonight."

"You better believe it."

They walked out of the room to find the pastor. It was time for a wedding.

Chapter Nine

CAROLINE WAITED NERVOUSLY in the waiting room for Fiona. They were giving Fiona some time alone with Hunter before they all bustled into his room and sprung a surprise wedding on him. Caroline couldn't wait to see Hunter. After Fiona finished her visit, she and Matthew were going to go in and see him and explain how they were going to get married today after all…in Hunter's hospital room. Caroline hoped he'd be happy, but first, she couldn't wait to see him with her own eyes to make sure he was okay.

Finally Fiona came into the waiting room. It looked like she'd been crying, but her lips were also swollen as if she'd had the stuffing kissed out of her.

"He's ready to see you guys now," Fiona said softly. Dude came forward and put his arm around Fiona's shoulders, giving her some non-verbal support.

Caroline stood up and grabbed Matthew's hand as he held it out to her. "Ready?" he asked.

"Yeah." And Caroline *was* ready. She was more than

SUSAN STOKER

ready. Caroline looked at the pastor who was sitting in the middle of the men and smiling. In fact, Caroline realized the woman had been smiling all afternoon, once she'd learned Hunter was going to be fine. She seemed happy as a clam to have been bribed...er...asked, to perform a wedding in a hospital room.

Caroline knocked once at Hunter's door and at his terse, "Yeah!" she pushed the door open.

Hunter was lying on the bed, wearing a scrubs shirt, the sheet pulled up to the middle of his chest. At seeing it was Caroline, he sat all the way up in bed, gingerly, and held out his hand. "Ice! Get over here."

Caroline smiled and let go of Matthew's hand and made her way over to Hunter's side.

"You look beautiful."

Caroline snorted. "Whatever, Hunter."

"Seriously. Okay, you have what looks like blood on your gorgeous dress, and your pretty hairdo is leaning a bit to the side, but for a man who saw a car coming straight for his head, you look perfect."

Caroline frowned a bit at that. But Hunter continued, "I'm pissed at the wedding thing, but don't worry, we had insurance on the reception venue, so we aren't losing all the money on that. We'll have to reassess about the flowers and some of the other stuff, but we'll figure it out. Give me a week after I get out of here and we'll have you two married in a jiffy."

Caroline sniffed and held back her tears by sheer force of will. Hunter didn't even care about himself, at the moment all he cared about was her wedding. She put her hand over Hunter's mouth. "Listen to me for a second." When Hunter nodded, Caroline took her hand away from his face and held it out to Matthew, who had been standing just behind her.

Caroline smiled at Matthew when he grabbed her hand and held it up to his lips for a quick kiss. Then she turned back to Hunter. "Okay, here's the deal. You did a shit ton of work for this wedding, and I'm not willing to give all that up. If it's okay with you, the pastor is here, I'm here, Matthew is here, you're here, all our friends are here...I want to get married now. Here. With you." When Hunter didn't say anything, but instead just lay on his bed and stared at her, Caroline stuttered, "If that's okay."

"If that's okay?" Cookie asked incredulously.

"Careful, Cookie," Wolf warned his friend, not understanding the tone of his voice.

Cookie spared a quick look at Wolf and briefly flashed their SEAL sign for "okay" to him. Wolf relaxed and put his hand on the small of Caroline's back in support.

"Caroline, come here," Cookie ordered. Caroline took a small step closer to the bed, and Cookie took hold of her hand in a death grip.

"I can't believe you'd do that. You should wait until you can do it right, until it's perfect."

Caroline sat gingerly on the side of Hunter's bed. "It's perfect today. I'm sorry the day didn't turn out like you planned it, but the bottom line is that I want to do this today. I've been looking forward to this day for the last two months. I don't want to wait. But I want *you* to be okay with it. For all intents and purposes, this is your wedding too."

Cookie reached up with both hands and brought Caroline's head down close to his. "I'm more than okay with it. I'm fucking honored you'd do this today here with me."

When Caroline sniffed with emotion, Wolf commented dryly, "If you two don't stop sniffling over each other, the doctors will discharge Cookie and all your plans for an emotional bedside wedding will be for naught, Ice."

Caroline laughed and looked up at Matthew. "Keep your pants on, Matthew."

They all laughed and Caroline stood up. "Okay, I'll send the rest of the group in. Matthew, you stay. I'll see you in a bit." She reached up and kissed her soon-to-be husband. She wasn't quick about it, and Matthew took advantage of her emotional state to deepen the kiss. Finally Caroline pulled away, kissed her fingertips, held them to Matthew's lips and backed out of the room.

"Is she wearing flip-flops?" Cookie joked to his friend.

"Yup."

"That's not what I bought for her."

"Nope."

"You okay with this, Wolf?" Cookie asked seriously.

"Fuck yeah."

"All right then."

The two men smiled at each other, both lost in their thoughts of the amazing woman that had come into their lives.

CAROLINE STOOD IN the hallway of the hospital wringing her hands nervously. The men were all inside the small hospital room where Hunter was lying on the bed. The pastor was also inside the room. Everyone was waiting for her to get in there, but Caroline wanted to have a moment with Fiona and Alabama first.

"You guys are the best friends a girl could ever have. I never had a sister, or even a close friend, but I thank God every day you came into Christopher's and Hunter's lives."

"Really? You're going to do this now?" Fiona mock-complained, wiping away her tears.

Caroline laughed and nodded. "No time like the present."

"Okay, then right back at 'cha. When I was locked inside that hut in Mexico, I didn't think I'd ever get out of there. You don't see me as broken, even when I literally descended into crazy-town right in front of your eyes."

Alabama chimed in as well, her words all the more meaningful because of her history. "I learned never to trust anyone, but you guys have shown me that people can be unselfish and genuine and I don't know what I'd have done without you, Caroline, when I was home-less."

The three women surged together as if they'd planned it. They hugged each other and sniffled. Finally Caroline pulled away and wiped at her eyes. "Okay, I know I started it, but I want to get married. Can we please put this mushy stuff away until later?"

Alabama followed Caroline's lead and wiped her face and Fiona did the same.

"Okay, Alabama, you go in first, then Fiona. It'll be just like we planned for the procession into the church, but only a much smaller aisle." They giggled, and Alabama got ready to open the door and walk in. She turned around at the last minute.

"Love you, girl. I'm so happy for you." And she was gone.

Fiona turned to Caroline.

"Oh, God, no more, I can't take any more."

Fiona laughed at Caroline. "All I want to say is thank you for grounding me back at the church. For a second my world was over, but then you were there, hauling me back to the real world and helping me get through minute by minute. Just like you did that day in the mall when I had that flashback. Thank you."

"You're welcome, Fiona. I know you'd do the same for me."

"Hell yeah I would."

"Okay, I'm going in." Fiona leaned over, kissed Caroline on the cheek, and she too was gone.

Caroline took a deep breath, she was ready. Without waiting for another moment, not even for dramatic effect, she opened the door to Hunter's room and squeezed in. It was a tight fit. The room wasn't big to begin with, but with all the SEALs, the pastor and her two friends, it was crazy crowded.

Matthew stood at side of Hunter's bed. The pastor stood by the door, ready to move into place once Caroline got to Matthew's side.

Caroline walked to Matthew and reached for his hands. Because she didn't have a bouquet, it felt awkward to just stand there, but Matthew didn't hesitate and engulfed her hands with his. The smile he bestowed down on her made her breath hitch. Matthew really was a handsome man, and in just a moment, he'd be all hers.

"We are gathered here today..." The pastor's voice

droned on, but all Caroline could see was Matthew's eyes. They were locked on hers and she could see the passion lying within them. She figured Matthew could see the same in her own eyes. Caroline tried to stay in the present, but the promise in Matthew's eyes was almost too much. All she could think of was the remembered feel of Matthew's hard length sliding inside her and the feel of his hands roaming her body.

Caroline started when Matthew reached into his pocket and pulled out two rings. She'd forgotten all about their wedding bands. Thank God Matthew hadn't.

When it was time, Wolf brought Caroline's hand up to his mouth and kissed her engagement ring. He slid it off, then pressed his wedding band down her finger until it nestled against the base. He replaced his diamond and once again brought Caroline's hand up to his mouth and kissed her finger again. Wolf lingered this time, savoring the feel and look of his mark on her hand.

Then it was Caroline's turn. It wasn't planned, but she couldn't stop the words that came out of her mouth. As she pushed the wide platinum band down Matthew's finger, she told him earnestly and honestly, "I know you probably can't always wear this when you're on your missions, and that's okay. I know you belong to me, you know I belong to you."

Caroline then followed Matthew's example and brought his hand to her mouth and kissed the wedding band that lay against his skin.

Caroline watched as Matthew mouthed the words, "I love you." She gazed into his eyes and once again tuned out the beautiful words being said by the pastor.

"I do."

The strength and certainty behind Matthew's words snapped Caroline back to reality. He brought her hand up to his mouth and kissed it.

Caroline listened to the pastor ask if she would take Matthew as her lawfully wedded husband. When it was her turn, she answered, "I do."

Knowing it was coming, Caroline could only smile stupidly at Matthew and wait for the words they both longed for. Finally the pastor put them out of their misery.

"I now pronounce you man and wife. You may kiss the bride."

Matthew put both hands on Caroline's neck, a position Caroline loved. Feeling his hands surrounding her, holding her still for his kiss, never failed to make her body ready itself for her man.

"I love you, Ice." Wolf's words were spoken against her lips.

"I love you too, Matthew." Each word out of her mouth brushed her lips against his. Before the last syllable was out of her mouth, Wolf completed the connection between them. He held her head still and tilted his mouth even more until he had Caroline right where he wanted her. Their tongues dueled with each other, tasting and teasing each other. It wasn't their first kiss by any stretch of the imagination.

But it was their first kiss as husband and wife. Somehow that made it completely different from any other kiss they'd ever shared before. It took the pastor clearing her throat for the third time to make Wolf pull away from his wife. He smiled down at Caroline and ran his fingertip down her reddened cheek. "Mine."

Caroline smiled up at him. "Yours," she whispered back.

"Lean down here so I can kiss the bride," Cookie demanded, interrupting their moment.

Caroline laughed and turned to the bed and leaned over. Instead of the chaste kiss on the cheek Caroline expected, Hunter kissed her hard on the lips.

"Hey!" Wolf snapped.

Caroline laughed and playfully smacked Hunter on the shoulder. "You shouldn't mess with him like that."

"But he makes it so easy," was Cookie's response.

"My turn," Dude stated, and turned Caroline to him. He too kissed her on the lips. "Welcome to the family."

And so it went. Each man on the team took his

turn, and said how glad they were that Caroline was now officially a part of their family.

When Caroline got back around to Matthew, she could see he was holding on to his temper by his fingernails. She tried to soothe him. "Hey, husband." Her words did the trick.

"Hey, wife." Wolf gathered Caroline into his arms and relaxed when she melted into him.

"Smile!" Fiona ordered, snapping a picture with her cell phone before either Caroline or Wolf could move.

"That's a good one!" she exclaimed after checking it out on her phone. "I've been taking pictures throughout the ceremony, but I think that's my favorite."

Alabama unexpectedly thrust her cell phone into Fiona's line of vision without a word.

"Okay, I lied. *That* is my favorite." Fiona took Alabama's phone out of her hand and turned the screen to Caroline and Wolf.

Alabama had snapped the photo as Wolf was kissing his bride. The passion he had for Caroline was clear. Caroline's head was bent backward at what should have been an awkward angle, but Wolf's hands at her neck prevented it from bending too far back. Both Caroline and Wolf had their eyes shut and Caroline's hand was cupped on the back of Wolf's head.

"Wow," was all Caroline could say at seeing the picture. "I definitely need a copy of that."

Wolf just leaned down and kissed Caroline's temple gently.

Fiona gave the phone back to Alabama, and sat on the bed next to Hunter. She put her hand over his and Caroline watched as Hunter turned his hand over immediately to grasp Fiona's hand tightly.

"So, is it time for the first dance yet?" Hunter asked with a tone just short of being snarky.

Caroline knew he was still irritated with her. It didn't matter how many times she reassured him that she had the song all picked out and had consulted with the DJ. The fact that Caroline refused to tell Hunter what song she'd chosen, really irritated him. He'd asked and demanded, then tried to guilt her into telling him, but Caroline had held firm. She'd wanted one thing to be a surprise.

"As a matter of fact, I think it is," Caroline told Hunter agreeably. She turned to Faulkner and held out her hand. "Thanks for holding my phone."

Dude pulled Caroline's phone out of his pocket and handed it over.

While Caroline was searching for the correct song on her music app, Cookie turned to Fiona. "Did you know what song she was gonna choose?"

"Don't bring me into this, Hunter," Fiona told him sternly, brushing her thumb over the back of his hand lovingly. It was obvious that she couldn't muster up any strength to be truly irritated with him. "She didn't tell any of us."

Caroline handed the phone back to Faulkner. "Okay, I'm ready. Hit play in just a second."

Caroline turned back to Matthew and walked straight into his arms. She looked up at him. "It's not a conventional song."

Wolf interrupted her, "I'd expect nothing different from you, Ice."

Caroline smiled up at him and started again. "I mean, it's not a conventional wedding song. Hell, it's not really even a good song to dance to, but the first time I heard it, I thought of us. I looked up the lyrics and knew it'd be perfect. It reminds me of you and me every time I hear it now."

The music started behind them and Caroline smiled as the Goo Goo Dolls song, *Come to Me* played tinnily out of her little phone's speaker.

They swayed back and forth listening to the lyrics of a love that started with friendship. Caroline didn't look away from Matthew's eyes as they swayed back and forth, but she knew everyone was watching them with smiles on their faces.

Caroline was floored when the song came to its crescendo, and Matthew sang the words to her, but changed them to fit their own current circumstances.

"Today's the day I made you mine, I didn't get to

the church on time. Take my hand in this hospital room, you're my wife and I'm your groom. Come to me my dearest love, this is where we'll start again."

"Oh my God."

Caroline heard the exclamation, didn't recognize the voice, but ignored it anyway. She had eyes only for her husband. "You know this song?"

"Yeah, Ice, I know this song."

He didn't expound.

"How?" Caroline demanded.

"Honestly? You left your phone out one night and I saw you'd been listening to it. I looked it up and downloaded it. I figured if you liked it, I should listen to it. It's a good fucking song. And now it's *our* song." He continued to surprise Caroline and semi-quoted the song again. "This is now our favorite song."

"Wow." The words had come from the nurse standing in the doorway. It was her voice that Caroline had heard after Matthew had sung to her.

"I think that's the most beautiful thing I've ever seen in my life."

Caroline smiled. She couldn't disagree with the woman.

When the song was over, Caroline turned to Hunter. "So? How'd I do?"

Cookie smiled at Caroline. "Good, Ice. You did good. I couldn't have picked a better song for the two of you."

Caroline grinned at the compliment and turned back to her husband.

"I love you, Matthew."

"I love you, Caroline."

Chapter Ten

WOLF SETTLED BACK against the headboard and smiled down at his wife. He'd kept their honeymoon destination a secret from everyone, and so far it'd been perfect. Caroline thought they were headed to a beach somewhere. As much as he wanted to see her in a bikini, Wolf had a different destination in mind. Caroline had dropped enough hints about hoping he was taking her to Maui that he vowed to take her there on vacation before too much longer.

His teammates had also tried to guess, and had thrown out ideas from Paris, France to San Francisco. Wolf had kept mum about where he was taking Caroline and he couldn't be more pleased with the results of his sneakery.

The only person he'd told was Fiona. Wolf needed Fiona to pack Caroline's bags with appropriate clothing and girly stuff. Wolf didn't expect Caroline would *need* many clothes. But he knew Caroline would want some of her own fripperies with her, so he'd told Fiona, and

Fiona had sworn that she wouldn't tell anyone, even Cookie.

They actually hadn't gone far from home. Wolf had taken them to Sedona, Arizona and checked them into a cabin high in the mountains. Wolf had researched it online and booked the most isolated room he could. He had plans to keep Caroline naked and in his bed for the entire week. The resort had room service, and that was all he needed. A bed, food, and his wife.

Wolf smiled. His wife. Jesus he loved the way that sounded. He stroked the hair back from Caroline's face and smiled as she snuggled further into him. She was exhausted, and Wolf knew it was all his fault. He'd apologize, but he wasn't sorry in the least.

Wolf thought back to that morning when Caroline had checked her email. He didn't want her to do it, but knew she worried about her friends. Fiona and Alabama had compiled all the pictures they'd taken of their wedding and emailed the link to the online album to Caroline. The pictures would certainly never make someone looking at them think it was a very good wedding, but Wolf fucking loved them.

Caroline's hair was mussed in every picture. Her dress had some random black stains around the bottom of it. It drug on the ground because she was wearing flip-flops instead of heels. Her shoes were now a part of their history, because in one of the pictures he had her draped over his arm backwards and her leg had come up and hooked around his waist. Her unconventional shoes were clearly visible.

Caroline's dress was also wrinkled and had some random red stains on it. Wolf knew he'd warned her, but thanked God she hadn't cared. Her makeup was nonexistent, but again, it was how Wolf saw her most of the time, and he loved that she looked like "her" in their wedding photos.

Fiona and Alabama looked just as disheveled as Caroline did, but they were also beautiful in their rumpledness. There was one picture of Fiona lying on the bed next to Cookie, with her left hand, wedding ring prominently displayed, lying on Cookie's chest. Her eyes were closed, but Cookie had been looking down at her as if she was the most precious thing in the world to him, which she was.

Alabama had also included a picture of her and Abe. Abe was standing behind her with one arm slung around her chest diagonally, and the other was around her waist pulling her back into him. Alabama was looking up at him and laughing at whatever he'd just said to her. Even with her lilac dress mussed and with a pair of sneakers on her feet, she was beautiful in her man's arms.

Caroline's friends had done a wonderful job in catching every moment of their impromptu wedding. From the guys kissing her, to them signing their marriage license. Hell, Alabama had even snuck a picture of Wolf handing the pastor a wad of cash to thank her for the inconvenience of having to spend all afternoon in the hospital. Of course the pastor had said it was no big deal and brushed off his thanks, but Wolf smiled, remembering how she'd pocketed the money mumbling about how it would go toward expanding the playground at the church for the children.

After they'd gotten married, Wolf had called his parents and explained what had gone on that afternoon. Caroline had been worried they'd be upset over missing their son's wedding, but Wolf knew they'd be okay with it. And they were. They were pleased as hell their son was happy, and it was more than obvious he was happy. They wrung a promise out of Wolf to bring Caroline over for dinner as soon as they could after they got back from their honeymoon.

Wolf's thoughts came back to Caroline. As much as he loved the pictures, he'd soon tired of looking at them and had shoved the computer out of the way and introduced Caroline to honeymoon-kitchen-table sex. She'd taken to it enthusiastically.

Neither of them shied away from showing each other how much they loved each other through sex. Caroline and Wolf had done a lot over the time they'd lived together, but they'd never had the luxury to completely let go and not have to worry about anything other than each other. There had always been work, or some sort of drama. First it'd been with Alabama and Abe, then it had been Fiona. Neither of them would ever begrudge their friends for what had happened, but it was heaven to not have to worry about anything other than being together.

Caroline tightened her grip on Wolf and then slowly opened her eyes and looked up. "Can't sleep?" she murmured drowsily.

Wolf laughed to himself. It was the middle of the afternoon. He was wide awake and nowhere near tired enough for a nap. "No, go back to sleep, Ice. You're gonna need it later."

Not intending his words to excite her, Wolf was pleasantly surprised when they did just that. Caroline shifted until she straddled him. They were eye to eye as he'd been leaning up against the headboard of the bed.

"You're not tired?" Caroline asked again, this time running her hands over his hard chest as she spoke. Her fingers teased his nipples for a moment before they slipped further down until she could hold him in her hand.

Wolf could feel himself grow hard at the first touch of her soft fingers against him. "Jesus Ice, you're gonna kill me."

"But what a way to go, yeah?"

Caroline shifted until she could take Wolf inside, and sunk down on him. Or at least she tried to. Wolf held her hips tight and wouldn't let her take him fully inside. "Are you ready for me, Ice? I don't want to hurt you."

"I don't want to be crude here, Matthew," Caroline panted, gripping Matthew's shoulders tightly as she looked him in the eyes as she spoke, "but I've still got your last orgasm inside me. You arouse me just by looking at me with those 'fuck-me' eyes of yours. So to answer your question, yeah, I'm ready for you. I'm *always* ready for you. I'm wet, you won't hurt me."

Wolf relaxed his grip and let Caroline drop down on him. She was right. She was soaked. Hot, wet, and tight. "How does this keep getting better and better?"

Caroline treated his question as rhetorical and ignored it. She started moving, not taking her eyes away from her husband's. "I love you, Matthew."

Wolf smiled. He'd never get tired of those words. "I love you too, Caroline. Now shut up and take me."

Twenty minutes later, Wolf smiled again. It seemed he couldn't stop smiling. They were lying sideways on the bed, the covers were nowhere to be seen, and Caroline was once again snuggled in his arms.

Wolf moved his leg, which had been propped up on the side of the bedframe and shifted higher onto the bed. Caroline groaned. "Hang on, Ice." Wolf straightened and shifted both himself and Caroline until they were both, once again, lying lengthwise on the bed. Wolf leaned over and snagged a pillow from the floor, where it'd lain forgotten in the midst of their lovemaking. He settled both of them again and sighed.

Wolf heard Caroline breathing deeply and kissed her temple. Her legs were tangled up with his and he could feel the heat of her body seeping into his own. The wet spot under his ass was annoying, but at the thought of what had made that wet spot, he knew he'd suffer through lying there for as long as it took for Caroline to wake up and for them to make another.

Wolf, finally feeling sleepy, thought about what he'd order them for dinner. He wanted to make sure they kept their strength up. They had four more days hidden away from the world. Wolf picked up Caroline's left hand and admired the rings on her fingers. It made him a caveman, but he loved having his mark on her.

Wolf closed his eyes thinking about his wife. His wife. He never thought he could be so lucky in his life. Before falling asleep, Wolf thought once more about the words to their wedding song. Truer words had never been sung. Caroline was sweet, and he sure as hell was grateful.

Look for the next book in the
SEAL of Protection Series:
Protecting Summer.

Discover other titles by Susan Stoker

SEAL of Protection Series

Protecting Caroline
Protecting Alabama
Protecting Fiona
Marrying Caroline (novella)
Protecting Summer
Protecting Cheyenne
Protecting Jessyka
Protecting Julie (novella)
Protecting Melody
Protecting the Future

Delta Force Heroes Series

Rescuing Rayne
Assisting Aimee (loosely related to DF)
Rescuing Emily
Rescuing Harley
Rescuing Kassie (TBA)
Rescuing Casey (TBA)
Rescuing Wendy (TBA)
Rescuing Mary (TBA)

Badge of Honor: Texas Heroes Series

Justice for Mackenzie
Justice for Mickie
Justice for Corrie
Justice for Laine (novella)
Shelter for Elizabeth
Justice for Boone
Shelter for Adeline (TBA)
Justice for Sidney (TBA)
Shelter for Blythe (TBA)
Justice for Milena (TBA)
Shelter for Sophie (TBA)
Justice for Kinley (TBA)
Shelter for Promise (TBA)
Shelter for Koren (TBA)
Shelter for Penelope (TBA)

Beyond Reality Series

Outback Hearts
Flaming Hearts
Frozen Hearts

Writing as Annie George

Stepbrother Virgin (erotic novella)

Connect with Susan Online

Susan's Facebook Profile and Page:
www.facebook.com/authorsstoker
www.facebook.com/authorsusanstoker

Follow Susan on Twitter:
www.twitter.com/Susan_Stoker

Find Susan's Books on Goodreads:
www.goodreads.com/SusanStoker

Email: Susan@StokerAces.com

Website: www.StokerAces.com

To sign up for Susan's Newsletter go to:
http://bit.ly/SusanStokerNewsletter

Or text: STOKER to 24587 for text alerts on your mobile device

About the Author

New York Times, USA Today, and *Wall Street Journal* Bestselling Author Susan Stoker has a heart as big as the state of Texas, where she lives, but this all-American girl has also spent the last fourteen years living in Missouri, California, Colorado, and Indiana. She's married to a retired Army man who now gets to follow *her* around the country.

She debuted her first series in 2014 and quickly followed that up with the SEAL of Protection Series, which solidified her love of writing and creating stories readers can get lost in.

If you enjoyed this book, or any book, please consider leaving a review. It's appreciated by authors more than you'll know.

Made in United States
Troutdale, OR
10/10/2023

13585224R00060

MARBECK AND
THE DOUBLE-DEALER

The Thomas the Falconer Series
by John Pilkington from Severn House

THE RUFFLER'S CHILD
A RUINOUS WIND
THE RAMAGE HAWK
THE MAIDEN BELL
THE MAPMAKER'S DAUGHTER
THE JINGLER'S LUCK
THE MUSCOVY CHAIN

MARBECK
AND THE
DOUBLE-DEALER

John Pilkington

Severn House Large Print
London & New York

This first large print edition published 2017
in Great Britain and the USA by
SEVERN HOUSE PUBLISHERS LTD of
19 Cedar Road, Sutton, Surrey, England, SM2 5DA.
First world regular print edition published 2012 by
Severn House Publishers Ltd.

British Library Cataloguing in Publication Data
A CIP catalogue record for this title is available from the British Library.

ISBN-13: 9780727895851

Severn House Publishers support the Forest Stewardship Council™
[FSC™], the leading international forest certification organisation. All
our titles that are printed on FSC certified paper carry the FSC logo.

MIX
Paper from
responsible sources
FSC® C013056

Typeset by Palimpsest Book Production Ltd.,
Falkirk, Stirlingshire, Scotland.
Printed and bound in Great Britain by
T J International, Padstow, Cornwall.

One

Marbeck was growing suspicious.

It wasn't merely the fact that he had lost three shillings in as many throws. Nor was it because the caster avoided his eye as he tossed the dice, or even because of the way the man appeared to block the light with his body most of the time. It was the air of suppressed excitement Marbeck detected in him whenever he called a number. This time it was seven.

'Seven, sir – alas! Come, your luck must change soon. How much will you hazard?'

'How much would you suggest?' Marbeck enquired.

His tone was gentle, though those who knew him might have noticed an edge to it. The caster, however, did not know him. He was a newcomer here – a traveller, he said. He summoned a grin.

'Well now, how can I answer that? You know what remains in your purse, sir, not I.'

'No?' Marbeck matched the other's smile. 'So you didn't do any rummaging, earlier on? Like asking the landlord who was staying here, what they might be worth, and so forth?'

'Nay, sir, you mistake.' A look of annoyance crossed the gamester's face. 'I'm a stranger here . . . I enjoy a game, and will play at Main Chance with any man who'll risk a throw.'

There was a lull in the inn's conversation. The

1

Dolphin, its air heavy with tobacco smoke and beer fumes, was noisy as a rule. Being outside the walls by Bishopsgate, the place drew customers from the Liberties, but some were travellers putting up for a night. It suited Marbeck to lodge here. Few asked questions – or, indeed, asked anything of him.

'The matter is, I've risked several throws now,' he said. 'And each time I've failed. Yet, whenever you play, you seem to throw a nick and win. What would it take to match your main, I wonder? A new bale of dice, perhaps?'

There was a cough nearby. Marbeck sensed eyes upon him, but kept his on the dice-caster's. A touch of pink appeared on the man's cheeks above his beard. He said: 'I dislike your words, sir. Were I of a suspicious nature, I might construe them to mean you name me a cheat.'

'Well, why not construe it?'

Now a silence fell. Outside, a bellman could be heard calling the hour; the doors of Bishopsgate had long since been shut for the night. In the tavern, drinkers regarded the two at the corner table warily. The man with the dice was a heavy-browed fellow, wearing a feathered cap. The other was lean but muscular, neatly dressed in a black doublet. His dark hair and beard were cut short, and he wore neither hat nor ruff. Some recognized him vaguely as a gentleman who had stayed there before. The landlord knew him as a man of unspecified business, who used the name John Sands.

'And if I should do so – what then?' the dice-caster asked. He wore a dagger at his belt, but

2

Marbeck had none. In fact he was unarmed, which struck some onlookers as rash if you were going to accuse another man of cheating.

'Then you have but two choices.' Marbeck leaned back from the table. 'You can permit me to examine your dice – to see there's no bristle set in a corner, say, nor a face filed down so that it tips over. I'll weigh them in my hand, in case they're fullams.'

The other man was frowning. 'My other choice?'

He shifted on his stool, then stood up clumsily, and in so doing knocked the table. The dice fell to the floor, whereupon he stooped to retrieve them – but at once Marbeck was on his feet, too. His hand shot out and grasped the other's wrist.

'Don't trouble to make the switch,' he said. 'It's the bale we were playing with I want to see.' He wrenched the fellow's arm up, while with his other hand he forced the man's fingers apart. There was a clatter as the second bale of dice dropped to the floor, but Marbeck didn't look. Instead, he snatched the first pair and thrust the fellow away. The dice-caster fell back – but as he did so he reached for his poniard.

'You whoreson knave—'

That, however, was all he said. With a movement so fast that those watching barely saw it, Marbeck banged the side of his closed fist against the other man's mouth. The fellow reeled and spluttered, still fumbling at his belt, but it was over. In a moment his dagger was taken and thrown aside, and he found himself shoved down on to his stool, from where he stared stupidly up at his assailant.

3

'Now, that looks interesting.'

Marbeck was holding one of the dice up to a nearby lantern, peering at it. Watched by what was now a small audience, he reached into a pocket and produced, of all things, a tailor's bodkin. Leaning over the table, he proceeded to pierce the die at one corner, working the point in. Then he shook it – and a groan went up from those nearby, as several shiny droplets fell on to the table-top.

'As I thought – quicksilver.'

He faced the cross-biter, who was glaring at him, blood about his mouth. 'Stopped dice,' he said. 'Nice workmanship. Who made them – Jacks, in Billingsgate?'

The other made no answer. Someone sniggered, which prompted others. The tension was broken.

'Well – I have another choice for you, master cogger,' Marbeck went on. 'Either return the shillings you took off me with your bale of fullams and leave, or I pass you over to the constable of this parish. I hear he dislikes biters – he'll likely serve you with a flogging for the pleasure of it.'

He dropped the die into his left hand and pocketed it, along with his bodkin. There was a pause, but the gamester knew when he had lost. With a savage gesture, he drew coins from his doublet and slammed them down.

'Best take that with you.' Picking up the man's dagger, Marbeck stuck it in the table, whereupon someone appeared at his side.

'I'll decide who stays and who goes, sir, if you please.'

The speaker was the Dolphin's landlord, a bulky

4

man with whom few cared to argue. Marbeck turned to him.

'As you wish, Master Hibbert.'

Hibbert glowered at the dice-cogger, then jerked his thumb in the direction of the doorway. But the man was already up. He drew his hand across his mouth, looked at the blood, then yanked his blade from the table and lurched away. The landlord watched him go out, before facing Marbeck.

'This is no thieves' den, Master Sands,' he said.

'I know it.' Only now did Marbeck relax, and the effect was striking: as if a mask had been pulled off. 'Indeed, it used to be more of a players' tavern, did it not?' he added. 'Before the ungrateful fellows went south of the river and built themselves a new theatre. To my mind, Shoreditch has never been the same since.'

Hibbert gave a shrug. 'I'll send the drawer over,' he said. 'Take a cup of sack for your trouble.'

'It was no trouble.' Marbeck scooped his shillings off the table. 'But it grows late . . . I'll walk up to my chamber. You may send me a mug there.'

'I will,' the landlord said. 'Is there aught else you need?' His eyes moved towards a figure across the room, who was looking at Marbeck. She wore a low taffeta gown, the breasts busked up so high they were almost exposed.

'Another time, perhaps.'

With a nod Marbeck walked to the stairs. His chamber was at the rear of the inn, facing north towards the Spital Field. Once inside he took off his shoes and sat by the window, leaving the door

5

ajar. Outside it was pitch dark, but he lit no candle. Instead, he waited for the drawer to come up, then took the mug of watered sack from him and closed the door. After taking a drink, he threw himself down on the bed and gazed up at the low ceiling.

'Well, Master Secretary,' he murmured, placing his hands behind his head, 'haven't you let me kick my heels long enough?'

As if in answer, there was laughter from downstairs. Marbeck listened for a while, then, feeling a yawn coming on, he closed his eyes . . . and an image rose up: of Sir Robert Cecil, the Queen's Secretary of State, seated behind a desk in his customary black suit and starched ruff. The little hunchback needed cushions to raise him, so as not to appear too short.

'Bravado's a poor cloak, Marbeck,' he was saying, wearing a quizzical look that might have conveyed a number of things. Just then it conveyed displeasure.

'If it were anyone else, I might have told you to quit my service long ago,' Master Secretary had continued. 'But I need you, despite your impetuousness.'

Tense as he was, Marbeck had kept silent. Both men knew the trip to Flanders had been a failure – as they both knew it had been no fault of his. What irritated Cecil was the loss of a good agent, caught only minutes before he was about to leave what had been a safe house in Antwerp. Marbeck was luckier: he had escaped with nothing worse than a powder burn to his arm – that and the sickening feeling that stemmed from leaving a fellow intelligencer in the hands of the Spanish. What had happened to the man since, he preferred not to think upon.

'Gifford knew we were in danger there,' he had said finally. 'I'd swear to it. He might have warned us – instead, I'll lay odds he was with his whore in Flushing. Now Moore's taken – likely racked, or worse – and I'm lucky to be alive.'

'Indeed you are.'

Cecil never raised his voice, nor had he then. His coolness was legendary. Fixing Marbeck with a steady eye, he had added: 'Forget about Gifford. I'll allow he has faults – but at least he follows my instructions. Whereas you seem to think . . .' He had paused, whereupon Marbeck had spoken up.

'What is it I seem to think, sir?'

'You deal too much in extempore, I was about to say.'

Master Secretary, who since the death of his distinguished father had become not only the Queen's right hand but many other things besides, had allowed a note of weariness to enter his voice. 'You could have been a player, Marbeck, or so I've heard. You enjoy taking roles – even at a risk to our main business, I might say. Were you indulging in some such foolery in Holland, when you almost got caught?'

Marbeck had merely shrugged, whereupon his master had glanced down at the document that lay before him. It was a lengthy intelligence report, written in spidery symbols, that would take his best code-breaker hours to decipher.

'That's Gifford's, is it?' Marbeck had said, his voice flat.

'It's not your affair. I've heard your version of events – now you will leave me to my work. But stay where we can find you. Use the letter-drop in Currier's Row if need be, or write to me as Coppinger at the Star in Cheapside.'

'For how long must I tarry?' Marbeck had wanted to know. 'There's some business I was . . .'

But he had broken off, for Cecil had reached for the small bell that stood on his desk. He was a busy man, and that was all the time he would give, even to his best intelligencer. He had rung the bell, the door had opened and Weeks had glided in.

'This man's leaving,' the Secretary of State had said.

Henry Weeks, Clerk to the Council, had blinked at Marbeck through thick spectacles, then looked at his master. 'Is there . . . remuneration due?' he had asked in his reedy voice.

'Not at the present time.'

Cecil had eyed Marbeck as if daring him to protest, but Marbeck knew better. In a matter of minutes he had left Whitehall Palace by a series of passages of increasing dimness and was shown out through a postern gate. He would have walked off, had Weeks not coughed to attract his attention.

'You're not the only one who grieves,' he had said. 'You lost a compatriot in Flanders, yet Master Secretary has lost both his wife and her unborn child, and his beloved father, too – all in

8

the space of a few years. Do you wonder at his temper?'

'I do not,' Marbeck had replied. 'And I've much respect for him, as I had for his father – whatever you may think, Weeks. Now, if you'll let me take my leave, I intend to get soused. And since I haven't been paid, I'd better find somewhere my credit holds, wouldn't you say?'

He had proceeded to work off his anger by striding to the Duck and Drake in the Strand, where he had indeed managed to get drunk.

That was a week ago. Now Marbeck's enforced idleness was starting to get the better of him. It was more than restlessness: at times it seemed to him as if England – nay, all of Europe – span about him like a whirlwind, while he stood helpless in the centre. A new century had dawned, filled with possibilities, but so far the year 1600 had brought little but woe. War with Spain dragged on as it had for fifteen years, while the one in Ireland seemed to go from bad to worse. His country was beset by troubles – and yet ruled by the cantankerous Elizabeth who, many believed, was losing her grasp of affairs. In her sixty-seventh year, it took the Virgin Queen's women hours to dress and paint her of a morning, to achieve a grotesque parody of the young maid she had once been. More, she had grown erratic – a sore trial to her Council, Marbeck knew, especially Cecil. Though if the man's patience was in short supply, as always he kept it well under control.

With a sigh, he turned his mind elsewhere. Despite everything, he refused to surrender to low spirits; such behaviour was mere weakness. Yet, for a man like him, wasting time was the worst kind of penance. There were other places he could be: a large house in Chelsea for one, where Lady Celia Scroop would be pleased to receive him. He saw her in his mind's eye, smiling expectantly. It had been months . . .

A loud knocking woke him. He sat up in near darkness . . . how long had he slept? Downstairs, the inn was quiet. He glanced at the window and saw a glimmer: dawn was breaking. Then came another knock, and at once he was up and opening the door.

'Prout. I should have known.'

Leaving the door wide, Marbeck walked in his stockings to the table where he had left his mug, drained it in one, then found his tinderbox. He struck a flame and lit the candle, and in its guttering light turned to the doleful-looking man in outdoor clothes who was closing the door behind him.

'I guessed you'd be here,' Nicholas Prout said. 'You need to find another bolt-hole. You'll become too familiar.'

'My thanks for the advice,' Marbeck said. 'What do you want with me?'

'I carry a message, from Master Secretary.'

'At this hour?'

'He's worked through the night.'

Suddenly, Marbeck felt relief: at last something was happening. Reining in his impatience, he waited while Prout drew a folded paper laboriously from his sleeve and handed it to him. It was an order in Cecil's own hand, instructing

10

him to go to the Marshalsea prison, collect intelligence from a person who had been questioned and bring it to him – not at Whitehall, but at his home in the Strand.

He lowered the paper. 'Do you know what this is about?'

Prout shook his head. 'But there was a codicil – a verbal one. He says Sangers will await you.'

He wore a look of distaste; the name of the Queen's most enthusiastic interrogator (nobody used the word *torturer*) was enough to dampen any man's spirits. Marbeck looked around for his shoes. As he sat on the bed to put them on, he found the messenger's eyes upon him.

'I heard about Moore – a bad business,' Prout said stiffly. Receiving no reply, he added: 'I've heard other things too, of late.' He was in full Puritan humour; Marbeck waited for the sermon.

'Your name's been linked to someone of substance – a married lady, whose husband is serving the Crown in Holland,' the messenger went on. 'Master Secretary dislikes scandal. It's . . .'

'Bad for business?' Marbeck eyed him. 'And do you know what I think, Prout?'

The other indicated that he didn't.

'I think you've become a tedious man. A decade ago you risked your life for Lord Burleigh – as many of us did. Now his son treats you like a lackey, and you're content to let him.'

Prout's expression hardened. 'And it looks as if he's treating you in the same manner.'

Having fastened one shoe, Marbeck turned his attention to the other. 'But, unlike you, I don't

11

care a fig for gossip,' he said. 'I take my pleasures where and when I can. You haven't forgotten how it is, I think?'

'Nay . . . I haven't forgotten,' Prout said, after a moment.

'That's well.' Marbeck stood up and met his eye. 'Stuffy in here, isn't it? I believe I'll take the morning air, before I make my way to Southwark. Will you join me, or do you have further business elsewhere?'

'I don't,' came the reply. 'Yet I'll not walk with you, Marbeck. I fear you may outpace a man of my years. Though I'll offer another word of advice, which you may heed or not: I'd take care which way you step, if I were you.'

'I'm always careful, Prout,' Marbeck said.

He saw the messenger out, waiting until his footfalls faded on the stairs. Then he moved to the bed, reached under it and drew out his basket-hilt sword in its scabbard. As he buckled it on, a feeling stole over him: one of anticipation. At least this time of inaction was over, even if, for the moment, his role seemed to have been reduced to one of despatch carrier.

But an hour or so later, when he had crossed London Bridge and arrived at the gates of the Marshalsea prison, the matter took on a different aspect.

Having been passed through various doors, he was finally admitted to a square chamber, where a short, squat figure in a leather jerkin stood. The room was dank and windowless, and hung with irons whose purpose Marbeck knew well enough. Noises assailed him through the walls, as he

12

stayed by the open door; the prison reek almost made his stomach turn.

'Master Sangers,' he said, and the man rotated his body towards him. 'I'm John Sands, sent by order of the Crown. Do you have information for me?'

The inquisitor squinted at him, an unpleasant grin appearing above his unkempt beard. 'That I do, friend,' he replied. 'It cost me a day's and a night's labour to get it, but I won through in the end. Then, I always do. I've uncovered a matter of grave import – worth a reward, I'd say. Mayhap you'll tell Master Secretary that when you see him.'

He waited, but Marbeck merely eyed the man.

'Aye – a grave business,' Sangers repeated, his grin fading. 'The subject's a Portugee: a physician – but I knew he was something more. Now he's made full confession.'

'Then I'll hear it, too – from him,' Marbeck said.

The other shook his head. 'That won't do. He's spent – you'll get naught out of him.'

'Nevertheless, I would speak with him.'

'But he's my prisoner, and I say not.' Sangers tensed like a wrestler, his shoulders swelling. 'There's only one piece of intelligence that matters in any case,' he went on. 'Everything else he spewed was chaff. Now, will you hear it from me or not?'

'If the intelligence is important, Master Secretary may want to question the man himself,' Marbeck persisted. 'And if he's near death as you say, you'd best make an effort to keep him alive until then – or it might be said you hadn't done your work properly.'

At that Sangers's cheeks puffed up like a bladder. He was fuming, but he sensed the other man's authority. He wet his lips and glared.

Suddenly, Marbeck understood. 'The poor wretch is already dead, isn't he?'

The inquisitor said nothing.

'Very well.' Marbeck sighed. 'You'd best tell me what you learned from this unfortunate physician, before he expired. And, for your sake, I hope it was worth the trouble.'

'Then hear this!' Sangers snapped. Turning aside, he spat heavily. 'What I learned, from yon whoreson papist, is that Master Secretary has an intelligencer in his service who's playing a double game: a cove called Morera, who's been feeding him false information. One who claims to spy for our Queen, yet takes his true orders from the Spanish. So go you, Sands – or whatever your name is – and tell your master that. And if I were in your place, I'd think twice before coming here again saying I'm not up to my work! Now, is that plain enough for you?'

14

Two

'The physician called himself Gomez,' Sir Robert Cecil said. 'But to his masters at the Escorial he was Salvador Diaz. His house has been searched, and it appears he was indeed in the pay of the Spanish. Though whatever else he might have told us, it's now too late.'

The spymaster stood beside a table spread with papers, in his private chamber at Burleigh House in the Strand. Marbeck stood nearby, towering a foot above him.

'Yet Sangers is thorough, if nothing else,' Cecil went on. 'And I'll believe Gomez's testimony, since he gave it in return for being allowed to make his peace with God – his last confession. Though he's given us only a code name: *Morera*. In Spanish it means "Mulberry".'

'So – one of our intelligencers is a double-dealer,' Marbeck said, though without surprise; after all, the Crown too used such people when necessary.

'Let's assume so,' Master Secretary replied. 'And whoever he is, we must flush him out – and quickly.'

It was unlike Cecil to state the obvious, Marbeck thought. But he sensed the man was rattled. 'In which case, sir,' he ventured, 'do you have—'

'Suspicions?' Cecil broke in. 'Suddenly, I find I have several. And, worse, I'm forced to the

15

conclusion that every report – every scrap of intelligence that has crossed my desk of late – might be false. The outcome could be disastrous . . . A storm has broken about our heads.'

'What will you do?' Marbeck enquired. 'Examine those who have entered your service in recent times? Men who've shown signs of discontent, or—'

'Or merely of loyalty.' The Secretary threw him a bleak look. 'I don't mean you, Marbeck,' he added. 'You may be a coxcomb at times, but my father trusted you – as do I.'

He looked away, and in the silence Marbeck thought briefly of Lord Burleigh, the Queen's beloved and most trusted minister. In the two years since his death she had aged ten, it was said. But Marbeck had no doubts about the abilities of his crippled son: a man who saw and heard everything. It was said he'd even had a spy in the house when his father lay dying, to eavesdrop on those who came to pay their respects.

'Tell me plainly—' Master Secretary's voice broke Marbeck's thoughts – 'do people still call me the Toad? I've seen what's chalked on walls, about the city.'

'Some do, sir,' Marbeck answered, straight-faced. 'Though I suspect they're of the Earl of Essex's party.' He would not have admitted to knowing the Queen's nickname for his master: *Elf*; let alone the more sinister one he had earned: that of *Roberto il Diavolo.*

Cecil allowed himself a trace of a smile. He picked up a paper, glanced at it and tossed it back on to the table. 'Just now, the Earl of Essex isn't

16

uppermost in my thoughts,' he said. 'A mountain of work lies ahead. My clerks and I will have to sift through everything – cross-referencing, double-checking . . .' He paused. 'Several recent despatches concern but one thing; a business that weighs heavily on me. I think you know what I speak of: the new ships the Spanish are constructing at Lisbon.'

'And at Corunna, or so I've heard,' Marbeck put in.

'Assuming such reports can now be believed,' Cecil said dryly. 'Though my man in Lisbon I've always found reliable.'

Marbeck considered. 'Do you truly think King Philip would repeat the follies of his late father? Send another Armada against us?'

'Why would he not?'

'Because, from what I've heard, Spain's almost bankrupt – not to mention racked with plague,' Marbeck replied. 'They say the new king has no stomach for the war. He's a pious young man, who spends half his time at prayer.'

'Indeed – leaving things to his favourite, the Duke of Lerma,' Master Secretary said. 'Who, like most of the Hotspurs of Spain, has unresolved business with us. Do you follow me?'

Marbeck followed only too well. In the last decade, the word *Armada* had acquired a near mystical power in England: enough to strike fear into every heart. It was twelve years since Francis Drake and the English seamen had seen off the huge Spanish fleet of Medina Sidonia, but since then no less than two others had been sent by the embittered King Philip II. Only luck and foul

17

Channel weather had saved the English, it was said – which was why panic had broken out only a year ago, when rumours of yet another Armada, sent by the late king's young successor, threw the country into turmoil. Rumour had sped in upon rumour: the Spanish had landed at Southampton – or was it the Isle of Wight? Trained bands were mustered, troops readied, chains strung across London streets . . . all to no purpose. *The Invisible Armada*, many now called it – a figment of someone's fevered imagination. Yet the words had a hollow ring, and no one could be sure whether the next rumour might turn out to be true.

'There's little doubt that another fleet is being readied,' Cecil said. 'Though it appears small, compared with those of the past. Hence we must discern its true purpose – and with good intelligence we will. But in the meantime—' he met Marbeck's eye – 'in the meantime, I need you to relieve me of my most immediate difficulty.'

'You want me to find out who Mulberry is?'

'I do. I'll instruct Weeks to pay you an advance. Fifty crowns.' He waited; the meeting was over. But Marbeck had another question.

'Those suspicions you mentioned . . .'

'Ah yes.' The spymaster frowned. 'There are two that come to mind just now. Men I'm unsure of, shall I say? Neither is known to you, I think. Their names are Saxby and Ottone – Prout will know where they may be found. I'll leave the manner of approach to you – and now, if you'll allow me, I need to do some thinking.'

* * *

18

That night, in his chamber at the Dolphin, Marbeck did some thinking of his own. He had no relish for the task that faced him: that of questioning two fellow intelligencers, either of whom might be a traitor.

He had been to Nicholas Prout and obtained the whereabouts of the men Cecil had named. One was Thomas Saxby, an ex-soldier who lived at Clerkenwell. The other was an Italian, Giacomo Ottone, who kept a fencing hall in Gracious Street. Both men would no doubt resent being objects of suspicion – wouldn't Marbeck himself? And yet it was imperative the matter be resolved, and promptly. The spymaster had left him to his own devices – but then the man knew he would trust his instincts, and make do with whatever cards fell to him. With that thought, he went to his bed and slept soundly, rising to a clear day. The weather was fair, and he decided not to ride but to walk through Moorfields and make his way to Clerkenwell by Smithfield. So, having taken a light breakfast, he went to seek out Thomas Saxby.

The ex-soldier, he discovered, lived in poverty in a tumbledown tenement by St John's. Ragged children fought and yelled in the narrow alley, where refuse had clogged the runnel to form a midden. Passers-by glanced at Marbeck, some men eying his good clothes and his sword, though he appeared not to notice. Arriving at the last house, he knocked. The door was opened by a blonde-haired woman in a faded frock, who flinched at sight of one who looked a gentleman.

'Tom's not here,' she said at once. 'I've not seen him for . . .'

19

Gently Marbeck took her arm. 'He's here, and he'll see me,' he said. 'Don't fret – I merely want to talk to him.' Steering her aside, he entered the hovel, which was devoid of any sort of comfort. At once a figure raised itself from a low pallet, and a male voice called out harshly.

'Come any closer, and I'll fire this!'

Sitting up in the gloom was a heavily bearded man in a sweat-stained shirt, an old wheel-lock pistol in his hand. Marbeck glanced briefly at it.

'Hadn't you better prime it first?'

The other glared but kept the weapon levelled.

'Master Saxby, is it?' Marbeck went on. 'Gunner Saxby?'

There was a rustle of skirts, and the woman brushed past him to stand beside the pallet. 'Jesu,' she breathed, 'not another recruiter!' And when Marbeck looked at her, she cried: 'He's done with fighting – are you blind, or what?' Stooping, she threw aside the coverlet. Marbeck looked down, then raised his eyes.

'I ask your pardon,' he said.

'Well you might!' Fiercely, she faced him: a spirited woman, Marbeck saw, with an intelligence belied by her shabby appearance. He turned his gaze to meet the ex-soldier's eye.

'I'll ask your pardon too, gunner,' he said.

'It's cannoneer,' the other man threw back. But he lowered the pistol, so that it rested beside his right leg. It had been amputated below the knee, the stump swathed in a cloth.

'Who are you?' he demanded.

'A friend,' Marbeck said, prompting a snort

20

from the woman. 'I'd like to speak with you –
nothing more.'

'About what?'

'Business.' He let his eyes rest on Saxby's
companion briefly, whereupon the man frowned.

'Who sent you here?' he asked. His tone had
changed, but he remained suspicious.

'Roger Daunt sent me,' Marbeck replied, and,
having used the code name, he waited. There was
a moment before Saxby looked to his companion.

'Help me up, Anne,' he said. 'Then you'd best
leave us for a while.' But when he turned back,
Marbeck was shaking his head.

'The Red Bull, at the top of St John's Street.
I'll await you there.' To Anne he said: 'Those
who've been wounded in service of the Queen
deserve succour. Please – take this.' Producing a
silver crown, he held it out.

She stared, then took it without a word, whereupon Marbeck got himself outside. He wore a
look which some would have interpreted as
distaste, at the squalor in which one of apparent
good breeding had found himself; others, however,
might have seen it differently. But a short while
later, when Thomas Saxby in his mouldy soldier's
jerkin entered the Red Bull tavern, he found
Marbeck seated by a window, composed and
seemingly in good spirits.

'Sit with me,' he said. 'Are you hungry?'

Saxby, who had manoeuvred himself in with
the aid of a crutch, shook his head. 'I'll have
beer,' he said as he eased himself down. 'But if
they'll sop some toasted bread in it, that'd be
welcome.'

Marbeck called the drawer and gave the order. It was early, and the tavern was almost empty. The mugs came soon, and both men drank in silence, until Saxby spoke first.

'Do you have a task for me? I know you not, but you named Roger Daunt . . .'

'So I did,' Marbeck said.

He looked hard at him: at the drawn face, the hollowed cheeks. This man had paid a heavy price for his service with Elizabeth's army. 'Where did you lose your leg?' he asked. 'The Low Countries, or—'

'Ulster,' came the terse reply. 'The bog of Europe . . . fit for naught but leeches.'

'So I've heard.' Marbeck gave him a grim smile. 'Who did you serve under?'

Saxby pulled a lump of soggy bread from his mug and thrust it into his mouth. 'Sir Arthur Chichester, at Carrickfergus,' he said as he chewed. 'He's the best man they've got over there – which isn't saying a great deal.'

'I've heard that, too,' Marbeck said. 'It's anger drives him . . . revenge, perhaps, for what the Irish did to his brother. Do you know about that?'

A frown creased Saxby's brow. 'Who doesn't know? The devils cut off his head – played football with it, so they say.' He swallowed and spat out an oath. 'I hope they pay – every last one of them.'

'Because they've rebelled against the Crown?' Marbeck enquired in a casual tone. 'Or because they're papists, or—'

'All of that – and this.' The ex-soldier banged a hand down: not on the table, but on his ruined leg.

'None would dispute with you,' Marbeck said, after a moment. 'And there's no reward for men such as you when they get home, is there? Those who are fortunate enough to return, that is.'

'Fortunate, you say?' As Marbeck had intended, Saxby's anger had risen. 'And what would a man like you know,' he growled, 'who, by the looks of you, never saw a battle, nor lifted a hand save to wipe your arse?'

'Tell me, do you know a man called Gomez?' Marbeck asked.

Saxby blinked. 'What?'

'Physician, lived over the river at Lambeth. Portuguese – know him, do you? Or *did you*, I should say. He's dead, poor fellow – died in prison, under torture.'

His words came quickly. The other stared at him, blank-faced. 'No, I never heard of him,' he said at last. 'And in God's name, what's this about?'

In a fair imitation of a stage conspirator, Marbeck glanced round, then leaned forward. 'He was working for the Spanish,' he said. 'That's what it's about, Saxby. Our masters are a little uneasy.'

He picked up his mug and took a pull. But Saxby merely continued to gaze at him. Finally, he drew a breath and said: 'Why do you ask if I knew this man?'

'Well, did you?'

'I've said I did not.'

'You're certain?'

'I'm certain.'

The man's anger had subsided; instead, he looked alarmed. But, then, Marbeck had seen performances just as convincing in people who

23

had lied to him with their every breath. Abruptly, he changed tack again.

'The drab,' he said. 'Can you trust her?'

The other gave a start, then gripped the handle of his mug until the knuckles showed white. Marbeck gazed into his eyes and waited.

'Anne is my wife,' Saxby said softly.

'But I ask again: can you trust her?'

A pause, then: 'She nursed me back from near-death, after I was shipped home. It was months before I could walk, by which time every last farthing we had was gone. She could have left me at any time – none would have blamed her. Yes, I trust her – with my life.'

'So that's why you turned intelligencer,' Marbeck observed. 'A matter of money, was it?'

There was a moment, but now Saxby understood. 'By the Christ,' he muttered. 'You're here to rack me. You think I'm a turncoat!'

'Well, I admit you seem an unlikely sort for what our Spanish foes call *un espia*,' Marbeck said mildly. 'You can hardly travel far, can you? What kind of service do you perform?'

Deliberately, Saxby lifted his mug and took a long drink, then put it down. 'If you're such a clever one, why not guess?' he said finally.

'How about prison louse?' Marbeck suggested. 'The sort that befriends papists in the Marshalsea, say, then draws out their secrets so they condemn themselves? A dirty task, but some are willing enough to do it. Or desperate enough.'

Saxby said nothing. Then he twitched, but it was a spasm of pain that had caused it. He leaned sideways, pressing a hand to his leg.

'And you,' the ex-soldier said with sudden weariness, 'in what way do you serve? For it looks to me as if you're playing a similar game yourself.'

'That's true enough,' Marbeck allowed. A moment passed, in which their eyes locked, but to Saxby's surprise his questioner sat back and relaxed.

'I ask your pardon once again, cannoneer,' he said in a different tone. 'I have other business, and I must leave you. This is for the reckoning.' He produced a coin and laid it down beside his mug. But Saxby didn't even notice.

'You sweet-voiced Judas,' he breathed.

Without looking at him, Marbeck got up and went out.

He walked steadily, a hand on his sword hilt, not towards the city, but westward by narrow ways until he reached Turnmill Brook. There at last he stopped, gazing across the turgid stream towards the fine manor house that stood beyond, in its walled garden: Ely Place – named for the Bishop who built it. Behind him came the din from packed streets, stretching down to West Smithfield. But ahead all was tranquillity and elegance: fruit trees poking above the wall, a wisp of smoke rising from a kitchen chimney. Just then, to Marbeck, the contrasts of London seldom seemed as stark as they did here.

He breathed deeply, gathering his thoughts. At times like these he had no difficulty focussing his mind on what he did, and why he did it. Though there were occasions . . . He frowned. Had his questioning of Thomas Saxby been one of them? If so, why? Because the man had suffered?

Impatiently, he turned away. Was it sympathy that moved him? What, then, of Giles Moore, facing torture in a Spanish prison? What of others who had given so much, even their lives, in furtherance of what all knew was merely warfare by other means?

He glanced back, at the smoke that curled from the chimney of Ely Place. For a moment it reminded him of another fine manor house, a long way from here: one where he had not been in years. Then, forcing the memory aside, he began to walk briskly, back towards the city.

Thomas Saxby, he decided, would be a most unlikely double agent; so now he must visit a certain fencing master in Gracious Street and sound him out instead.

Three

Giacomo Ottone was a surprise. Marbeck had expected a bombastic swordsman, with a pointed beard and a swagger. Instead, he found a slim, clean-shaven man with oiled hair tied back and, alarmingly, a hand that shook, almost as if he were palsied.

'You are new here, *signor*. How may I serve you?'

The fencing master regarded him somewhat warily, Marbeck thought. They were in a bare room with benches around the walls, hung with enough swords to arm a small regiment. Ottone wore a loose shirt and breeches, and a mail glove on his right hand.

'I came on recommendation,' Marbeck said. 'From a friend – Roger Daunt. I think you know him?'

To his surprise the other gave a start. He looked quickly towards the far end of the hall, where several young men were practising their swordsmanship.

'I cannot talk with you now,' he said, speaking low. 'You should come later, after dark . . .'

'I don't have the time for that,' Marbeck told him. His eyes strayed to the walls, and, placing a hand on his own sword hilt, he said: 'Why don't we talk while we fence? I could do with a little practice.'

Ottone frowned. 'Well . . . if you wish.'

27

He gestured to the centre of the room, where a circle was marked out on the floor. As Marbeck unbuttoned his doublet, the other went to a rack and selected a light rapier. He took it down, hefted it, threw it up and caught it in his mailed hand. Then he walked back to the circle. Having laid aside his outer clothes, scabbard and dagger, Marbeck approached him and showed his own rapier. Their eyes met briefly, before the Italian lowered his gaze. He was clearly nervous; Marbeck wondered why.

'Your blade is unbated, *signor*.' Ottone indicated the point of his sword. 'And I am not padded . . . you must take care. Or our conversation may be short, eh?'

He gave a quick smile, which Marbeck returned. 'I'm noted for my care, Master Ottone,' he said. 'As I am for—' Then he broke off. With lightning speed, the other man had lunged, so that his rapier struck Marbeck's chest. If its point had not been fitted with a small cork, the blow could have been fatal. Marbeck breathed in, eying his opponent.

'Your *stoccata* is impressive, master,' he said. 'As fast as I've seen anywhere.' Then he too made a thrust, though not as quickly. As he expected, it was parried expertly.

'I cannot say the same for yours, *signor*,' Ottone said. 'Perhaps you will show me your *punta*, and your *pararla*. I would like to know the measure of the man I face.'

There was a moment as each regarded the other. But Marbeck nodded and executed a few simple moves. The fencing master watched with a keen

28

eye. Suddenly, his sword hand shook. Marbeck feigned not to notice.

'*Basta* – enough.' Ottone lowered his rapier. 'You fence well. Who was your teacher?'

Marbeck gave a shrug, but made no answer. Aware that he was being observed, even judged, the other returned his gaze.

'What is it you want of me?' he said then, with a glance across the room. The young men were talking among themselves, paying no attention to what went on elsewhere.

'I heard you were in France, a while back,' Marbeck said. 'Whereabouts, precisely?'

'In Paris,' Ottone replied. Suddenly, he went into a crouch, levelling his blade. 'Come, we must fence. Say what you came to say. Is there a message?'

Marbeck bent his knees and raised his own weapon. The two men circled each other, trying a few thrusts, though at every turn the Italian seemed to read Marbeck's move before he had even made it. But it was well, he thought: sharp as his wits were, just now he needed them to be even sharper.

'The man Gomez,' he said suddenly. 'He's been taken, put to torture. He's spilled everything.'

Ottone gave a jump – or so Marbeck thought. But the fellow's reactions were so jerky, he could not be certain. What was certain was that the next second he found the other's blunted rapier pressed against his shoulder.

'Who is Gomez?'

As fast as he had lunged, the fencing master drew back, his dark eyes fiercely alert. So

Marbeck took a breath and told him, or as much as he had told Thomas Saxby. While he spoke, he made several thrusts, allowing each to be warded off. Then, judging his moment, he made a rapid crosswise sweep from left to right which caught the other off guard. To his own surprise, Ottone found his opponent's sword only an inch from his throat, where it stayed.

'Well . . . your *mandritta* is better than your *stoccata*, *signor*,' he breathed. His eyes flicked from the weapon's point back to Marbeck. 'If you meant to scare me, you have succeeded.'

After a moment Marbeck lowered his rapier. But he kept his eyes on the other man's face, until he flinched. Again his hand shook, and this time Marbeck made a point of noticing.

'I can see that,' he said.

'I ask again,' Ottone said sharply, his blade trembling. 'What do you want?'

'I want to know what you know of Gomez.'

'Since I never heard this name, I don't know anything of him,' came the snapped reply. 'And you seem to think ill of me, *signor*. To insult me would be most unwise.'

'I imagine it would,' Marbeck allowed. 'Though I'm curious to know what happened to you in France. No insult intended, master, but you strike me as a frightened man. Why so?'

Ottone did not answer immediately. Unlike Saxby, if this man was angry, he knew how to control it. He crouched again and made a lunge which he permitted Marbeck to parry. Then in a low voice he said: 'Such details are not important. I did my work, and I came back. What my

30

commission was I would never tell. You know that.'

'Very well.' Marbeck lunged himself, keeping his blade well clear of the other's body. Then, drawing back, he said: 'Where are you from, master? Genoa, isn't it?'

'No . . . Livorno.' Breathing steadily, Ottone made a thrust, which connected with his opponent's abdomen. As he did so, he threw him a look, the meaning of which was clear: but for the existence of a tiny lump of cork, Marbeck would be mortally wounded.

'And before you go further – *si*, I was born of the Roman faith,' he added. 'I never hide it. I'm *recusanto*, one who pays his fine every week instead of going to church. Is that where your mind moves?'

'Do you know what *Morera* means?' Marbeck asked him.

Ottone looked puzzled. But Marbeck waited, until at last the other said, 'In Italian, it is *La Mora*.' He pronounced it in an exaggerated manner. 'Yes, *signor*, I know what it means.'

The two eyed each other again. Then Ottone glanced aside, and Marbeck followed his gaze. A silence had fallen at the other end of the room, where the young fencers were looking curiously at them both.

'What is it?' Immediately, the fencing master turned and strode swiftly across the boards. 'You boys think Ottone has time to waste?' he shouted. 'Go on with your exercises – *subito*! To work!'

The youths needed no further prompting, but fell to their swordplay with gusto. Ottone stood over them, barking criticisms, but his anger was directed at Marbeck, and both of them knew it. The performance lasted minutes, before the master left his pupils and returned to the circle.

'Your temper is short, sir,' Marbeck said mildly.

'Only on occasions, *signor*,' came the rejoinder. 'Now, have you further questions for me? About fruits, perhaps – or about Paris? What more can I tell you?'

'Nothing more, for the present,' Marbeck replied. 'I believe I've learned all I need to.' He inclined his head. 'I thank you for the lesson, *signor*.'

He walked to the bench where he had left his belongings. There he sheathed his sword and busied himself putting on his doublet. After a moment the fencing master took a few steps towards him. His manner had changed.

'I think I know you now,' he said quietly.

Marbeck buckled on his sword belt, but said nothing.

'I do not wish to fight you again,' Ottone added.

'No?' Marbeck raised his eyebrows. 'I think what you mean is it's I who shouldn't fight you again. For I might get hurt . . . if the stop should fall off your weapon, perhaps. I'm sure you'd be filled with remorse if that happened.'

The other gave a thin smile. 'We understand each other, *signor*,' he murmured.

'I wouldn't be too certain of that,' Marbeck said.

At the door he looked back to see Ottone gazing at him, rapier still in his mailed hand. The fencing master raised the weapon in salute, then made

32

him an ironic little bow before turning once again to berate his pupils.

Later that day, after mulling things over, Marbeck went looking for Nicholas Prout.

Having failed to find him in places he expected, he was about to go and take some supper when, on impulse, he decided to walk to Aldgate Street, to the church of St Andrew Undershaft. The bell was tolling, and among those gathering for evening service he found Cecil's messenger in a sombre suit of grey. Prout saw him at the same moment and made as if to hurry into the church, but he wasn't quick enough. Marbeck waylaid him by the door, and bent close.

'A word with you, please.'

'Not now – not here,' Prout said with a frown. 'I'll come to the Dolphin as before.'

'There's no need: I want a location, nothing else. Give it me and I'll be gone.'

'Whose?'

'Joseph Gifford's.'

The messenger hesitated. 'I like it not,' he said after a moment. 'There's bad blood between you and he . . . I sense a settling of scores.'

'Now, I thought you knew me better.'

'Do I?' The other met Marbeck's eye. People moved past them into the church. Overhead, the bell still clanged.

'To the devil with your punctilious ways, Prout,' Marbeck said. It had been a long day, he was hungry and his temper was short. 'I want to see him – it's important.'

'It always is, isn't it?' The messenger sighed.

'I'll give you known whereabouts, but in the morning I'll be making report of it. No offence, I'm—'

'You're arming yourself,' Marbeck finished. 'God forbid that anyone should hold you to account if the man was found with his throat cut – or even with a black eye. Is that it?'

Prout bristled. 'You'll not use God's name in that manner, Marbeck,' he said. 'Not here, at my church—'

'Then tell me where to find Gifford, and I'll be gone.'

A pause, then: 'You'll have a long walk ahead of you, I fear: he's in Dover. Try Mother Sewell's house, near the castle. Now – can I go to worship?'

Morning found Marbeck stepping out of the back door of the Dolphin Inn and walking to the stable. It was barely dawn, but the ostler was already up. When the door creaked open, he gazed in surprise at the man who entered, carrying a light pack.

'Master Sands – d'you want me to fetch Cobb?'

'I'll do it, Zachary,' Marbeck said. 'Though if you'll look out a bag of feed for him, one I can tie on my saddle, there's a two-penny piece for you.'

Zachary peered through rheumy eyes. 'You going far?'

'Middlesex, on business.'

The old man shuffled away to do his bidding, while Marbeck went to the stalls. Soon he had loosed a fine roan horse and was leading it out. Cobb was of pure Iberian stock: strongly built and compact, with a thick mane and tail. At the

34

prospect of exercise, he was quickly alert. As he tightened the girth, Marbeck spoke softly, rubbing the animal's flanks. 'Sixty miles to Dover, as the crow flies,' he murmured. 'What say we do it in a day and a night?'

The horse turned its head, which seemed a good enough answer. Marbeck was soon upon his back, walking him out into the chilly air. A short time later he was leaving Southwark, with the sun rising at his left. At his urging, his mount began to trot, then to canter. By mid-morning they were well on the Dover road, whereupon, with the open country about him, Marbeck at last began to think about how to proceed – and about what had happened the day before, when he had begun the hunt for the traitor known as Mulberry.

He had dismissed Saxby already, and finally, after some rumination, he had dismissed Ottone, too. He wasn't sure why, for it seemed clear the man was hiding something. But as one who might be a double-dealer, he fell short. Not because he lacked courage: he did not. What he did lack, Marbeck thought, was guile – or enough of it to mark him out as a traitor. So his instinct told him, and for now it must serve.

The man he was riding to see, however, lacked neither courage nor guile. He and Marbeck had known each other for years, and their rivalry was common knowledge. He knew, of course, that Gifford was not under suspicion. And despite what had happened in Flanders, he had no reason to think badly of the man . . . yet there were times when he did; perhaps because, with Gifford, his feelings went deeper.

35

It had come upon him yesterday, in the late afternoon: the need to disregard Sir Robert Cecil's words, and to seek out the man who he believed had failed him. And once that urge had taken hold, nothing would stop him.

Now, as the hop-fields of Kent flew by, Marbeck gripped the rein and bent low along Cobb's neck. 'A day and a night,' he repeated, while the horse's mane whipped past him. 'And you'll have a warm stable to rest in, while I find our man Gifford. Then let's see how the dice fall, shall we?'

Four

In the early morning Dover Castle lay ahead, its bulk dominating the sprawling town below.

For the past few miles Marbeck had tasted a salt breeze from the Channel; now it stretched before him, a sparkling sheet of grey-blue. He drew rein, peering at the distant horizon. On some days you could see the French coastline, it was said; but as usual all Marbeck saw was mist, and seabirds wheeling. He yawned and walked his tired mount on, along the last stretch of rutted road that had brought them by Rochester, Sittingbourne and Canterbury to the edge of England.

In the town he found stabling for Cobb, and, having seen to the horse's comforts, made his way to the sea wall to stretch his legs. Dover was astir, with fishing boats setting out. Looking westwards to the harbour, he saw large ships moored, while on the far strand lay several hulks that spoke of past dangers: Spanish vessels left to rot, their beams like skeletal ribs. Drawing deeply on the sweet air, he turned from the water and went in search of breakfast. The inns were open, for Dover was used to travellers. He ate in the Woolsack, paid his reckoning and left. *Near the castle*, Prout had said; and that was where he would start looking for the house of Mother Sewell.

Below the castle's west wall lay a cluster of

small streets. People were about, but Marbeck paid them little attention. With a casual air, he strolled the narrow ways until he found what he was looking for. It was a large corner house, somewhat rickety, with an upper storey that looked out over the sea lanes as well as the road to London – just the sort of place Gifford would pick. Having learned from a passer-by that this was indeed the house he sought, he went to the door and knocked. Soon it opened a few inches and a face peered out, framed by a linen hood.

'Mother Sewell?' Marbeck enquired.

'Nay, sir – she's busy.' The maid held on to the door tightly. 'If you're wanting a room, they're all took. Try the Swan, over by St James's.'

'I seek a friend,' Marbeck said. 'I believe he lodges here.'

The girl shook her head, and the conversation would have ended had he not remembered the cover name Gifford used.

'His name's Porter – Edward Porter. Is he within?'

'Master Porter's abed, sir,' the maid answered, after a moment's hesitation. 'If you care to leave a message, I'll tell him when he rises.'

She looked embarrassed – and at once Marbeck knew why.

'Tell him John Sands is here,' he said, and pushed the door inwards, forcing her to step back. Flustered, she stood aside while he entered a hallway with stale rushes underfoot.

'It's best that I wait here, isn't it?' he added, with eyebrows raised. 'I wouldn't want to blunder

38

into his chamber and upset whoever else might be there.'

The maid was a spindle-thin girl of fourteen or fifteen. With an up-and-down glance at him, she grabbed her skirts and hurried to the stairs. There wasn't long to wait; voices were heard, floorboards creaked, then someone padded to the stairhead and looked down.

'By the Christ, what foul wind swept *you* here?'

Unhurriedly, Marbeck glanced up. 'The same one that brought you, I expect.'

As their eyes met, he felt both pleasure and irritation: the mixture Joseph Gifford often aroused in him. Already the man's brow had creased into a familiar expression, one of pained amusement. 'You'd better come up,' he said.

Marbeck climbed the stairs. As he reached the landing, he saw a door closing and heard female voices beyond it. One was the maid's; the other, he guessed, belonged to Mother Sewell, who had just made herself scarce. With a thin smile, he followed his fellow intelligencer through another door into a cluttered chamber, where one glance at the rumpled bed was enough.

'Does the hostess charge you extra for body services?' he enquired, closing the door behind him.

Gifford was at the window, pulling curtains back. As sunlight flooded in, he turned, a grin in place. 'You know I never pay for it, Marbeck,' he said. 'She's a widow – past forty years, but firm of flesh; not too old for barley-brake.'

He was a handsome man – one of those with a high forehead, his blonde hair worn long at the

39

sides. He was barefoot and had thrown a morning-gown over his nightshirt.

'Will you take some Rhenish, while I dress myself?' He gestured to a small table where a jug and cups stood.

'I won't,' Marbeck said. 'A clear head's best for discourse.'

Gifford paused, then moved to the bed and sat down facing him. 'Why have you come down here?' he asked warily. 'To rake over the Antwerp business?'

When Marbeck made no answer, he let out a sigh. 'Have you not spoken with others?' he demanded. 'I knew nothing of that house being watched – I'll swear to it. My warrant was to stay in Flushing, watch vessels coming and going – as I do here. There's a flow of illicit books, papist tracts and the like. I've orders to break it, come what may—'

'What about Moore?' Marbeck broke in sharply.

The other looked away. 'Regrettable,' he murmured. 'And yes, I know it could have been you in Spanish hands – as it might have been me, on other occasions. Such risks we all take, Marbeck.'

'I'm John Sands, just now,' Marbeck said gently.

'But of course you are,' Gifford retorted. '*Shifting Sands*, someone called you – did you know that? Always on the move.' He put on a wry look. 'Just what is it that's chasing you now?'

'There was a physician, called himself Gomez,' Marbeck said. 'He was racked in the Marshalsea. Before he died, he spilled a tale – about Mulberry.'

40

The grin left Gifford's features, and a knowing expression appeared. 'So that's why you're in Dover,' he said finally. 'To do a little fishing.'

The two eyed each other . . . and, for Marbeck, a dozen years suddenly fell away. A memory sprang up: two youths in black gowns rolling out of a Cambridge tavern, stumbling along a lane towards the river. Then shouts from behind, running feet – and in an instant they were set upon by half a dozen town bullies. There, beside the Cam, the fight had raged: fists flailing, blood welling, cries and curses loud in the night air, until at last the assailants backed off, surprised by the resistance they had met. Two of their number lay on the grass; another knelt, hugging his ribs . . . while Martin Marbeck and Joseph Gifford, students of St John's, stood blooded and breathless, but unbeaten. A day to remember, they said later; they'd vowed to keep its memory . . .

'Fishing?' Marbeck drew breath. 'Well, why not?'

'So, is this Master Secretary's bidding you do? Nay . . .' Eyes narrowing, Gifford shook his head. 'This is some whim of your own, I wager. And who – or what – is Mulberry?'

For answer, Marbeck wandered to the window and looked out. 'You've a fine view of the Channel,' he observed. 'How far is it across to Dunkirk, would you say? Forty miles? Forty-five?'

Gifford watched him.

'Forty or forty-five – what does it matter?' Marbeck went on. 'That's how close the Spaniards are: but a few hours' sail, with a favourable wind.' He turned round abruptly. 'Who do you think betrayed us? One of the English renegades? Or

41

some merchant perhaps, happily doing business with both sides? Which reminds me: I hear you've a Spanish whore in Flushing – is that true?'

There was no answer.

'Was it she you lay with, when Moore and I were trapped like rats in that house in Antwerp?'

Again nothing.

'They work differently from us – the Spanish, I mean.' Marbeck's tone was conversational. 'The French, too. Catherine de Medici had some pretty female agents in her service, I believe. Men like us must be careful whom we bed.'

'And careful whom we accuse, too.' Gifford spoke low, and his face was taut. 'I thought you knew me better, Marbeck.'

'I thought I knew Tom Standish, too,' Marbeck replied. 'Remember him? Yet there he is, over in Rouen: a papist down to his soles, they say, spitting fire at his own countrymen any chance he gets.'

In an instant Gifford was on his feet. 'If you mean to name me a traitor too, then do so!' he snapped. 'Though in God's name, I can't think why you would.'

'No?' Marbeck's voice was harsh too. 'Then why take a Spanish drab to bed, when there are Dutch aplenty?'

Angrily, the two faced each other. Outside, footsteps descended the stairs; Mother Sewell was now dressed, Marbeck surmised. Then he frowned slightly. A look had come over Gifford's face that he knew well enough.

'You haven't seen her, Marbeck,' he said with a sigh. 'If you had, you wouldn't need to ask.'

42

He lowered his gaze and indicated a stool. 'Now that we've done with the pleasantries, will you sit while I attire myself? Then I think we should get some air, don't you?'

It was a long day, but by evening matters had been settled. Marbeck would send a despatch to Sir Robert Cecil and await his reply. Because for the present, he knew, his investigation had stalled.

He had taken a room at an inn Gifford had named: the Greyhound in Biggin Street, close to the harbour. There he penned his report to the spymaster, using a cipher and signing it with his number, twelve. There was a post-horse service to London, for servants of the State; a rider was leaving at first light. Having delivered the sealed letter, he took his first proper rest in two days, awaking next morning to the harsh cries of seagulls.

Restlessly, he got up and went to the window. Gazing out over the bustling little town, he began to think. He would not seek out Gifford; the two had agreed it was best they weren't seen together again. But their stroll by the harbour, which turned into a longer walk along the sea strand, had revealed troubling news. It seemed that in Dover there were more rumours of a planned landing by the Spanish: not from Spain, but from their territories in the Low Countries.

'My orders were to watch incoming ships, for one who's posing as a merchant,' Gifford had told him. 'He's the one likely bringing in the literature. Him I could deal with – but what must I do if an entire fleet appears in the Channel?'

43

They had talked through the morning, and as always Marbeck's anger with the man had abated. Gifford had his own troubles; and in the end the intelligencers had pooled what knowledge they had, even sharing a jest about Sir Robert Cecil. But after they parted Marbeck found himself in sober mood. His journey here, he knew, had been on a whim. He was no closer to finding out who Mulberry was, and the trail was cold.

He threw the window open, letting in a gust of sea air, and began to dress. The prospect of kicking his heels in another inn was not to his liking; he had done it often, and frequently to little purpose. He thought of his meeting with Cecil, and about the quandary the spymaster faced. If Mulberry had indeed been feeding him false reports of enemy plans, which ones could be believed? Would the Spanish really come again – and, if so, from where? The south coast of England was long, and landing places were many. Here at the very tip of his country, with the sea stretching to the horizon, Marbeck felt its vulnerability. That feeling wouldn't go away, he knew; not until he had uncovered something of use.

But that day brought a surprise – and a change to his plans. It came with a knocking in the afternoon, as he lay on the bed dozing. He went to the door, to find not a maidservant but an ostler in dirty fustian.

'Your pardon, Master Sands.' The man touched his cap. 'Only a messenger just came into the yard – ridden hard and fast, by the look of him. He said you should have this at once.'

44

He held out a sealed paper. With murmured thanks, Marbeck took it and closed the door. Going to the window, he broke the seal, unfolded it . . . and blinked.

Brittany?

He mouthed the word, as he read the short missive to its end. He knew his report couldn't have got to Cecil so quickly, let alone brought such a prompt reply, but when he looked at the date he understood: Prout, of course.

He lowered the letter. Prout knew he'd gone to Dover – it wouldn't take long to enquire at the inns for John Sands. In any case, the Greyhound was the one Gifford had used before he found more congenial lodgings. He sighed. His own despatch, in any case, was now superfluous. Here were new orders telling him to cease his present task and leave at once for France.

He re-read the letter. It was coded, of course, as was his master's name. Anyone else who happened to see the message would have noted references to goods being shipped, friends to be remembered and other everyday matters. But to Marbeck, Cecil's meaning was clear: there was rumour of a build-up of Spanish troops in Brittany. Marbeck spoke French, hence he must go there and assess the situation. As for Mulberry . . .

Mulberry wasn't even mentioned; all at once, priorities had changed. A few days ago, he mused, a threat was perceived to be coming from the new fleet being assembled at Lisbon. Next, according to Gifford, an invasion might be launched from Holland . . . Was Brittany now the source?

45

He moved to the bed and sank down upon it. So, he was bound for France – at least he would not be idle. He could sail from Dover, which was no doubt what Cecil expected him to do, then make his way along the French coast by barque from Calais. Or he might get himself to Portsmouth and cross to Dieppe. Either way, it meant leaving Cobb here in Dover. He would have to leave instructions for him to be exercised – and money, too. It was fortunate that he had a full purse . . .

He sat on the bed, thinking rapidly: there was another way that was better. Small boats left from Dover, and skirted the south coast as far as Plymouth. From there he could take ship directly to Brittany; the crossing was longer, and there was the risk of meeting Channel pirates, but he liked the notion. He was unknown in Plymouth – but Edmund Trigg was there, or had been the last Marbeck had heard. He could lodge with him while he arranged passage.

He folded Cecil's message up tightly; he would dispose of it later. Briskly, he stood up, went to the window and threw it wide, letting in a blast of sea air.

Plymouth it would be, then. And from the tone of the spymaster's letter, it seemed there was no time to lose.

Five

Grey clouds scudded in over Plymouth, and as soon as Marbeck stepped ashore, three days after leaving Dover, he sensed an air of unease that seemed to permeate the very stones of the old walled city. Stiff, salt-stained and windswept, he stood on the busy harbour with the reek of tar and fish in his nostrils and looked about. Somewhere a bell was tolling – then he remembered it was Sunday. He was surveying the cluttered quayside, when a raggedly dressed boy appeared at his elbow.

'Us'll teck your baggage, sir . . . find 'ee a tavern, if you wish it. Say, a halfpenny?'

'I seek a friend,' Marbeck said after a moment. 'Scholarly fellow, bald as an egg. Keeps a little shop hereabouts—'

'Name of Trigg?' the lad broke in. When Marbeck gave a nod, he put on a sad expression.

'Lost his shop, Trigg did. Couldn't make a fist of it . . . Heard he took a lodging over by St Andrew's church.' He brightened. 'But I can take 'ee there, maister – for a penny?'

Marbeck appeared to think about it. It may have been Sunday, but two or three vessels were being loaded. 'Where are those ships bound for?' he asked, pointing. 'Ireland? Supplies for our troops is it, or reinforcements?'

'Mayhap, sir,' the boy answered. 'There's been

47

a deal of toing and froing these past years. Soldiers billeted in town. They fight sometimes – folks are mighty sick of it.'

There was movement nearby. More people from the Dover boat had disembarked, and now an official-looking figure approached them. Marbeck glanced at the harbour waif, who gave a nod.

'That's the mayor's man,' he said helpfully. 'They always question travellers nowadays.'

The church bell had ceased tolling. With a swift look at the distant spire, Marbeck asked. 'Is that St Andrew's?'

'Aye, maister.' The boy grinned. 'Does you want to go and find your friend?'

'I does,' Marbeck said. 'And if you want to earn that penny, you'd best step lively.'

The other nodded eagerly. Soon the two of them had ducked into an alley, left the harbour and skirted the city's south wall, to come by twists and turns to a narrow street near the church. There Marbeck paid off his guide, finding himself outside a tumbledown house, then in a passageway that smelled of mildew. Having taken the boy at his word, he walked to the end door and knocked.

'By the Saints . . . Marbeck!'

Edmund Trigg stood in the doorway of the dimly lit room. He was stooped, lowering his tall frame by several inches. His old gown, spattered with stains Marbeck didn't care to speculate about, hung loosely on him. He looked like a man who hadn't had a proper meal – or a wash – in weeks.

'Trigg.' Marbeck nodded a greeting. 'Forgive the intrusion. I was going to beg a night's lodging . . .' He broke off, for at once the other grew animated.

'Of course – pray you, come in! I get so few visitors.'

The man's eagerness was genuine. Excitedly, he drew Marbeck inside the untidy chamber and fussed about, clearing a stool for him to sit. The place stank of unwashed clothes and bedding, and of mouldy paper. Books and documents lay scattered in corners, on a tiny table, on the floor. Eyebrows raised, Marbeck looked round.

'I hear you've given up your shop,' he said finally.

'Oh, that!' Trigg dismissed it. 'Too much trouble – I've no bent for commerce. I've returned to my true muse: poetry. I'm tutor to an alderman's son – there are some who value real scholarship, even here beyond the pale of civilization!' He forced a smile through his beard, which was in need of trimming. 'But please, seat yourself . . .' He paused. 'You're on, ah . . . London business, I expect?' When Marbeck shrugged, he ran a hand over his bald pate. 'And how fares Master Secretary? I hear he's still at loggerheads with that popinjay Essex.'

'There are other matters to occupy him just now,' Marbeck said, stifling a yawn. He sat down heavily upon the stool. The voyage along the coast had been uneventful, but he never slept well on board ship. He glanced up and found Trigg gazing at him.

'Saints above,' the scholar muttered. 'It's pleasant to see a face from the old days. What joys once, eh?' But the words caught in his throat

49

– and the next moment, to Marbeck's embarrassment, the man was close to tears. He sniffed, wiped his nose with his sleeve, then threw his arms out helplessly.

'As you see, this is no place to converse,' he said. 'But a few pennies will buy pilchards at an ordinary. If perhaps you could . . .' He trailed off. To his relief, Marbeck was nodding.

'Away with your pilchards,' he said. 'Does a beef dinner not tempt you, with a pint of claret beside it?'

Trigg's mouth fell open, and something like a shudder passed through him. '*Ecce Aurora!*' he said, and opened his hands as if in benediction. '*Ecce Aurora, fide amice!*'

Marbeck sighed and got to his feet.

They ate quickly; Marbeck because he'd taken nothing since the previous night, Trigg simply because he was ravenous. Finally, the scholar leaned back from the table, drained his cup of wine and eyed his host. 'Now we may talk, if you wish,' he said.

The ordinary was quiet, and they sat in a corner booth. Marbeck took a drink and eyed him. 'What's afoot here?' he asked. 'I know fear when I smell it – and I smelled it the moment I came off the boat.'

Trigg looked surprised. 'You must have heard the rumours, surely? The place is on tenterhooks – sentries posted, patrol boats manned. Everyone keeps an eye out for the Spanish.'

'Will you elaborate?' Marbeck asked, after a moment.

50

'By the Saints!' Trigg frowned. 'Have you forgotten what happened down here, five years ago? Galleys sweeping inland, villages burned – even Penzance was aflame!'

'That was in Cornwall,' Marbeck said. 'A small raid – four ships, wasn't it? Plymouth's well fortified.'

'Not many troops now,' Trigg said, with a shake of his head. 'This isn't the main departure point for Ireland – Chester fills that duty. Levies get sent to Barnstaple. Plymouth's a supply port now – surplus grain, mostly.'

'So what's the source of these rumours? You know invasion scares are common as fleas – have been since eighty-eight.'

'Ah, but there's intelligence, too.' Trigg leaned forward. 'I've a report for Cecil back at my lodgings, half written. I've set it all down.' Suddenly, his face twitched. 'I know he thinks me a third-rate informer – perhaps that's why he seldom pays me. But my eyes are as sharp as yours, Marbeck – my ears, too. And I can still tell the difference between gossip and fact!'

Drink had enlivened the man, but Marbeck let him talk. Soon, flushed and animated, Trigg was holding forth about a Spanish plan to invade England from the west. This time, he was certain, they wouldn't attempt to sail the length of the Channel. Instead, they would land at Cornish ports like Falmouth and Fowey, then send troops inland while other vessels made for Plymouth.

'They could have done it in ninety-five!' he exclaimed. 'If they'd crossed the Peninsula, Bristol would have been threatened. And Welsh

51

renegades would have joined them to attack us! Don't you see?'

'I didn't think the Welsh posed a serious threat,' Marbeck observed dryly. 'Some of them are fighting for us in Ireland.'

But his words only aroused Trigg further. 'What matters that?' he exclaimed. 'Why, it's but fifty years since the Cornish rebelled against the Crown, back in King Edward's time. Meanwhile, a hundred miles west – as you say yourself – the Irish are at our throats!' He seized the wine jug and poured himself another cupful. Then, taking a slurp, he levelled a finger. 'Never trust a Celt, Marbeck – they're as bad as the Spanish, and as wily as the French!'

A sigh escaped Marbeck's lips. 'Is that the substance of your next despatch to Master Secretary?' he enquired.

'What – do you scoff at me?'

There was a moment, then Trigg set down his cup. 'Pray forgive me . . . I've made free with your hospitality,' he said, with an attempt at dignity. 'Yet poor as I am, I've not lost my reason. I fed on logic at Oxford – just as you did, at the other place.'

'Very well.' Marbeck met his eye. 'Then let's apply reason and logic, shall we? These rumours of a Spanish landing in the west – where do they stem from?'

'I've said I had intelligence,' Trigg replied. 'It was no idle boast. My informants are few, but trustworthy. The fishermen go far afield – to the Bay of Biscay, even. And there are pinnaces out at sea, ready to board Breton boats.' He grew

52

animated again. 'Papists sneak in by the back door, you know. Think of the Bretons – they're Celts too, aren't they? What did I tell you?'

'Your source,' Marbeck said wearily, 'for this talk of a Spanish landing?'

'The source? It's in Brest,' Trigg told him. 'A hundred miles south of us. Cecil has a man in Brittany . . . but you'll know that, I expect.'

Marbeck nodded briefly. And seeing he would add nothing, Trigg talked on. 'He's a merchant, I think,' he said. 'Or something else . . . Anyhow, he uses the name Cyprien. Two weeks ago he sent word to me that—'

'Two weeks?' Marbeck had lifted his cup; now he put it down with a thud. 'And you've not yet penned your despatch?'

'It's almost finished,' Trigg said quickly. 'I've a lot to do here, you know. My mind's seldom still . . .' But as the other's impatience showed, he lowered his gaze.

'By heaven, Edmund,' Marbeck breathed. 'These are dangerous times. Cecil's desk is awash with reports of Spanish activity. All intelligence is valuable – perhaps yours more than most! Have you forgotten that?'

'Of course not!' The scholar gulped. 'See now, I'll finish my report today – this very evening. Perhaps you can take it back with you, when you leave for London?'

But Marbeck shook his head. 'You must use other means. I'm not going back – not just yet.'

The other swallowed. There was a dullness in his eyes as he stared down at the table. He not only looked tired: Marbeck saw a man clinging

53

to the remnants of his self-respect. He spoke again, in a gentler tone.

'Send your despatch, and make mention of my visit,' he said. 'Tell our master I was en route – he knows where. Say I'll report when I can. Will you do that?'

'I will.' Trigg nodded, then lifted his gaze. 'I . . . I won't ask where you're going. I'll merely say *cave, fide amice*. You've not forgotten your Latin, I hope?'

'I've not forgotten.' Marbeck raised his cup and drained it. 'I'll not trouble you for a bed for the night, after all. I have arrangements to make. Perhaps you can point me to someone who'll sell me some ducats?'

'Of course.' The scholar showed his disappointment. 'I'll walk as far as the port with you.' He reached out suddenly and caught Marbeck by the sleeve. 'Speaking of money, has Master Secretary provided you with a goodly purse? I hate to raise the matter, only . . .'

'Save your breath,' Marbeck replied. 'Would five crowns be of any use to you?'

The other's face lit up briefly. He looked away and mumbled a quotation, adding: 'Cicero.'

'I know,' Marbeck said, and called for the reckoning.

A day later, and the wind had risen; as he had feared, the sea journey was somewhat rough.

He had sailed the English Channel often enough, but his crossings had been at its eastern end, where the distance was mercifully short. The voyage from Plymouth to the Breton coast was of a different

54

nature: a hundred miles of dangerous water, open to the great Atlantic. And for the first time in years Marbeck felt the threat of seasickness.

To allay it, he ventured on to the open deck. The seamen were busy at their work, hurrying about the little vessel, and paid him no attention. She was a fishing smack, bound for the waters of Finisterre, but for a price her captain had agreed to put Marbeck ashore on the western tip of Brittany. A Devonshire sea-dog, heavily bearded, he stood behind the wheel, gazing at Marbeck who was clutching a stay for balance. Finally, he beckoned, so Marbeck ventured over to him unsteadily. The captain stifled a laugh.

'I advise 'ee to get below, sir,' he said, raising his voice against the spray. 'We've more than a day's sail before we strike Ushant – that's an isle off Point St Matthew. Another hour or two more, to get you to Conquet.'

'I fear a flux of the stomach,' Marbeck told him. 'I believe it's best to stay in the open air.' He staggered to the rail again and quickly found a place to steady himself.

To occupy his mind, he ran over recent events. It was several days since he had sent his last despatch to Cecil, from Dover. Now Trigg would send his; he was confident of that, despite the man's laxity. They had parted as friends, yet he was uneasy: he would have no choice, once he returned to London, but to speak to the spymaster about his agent in Plymouth. The times allowed no room for sentiment.

He thought of Gifford, and then of Saxby and Ottone. A short while ago he had been charged with unmasking a traitor called Mulberry; now he was about to set foot in France, to another purpose. He wondered what he might find. It was two years since the French and Spanish kings had signed their peace accord at Vervins, after decades of strife. Now the Spaniards were supposed to have left, yet reports still spoke of ships criss-crossing the Bay of Biscay, and Spanish voices heard in the coastal villages. His mouth tightened. Once ashore, he must move swiftly. From Conquet he would travel east to Brest, and make contact with Cecil's agent.

He had chosen not to discuss Cyprien with Trigg. He had never met the man, but, thanks to coded information in Cecil's letter, he knew how to find him. The fellow was said to be reliable; hence intelligence that came from him must be taken seriously. But a Spanish invasion in the west?

To Marbeck that made no sense. It would mean a two-hundred-mile march to London, giving Elizabeth's commanders time to prepare defences, and the Spanish generals were too clever for that. There must be more to the matter; had Trigg misunderstood? Or was it misinformation? His thoughts leaped back to his conversation with Cecil. *Every scrap of intelligence that has crossed my desk*, Master Secretary had said, *might be false . . . a storm has broken about our heads . . .*

Suddenly, Marbeck almost laughed. Standing on the tilting deck with sea-spray in his face, he preferred not to think upon storms. He took a lungful of salt-laden air and cheered himself with the prospect of dry land. He pictured an inn, a warm fire and a cup of good wine.

But his optimism, it transpired, was short-lived. For at eventide a day later, as he finally clambered ashore in Brittany with a queasy stomach, two things struck him. The first was that in the village of Conquet nobody seemed to speak French; or, at least, nobody he encountered would admit to knowing any other tongue than their native Breton. Moreover, the inn was cold, and even the claret not to his taste.

But the surprise that awaited him the next day was more serious. Having begged a ride from a carter travelling eastwards, he arrived at last in the town of Brest – and found that Cyprien was dying.

Six

In France he was not Marbeck; nor was he even John Sands. He was Thomas Wilders, a merchant of mixed Dutch and English blood. Thomas Wilders had few morals, and even fewer scruples about how he did business – or with whom. The persona had served him well in the past, in Paris and elsewhere, and it should serve him in Brest, too. With that in mind, he took a room at an inn, then ventured out to get his bearings.

The town was old and had seen much conflict. It occupied the steep banks of the Penfeld River, and the visitor's eye was soon drawn to the castle at its mouth. But Marbeck's was on a round tower, the *Tour de Tanguy*, a short way upriver. Near it stood the home of the man he sought: a French Huguenot, who used the name Cyprien.

But he would not go yet. First, he strolled about, as any traveller might. He heard both French and Breton spoken, but no Spanish. Walking near the castle, he peered across the inlet, the *Rade de Brest*, and glimpsed the outline of the old Spanish fortress, the *Castilla de Leon*. A desperate battle had been fought here, six years ago, but that was when Spain and France were still at war. Now Marbeck was struck by how peaceful the town was. Having taken its measure, he returned to the inn. Then, as evening fell, he made his way

58

to the Tour, and in his passable French asked for the house of a man with a white streak in his hair . . . only to receive a shock.

That would be Louis Orme, he was told; his informant, an old woman, sighed and crossed herself. The *monsieur* must seek him at the convent of La Madeleine – in the hospital.

Dusk was falling, and briskly Marbeck walked as the woman had indicated, to a building which was unmistakable. At its entrance he found an aged Carmelite nun, and asked permission to visit his friend Louis Orme, who he had heard was gravely ill. The *religieuse* looked him over, before admitting him. So at last he came to a small, candlelit infirmary and was conducted to the bedside of one who appeared to be unconscious. But as the nursing sister moved away, the man opened his eyes.

'*Qui êtes-vous?*'

'I'm Thomas Wilders,' Marbeck said, speaking French. 'I've come over the water, with greetings from my friend Roger Daunt. He begged me to seek out his old comrade – Monsieur Cyprien.'

The other's eyes widened. He searched the visitor's face, but made no reply.

'I'm saddened to find you in this place,' Marbeck said. 'Is there anything I can do for you?'

He took in the man's shrivelled appearance. Cyprien's face was haggard, while the snow-white streak – his distinguishing mark – was now invisible, since all his hair had become the same colour. His eyes strayed to a stool by the bed, where stood a pitcher and an earthenware beaker. Marbeck poured water and brought it to the man's lips. After he had drunk, Cyprien sank back feebly upon the pillow. Then he spoke.

'Wilders . . .' He pronounced the word as if testing it.

Marbeck glanced round. The occupants of the other beds appeared to be sleeping. A sister sat by the door, fingering her rosary. But when he looked back, the invalid was trying to lift his hand. He took it, feeling its clammy warmth. But there was no grip; the man was as weak as a sparrow.

'Well, Thomas Wilders . . .' A faint smile appeared. 'I never thought my last confidant would be an *Anglais*. How does your good Queen Elizabeth? Rumours abound in France that she too lies close to death.'

With some relief, Marbeck smiled back; the man was not delirious as he had feared. He said: 'Rumour's a fickle jade, my friend. The last I heard, the Queen was dancing galliards at Richmond Palace and bantering with ambassadors.'

The other wheezed; an attempt at laughter. 'If only France had been blessed with such a monarch . . .' He gave a sigh. 'Well, monsieur . . . you come to learn what you can from me, before I change this bed for a coffin. Is it not so?'

Marbeck made no reply.

'Your silence is answer enough,' Cyprien breathed. 'So . . . will you tell me how goes the war? Perhaps I should say *wars*. I've been here some weeks . . . or so I believe. I was mad for a while, the sisters tell me. Now I am sane, but

60

helpless.' His face clouded. 'This sickness is beyond even their skills.'

Marbeck cleared the stool and moved it closer. 'I'm come from Plymouth,' he said as he sat down. 'There I spoke with another friend – you'll remember him as the Shopkeeper. He told me the tidings you sent, two weeks ago.'

'Was it so?' Cyprien frowned. 'I was already sick . . .' He gave a cough. 'Yet, now I remember. You English must make ready – the Spanish aren't done with you yet.'

'We know it,' Marbeck said – and before the man could speak again, he raised his hand. 'Please, save your strength. Let me talk.' And with that he gave him a very brief account of recent affairs. Dunkirk was still in Spanish hands, despite the Dutch victory at Nieuwpoort under Maurice of Orange. In the Low Countries the war raged on, as in Ireland. Rumours crossed and re-crossed the Channel, so that few knew what to believe.

'Enough – I pray you.'

Cyprien was wearying. Drawing a rasping breath, he said: 'The report I sent on to Plymouth came from someone I always trusted. She it was who spoke of this plan the young Philip's admirals have . . . I mean men like Brochero and Zubiaur. They wish to sail again to England and land in the west – that is why they build new ships at Lisbon—'

'I don't believe that,' Marbeck broke in. And when the other showed surprise, he outlined his objections.

'You think the tidings I sent were lies, then?'

61

Cyprien looked aghast. 'To lure your masters in the wrong direction?'

'Such practices are common enough in wartime,' Marbeck replied. 'Your source – you said "she"?'

Feebly, the sick man nodded. 'She would not fail me. And she is close to the Spanish – too close, some have claimed.'

'That's why I'm here – to get close to the Spanish,' Marbeck said. 'To find out why they're building up their troops in Brittany. It puzzles me . . . I understood that by the treaty of Vervins they'd agreed to leave—'

'But, my friend, they have done so.' Cyprien's face glistened with sweat, and his breathing was laboured. 'There are no Spanish here now,' he went on. 'A few ships down south, perhaps, on the Blavet.' He sighed. 'Perhaps they may wish your government to think they're still here in large numbers, when their troops are in Spain and Portugal.'

'But if that's true . . .' Marbeck thought quickly. 'If they're not here, then they're preparing to embark in the new fleet that's being built. Which means . . .'

Then he saw it; and at once he realized that he had known it all along.

'Which means?' Cyprien echoed.

'The Spanish fleet is bound for Ireland. It must be.'

The dying man frowned. 'Well, it was always the back door to England – everyone knows it. And the rebel Tyrone has been asking for Spanish help for years . . .'

He broke off then, as one of the convent's other

patients called out – a wailing cry. Marbeck looked round to see the sister moving to his bedside, then turned back to Cyprien.

'Indeed, some may wonder why it's taken them so long,' he said dryly.

'But . . .' Cyprien looked dismayed. 'I ask again: do you tell me the intelligence I took such pains to pass on is merely lies? I cannot believe such. I repeat: my source is true – she is a woman of courage and honour.'

'Will you tell me who she is?' Marbeck asked.

'You would go to her?'

'I have no time,' Marbeck replied with a shake of his head. 'Besides, what you've told me is enough. My master must hear of it.' He placed a hand on Cyprien's shoulder. 'England owes you much for your pains,' he said. 'Even now, at the very last.'

But the man had grown agitated. He coughed again, then said: 'Thomas Wilders – if such is really your name – please listen to me. My homeland of France – she is torn and bleeding. Do you know how many of her people have died, these past two score years? One million, or so they say.' He gave another sigh. 'Will we ever know peace? Why, it's but two years since the law gave rights to such men as me. That's why I'm permitted to lie here, instead of dying in the street!'

'The sisters are merciful,' Marbeck said. 'Taking in a Huguenot.'

'It's not only that.' Cyprien gazed fiercely at him. 'I speak of sacrifice – you understand me, I think . . .' He hesitated. 'I ask you now to do

63

me a service, my friend. It will be my last wish. I ask you to ride to this woman I spoke of, and tell her of my death. Tell her she was in my thoughts at the very last, as always . . . and besides, you may learn matters to your advantage. Where these tales come from, perhaps.'

In his eagerness, the man had raised his head slightly. Now he fell back in exhaustion, but his eyes peered into Marbeck's. A moment passed, then:

'Where should I go?' Marbeck asked quietly.

'To the Château des Faucons, on the Scorff River,' Cyprien answered. His relief was such, he even smiled. 'It's two days' ride, to the southeast. There you will find Marie, the Comtesse de Paiva. I was once her groom . . . and, in my private thoughts, I longed to be more.' His smile faded. 'But confide in her only – not her husband. She can tell you of the Spanish, more than you would learn elsewhere. So – will you make me this promise, my friend? Will you swear it?'

He waited, until at last Marbeck nodded. Then with a sigh, he closed his eyes.

The horse was named Chacal. Marbeck had been told so by a widow who kept a tiny stable close to Louis Orme's cottage near the Tour de Tanguy. The cottage, Marbeck learned, was to be hers; Monsieur Orme was a widower who had no relatives living. In return, she agreed to carry out the last wishes of her friend, as set out in the letter Marbeck showed her, and provide him with a mount. The letter was in his own hand, but at its end was a scrawled signature – all the dying man had been able to manage. Fortunately, it was recognizable. Which was how, mounted on a stubby French pony, Marbeck came to leave Brest the following day and ride up the Elorn Valley. At Landerneau he crossed the river and turned southwards, to begin his journey to a château on the Scorff, where lived the Comtesse de Paiva.

He was thoughtful as he rode. It was a promise to a dying man, he told himself – several times – but it didn't help much. He had to get a despatch to Cecil, at the first opportunity. Though at least he could reflect while he travelled. Part of him insisted that the journey could prove useful, perhaps shedding light on Spanish activities. He might even uncover the source of what he felt certain was false intelligence – and which, bizarrely, seemed to have emanated from the French interior, before coming thence to the west of England via Brittany.

Other thoughts pleased him less. This was a fool's errand, another part of him reasoned, which stemmed from a moment of weakness. Or had he simply been intrigued by the dying Cyprien's account of the Comtesse de Paiva, whom he seemed to adore? The woman was *close to the Spanish*, the man had said . . . in which case, perhaps, a visit might prove fruitful. As Thomas Wilders, he would pose as a dealer in ordnance – a man with access to cannons that had gone astray from Elizabeth's navy. He had used the story once before; English guns were prized and much sought after. But he must speak to the Comtesse alone, Cyprien had told him. Might her husband pose a difficulty?

He looked about him. The sun had risen, and ahead in the distance was a range of hills: *Les Monts d'Arrée*. Beyond them was another range he must cross, *Les Montagnes Noires* – the Black Mountains. A hilly country of farms and forests lay beyond, before he would eventually strike the valley of the River Scorff. The river flowed down to join the estuary of the Blavet; there, the Spaniards had once based a fleet. If Cyprien's suspicions were correct, they might yet have vessels in the region.

That at least would be something to tell Sir Robert Cecil, he thought, when he eventually made his way back to London. He could say he had travelled through the heart of Brittany, and made certain that the Spanish had truly departed – hence confirming that intelligence to the contrary was false. It might just persuade Master Secretary that his journey had not been entirely wasted.

With that in mind, he made good speed, heading deeper into the rural interior. The air was sweet and the countryside fair; and so, on the evening of the following day, after a journey of more than seventy miles, he emerged at last from a line of trees and reined in. He was looking down a gentle slope at the valley of the River Scorff – and there below him was the Château des Faucons.

It was smaller than he had expected: the seat of a minor member of the nobility. He scanned the walled gardens and outbuildings. Cattle grazed the surrounding fields, while on the river beyond he saw a landing stage, with small boats drawn up. It was a scene of tranquillity. Why,

66

then, Marbeck asked himself, this feeling of foreboding?

For unease had come upon him the moment he left the tree-line. Alert, despite his weariness, he eased the pony forward and rode down the slope until he struck a road which approached the château from the south. By the time he neared the gates, which stood open, dusk was falling. Nobody challenged him, so he passed under an archway into an enclosed courtyard and halted.

There was no one about. The only sound, a soft cooing, came from a dovecote that stood in the centre of the yard. The surrounding windows were dark – save for one on the upper storey, where a light showed. He glanced round in the saddle. The main entrance was ahead of him, approached by a broad flight of steps. After a moment he called out in French. There was a brief silence, then to his left a door clattered open. He swung round, to see a figure stumble out.

'*Monsieur . . . c'est vous?*'

The servant was elderly, with long white hair. Torchlight spilled from the doorway behind him. Marbeck stayed in the saddle as the old man hurried towards him, bowing obsequiously. But when he drew close, squinting upwards in the gloom, he gave a start.

'*Non – c'est un autre! Qui va lá?*'

At once Marbeck assumed the manner of a man of status addressing a lackey. In clipped tones he announced himself as a merchant who had business with la Comtesse de Paiva. Then, without waiting for reply, he dismounted and held out the pony's reins. 'I've had a long ride – see my mount's well cared for,' he said. 'Will someone conduct me to la Comtesse?'

The servant stared, then took the reins automatically, whereupon another figure appeared in the doorway.

'Qu'est-ce que c'est?'

The voice was female. Marbeck strode past the old man to greet one he assumed was a woman-in-waiting. He gave his name and business, and mentioned a message he carried. It was private, for *la Comtesse*, he went on . . . then he looked into the woman's face, and fell silent.

'I'm Marie-Clothilde, Comtesse de Paiva.'

She said it in English. Marbeck gazed at her, concealing his surprise, and made his bow.

'Your pardon, madame,' he said. 'I thought—'

'So I surmise.' The lady peered at him with large eyes, though her expression gave nothing away. Then she glanced at the elderly servant, who was still standing beside Marbeck's horse. In a few words she instructed him, whereupon he led the animal away.

'Matthieu has poor eyesight,' she murmured. 'He thought you were my husband.'

Marbeck inclined his head. Sugared phrases rose to his lips, but he held them in. This woman, he sensed, would not be susceptible to flattery. Instead, he said: 'Then perhaps I arrive at the right hour. For the words I carry are for your ears alone, madame. I have brought them from the convent of La Madeleine in Brest . . . from the bedside of a dying man. He begs to be remembered to you; his name is Louis Orme.'

The Comtesse continued to gaze at him, and, in spite of himself, he was impressed. She was rather beautiful.

'Wilders,' she murmured. 'Is that a Dutch name?'

'Anglo-Dutch, madame,' Marbeck said. 'Yet my loyalties are to none but myself.' He was hungry and thirsty, his body sore from riding. Yet he watched her and waited – and all at once the woman frowned.

'He's dying . . . Louis is dying?'

'I fear so,' Marbeck answered. 'I was at his side . . . He had but days to live.'

Only now had the news struck home, he realized. 'But that is terrible . . .' The Comtesse looked round and called towards the open doorway. A voice answered.

'You need rest after your journey,' she went on, facing Marbeck again. 'But first you must take food and tell me of poor Louis. You are a friend of his?'

'I am, but not a close one,' Marbeck replied.

'Yet you came all this way, only to bring his respects?'

He hesitated. This wasn't the time – yet when would there be another? It seemed the Comtesse's husband was expected at any moment; he drew a breath.

'In fact, it's not only for that. I'm a man of business, madame, and I've heard you may be able to help me.'

A moment passed . . . then, to his relief, the woman nodded.

'I understand, Monsieur Wilders,' she said stiffly. 'Will you please to enter my house?'

Seven

The Château des Faucons was ancient, it seemed, and had changed hands many times before coming into the possession of the Comte de Paiva. So the Comtesse told Marbeck over an excellent supper, in a small chamber on the upper floor of the house. His hostess had already dined, but nevertheless kept him company while he ate, taking a cup of sweet wine herself. The only others present were two male servants who waited on them. The atmosphere was congenial; indeed, Marbeck's welcome had been warmer than he expected. Which was why, as he enjoyed roast quails and stewed carp, he began to wonder why he was being treated like an honoured guest.

He soon exhausted his tale of Louis Orme, whom he described as a friend he had not seen in years, before finding himself by chance at his sickbed in Brest. It was the dying man's wish, he explained, that he should tell the Comtesse his last thoughts had been of her, and of happier times. This the lady acknowledged politely; her manner, he thought, had become markedly cooler than earlier. Finally, having declined a rich pudding, Marbeck declared himself sated and changed the subject.

'Your husband, madame – you expect him home soon?'

'He has been out two days on Domain

business,' the lady replied. 'He will return by nightfall.' She glanced towards the window. 'And yet the night draws in already . . .' She favoured Marbeck with a smile. 'The roads are poor hereabouts, Monsieur Wilders – you will, of course, be our guest. I have ordered a chamber to be readied for you.'

Taken aback, Marbeck expressed gratitude. 'Your kindness is such, it pains me to speak of mundane matters,' he ventured. 'Yet I would beg your indulgence. I've said I'm a man of business, madame. I came to Western France in hopes of finding representatives of His Royal Majesty . . . I mean not your King Henri, but the King of Spain. I was told you might number such men among your acquaintance?'

He touched a napkin to his mouth. The room was warm, lit by a log fire as well as numerous candles. He longed to unbutton his doublet. La Comtesse, for her part, displayed a neck and shoulders bare of anything save jewellery and puffed sleeves of silver gauze. Keeping his eyes on hers, Marbeck waited.

'Was it Louis Orme who told you so?' she enquired, raising her eyebrows. 'I ask because it's some years since he and I saw each other. Times change . . . as do circumstances.'

'They do,' Marbeck agreed. 'I know that since the peace treaty the forces of Spain have withdrawn from Brittany. Nevertheless, I suspect there are some not too far away, whom I could do business with.' He met her eye. 'Or do I presume too much?'

There was a silence. Then the Comtesse smiled

71

again, somewhat archly, and fingered a ruby pendant that lay upon her chest. Inwardly, he tensed: was she now flirting with him?

'Might I ask what, precisely, is the nature of your trade, Monsieur Wilders?'

The question sounded casual. But knowing that opportunity might be lost at any moment, Marbeck seized it.

'Ordnance, madame,' he said. 'More precisely, cannons that once saw service on English ships – the same ships that vanquished the late King of Spain's fleet, a dozen years ago. I'm a peddler, if you like – a dealer in instruments of destruction.'

'That is a dangerous activity,' the lady observed.

'It is,' Marbeck allowed. 'Yet as long as men wage war upon one another, it remains profitable. It has taken me to many places: to the fringes of Europe . . . even to the Palace of the Grand Sultan, in Constantinople.'

'And was that visit profitable?'

Perhaps she wasn't flirting after all, he thought, but testing him. It was time to produce some cover.

'Not as much as I'd hoped,' he answered amiably. 'The Turks are fierce bargainers. The Spanish, on the other hand, can be generous. Ten years ago they were paying twenty English pounds a ton for our cannons – cast-iron, of course. Now I'm asking twenty-five for culverins – eighteen-pounders, splendid guns cast in the Forest of Dean. I can also lay my hands upon demi-cannon – thirty-pounders.' He smiled. 'But I'm sure you've no wish to hear such petty details.'

'On the contrary, it's most interesting.' La

Comtesse gazed steadily at him, and it was then that Marbeck made a slip. It was unlike him, but he was weary and the wine was strong, and though he had tried to drink little, it had taken its effect.

'Our friend Cyp—'

Quickly, he turned it into a cough. 'Forgive me, madame.' He patted his chest and made a gesture of self-deprecation. 'I've ridden far, and your table is so fine . . . I grow sluggish. Perhaps we may speak further tomorrow?' Then, feeling he should mention her husband, he added: 'I would naturally wish to pay my respects to Monsieur le Comte.'

There was no reply. Marbeck waited – then gambled.

'Although . . . Louis Orme did suggest it was you I should confide in,' he went on. 'You are, he said, close to the Spanish. Forgive me, but those were his words.'

'Were they indeed?' The lady gazed at him. 'And what, Monsieur Wilders, did you take them to mean?'

'Merely that you were acquainted with men of rank and status, during the Spanish occupation,' Marbeck answered. 'Their ships were downriver, I understand?'

'At Blavet.' The Comtesse gave a nod. 'The town was returned to French control two years ago. Did you not know that?'

'Of course.' Marbeck nodded, too. 'Yet a man who conducts my sort of business must look beyond the obvious, madame. I seek a market for my wares – nothing more. I deal where I can, and judge no man provided he pays. Do I make myself clear?'

There was another silence. The fire had sunk low, and several candles had gone out. He looked round, expecting a servant to replenish them, and only now realized that he and the Comtesse were alone. Then he felt a hand on his, and turned sharply.

'It grows late . . . I must go to my bed.'

The lady had leaned forward and laid her bejewelled hand upon his wrist. When Marbeck met her eye, she added: 'On nights when my husband returns this late, his custom is to go straight to his chamber and have a supper brought there. He will fall asleep at once, and not rise before midday.' She allowed the words to sink in, then: 'You will be conducted to the Cerise room. It is small, but it has a unique feature: a hidden panel in one wall. If this should open during the night, would you be alarmed?'

'It would depend on what – or I should say who – came through the panel, madame,' Marbeck said, after a moment.

'Who would you hope might come through it?'

'I hesitate to voice it.' He appeared flattered, but he was on his guard. This was not what he had intended, nor did it feel comfortable. But when he asked himself what Thomas Wilders would do, the answer came immediately.

'Yet if I may make bold,' he added, 'I would hope to see the person I see before me now – the most beautiful woman I have encountered in a long time.' He smiled. 'Though I would have to pinch myself, to be sure I was awake.'

74

He waited, smile still in place, whereupon la Comtesse withdrew her hand.

'Very well,' she said, in a tone that bordered on the businesslike. 'Now, if you will excuse me . . .' She turned and snapped an order. The door opened, and a servant hurried in to stand behind her chair. As she rose, he pulled it back skilfully. 'Until tomorrow, Monsieur Wilders,' she said coolly, and stretched out her hand.

Marbeck got to his feet and bent to kiss it. Then he was alone, with the fire sinking to its embers.

The Cerise room was indeed small, and half filled by a large, ornate bed. Tired as he was, Marbeck slept fitfully, before waking in darkness. For a few seconds he struggled to get his bearings, then sat bolt upright. The single window had curtains, but he had pulled them back before retiring. With nothing but starlight to see by, he scanned the room, his eyes resting finally on the wall-panel.

It was narrow and little more than five feet high; he had already examined the wall and found hairline cracks. There was no catch of any sort: it must open from the other side. Briefly, he wondered how many times la Comtesse had used it in the past. Then he began, once again, to run over the details of the past evening.

He was uneasy. Was this really the woman Cyprien adored – his former employer, whom he had described as a woman of honour? Thus far, she struck Marbeck as a bored and flirtatious member of the provincial nobility, perhaps married to a man much older than herself. Such women could be found in any country in Europe;

was his friend Lady Celia Scroop not one of them? But Lady Scroop, he knew, would never have behaved as precipitately as la Comtesse had done, with a man she had just met. The more Marbeck thought about it, the more suspicious he became. Hence, any intelligence this woman may have passed on, he thought, should be treated with caution. In fact, he was close to convincing himself that she had indeed been spreading misinformation. For how long she might have done so, he couldn't know.

Restlessly, he threw the covers aside and got out of bed, to stand in his shirt. Not many hours ago, he had planned to question the Comtesse de Paiva about a rumour she had passed to Cyprien, concerning an impending Spanish landing in the west. Yet his instincts had held him back. How he should behave now, if she indeed appeared through the wall at any moment, he was uncertain. He had enjoyed women's company in curious circumstances before, of course, but not quite like this. Though when he pictured the lady at supper, her neck and shoulders shiny in the firelight, he believed he could do justice to the occasion . . .

A sudden noise, far louder than expected. He turned, his eyes on the wall. Then came a clanking, but from a different direction; he whirled round – too late.

It was not the wall-panel that flew open, but the door. A flame sputtered, and heavy shapes lurched into the room. Boots thudded, torchlight flickered on helmets and steel cuirasses – and before Marbeck could leap for his sword, they

76

were upon him. In the gloom, brawny arms seized him; he struck out with a fist, felt it connect, heard a grunt. But someone else grabbed his wrist . . . There were three men. He struggled harder. His arms were being pinioned. He kicked, but since he was barefoot the effect was feeble. In a moment he was held, wrists forced upwards behind his back . . . then something cold and sharp was pressed to his neck.

'*Basta!* Be still – you are a prisoner!'

The speaker was Spanish. Breathing hard, Marbeck looked round into a black-bearded face.

'You mistake!' He snapped. '*Erroneo, si?* I'm a guest of la Comtesse – I came here to meet with servants of *el Rey Philip*—'

He broke off, hearing a click. It was followed by a squeal of rusty hinges, and the wall-panel swung inwards to reveal another figure bearing a light. This one was quite short, however, and not garbed as a soldier. Stooping, he lifted the torch, and at once Marbeck knew who he was.

'Monsieur Wilders?'

The newcomer was grey-haired and grey-bearded, richly dressed in a suit of dark brocade and lace. With some difficulty, he manoeuvred himself through the narrow opening and stepped into the room. As he did so, the two Spanish soldiers who held Marbeck thrust him against the wall. There he remained, while the third man, their captain it seemed, held a poniard to his throat.

'I am Henri, Comte de Paiva.' The grey-haired man wore a look of some amusement. 'You were expecting someone else, I think?'

77

Marbeck merely gazed at him.

'I hope you enjoyed your supper,' the other went on. 'My wife has told me you were most desirous of meeting with Spaniards.' He put on a thin smile. '*Alors* – now you have your wish.'

'Monsieur le Comte – this is intolerable!' Quickly Marbeck summoned a bewildered look. 'I'm a merchant . . . I've come here to—'

'No, monsieur – you are a spy.'

Moving carefully in the cramped room, the Comte took a step forward. There was a sconce on the wall, and he placed his torch in it. He looked at the Spanish captain and muttered a few words. Marbeck knew a little Spanish and understood that he was to be taken away at once.

'A spy?' he echoed, with incredulity. 'Monsieur, that's absurd! I'm a man of business, a citizen of Antwerp—'

'Indeed? Then, pray, address me in the Holland tongue.'

'Gladly,' Marbeck said. And he would have uttered what words of Dutch he knew, but he was not given the chance. An order was barked, and he found himself shoved towards the bed. Someone picked up his clothes and threw them at him.

'Dress yourself,' the Spanish captain said in English. He glanced round, saw Marbeck's shoes and kicked those towards him, too. 'Be quick!'

The room had become warm, and smoky from the torches. Marbeck sat on the bed, and, as he dressed, risked a look at the soldiers. Both were professionals, muscular and alert. Having assessed his chances, he faced the Comte.

78

'Monsieur, please listen. I am in your power, yet I insist there has been some fearful misunderstanding. I'm a dealer in ordnance – I came here to make contact with men who will buy my wares . . .'

But he fell silent; the Comte wasn't even listening. With a casual movement, the man pushed the secret panel by which he had entered. It closed with a click, whereupon he moved to the door, which was still ajar.

'You and I are unlikely to see each other again,' he said, with a final look at Marbeck. 'But allow me to offer you some advice. Before you enter a seigneur's house, enjoy his table and dally with his wife, it's wise to ascertain what kind of people you abuse. But then—' he gave a shrug – 'it's futile to expect a man to change his ways – especially one who has so little time left.'

Then he turned on his heel and went out.

There was a boat tied up by the river: a larger one than Marbeck had seen on his arrival. By torchlight, he was marched along the jetty and made to clamber in. It was difficult, since his hands were bound, but he was soon seated in the stern, facing the Spanish captain, while behind him his men took their seats. In a short time they had cast off and began to row, heading downstream. There was a faint light: dawn was near.

Woods and fields drifted by; water birds flapped away, and somewhere a fox barked. The rowers began easing the small boat to their left – and now there was a change in the sound of the water: the stream had widened. Marbeck peered ahead, and saw that they were emerging from the mouth of the Scorff, into the River Blavet.

His face was blank: a mask, hardened by practice. To a casual observer, he appeared to have retreated into himself, but he was watching. He eyed his captors: the soldiers straining at their oars, the sharp-faced captain. He also watched the banks, noting any landmarks. He had not yet formed a strategy, but one thought took hold: that he was not yet finished with the Château des Faucons. If it proved possible, he would return . . . and when he did, he would be seeking answers from Marie-Clothilde, Comtesse de Paiva.

One of the soldiers muttered something, whereupon their captain glanced behind. Picking up speed with the current, the boat scudded out into the Blavet. Marbeck gazed ahead, squinting in the gloom, and saw the ship.

It was small; the river, he supposed, was too shallow for a vessel of larger draught. A lantern showed at its stern, where he made out a large, red-and-gold standard. As they drew nearer, he heard the creak of ropes and timbers. The captain put his hand to his mouth and gave a shout, and there came an answering call from the ship. As Marbeck watched, another light danced above, at her side. He peered upwards as they rounded the stern, and saw the name in large, elegant letters: *Delfin*.

Dolphin? Despite everything, he wanted to laugh. Not long ago he had waited, bored and restless, kicking his heels in an inn by Bishopsgate which bore that name. Now he was about to board a

Spanish ship of the same name, where he faced another challenge . . . though one that was going to tax him a good deal more severely. Unless, of course, he was able to change his circumstances.

To most people, the chances of that might have looked somewhat slim. But Marbeck had a few ideas; all he needed was the opportunity to put them into practice.

Eight

He was put below the forward deck, in a sail-locker. The only light in the cramped space came from gaps in the boards, through which he could hear footsteps and voices. As the sun rose, noise and movement increased, and his main fear was that the vessel would make sail: if he found himself at sea, he would be in serious difficulty. But there was no sign that the *Delfin*'s master intended to disembark. The ship swayed gently at anchor, while Marbeck lay on a pile of sailcloth and assessed his chances. The prospect, he knew, was bleak: interrogation, probably soon and probably with torture, followed by an ignominious death. In which case, he had better make himself busy.

First, his wrists: they were tied tightly, but it had been done hastily. He worked his hands and found a little leeway. There was no means of cutting his bonds, hence he would have to employ one of Ballard's tricks. Ballard was a player, whose company had sometimes visited Marbeck's home. As a boy, he had been enthralled by the antics of the clown and tumbler. What nobody realized was how much he had learned from him, let alone how useful those skills had proved in the years since. Now, with one ear cocked towards the deck, he set to work. Using the bulwark to brace himself, he shifted to a kneeling position, then began to rock back and forth. As he did so, he tugged his bonds, one way then another, grunting as the cord dug into his flesh. Soon he had loosened them, but only slightly. Further effort followed, until he judged the time was right. He flexed the fingers and thumbs of his left hand several times, before grasping it firmly with his right; then he squeezed.

It worked best with his left; he'd found that out long ago. He had his mother's hands, people said; too slender for a man's. His brother had mocked him often enough for it . . . Memories flew up while he worked, breathing faster, ignoring the rough cord as it chafed him. Slowly and painfully, he worked his hand free. He wrenched and twisted, until finally his knuckles slid through the last loop, and it was done. Then he sat back against the wall, brought his hands round and assessed the damage. His wrists were raw, but they were unfettered. He worked the muscles of his aching left hand, then busied himself untying his right. Soon, to his relief, he was able to loosen the knots and shake the cord off. What happened after this, he knew, would depend partly on luck; Ballard's Luck, Marbeck called it. Silently, he mouthed thanks to the old player, dead these past five years, before turning his thoughts to a special weapon that was sewn into the waistband of his doublet.

Working with difficulty in the poor light, he unpicked the stitching. Then his fingers probed until they found the end of the cord: a very different cord from the one he had been bound with. It was a lute string; a Roman string to be exact, that would tune to a low F. Thirty inches long and made of sheep's gut, it had been treated and twisted until it was as strong as wire. Gently, Marbeck pulled, teasing it out until its end protruded from his clothing by a fraction of an inch. He would likely get just one chance to draw it, and it would need to be done quickly. Thus prepared, he sat back and waited.

To his discomfort, he waited all day. Why that should be, he could not know. Perhaps the Spaniards were in no hurry; they knew he couldn't escape, just as they knew that, under hard questioning, he would tell what he knew, sooner or later. He refused to dwell on that. By late afternoon he was hungry and thirsty, and doing his best to conserve his strength. He would need every scrap of it.

He was dozing when they came for him, at sunset. There was a clatter as the hatch was opened. Shapes loomed, arms seized Marbeck and yanked him out on to the open deck. There he stood, hands behind his back, blinking in the evening light.

To his captors, his bonds appeared as they had been when he was first taken, in the Château des Faucons. Had any man looked more closely, however, he might have noticed they were now tied with a different knot: one that could be pulled loose by a simple jerk of the hand. But nobody looked. Marbeck was marched to the stern of the vessel, under the poop deck. Sailors looked over the rail, staring belligerently at him, before he was pushed through the doorway of a well-lit cabin that filled the entire width of the ship.

The room was low-ceilinged and dominated by a large table. Behind it, his back to the ship's rear windows, sat a figure of unmistakable authority dressed in a coat of black and gold. As the door closed behind Marbeck, the man spoke in the thick accent of southern Spain.

'Welcome, señor. Are you thirsty?'

After a moment Marbeck nodded, whereupon someone stepped from behind and tipped a leather flask to his lips. Eagerly, he swallowed the tepid water before it was snatched away. He glanced round, saw two armed men in jerkins and helmets. But as he turned to face the officer again, his eyes fell on another man standing by a side bulkhead. He knew that look: here was the one who would serve as interrogator, and at once he thought of Sangers, back in the Marshalsea. The man even had the same bull neck, the same piggish eyes that bored into Marbeck's.

'Come closer, please.'

He took a step. He was facing a handsome man in his thirties, with a neat beard and a gold earring; for a moment he reminded Marbeck of the Earl of Essex. But the *comandante* of the *Delfin* was no vain swaggerer. He eyed his prisoner coolly, then flicked a hand to indicate the interrogator.

'Now, señor, you are not a fool, I think. You know what we can do, to make you speak. So, you will begin by telling me who you are and why you came here. I believe you are English, as I believe you are a spy for your Queen Elizabeth. So talk, and save yourself much pain. You understand?'

Marbeck glanced at the interrogator; then he coughed and looked down at the floor. His intention was to look as scared as his captors expected him to be.

'My name is Wilders, sir,' he said. 'But I swear to you I'm not a spy. I came here to make contact with men I can do business with. I have access to English guns – falconets, culverins, demi-cannon . . . Profit is my only spur. I implore you to believe me—'

'*Cavador, avante.*'

The officer's snapped instruction cut him off. The bull-necked fellow stepped towards Marbeck, holding a short length of rope fashioned into a loop. It was a simple device, but an effective one: when placed around a victim's head it would be twisted tightly, until the pain was unbearable.

'Wait, please – there's no need. I will speak!' Marbeck swallowed, then: 'It's true – I am English,' he said hurriedly. 'But I swear I'm no spy. I carry tidings from La Rochelle, to men of business like myself. They tire of the war – who doesn't?'

In part, he spoke the truth. It was no secret among intelligencers that overtures of peace had been going on throughout the conflict, through private intermediaries. Trade had suffered badly, and many were indeed tired of it all.

'And there's more, Capitán . . .' Deliberately, he looked round, before facing the man again. 'But not before common soldiers,' he went on. 'Such matters are not for their ears. You understand me, sir?'

It was a gamble, but he knew enough about the

86

Spanish aristocracy to think it might work. The officer was a *caballero*, who sensed he was being addressed by another gentleman. And when a look of doubt flickered across the man's features, Marbeck pressed his advantage.

'I speak of affairs of state, sir . . . secrets. You will soon know I speak truly. I won't bluff – how could I?' He nodded at the interrogator. 'I see this man knows his task – how to sift the truth, and how to keep silent. Let him stay if you wish, but permit me to address you, as one man of substance to another. Please . . . what is your answer?'

A silence fell. The guards stirred, not liking the suggestion at all. Neither did the interrogator, who glowered at Marbeck, fingering his implement of torture. To his master he spoke rapid Spanish, from which Marbeck gathered that he believed the prisoner was stalling, and he would soon put an end to it. But when the officer spoke, relief swept over him.

In a few words the soldiers were ordered to withdraw. Without further word, they did so, but as they went out the interrogator seized Marbeck roughly by the arm. With the man's sour breath on his face, he waited until the door had closed. Silently, he counted to five . . . then he struck.

First, his shoulder slammed into the interrogator's chest. Then, even as the man registered the blow, Marbeck jerked his head back and banged it into his face. The fellow staggered backwards, but immediately the officer behind the desk jumped to his feet. Marbeck had barely a moment to jerk his hands out of the cord – but once they were free, he could set to work. Three blows in rapid succession pummelled the already blooded face of the burly interrogator, who fell with a groan.

Dropping to a half-crouch, Marbeck whirled round to face the Spanish commander – to be met by a roar and a spurt of flame. The shot was close; he heard the ball whistle by his ear and smack into the bulwark behind him. Dropping his pistol, the man leaped aside. Marbeck saw the sword in its scabbard, hanging from a beam. But instead of preventing him reaching it, he used those seconds for a different purpose: to secure the room.

The shot had brought running feet; he heard shouts from outside, and just had time to reach the door and turn the key before someone rattled the handle. Then came a shriek of steel as sword left scabbard, and he turned back to his assailant.

The *comandante* came at him, his face livid with anger. His first thrust was deadly, and Marbeck was hard-pressed to dodge it. The blade then rose and fell, cleaving the air, but this time he anticipated it. It flew past his shoulder, throwing its owner off balance – whereupon Marbeck's hands shot out to seize the man's forearm, which he bent backwards with all his strength. There was a fearful crack as the bone snapped, followed by a cry of pain. The rapier clattered to the floor.

A tense moment followed. Marbeck kicked the sword away and stepped back, but he saw the officer was beaten. Numb with shock, the man

88

slumped to the floor, fingers clawing his shattered arm. Meanwhile, shouts came from beyond the door, and blows rained upon it. Marbeck's time was short, and he had one chance of escape: the stern windows, through which a soft evening light filtered . . . He believed he could squeeze through. But first he had a task, for the interrogator was recovering.

Flushed and bleeding, amazed at the speed with which events had unfolded, the heavy man was struggling to his feet. He had dropped his length of rope and was reaching for a poniard at his belt. Marbeck put his hand to his waist and drew out the lute string, then stepped forward and kicked the torturer's leg from under him. As the man swayed Marbeck shoved him to his knees, darted behind him, threw the string around his neck and pulled.

It took longer than he had expected, and a deal longer than he liked. The big man thrashed wildly, his fingers clutching at Marbeck's wrists, but he was weakening. Then he was gurgling, as the tough string crushed his windpipe. Marbeck looked over his head at the officer, who was still seated on the floor. Though dazed with pain, the man was looking him in the eye.

'You had better kill me too, señor,' he panted. 'Or else I will remember you . . . and one day I will find you, and put you to a terrible death!'

But Marbeck's ears were bent to the thudding on the cabin door. Though stout, it wouldn't last much longer. Keeping his grip on the garrotte, he eyed the Spaniard.

'I've never killed in cold blood,' he snapped.

'Though I could make an exception for this man, who would have racked me until I was broken.' Abruptly, he looked down: his victim had gone limp. Straightening up, he removed the lute string and thrust it in his pocket, allowing the body to fall. Though senseless, the interrogator still breathed.

'Your name!' The *comandante* glared at him. 'Tell me your name . . . I ask you, as a gentleman—'

But he broke off, for Marbeck was hurrying to the windows. They were well made and set in oak frames, designed to allow a fresh breeze into what could be a stifling interior. He opened one wide and placed his foot on the sill. Then he turned round and threw a last look at the man who had briefly been his jailer.

'My name? I told you: it's Wilders. And I don't expect our paths will cross again – so all that remains is for me to bid you *adiós*!'

With that, he bent himself double and squeezed into the opening. Sweet air filled his nostrils as he forced his body through, his feet resting briefly on a narrow ledge below the window; then he was dropping like a stone. As he fell, he heard the crack of splintering timbers: the cabin door had at last given way. There was a great splash as he hit the water, and the Blavet closed over his head.

It was the twilight that saved him, he thought later; that and the thick reeds that bordered the river. Once underwater, he struck out, swimming until his protesting lungs forced him to surface. The chill of the river was a shock, but it revived him. Gasping for breath as he came up, he looked round and found himself barely twenty yards from the ship. The word *Delfin* loomed over his head. He was no dolphin, he thought, but he would try . . .

Something hit the water, inches from his face; a crack followed. His eyes flew to the windows of the master's cabin, where a puff of smoke showed. Even as Marbeck looked, a second caliver was being aimed. He drew breath and dived.

Whatever it took, he had to reach the bank. He was sluggish in his clothes, especially his shoes, but there was no time to take them off. Besides, he had walking to do; the thought gave him hope and strength. He lashed out, his hands dragging at the water. Weeds brushed against his legs – then suddenly there was gravel under his chest. For a moment he floundered, clutching at stones and mud, before his head broke the surface. He was on his knees; reeds towered above him, dull grey in the gathering dusk.

Grasping the foliage, Marbeck pulled himself out of the shallows and fell flat. From a distance he heard another shot fired, but there was no sound of the ball hitting water. With what strength he could muster, he rolled aside, seizing reeds as he did so, and cocooned himself. Then he lay still and began to catch his breath.

He could not delay, of course; they would send a boat and hunt him down. Their shame and pride would drive them, coupled with their hatred of the English. But his hope was that they would expect him to follow the coast, to east or west. What they would not expect Marbeck to do, he reasoned, was return the way they had brought him: back up the Blavet into the Scorff – and thence upriver to the Château des Faucons.

It was foolhardy, of course. But he was stuck in Brittany with no immediate means of making an escape, or even of defending himself. His horse and his sword were at the château. His mouth tightened. There, too, was the woman who had betrayed him: the Comtesse de Paiva. Lying swathed in coarse grass, exhausted and shivering in his soaking-wet clothes, Marbeck peered up at a patch of darkening sky and swore an oath; he was not yet done with la Comtesse.

He waited a few minutes more, alert for sounds of pursuit, but there were none. Finally, his breathing restored, he freed himself from his concealment, got to his knees and slowly lifted his head, to see the *Delfin* riding peacefully at anchor. Already it was hard to make out its standard, while the lettering on the stern had disappeared in the gathering gloom. There was no sign of movement; then he saw a flame above the poop-deck, and knew someone had lit a lantern.

Carefully, he backed away from the river-bank, keeping low, until the reeds petered out and he found himself in a grassy meadow. He looked round, saw a row of poplars and loped towards them on all fours. Only when he had reached the tree-line did he stand and draw breath. Then he began to walk, parallel to the river, with the sunset fading at his left.

An hour, he estimated, would take him to the mouth of the Scorff. He was on the wrong side of the Blavet, but was sure he could cross it at some point. Then, following the narrower stream, he would have to find his way in the dark, back to the château.

As yet, he was uncertain what to do once he reached it. But by the time he got there he knew he would have decided. With that goal in mind, he began a steady jog-trot through sweet-smelling grass, while dusk fell about him.

Nine

The archway showed stark against the night sky, as Marbeck made his way stealthily towards it. Above him loomed the château, but no lights showed. He reached the gates and was unsurprised to find them shut. As he had expected, he would have to climb.

He squinted upwards. There was just enough moonlight to see by; otherwise his journey here would have been longer. As it was, he knew it had taken most of the night. His clothes, streaked with mud and soaked from crossing the river, clung to his skin. But, though cold and weakened, he was unhurt. He had enough strength, he thought, to gain entry to the château and locate the Comtesse's chamber, provided his luck held. But first he needed to prepare for his escape.

In silence he worked his way round the courtyard wall, seeking a point of ascent. He found it on the side nearest the river. Prodding the crumbling masonry, he was able to mark out footholds, after which it was short work to clamber up the wall and gain the top. He straddled it briefly, then eased his other leg across and dropped down inside the yard.

He landed with knees bent and flattened himself against the wall. As his eyes adjusted to the gloom, he picked out the dovecote and, away to his right, the stable. Straightening up, he padded towards it.

The latch lifted with a squeal. He stiffened, but the only sound was the distant call of a nightbird. Then he was inside, with the warm scent of hay and horses about him. There was a stir as the animals sensed his presence, hooves thudding softly on straw. Standing by the door, Marbeck gazed about until he could make out the stalls, whereupon a grunt startled him. He looked round to find himself face to face with Chacal, the hill-pony that had carried him here.

He stroked the animal's neck, murmuring soft words. The horse shook its head and snickered as he untied its halter, but made no further noise as he led it from the stall. It was bridled but without a saddle, and Marbeck had no time to search for one. His purpose was to get the animal outside, across the courtyard and through the gate without waking the household, which meant he must muffle its hooves.

Working quickly in the semi-darkness, he gathered up handfuls of straw. Soon he had bound Chacal's feet, using baling-twine which he severed with his teeth. Then, with one hand grasping the animal's mane, he led it out of the stable. They crossed the courtyard, passed the dovecote and drew near the entrance, where Marbeck stopped to peer at the gates. They were secured with a simple draw-bar; it was an easy task to slide it clear and heave one gate open.

Without looking behind, he led the horse through. Twenty yards from the gateway he moved off the road, tethered it to a bush, then stepped away. To his relief, it dropped its head and began cropping grass, whereupon he turned and walked softly back towards the château.

Once inside the courtyard again, he approached the side door where he had first encountered the Comtesse. He tried the door: it was locked. He looked for other means of ingress, but there were none, and the windows within climbing reach were too narrow. Then his eyes fell on the imposing main doorway, with its flight of steps. It was the last entrance an intruder would think of using . . .

He mounted the steps and found a solid door with a cast-iron handle. To his surprise, it opened; the lock, he decided, was so old the key had been lost. He slipped through, finding himself in the wide, flagged hallway; ahead was the main staircase.

Silently, he moved towards it and began to ascend. On the first floor, where a rushlight burned in a niche, he paused to get his bearings. A passage opened nearby, to another part of the château; there, Marbeck remembered, was the Cerise room where he had been captured. He saw closed doors, and, at the far end of the landing, stairs rising. Instinct told him that way led to the Count's bedchamber, but where would the Comtesse sleep?

He hesitated, knowing he had no choice but to open doors until he found her chamber. So he took a breath, approached the nearest one and opened it. When he looked inside, however, the room was empty. He made out a bed, chest and chair, all covered with dust sheets.

Outside again he listened, but the house was

quiet. The servants would sleep below stairs, but some might not: a lady's maid, a servant to the Comte . . . and did the couple have children? He moved softly down the passage and stopped at another door. Its handle turned noiselessly. Gently, he pushed it ajar until he could pass through, to find himself in a large room hung with heavy drapes; at the same time, he grew aware of the sound of gentle snoring. On a chest by the wall candles burned, and there were two beds: an ornate four-poster, fully curtained, and at its foot, set at a right angle, a small truckle-bed. In it a young servant girl lay on her back, snoring peacefully.

He had found the room, but there were two occupants – and again only one course of action presented itself. After closing the door carefully, Marbeck hurried forward, dropped to one knee beside the truckle-bed and clamped a hand over the girl's mouth.

The effect was instant: her eyes flew open, and a look of terror appeared. With muffled squeals, she began to struggle. In silence, Marbeck clamped her wrists together and held them fast in one hand. Then he raised a closed fist, scowling like a playhouse villain. It worked; the petrified servant went limp and shook her head – but at the same moment there came a sound from the four-poster. Sheets rustled, and a voice he knew at once murmured: *'Agathe . . . c'est toi?'*

Now his choice was stark: knock the maid out or gag her – or both. He chose the gag. Whipping the sheet from under her body, he rolled the girl into it and trussed her like a chicken. She yelped

97

as the ends were tied about her neck, then lay quivering with fear. At once Marbeck was up, with barely time to reach the other bed. The curtains moved, parted – and a figure appeared in a loose shift, long hair falling about the shoulders.

Immediately, she saw him, and would have screamed had he not put a hand over her mouth. Seizing her arm, he thrust her backwards on to the bed . . . whereupon mayhem broke out.

He should have expected resistance, he realized; overpowering the servant had been too easy. What he had not foreseen was the ferocity with which the Comtesse de Paiva set about him. Now, he found himself in hand-to-hand combat with an opponent who fought to kill or maim. Her left hand clawed at his cheek, narrowly missing his eye. With his free hand, Marbeck seized it and forced it down – but her right hand became a balled fist, with which she began beating him on the nose and mouth. He tasted blood – then her knee shot up, seeking his groin. He managed to pin it with his elbow, though in doing so lost his balance . . . and before he knew it, he was on the floor. He still clutched the Comtesse's hand, but now her mouth was uncovered. Even as she fell atop him, her jaws opened. He grabbed at her, then grunted with pain. Like some succubus, the woman had bent across him and sunk her teeth into his ear.

It was becoming a comedy, Marbeck thought vaguely; only there was no audience. He felt warm blood on his cheek, even as he caught the Comtesse by the hair. He yanked her head back and saw her face in the candlelight: the face of a gorgon.

'*Diable!*' she cried. 'I will tear your neck, you—'

But she was cut short, for Marbeck was at the end of his tether. In exasperation, he seized a handful of her hair and stuffed it into her mouth. As she gasped and gagged, he pushed her aside and got to his knees. The next moment, the lady's hands were behind her back, being tied with cords ripped from her own bed-curtains. The legs followed, and, kick as she might, she was soon bound like her servant. Only then, breathless and bleeding, did Marbeck trouble to unstop her mouth.

'Enough!' he panted, kneeling beside her. 'If you shout or scream, I'll stuff your gorge again.'

Gasping, eyes bright with hatred, she spat the words out. 'What do you want?'

But she was shaking, imagining the worst. From the truckle-bed, the maid could be heard whimpering. Silently, Marbeck cursed himself; he was no violator of women, and he had made a poor fist of the situation.

'That depends,' he murmured. Lifting his head, he listened – surely the noise of their struggle had wakened someone? He glanced round, and his eyes fell on a door in the far corner: the Comtesse's closet. He stuffed hair into her mouth again and got to his feet. Hurrying to the door, he wrenched it open, found a *garde-robe* lined with gowns and petticoats. Then he was lifting the maid and carrying her like a child into the closet. Laying her down gently, he raised a finger to his lips.

'No harm will come to you, or la Comtesse,' he murmured in French. 'Provided you stay still and keep quiet. Agreed?'

The terrified girl nodded, whereupon he closed the door and returned to her mistress. She lay where he had left her, beside the huge bed. Leaning down, he cleared the hair from her mouth again. She retched, and threw a baleful look at him.

'You can never leave here alive,' she gasped. 'My husband will stake his honour on it!'

'Your husband's not my concern, madame,' Marbeck said. He gave his voice a cruel edge: Thomas Wilders would have no pity. 'And I have little time,' he went on. 'So, are you going to tell me where your intelligence came from – the false rumour you passed to Louis Orme? I speak of a non-existent build-up of Spanish troops in this province – and of their plans to invade the west of England.'

She froze, her eyes widening. 'Who are you?' she whispered.

'It matters not.' Marbeck leaned over her. 'Speak!'

'And if I refuse?'

He sighed. He disliked having to pretend such brutality, but there was no other way. Roughly, he put his hand down, found the hem of the Comtesse's shift and yanked it upwards to her waist. She flinched as if struck.

'Do you really want an answer?' he hissed.

For the first time abject fear showed in her gaze. 'You would not dare . . .'

'Are you certain?' Summoning a bleak smile,

100

he began to unlace his doublet. The woman let out a gasp, whereupon he seized her hair again and prepared to stop up her mouth.

'No . . . please!' She shook her head quickly. Desperately, her eyes flicked away, towards the door.

'Your maid's gagged and confined,' Marbeck said. 'Help won't come soon enough . . . so – for the last time – speak.'

A pause, then: 'If I do, will you leave at once?'

'I haven't decided yet.' He bent closer, making her recoil. 'But tell me something I can believe, and we'll see.'

She swallowed, then looked down briefly before meeting his eye. After a moment, he pulled her shift back to cover her modesty. A shudder passed through her; then she spoke.

'Louis Orme is nothing to me . . . his death is nothing.'

Her voice was cold as ice. 'He was a child in Paris, on the Day of Saint Bartholomew,' she breathed. 'His parents had been slain. My father took pity and gave him refuge in our house . . . he became a kitchen-boy, then a groom. He's a simpleton.'

Marbeck frowned. He had been a small child back in 1572, when, in that terrible August, Protestants had been massacred throughout Paris. Yet the very name of Bartholomew evoked horror in him, as it did in every Englishman.

'You mean, you kept his religion secret – made Louis your devoted servant?' He drew a breath. 'He trusted you – he called you a woman of honour.'

There was no reply.

'So you used him,' Marbeck went on, thinking fast. 'And later on you fed him false rumours in Brest, no doubt with enough truth mixed in them to allay suspicion. When did that begin – after Henri of Navarre came to the throne? Did you and your husband profess loyalty to the new king, as others did – knowing one day he would renounce his religion and return to the papist fold? Of course you did! What was it Henri said, when he switched sides – *Paris is worth a mass*?'

His anger was real, and the Comtesse saw it. 'One had to do such things,' she said quickly. 'They were desperate times . . . My husband—'

'No.'

Marbeck bent over her. 'I don't believe you care much for your husband,' he murmured; all at once things seemed to be falling into place. 'Close to the Spanish, Louis said . . . I think you're close to someone in particular: someone younger and more handsome than Monsieur le Comte, perhaps? You spoke of Paris – do you often go there?'

But she refused to answer, until he seized her wrist and gripped it hard.

'My husband has a house in Paris!' she cried. 'I am sometimes there . . . Let go of me!'

'So, whom do you visit?' Marbeck demanded. 'Who is your lover, whose bidding you do? Or does it merely amuse you, to dabble in matters of state? Tell me!'

Her chest rose and fell rapidly, but she kept

102

silent. Then suddenly she stiffened. Somewhere a door had banged – and now a male voice called; at last, Marbeck's luck had run out.

He stood up and drew the Comtesse to her feet. Then, gripping her by the shoulders, he thrust his face close to hers. 'Give me a name and I'll leave,' he said. 'Refuse or play me false, and I'll break your neck. Do you doubt it now?'

He placed his hands about her throat, thumbs to her windpipe. She shook, but made no sound, while outside someone called from the stairhead.

'Then *adieu*, madame,' Marbeck muttered.

It was his final throw: already his thoughts were on his escape. But keeping to his ploy, he began to squeeze. The woman let out a gasp, then:

'His name is Juan Roble!' she said, her voice cracking at last. 'And he is a match for you, monsieur. I pray that he kills you, and tears out your heart—'

But she broke off, as Marbeck let her fall. Even before her body hit the floor, he was turning: footfalls sounded at the door, and he had only time to spring aside as it opened. Fortunately, he was behind it. A candle appeared, borne aloft by a grey-headed figure in an ornate floor-length robe.

'*Qu'y a-t'il?*'

The Comte de Paiva gave a start and stopped in his tracks. His wife, for her part, let out a blood-chilling scream – but Marbeck was ready. With a single blow to the back of the man's head, he felled him. Then he ran out, down the stairs – straight into the ageing servant whom he had seen on his first arrival. Mathieu, however, had only

103

time to register astonishment as Marbeck ducked past him.

In a moment he was crossing the hallway; then he was through the door and flying down the steps. Shouts came from the house, but his eyes were on the gates. As he crossed the yard, he was aware of a startled flurry, of doves flapping in their cote. Then he was out of the château, running in the moonlight.

Some distance down the road he stopped: for a moment he couldn't find his bearings. He peered about in the gloom until, a few feet away, Chacal snickered. In a moment he had untied the horse and was scrambling on to its back.

He tugged at the halter, using his knees to urge it forward. But the animal jerked nervously, unwilling to obey, until Marbeck flatted himself along its neck and spoke softly. Soon it began to walk, then to trot . . . and at last, clinging to its bare back, he was able to guide it up the slope towards the trees.

At the tree-line he reined in and dismounted, to free Chacal's hooves of their muffles. He was shivering: whether from exhilaration, hunger or cold – or perhaps all three – he didn't know. But swiftly he remounted and pointed the animal's head to the north. He would ride up the valley of the Scorff, then cross the river and turn eastwards, in the direction of Rennes.

How long it would take him to reach Paris, he did not know; hundreds of miles lay ahead – half the width of France – but reach it he would. He was without weapons, apart from a lute string; but he had a mount, he spoke the language, and he had money. The Spaniards had taken his purse, but failed to make a thorough search of his clothing: the lining of his doublet held enough ducats, he believed, to see him through.

His task now was to put enough distance between himself and the Château des Faucons. Then he needed food and rest, a change of clothes and a sword, but such things could be purchased easily enough. What had been harder to purchase was information – that and his freedom. He tasted it now, drawing in lungfuls of air, and a smile tugged at his mouth: the first real smile he had allowed himself in days. At the same time, he became aware that the night was ending: through the trees to his right, a grey light showed.

He gazed down at the château, the seat of the Comte and Comtesse de Paiva. Briefly, he thought about the name: surely it was not French but Italian? Now, however, he had a new name to ponder – a Spanish name: Juan Roble. It intrigued him, and not least because of the way the Comtesse had spoken of the man: a match for him, she had said.

'We'll see, shall we?' he said to himself. Then he dug his heels into Chacal's flanks and urged the horse forward into the trees.

Ten

The journey to the capital took three long days.

The first was the hardest, for Marbeck could not be certain he was not being pursued. Though hungry and weary from lack of sleep, he forced himself to keep riding, pausing only at streams to wash the blood from his face and to water his mount. By afternoon the horse was tiring, and he was forced to slow his pace. He was tempted to beg fodder from a farm, but knew his appearance might attract unwelcome attention, as his lack of a saddle did. That, Marbeck decided, was his worst discomfort; he would have to obtain one soon.

Yet, despite everything, the journey passed without incident. The sun dried his clothes, as he rode north-east through wood and pasture until he struck the main highway that led from Brittany to Paris. Travellers on foot and on horseback stared at him, but he avoided their gaze, his eyes on the horizon. Finally, as evening drew in, he walked his exhausted mount into the great cathedral city of Rennes. They had covered more than eighty miles.

In Rennes, he moved through bustling streets, leading Chacal by the halter. Mercifully, it proved easy enough to find an *auberge* with stabling. Having seen the horse bestowed, he took to his chamber, ordering a supper to be brought up along with a pail of hot water. Thereafter, after bathing and feeding himself, he fell into a sleep that lasted until morning.

Once up and breakfasted, stiff in limb but restored, Marbeck set about improving his lot. His clothes were ruined and drew many odd looks. So he purchased a plain costume from a dealer in hand-me-downs – blue coat and breeches, grey hose, shoes and belt – and discarded his black doublet. He also bought a cheap sword and, after some hard bargaining, a poniard to go with it. Finally, he found a saddler and, after more bargaining, bought a well-worn saddle with stirrups. Thus equipped, he paid his reckoning at the inn and left Rennes by mid-morning.

Now, travel was easier. Fougères, with its ancient castle, marked the boundary of Brittany, and Marbeck could not help feeling relieved as he passed into Normandy, where the terrain grew hilly. Now and again he saw signs of the long years of civil war: ruined houses and bridges, devastated fields. The road, however, was good; by afternoon he was in Mayenne, crossing the river of the same name. Alençon was less than forty miles further, or so he learned when he stopped to water the horse. By nightfall he had reached the old town, pleased with his progress. One more day, he told himself, as he clattered through cobbled streets; one more day and he would reach Paris.

That night, in a run-down hostelry at Alençon, Marbeck borrowed pen and ink from his host and wrote a report for Sir Robert Cecil. During the long ride, he had pondered the sequence of events that had marked his time in Brittany – an experience he did not care to repeat. Sitting up late in his chamber with sounds of revelry below, he set down what he had learned, mentioning in particular the name of Juan Roble. This man, whoever he was, appeared to be the source of false intelligence that had found its way via the Comtesse de Paiva to poor Louis Orme in Brittany, and hence across the Channel to Edmund Trigg. Like all such reports, it was designed to sow confusion in the minds of the English. It would irritate Master Secretary, Marbeck knew. He had no means of sending the despatch before he reached Paris, but hoped this account might serve to justify what had become a lengthy sojourn in France.

There was an English embassy in the capital, of course: Sir Henry Neville, the ambassador, had a house on the Quai de Tournelle. But Marbeck would not announce his presence: Neville was an officious man, he had heard, who might want explanations that would slow him. Instead, he planned to seek out Cecil's agent, one who used the name George Ingle. He had never seen Ingle and knew little of him, yet he needed to share intelligence with someone who knew the territory. Ingle might know of Juan Roble too, he reasoned: if not, it was time he did.

Having finished the report, he folded it and secreted it in the lining of his coat. He had already threaded his lute string into it. He had one regret: that when the Spaniards searched him, back in Brittany, they had taken his tailor's bodkin. It was a tool that had proved useful more times than he cared to remember. He even thought about purchasing a new one, then dismissed the idea: his money was almost gone. He hoped Ingle could loan him enough to find his passage home.

With that thought, he went to bed and was asleep within minutes. When he awoke, he thought for a moment he was back in his room at the Dolphin by Bishopsgate. Then he arose, stiff in every limb, and resigned himself to one more gruelling ride.

Paris may have been bigger than London, and fairer too, but one thing the two cities shared, Marbeck thought, was the smell.

With the sun sinking at his back, he passed via the West Porte into noisy streets, and a familiar odour assailed him. It was made up of many things: the smells of ordure, offal and wood smoke, mingled with that of the river; Thames or Seine, it made little difference. Soon, however, Marbeck paid it no heed; like the horse plodding beneath him, he was close to exhaustion. The last part of his journey had taken longer than he expected: at Dreux he had been stopped by soldiers and asked to account for himself. Only quick thinking had saved him: he was a traveller, he said, who had come by Cherbourg and Caen, meaning to visit Paris by a scenic route. He was expected at the embassy on the Quai de Tournelle – the *messieurs* could check, if they wished. The name was John Sands, Marbeck added, having decided to leave Thomas Wilders behind. It was something of a relief; though not so great a relief as when he was finally believed and sent on his way.

Now he walked Chacal along the teeming thoroughfare that crossed the great city from west to east, all the way to the Bastille. He had a few small coins left, which would barely buy a supper; he needed to find George Ingle, ideally before nightfall. He had a half-remembered street name in mind: the Rue de Braque, which he thought was in the north-east part of Paris. So, with the distant sound of the huge bells of Notre Dame in his ears, he rode as far as the Rue des Haudriettes, before finally coming to a halt.

Here he dismounted and looked about. People hurried past, all of them seemingly men in hats and dark robes. Then the penny dropped: he was in the Jewish quarter. Some eyed him suspiciously, but at his request one old man stopped. Yes, he said, the Rue de Braque was nearby, but he knew of no Englishman living there. There was one who looked like a Turk . . . a foreigner, anyway. He gave directions, whereupon Marbeck thanked him and led the horse away.

Dusk was falling as he stooped outside a low, narrow-fronted house in a dark street. The window was shuttered, but a light showed through cracks. Half prepared for disappointment, he banged on the door and waited; already he was pondering how he might get Chacal fed and stabled. Then came the noise of a bolt being drawn, and the door opened a few inches.

'Master Ingle?'

The person carried neither candle nor lantern. Marbeck looked closer and realized he was addressing a woman: blowsy and overweight,

110

with long greasy hair. She stared back at him with a sullen expression.

'I seek George Ingle,' he told her. 'I'm a friend from England – the name is Sands.'

From somewhere in the house came a shout. The woman turned and yelled back, to receive another shout in reply – whereupon a torrent of abuse followed. To Marbeck, it sounded like the continuation of a running battle. With a sigh, he put a hand on the door and shoved it inwards.

'Does he live here or not?' he asked wearily. 'If not just tell me, and I'll be gone.'

'He does. What do you want?'

The words were in English. Marbeck looked past the blowsy woman at a shambling figure, who lurched forward, pushing her aside. With an oath, she squeezed past him and vanished.

'I'm John Sands, from London,' Marbeck said. He looked into a dark, heavily bearded face and saw why some might think this man a Turk. 'Roger Daunt sent me.'

The other sniffed. 'Jesu, what's afoot?' he asked sourly. Marbeck smelled strong drink on his breath.

'You're Master Secretary's man?' he asked. 'I confess I expected—'

'What?' Ingle interrupted with a scowl. 'What did you expect – a hearty welcome?' He looked Marbeck up and down. 'By the Christ,' he added. 'Fought your way here, did you? Where have you come from?'

'A long way off.' Marbeck eyed him blearily. 'I'm on Crown business. I need a place to sleep

111

and stabling for my horse. And money, too. Can you aid me, or not?'

Ingle hesitated. Through eyes heavy-lidded under black brows, he squinted past Marbeck to where Chacal stood, a picture of weariness. Then he fumbled in his clothing.

'Here.' He found a purse and shook out some coins. 'There's an inn two streets away – *La Chèvre*. Get a room and see to your nag. Come back tomorrow . . .' But he broke off, for Marbeck was shaking his head.

'I'll stable the horse,' he said, taking the money. 'But then I'll return. I've things to ask you – and I don't want to stay here longer than I must.'

Ingle swore under his breath. Spreading his hands, he said: 'The house is unfit. There's nowhere for you to sleep, save the floor – and others won't like it.' He jerked a thumb over his shoulder, leaving no doubt who was meant. But already Marbeck was turning away.

'I'll be back within the half-hour,' he said.

And so he was. Having unsaddled Chacal and seen him made comfortable at *La Chèvre*, he returned to the Rue de Braque and knocked again on Ingle's door. This time, however, the man was ready for him. He was admitted and found himself inside the most noisome dwelling he had entered since that of Thomas Saxby, in Clerkenwell. There too, he recalled, he had been greeted by a hostile woman. But the ex-soldier's wife, he thought, was a gentlewoman compared with the one who shared Ingle's company.

'There's bread and cheese . . . it's all we have.' Ingle, in shirt sleeves, stood in the middle of the

112

single downstairs room and pointed to a table. 'Apart from the burgundy,' he added, indicating a jug. 'It's poor, but drinkable.'

Marbeck moved towards the table. The house stank; it hadn't been cleaned, or even aired, in months. As he sat down, he threw a glance at the woman, who sat in a corner glowering at him. She had needlework in her hand, though the light was so poor he could barely see it. But he marked the loose, low gown she wore, and guessed how she earned a living.

'Berthe will make up a pallet later.' Ingle waved a hand vaguely, then shuffled over and sat down facing him. 'Are you known here?' he asked. 'I mean, are you in flight, or—'

'The answer's no, to both questions.'

Somewhat gingerly, Marbeck broke a crust off the hard loaf and bit it. Finding it passable, he took some cheese and found that better. Soon he forgot his surroundings and ate hungrily, fortifying himself with the watered wine. His host and hostess watched him in silence, until finally he paused.

'Does she speak English?' he asked, without looking up.

'Not a word,' Ingle replied. 'That's why I keep her.'

'You keep *her*?' Marbeck couldn't help looking sceptical.

'That's what I said,' the other retorted. 'I pay my way. I give lessons in rhetoric, to the children of a seigneur. I have to,' he added. 'Master Secretary, bless his crooked little frame, barely sends me enough to pay the rent!'

113

He lifted the jug and poured wine into a second cup, and as he did so, Marbeck saw his hands tremble. Inwardly, he sighed; Ingle was a drunkard, of the kind that is beyond saving.

'I've come from Brittany,' he told him. 'The Spanish are gone – most of them, anyway. But there are rumours, some of them conflicting. You might know of the new fleet they're building, in Lisbon. We need to discover its true purpose . . .'

He paused, for Ingle was staring at him. 'You rode from Brittany on that broken-down nag?' the agent muttered. 'It's more than a hundred French leagues.'

'I know,' Marbeck replied. 'And the horse isn't broken-down – he served me well.' Having eaten his fill, he pushed the plate aside. Weariness surged through him; he needed rest badly. 'I got a name, while I was there,' he went on. 'Juan Roble. Spanish, I assume. Do you know it?'

An odd look came over Ingle's face. 'Yes . . . I know it.' He was silent for a moment, then: 'You're not Sands, are you? You're Marbeck.'

Receiving neither confirmation nor denial, he shrugged, took another drink and wiped his mouth with the cuff of his dirty shirt. 'So, what else have you heard?' he asked.

'About Roble? Nothing.' Marbeck eyed him unfavourably. 'I was hoping you could tell me more.'

There was a sound from the corner. Berthe had got up from her stool and was looking pointedly at him. Her habitual scowl seemed to have given way to a lopsided grin, and for the first time he noticed a bruise on her cheek. Frowning, he met

114

the woman's eye, before swinging his gaze to Ingle, whereupon he blinked.

'You can go upstairs with her, if you like.'

The man had put on a leery smile. 'I'm content to lie down here,' he added. 'She's not poxed, by some miracle. She foins well enough . . . afterwards, you'll sleep like an infant.'

In the guttering light, Marbeck regarded him stonily. 'I'll sleep here, Ingle – alone,' he said. 'But first you'd better tell me all you know about Juan Roble, and any other intelligence you've bothered to gather of late. At first light I'll be gone. I'll ask Master Secretary to reimburse you for the loan. Does that sit well with you?'

There was a brief silence, as Ingle's smile vanished. Then, abruptly, he slapped a hand on the table. 'Don't you judge me, sir!' he snorted. 'You know naught of what I put up with in this city! Lied to and threatened, surrounded by people who despise me – never knowing if I can rest safely at night—'

'Enough!' Marbeck's patience was spent. 'You're here to serve, as I am,' he went on. 'I need any intelligence you have on Roble. Then I'm leaving – tomorrow. So send your woman off to bed, and we'll talk. Will you do that?'

Ingle blinked at him, then all at once the man's anger seemed to melt away. With a sigh, he turned to his companion and muttered a few words. Berthe stared at him, then at Marbeck, who braced himself – but there was no retort. Instead of going upstairs, however, she took a shawl down from a peg and went out. The house door banged behind her.

Without comment, Marbeck faced his host, but the man wouldn't meet his eye. Eyebrows knitted, he gazed down at the table. Finally, Marbeck said: 'This man Roble . . .'

'He's a fable.'

At last Ingle looked up, a thin smile on his lips. 'You've been spun a yarn, my friend,' he went on. 'Roble's a bogey-man . . . or if he exists, no one's set eyes on him. I've heard a dozen tales about him, none of them worth a cannikin of spit.'

Marbeck leaned back slowly. Suddenly, he saw the face of the Comtesse de Paiva, and recalled how she had cried out the name of the man he'd assumed to be her lover. Had she lied? Well – the name existed, at least. Fighting disappointment, he said: 'Will you tell me what you've heard, in any case?'

Ingle shrugged and poured more wine into his cup. He waved the jug at Marbeck, who brushed him aside.

'He's said to run intelligencers here in France.' He took a gulp, then sniffed. 'Don't let that treaty the Spanish have signed fool you,' he muttered. 'They don't trust the French, any more than we do. King Philip's people have eyes and ears in every province, especially in Paris and the ports. Juan Roble – if he exists – serves Juan de Velasquez, Spain's chief spymaster.'

'Well, I've another name for you,' Marbeck said. 'The Comtesse de Paiva.'

'Ah, *la Comtesse volage* – the flighty contessa.' Ingle gave a nod. 'We think she's linked to Velasquez's man in Brittany. Breton ships are

116

carrying English traitors to Spain, through La Rochelle and San Sebastian.' He shook his head. 'It's a maelstrom here, Marbeck – you should trust no one.' He drank again, then gave a snort. 'How's this for a jest? I've heard that Roble gives his men the names of fruits! *Uva* for a grape, say, *Higo* for a date . . .'

'And *Morera* for Mulberry?'

Ingle gave a start. 'Perhaps,' he replied, in some surprise. 'What – have you heard this, too?'

'Not quite.' Marbeck sat rigid, his tiredness forgotten. Briefly, he recounted the events of almost a fortnight ago that had led him to seek the traitor known as Mulberry, before Cecil had ordered him to Brittany. 'What do you know about the Spanish plans?' he asked. 'There's talk of another Armada. I've a notion it's destined for Ireland . . .'

Ingle looked sceptical. 'For O'Neill? It's possible, I suppose. But I've only heard rumours of Spanish troops entering Brittany again, poised for another landing in England. In Devon, or Cornwall . . .' He shrugged. 'Who knows what to believe? But I sent a report to Cecil anyway.' He caught Marbeck's expression. 'You've heard the same?'

'Where did that come from?' Marbeck asked sharply. 'Tell me – it's important.'

'So it would seem.' Ingle sniffed, wiped his nose again and frowned. 'To tell you truly, I'm hard pressed to remember.'

'Well, try, can't you?' In exasperation, Marbeck leaned forward.

'I believe the report stemmed from the south – from Bordeaux, perhaps . . .' Ingle groped for

117

a memory. 'But the man I got it from was an Italian who was here – a papist, of course, but one of ours.' He yawned. 'Yes, I remember: odd fellow, jumpy . . . hair tied up like a woman's. He was here a month or so back – at least, I think it was then . . .'

Ottone.

Suddenly, Marbeck was elsewhere: in a fencing hall in Gracious Street, bandying words with the man Ingle had just described – the one he had dismissed from his thoughts. He sighed; a weight seemed to settle upon him.

'What's wrong . . . are you ill?' Ingle was frowning at him.

'Not ill – sick at my own foolishness . . . my haste . . .' Marbeck put a hand to his head: it all made sense. Ottone was the double-dealer. That was why he was so nervous . . . the shaky hand, the sharpness of his speech. Marbeck had had the man within his grasp, and he had let himself be fooled. Ottone was Mulberry – and for all he knew, he had now left London and made his escape . . .

'What did he tell you, this Italian?' he asked quietly.

Ingle gave a shrug. 'Merely what I said. He had strong intelligence the Spaniards were planning a landing in the west, he said. They did it a few years back, didn't they? Burned Plymouth, or somewhere.'

'Penzance.' Marbeck gazed at him without seeing. 'I must get to Cecil at once,' he said abruptly. 'Tonight.'

'Tonight?' Ingle echoed. 'Are you mad? It's a

118

hundred miles to the coast. You need rest. So does your nag.'

But Marbeck had lurched to his feet. Vaguely, he looked around – the room had begun to swim. For the moment he seemed to have forgotten where he was. 'A bodkin,' he muttered. 'I need to buy one . . . that and a saddle . . .'

Then his legs gave way, and he sat down on the floor with a thud. Someone loomed over him; when he looked up, his eyelids felt like lead.

'I'll make up that pallet,' Ingle muttered.

Eleven

In mid-morning, with the sounds and smells of Paris about him, Marbeck led Chacal out of the stable of *La Chèvre*. Then he was in the saddle once again, walking the horse through busy streets towards the city's northern wall. Soon he had passed through the North Porte into gardens and orchards, and was striking the road for Dieppe.

Since rising he had barely exchanged another word with Ingle. He'd slept as only the dog-tired can, waking once in the night when Berthe came in and fell over him. When he finally awoke, the sun had risen and Ingle was at the table drinking, his face haggard in the morning light. Thereafter, after a brief conversation, the two men had parted. Ingle would attempt to find out more about Juan Roble – or so he promised; Marbeck expected little progress in that direction. He, meanwhile, would head for the coast, take ship for Dover and get himself back to London.

As he rode, he reflected on what he had learned, but found little comfort. There was a shady, if not invisible Spanish spymaster in Paris . . . but, then, wasn't there one in every capital in Europe? And if the Comtesse de Paiva was indeed his lover, what did it matter? That the false intelligence about Spanish activity originated from Juan Roble seemed in little doubt. Most troubling was the discovery that Giacomo Ottone had been the means by which such information had been passed to Ingle, and through him to Sir Robert Cecil.

Once again, Marbeck reproached himself for laxity in his questioning of Ottone. Yet his instincts had told him the man had not the stamina for the role of double agent; and sifting the matter now, he found he reached the same conclusion. Ottone had been nervous and seemed to hold something back, but a difficult mission in Paris might have accounted for his manner. Cecil might know more, of course; though what Master Secretary would say now if Mulberry had indeed fled, Marbeck didn't like to dwell on.

Instead, with an autumn chill permeating his thin clothes, he sat hunched over the reins and forged ahead. By evening, finding that he was yet some distance from the coast, he was forced to stop for the night. A wayside farmer proved amenable, however: for a small remuneration he fed both man and mount, and allowed them shelter in his barn. The following day Marbeck at last reached the busy port of Dieppe and sought passage on the next ship crossing to Dover. Luckily, there was a merchantman leaving in the morning. So, at last, on a windy afternoon with black clouds scudding in, Marbeck finally stepped on to English soil again. It was the twelfth day since he had left Plymouth.

In Dover he had little choice but to seek out Joseph Gifford; he could only hope the man was still here. His money was gone, and there was the small matter of retrieving Cobb from the stable: the reckoning would be large. To pay for his passage, he had sold Chacal in Dieppe to a dealer who, sensing Marbeck's plight, forced him to accept a humiliating price. With regret, he had taken farewell of the spirited little pony, before setting his face grimly to the sea crossing.

Evening was near by the time he made his way through the knot of streets below Dover castle and found the corner house. He knocked and was greeted by the same maidservant as before, who seemed not to remember him. But when he asked for Edward Porter, recognition dawned.

'You was here a fortnight ago,' the girl exclaimed, drawing back. 'I've got orders from Mother Sewell not to admit any more friends of Porter!'

'So, he still lodges here?' Weary as he was, Marbeck tried a smile. 'I have urgent business with him—'

'He do and he don't,' came the snapped reply. 'That's to say, the room's still his, but he don't always use it.' She made as if to close the door, then added: 'There's some men think once they've made free with a place, they own it and everyone what lives here. In any case, he's out!'

With that she slammed the door. So Marbeck made his way back to the town, presently finding himself outside the Greyhound where he had lodged previously. He was on the point of trying to bluff his way to a supper, when someone called out from a short distance away. He turned quickly, hand going to his sword hilt, then blinked. There stood Gifford, wrapped in some kind of seaman's cape. At once Marbeck walked across the street towards him.

'I never thought to find you a saviour,' he murmured. 'But I could do with your aid. I tried your lodgings.' He raised an eyebrow. 'Outstayed your welcome there, have you?'

'Let's say boredom set in,' Gifford said with a shrug. 'I've been visiting a woman in the town.' He looked Marbeck up and down. 'What in God's name are you wearing?' he added. 'Have you pawned everything you had?' Then, taking a closer look, he frowned. 'Ah . . . long story, is it? Would you care to tell it over a meal?'

'I would,' Marbeck answered. 'Only I haven't a farthing . . . or a sou, for that matter. Can you bear the cost?'

The other gave a thin smile and led the way.

Once supper was over, the two intelligencers took themselves to the inn's taproom and found a quiet corner. Having told Gifford of the events of the past two weeks, Marbeck now spoke of Juan Roble, and finally of Ottone. He was glad to unburden himself to one who understood the significance of such matters. But when Gifford heard the last part of Marbeck's tale, he was puzzled.

'The fencing master? I know him. He's loyal – I'd have staked a crown on it.'

'I thought so, too,' Marbeck said. 'Yet he's the one who passed a false report to Ingle. Ingle may be a sot and a wastrel, but he's no traitor. I've turned it about a dozen times since I left Paris, and I see no other explanation.'

'So this devil Roble works the strings over there, does he?' Gifford mused. 'The word means "oak", as I recall. Probably a code-name, like the ones he gives his minions. Fruits?' A sneer showed. 'Not very original, is it?'

'Hardly,' Marbeck said absently. It still irked him that one such agent, code-name Mulberry, had been within his grasp and had outwitted him.

'But what's the broader picture?' Gifford wondered. 'If the Spanish are set on a landing in Ireland, shouldn't we have other intelligence of it? Your old friend Trigg, for one – he keeps his ear to the ground, doesn't he?'

Marbeck sighed, and gave a fuller account of his time in Plymouth.

'Jesu . . . but then he's not the first to end up in that condition,' Gifford observed with a frown. 'Some bear the strain better than others . . . drink, gaming or women – or all three. We each choose our means of solace, don't we? You're no Puritan either, Marbeck,' he added dryly. 'Do you still dally with Sir Richard Scroop's wife, while the poor man serves our Queen in Holland?'

'You shouldn't listen to gossip,' Marbeck said.

'But what else should I do?' the other countered. 'Rumour and hearsay, with the occasional nugget of hard fact – that's our usual fare, isn't it? That's why I'm still kicking my heels in this town, instead of getting myself to London.'

Marbeck said nothing.

'By the Christ . . .' Gifford sighed. 'There are times I wish I was back at Cambridge, with a quart of cheap ale inside me and a pretty wench on my lap . . . don't you?'

'I used to,' Marbeck admitted, after a moment.

'Though a man has to do something more, doesn't he?'

'Do you ever go home?'

The question caught him off guard. He looked into Gifford's face, but saw only curiosity. Few men would have asked that of him. He shook his head.

'There's nothing for me there.'

'Because your brother rules the roost?' Though sober, Gifford was in expansive humour. But Marbeck never talked of his family, nor their country seat in distant Lancashire. He shrugged again, unwilling to pursue the matter.

'Well, I know enough about the fate of younger sons,' Gifford said. 'Especially when there's a father who refuses to die, and a greedy sibling who's set to inherit everything.' He paused. 'What is it they think you do?'

'I serve our Gracious Majesty, of course. A minor Court post, to do with arranging jousts and pageants.' Marbeck allowed himself a smile. 'It's no secret that I always liked spectacle.'

'You did,' Gifford agreed. 'And had a fondness for plays and players, I remember. You enjoy it, don't you?'

'Enjoy what?'

'Pretending to be someone else.'

Marbeck considered. 'Don't you?'

'At times, perhaps.' Gifford yawned, leaning back in his chair. 'Well, anyhow, you'd best come back with me to Mother Sewell's. I'll have to flatter the old buzzard, but I expect she'll let you spend the night on my floor. The bed will be mine . . . and before you ask, she won't be sharing it.'

125

'That's a relief,' Marbeck said.

'But, for now, tell me again of the Comtesse de Paiva,' Gifford said, with sudden interest. 'She sounds like a woman I'd like to know.'

Three days later, on a wet Monday morning, Marbeck entered Sir Robert Cecil's private chamber in Whitehall Palace, where his welcome was even chillier than he had expected. As always, Master Secretary wasted no time.

'I have your report,' he said, fingering the badly creased paper that Marbeck had penned, back in the inn at Alençon. 'It's somewhat scant. Would you care to fill in the substance of what occurred after that?'

Not being invited to sit, Marbeck stood before the spymaster's table and gave his account. He spared no detail, even down to Gifford loaning him money to recover his horse. By the time he had finished, Cecil was looking as stony-faced as ever.

'Forgive my pedantry,' he said, 'but, in my last despatch to you, I ordered you to find out whether or not any Spanish were still in Brittany. Not to chase rumours across half of France, as to the possible identity of Mulberry. Do you truly think it has merited the time and expense?'

'I've set down my reasoning, sir,' Marbeck said stiffly. 'I followed my nose. The scent led me to Paris, and—'

'I see that,' Cecil broke in. 'I also received Trigg's report, soon after you left Plymouth. Filled with apologies and the most flowery language. The man's a fool. And more, if Cyprien's dead by now as you surmise, that is a bitter blow. As for

126

Ingle . . .' He sighed and looked down at his desk, which was strewn with papers, and a frown appeared. 'How can I rely upon him now? Even though it appears he's not the only one who was duped, is he?'

Stung, Marbeck remained silent.

'I was unsure of Ottone, as you know,' Master Secretary added. 'Yet I never truly believed him a traitor. Hence, I hope your suspicions warrant what I'm about to do with him.'

At that Marbeck showed surprise. 'You mean he's still here, in London?' he asked. 'I thought he would have fled; he must know he's suspected, after I spoke with him.'

'Yet he sent me a report, only two days ago,' Cecil replied, raising an eyebrow. 'While you were still en route here from Dover. As far as I'm aware, he continues to instruct the sons of gentlemen in the Italian style of fencing. Hardly the behaviour of one who fears capture, is it? Unless he's cleverer than you thought, and has some elaborate bluff in mind.'

'No.' Marbeck shook his head. 'He hasn't the nerve for that – there must be another reason.'

'Well, he has a wife, and a house in Mark Lane,' Master Secretary said. 'But even that's not enough to make a man brave interrogation. I speak of a torture warrant,' he added. 'I believe the Queen will grant one. Ottone would know what to expect, at the hands of someone like Sangers.' Seeing Marbeck's expression, he frowned again. 'What is it?' he asked. 'A while ago you were sure you'd unmasked Mulberry; do you now harbour doubts?'

'This report of Ottone's,' Marbeck said. 'Does it concern—'

'Spanish activity? Not in the slightest degree. It's routine matter: talk of someone in the French ambassador's train, who may or may not be in contact with a priest hiding in the north. Barely worth the trouble of setting it down.'

'Then, let me visit him again.' Marbeck spoke more sharply than he had intended. 'I'll get the truth out of Ottone if—'

'You would if I allowed it – yet I do not.'

The spymaster's tone brooked no argument. Biting back a reply, Marbeck waited.

'For now, you may rest easily,' Cecil went on. 'I've already set a watch on Ottone: on his hall in Gracious Street, and his house. There's been no sign of anything unusual.'

Though relieved, Marbeck remained troubled. Suddenly, the conclusions he had come to in France seemed in doubt. He began to run matters over rapidly in his mind, but Cecil cut through his ruminations.

'However, I'm sending Prout – tonight. Along with a pair of pursuivants,' he added. 'They'll bring Ottone in.' He gave a sigh. 'I repeat: I can but hope your instincts prove true. About the other matter, too. I speak now of Ireland.'

'You mean, the new Armada being destined for O'Neill?' Marbeck was suddenly glad to talk of something else. 'I would stake anything on it. Indeed, the more I ponder it, the more likely it looks.'

'Well, there we're in agreement.' Master Secretary paused – then, for once, showed his irritation. 'I

128

curse the day the Queen ever committed troops to that land,' he said, with sudden vehemence. 'It will bankrupt our nation – indeed, it's halfway to doing so already!'

He fell silent, whereupon Marbeck seized the opportunity.

'Sir . . . I pray you, let me go with Prout tonight. I need to see Ottone: to look him in the eye once more and know the truth.'

There was a moment while Master Secretary appeared to consider. But when he spoke, he was on a different track. 'This Juan Roble . . . do you think he exists?'

'I believe so,' Marbeck answered, taken aback. 'The Spanish have always had spies in Paris. Though who the man really is, I cannot say.'

'Well, whoever he is, he's been getting intelligence from us, as well as laying false trails,' the spymaster mused. He was thoughtful, then suddenly he grew brisk. 'Very well – go with Prout tonight,' he went on. 'Gaze at Ottone all you wish. But forbear to lay a hand on him: it's Prout's commission, and you'll follow his lead. No swordplay – you understand?'

Marbeck let out a breath and nodded.

After that, the night couldn't come quickly enough.

Back in his room at the Dolphin, he paced about, racked with impatience. All day he had striven to keep himself occupied: seeing to Cobb, getting rid of the travel-stained clothes he had purchased in France, garbing himself in his preferred black. The sword would have to serve for the present, since he had no money for a new one. He had been so eager to leave Cecil that morning that he had forgotten to ask for a payment. Fortunately, his credit at the inn held firm.

By the time dusk fell, having taken a quick supper and a mug of sack, he could wait no longer. He left the Dolphin and walked through rain-washed streets, into the city by Bishopsgate. Curfew had sounded, and the gates would soon be shut. His orders were to await Nicholas Prout in Fenchurch Street by the Clothworkers' Hall, from where they would proceed to Ottone's house in nearby Mark Lane. But as he reached the crossing with Cornhill, he saw a body of men coming towards him and stopped.

'There's been a turnabout,' Prout said, as if he had seen Marbeck only that day instead of weeks ago. 'Our man's not at home, and his wife doesn't know where he is. She looks like a worried woman.'

'Then, we go to the fencing hall?'

Marbeck eyed the messenger, before glancing at the men who accompanied him. Both were seasoned soldiers, well armed, faces hard as flint. He faced Prout again.

'We do,' Prout said. Returning Marbeck's gaze, he added: 'It's my warrant, and you're a bystander. Is that plain?'

'It is,' Marbeck nodded. 'See – I'm not even wearing a sword.'

Prout didn't bother to look. He gave the order, and they trooped back the way they had come with Marbeck in the rear. They passed the Cross Keys Inn and stopped outside Ottone's fencing hall. It was in darkness, and the door was locked.

130

Marbeck stood on the edge of the group, fighting dismay. The man had bolted: suddenly, he felt certain of it. In the weeks since he had questioned him, he had been making plans, sending in a report to Cecil merely to give the impression that all was normal. He was Mulberry – and cleverer than either of them had imagined.

'Is there a back entrance?' Prout asked one of his men.

The soldier shook his head. 'There was a yard once, but Ottone built over it when he extended the place.'

'Very well – force an entry.'

It was easy enough. After a few kicks, the lock gave way. The door crashed inwards and the Queen's servants piled in, boots thudding on the bare floorboards. With little hope, Marbeck followed. One of the men had a lantern, which he lit at once. The four of them stood in the middle of the wide room and looked about, but it was clear the place was empty.

'He's flown,' Prout said, in his most phlegmatic voice.

The other two began poking in corners, but there was nothing to see: only rows of swords hanging up. His spirits sinking, Marbeck moved to the wall – to the spot, he realized, where he had once made ready for a fencing bout with Ottone.

'What's through there?' Prout was pointing.

Without interest, Marbeck followed his arm towards a doorway at the end of the room. He shrugged . . . then stiffened: he had smelled the iron tang of blood. He started for the opening.

The man with the lantern was already walking towards it.

'You've been here, haven't you?' Prout was saying. 'Are there more rooms, or—'

He was cut off by a shout. The soldier was holding the lantern up, peering inside. In alarm he stepped back, just as Marbeck came up. Together they stared down at the grisly sight.

It was a tiny back room, containing only a low bed. On the bed lay Giacomo Ottone, his body rigid and soaked with blood. The man was as Marbeck remembered him, clad in breeches and shirt. There was no mail glove on his hand – but there was a knife in it, his fingers clenched about its handle. His throat had been cut from ear to ear.

And his eyes, which were open, seemed to stare directly at Marbeck.

Twelve

Ottone had taken his own life; at least that was Prout's first thought. But Marbeck knew that he hadn't.

'It looks utterly wrong,' he insisted. 'No one could have made a cut like that – not even a skilled rapier-and-dagger man like Ottone. It was done from behind – by the same person, I expect, who laid him on the bed and placed the knife in his hand. It's murder.' He thought for a moment. 'By the hand of someone he knew, I'd say – the killer locked the door when he left.'

Prout glowered at him. They were standing in Gracious Street, outside the fencing hall. On his orders, the soldiers had remained inside, but for the moment the messenger seemed at a loss. He looked more shaken than Marbeck had ever seen him. Then it struck him: Prout simply looked old. Finally, he said: 'I'll make my report. But now we'll get rid of the body and clear up, before the constables of Bridge Ward get to hear about it. Whether suicide or murder, there'd be an inquest, and we don't want that.' He shrugged. 'Ottone will just have to disappear.'

'I'd like to ask something of you, Prout,' Marbeck said.

The other gave him a bleak look.

'Someone should tell Ottone's wife. Will you

let me do it? Master Secretary would agree, I'm certain.'

He expected resistance, but instead the messenger seemed relieved. 'Go to her, then,' he said. 'Her name's Margaret – English, not Italian. But have a story ready. She won't be able to claim the body, or even see it . . .' He broke off, finding his own words distasteful. He was a devout man. With a nod, Marbeck left him.

He walked along Fenchurch Street to Allhallows, then turned into Mark Lane, with the Tower looming over the rooftops. It was not yet late, and people were about. Having been directed to the house of the fencing master, he knocked. Soon the door was flung open, and an anxious face appeared.

'Mistress Ottone?' Marbeck bent his head; she was small and barely reached his shoulder. 'I'm John Sands, a friend of your husband. I have some news. Might I come in?'

At once Margaret Ottone's hand went to her mouth. 'What's become of him?' she demanded. 'There was another here, asking questions. Tell me, quickly.'

'I will,' Marbeck said. 'But indoors, if you please.'

She hesitated, then turned about. He followed her inside, closing the door. He was in a comfortable, well-appointed room. On the wall was a crucifix, and beside it a splendid sword: silver-hilted and chased with gold. A prize, perhaps; too good for use in the fencing hall.

'He's left me, hasn't he?' she said at once, her face taut. 'I knew he would; indeed, it's as if he had done so already!'

She stood facing him, hands clasped. She wore a black gown with a high neck, her hair pinned up and covered. She was younger than Marbeck had expected – a good deal younger than her husband. He regarded her calmly; just now, feelings were a hindrance that must be set aside.

'Left you?' he echoed. 'Why do you say—'

'You know what I speak of, sir!' Suddenly, she was angry. 'He's with someone, is he not? You need not spare my feelings, for I know my husband better than you do – friend or no. If he has gone with a man – or a pretty youth, more likely – then tell me so!'

Surprised, Marbeck hesitated. A moment ago he had been concocting a tale to account for Ottone's disappearance; now it looked as if the man's widow was about to save him the trouble.

'He's gone, mistress,' he said finally. 'I fear he will not return.'

She stared, then slowly her face crumpled. 'He always meant to abandon me,' she said. 'And lately – since he came back from Scotland – he was resolved to carry it out. He denied it, but I knew he lied. What wife wouldn't know the truth when her husband shuns her – forbears even to touch her?'

There was a stool nearby. She sat down and began to weep, her shoulders heaving. Marbeck could only watch her.

'Do you face difficulties?' he asked presently. 'I mean, with regard to money?'

She looked up sharply. 'Master Sands . . . is that your name?' Plucking a kerchief from her sleeve, she pressed it to her face. 'Pray, forgive

135

me – you at least came to tell me. Others of his acquaintance would not have troubled themselves.' Her chest rose, but she was reining in her emotions. 'If you mean has my husband left debts,' she went on, 'you may rest assured he has not. He was – is – a man of substance. A master swordsman and a good tutor.'

'Indeed, that's true.'

Suddenly, there was nothing more to say. This unfortunate woman knew less about her husband's life than she could imagine, Marbeck thought briefly. But it was ever thus, with men of their profession.

'Is there someone you can turn to?' he asked.

'My brother . . .' She faltered. 'I would have named my father too, but I will not. He'll shed no tears . . . he will be glad. He never wished us to marry. Nor did he trust Giacomo.' She looked away. 'Perhaps I should have listened to him.'

She lapsed into silence; it was time to leave. A moment ago Marbeck's intention had been to press her further, but for now he had learned enough. After expressing his regrets he went out, leaving her alone in the room with the silver-hilted sword.

To gather his thoughts, he walked – across Tower Street to Thames Street, then along the river. As he drew near to Billingsgate, it was all becoming clear; by the time he reached Dowgate, he was certain. Everything fitted. Ottone's sexual tastes, which his widow had just revealed – and which Marbeck cursed himself for not suspecting earlier – had been his downfall. Such tastes made him

136

vulnerable: in fact, they had laid him open to blackmail. And the man's recent excursion, he saw – not to Scotland, as he'd told his wife, but to France – had resulted in his being forced to act against his will: in effect, to turn traitor.

Even as he pieced it together, Marbeck pitied him. Ottone, he guessed, had had no choice. He could imagine how it had been arranged: a fair young man in a Paris *auberge* . . . a jug of wine, the offer to go somewhere private – then the trap would be sprung. All he needed to do, he would have been told, was carry a certain report to the English agent. But refuse to cooperate, and word of his dalliance with this *pédéraste* would be spread – not merely to his wife, but all over London. In England, where such congress was a crime punishable by death, his reputation would be ruined – Ottone would have been ruined. Hence his nervousness when Marbeck had questioned him. And hence his suicide – or so it had been made to appear. But he had not taken his own life, which meant . . .

He stopped, staring down at the cobbles. Ottone wasn't Mulberry. Someone else was – most likely the one who had silenced him. Ottone was only a frightened man, who may have despised himself for what he had been made to do. Perhaps he had even been approached in London, and refused to cooperate further. Whatever the facts, not only had he outlived his purpose, but he posed a threat. Mulberry could have been instructed by his spymaster to remove that threat.

So, the search must continue. Standing in the dark street with the smell of the river in his nostrils, Marbeck cursed silently. Ahead, he saw further toil, of a kind not to his liking: yet another audience with Sir Robert Cecil, perhaps more suspects to be questioned, their every word examined . . .

He sighed. He wanted to go back to the Dolphin, but the city gates would be shut. Then he thought of the street he had left: in Mark Lane was a tavern called the French Lily, kept by a real Frenchman. He knew Charbon slightly – it would serve. He turned about and retraced his steps.

The landlord greeted him cordially but warily. Charbon was a suspicious man by nature, as befitted one who claimed to have survived the bloodbath of Saint Bartholomew's Day. He gestured Marbeck to a table and asked him his pleasure. The French Lily was busy, the air filled with laughter and chatter, together with the strains of a lute. Since his credit would not serve here, and having little money at his disposal, Marbeck ordered the cheapest ale. But no sooner had he taken a stool than a figure appeared and sat down beside him.

'John Sands . . . you've been a stranger of late, haven't you?'

'Grogan.' Marbeck sighed. 'No offence intended, but may I make a request? Take yourself some-where else – I'm in no humour for playhouse gossip.'

But his reply was a broad smile. Augustine Grogan, once of the Lord Admiral's Company, was always difficult to get rid of.

'Very well – what sort of gossip would you prefer?' the player countered. 'The Earl of Essex

138

is always a rich source . . . or how about Lady Willingdon and her steward?'

With a sigh, Marbeck found his purse and shook it. 'Let me buy you some ale,' he said, as coins fell on to the table. 'Or better still, slip over to Bankside and find someone to tug your yard.'

'You are tetchy, sir!' Grogan raised his eyebrows in mock dismay. 'What's the cause of your ill humour? Come, tell me all – I'm everyone's confidant.'

'Here's two pennies,' Marbeck said. 'Take them and go, while the offer stands.'

As if in alarm, the player drew back. 'I believe you're in earnest,' he said. 'Indeed, I think I see a troubled man.' He put on a look of concern. 'A matter of the heart, perhaps?'

But the drawer arrived then and placed Marbeck's mug in front of him. He lifted it – and a vision swam before him: Ottone's blood-soaked body, his dead eyes. He drank, and carried on drinking until he had drained the cannikin. He set it down, to find Grogan still watching him.

'The offer's withdrawn,' Marbeck said. Then, as he was about to scoop up his money, a thought occurred. 'But see now . . . perhaps we might exchange a little news,' he added. 'How is your swordplay these days?'

'Verbal or literal?' The player grinned at him. 'Not that it makes a great deal of difference. I was said to be the Admiral's Men's best fencer.'

'So I heard,' Marbeck lied. 'Where do you practise? Didn't you use Kemp's old hall? Or, now I think on it, perhaps it was Ottone's, in Gracious Street.'

'I used to fence there.' Suddenly, Grogan wagged a finger. 'I wonder where you lead with this, Sands?' He put on a knowing look. 'You're a man who pokes about. It'll get you into trouble one day – you may take my word upon it.

'I thank you for that,' Marbeck said, and waited.

'But since you ask—' the player shrugged – 'I still use Ottone's sometimes. He's the best for the Italian school – when he's here. He's often absent . . .' Suddenly, the man leaned forward. 'But if you want to hear matter of a more serious nature – about him, and the sort of men he favours – it will cost you more than a can of ale.'

He leered . . . and gazing into the man's face, Marbeck was suddenly ashamed. Ottone was dead, and he knew why. Yet here he was, digging for scraps of intelligence from force of habit. He snatched up his mug and found it empty. A curse on his lips, he faced Grogan.

'I've changed my mind,' he muttered. 'Save your words for someone who cares. But first call the drawer back, will you?'

'Ah . . .' The player relaxed. 'It's a quart-sized difficulty you face, rather than a pint-sized one, is it? I know the signs.' Eagerly, he grabbed a coin from Marbeck. 'Well, if you mean to get yourself soused, sirrah, I'm game for it.'

'I don't,' Marbeck said.

But he did. In a short time he had downed several mugs of ale and two of watered brandy, until his last halfpenny was gone. It was not his habit, and for a man like him it could be dangerous, but he felt reckless. In the last month, he realized, he had travelled in a great, flattened

140

loop: down one side of the English Channel, across to France and back up the other side – and what had he to show for it? He was no nearer to finding Mulberry. But one intelligencer was dead, while over in France a Spanish spymaster mocked his efforts. In frustration, he brought his fist down upon the table-top.

'Fools,' he muttered. 'The whole pack of us!'

Nobody answered him. He swung his gaze round and found himself alone. For how long, he had no idea. He squinted through the smoke, now an almost impenetrable cloud, and saw no sign of Augustine Grogan. Instead, another shape was moving towards him. Blearily, he looked up.

'Master Sands, I think you 'ad enough now.' Charbon looked down at him, wearing a look of disapproval.

'You mean my money's gone, and I'm no longer welcome,' Marbeck grunted. He took up his mug, tilted it, then let it fall. 'Very well, Monsieur Charbon,' he went on, easing into French. 'It would seem there's no other course than for me to forgo your company and take myself off, *n'est-ce pas?*'

'It seems best – sir.' Deliberately, Charbon spoke English. Marbeck got to his feet and swayed slightly. But when the landlord went to take his arm, he was pushed away.

'I don't need your help,' Marbeck told him.

The landlord regarded him, a glint of anger in his eye. But after a moment he backed off, allowing Marbeck to make his way to the door. The strains of the lute followed him.

Outside, he stepped into cold, rain-washed air.

There had been another shower, he decided. He turned away from the door of the French Lily and started to walk. He was unsure where he was going, but it didn't seem to matter. He would find somewhere . . . there were acquaintances he might call upon. He reached a corner and realized he was at Hart Street, by St Olave's.

'Why, that's Prout's church,' he muttered to himself. Then he stopped, shaking his head. Of course it wasn't; that was St Andrew's Undershaft . . . Then he stiffened. There were footsteps, coming up fast. Alert at once, he turned, reaching for his sword, and found only thin air. *See – I'm not wearing one*, he'd said . . .

Then something hit him, very hard. There came a rushing in his ears, and wet cobblestones tilted up to meet him. And after that, all was dark.

Thirteen

He woke up seconds later, or so it seemed; then he realized it was considerably longer. He wasn't on the corner of Hart Street . . . he wasn't in any street. He was in a dark room, stuffy and seemingly windowless, sitting on the floor with his back to a wall. And there was someone else present. He gave an involuntary start, whereupon a voice addressed him.

'You're awake at last, sir. Would you like some water?'

His head ached. He lifted a hand, felt a painful lump on the back of his skull.

'I regret the means by which you were detained,' the voice said. It was male, and bore an accent Marbeck couldn't place. 'It was a matter of expediency.'

He peered about, but could see nothing. Then he caught a whiff of sulphur and stiffened.

'You smell the match,' the voice continued. 'There is a loaded pistol, primed and aimed at your head.'

His mouth was dry. He swallowed and took a few breaths, tried to collect himself. Only now were things coming into focus.

'There is a can of water to your left.'

The man spoke calmly, with an air of authority. Marbeck groped, found the mug. He took it up, sniffed and hesitated.

143

'It's merely flavoured with a little rose-water,' the voice informed him. 'But leave it, if you wish.'

Against his better judgement, Marbeck drank. He needed to gather his wits, and to restore his strength. How long had he been unconscious? He took just enough to slake his thirst, then spoke into the gloom.

'Your accent . . . French, or Spanish? Who are you? The one who's replaced Gomez?'

A silence followed, and all at once Marbeck sensed the presence of another person. He tilted his head, trying to see.

'My name is Silvan,' the man said. 'And yours is Marbeck.'

'You're mistaken,' Marbeck said automatically. 'It's John—'

'Please don't take me for a fool, sir,' the other broke in. 'I know who you are and what you do.'

There was a stir, some yards away; whoever was there had shifted slightly. The two were seated, a few feet apart. Marbeck saw a crack of light; there was a door between them. He thought he could smell the river; were they near the quays?

'If you know so much,' he said, 'what is it you want of me?'

But a suspicion was forming. This was no interrogation: instead, he suspected that a bargain was about to be offered. It wouldn't be the first time someone had tried to turn him. He wondered how long they had planned for this opportunity.

'I gather you're woefully short of money, sir.' Silvan, whoever he was, became affable again.

144

'That must be a sore trial, for a man of taste and breeding like you.'

'I get by,' Marbeck said, in a similar tone. 'I'm not without resources, or friends.'

'So I have heard,' came the reply. 'But ladies of fashion seldom grant largesse along with their favours, do they?' A pause, then: 'It must grow tedious, badgering Sir Robert Cecil for the sums due to you. Like a servant, in thrall to a skinflint master.'

It was the other one who held the pistol, Marbeck guessed. His eyes were adjusting to the gloom, but he could see only vague shapes. He said: 'Your pardon, but might we postpone this discussion for another time? I'm sore and would like to take some air.'

'Don't be tiresome, Marbeck.' Silvan's voice grew sharp. 'I'm empowered to make you a most attractive offer. Besides, what good will you be to your masters, once your identity becomes known?'

'Who's *your* master? Marbeck enquired. 'Juan Roble?'

A brief pause, then: 'Who is that?'

'You spoke of identities becoming known. I thought I'd mention another whose name is no longer secret. I wonder how long he'll last, before de Velasquez recalls him from Paris?'

But his attempt to rattle his opponent failed. 'It's good to see your wits aren't dulled, Marbeck,' he replied. 'Raillery, however, will avail you nothing. Come – you know what I ask of you. In return – depending on how reliable is the intelligence you give us – you'll receive

145

generous payment. In crowns or ducats, it matters not—'

'Rixdollars?' Marbeck broke in. 'Why not livres or Dutch florins – or escudos?'

'Whatever you prefer.'

'You sound somewhat desperate,' Marbeck said. A moment passed. He could still see nothing, but the pistol, he sensed, remained pointing his way. Then Silvan's next words brought a shock.

'How is your good friend Giles Moore?'

He kept silent.

'But, of course, how would you know?' Silvan went on, with a note of mockery. 'You haven't seen him since Antwerp. You were a little careless there, weren't you?'

So that was it. Under torture, Moore had given way – what man would not? The only question was how much had he told? With his head throbbing, Marbeck went on the offensive.

'Though it pains me to disappoint you, Silvan, Moore is yesterday's man,' he said. 'We've adjusted our plans . . . and, as you know, intelligence squeezed out by force may well be false in any case.'

'Indeed? Then I ask your pardon,' the other answered smoothly. 'You're not the Marbeck who is second son to Sir Julius Marbeck, of Bindels Manor in the North Country. You have no brother, and no sister . . . I speak of the fair Justina. You miss her, do you not? The only one you truly care about. I wonder whose bed she shares while we converse?'

'We're not conversing,' Marbeck retorted. 'You're spewing idle chat; I'm merely waiting

146

until you've done. If you were going to despatch me, you'd have done so already. So why not blindfold me, or whatever it is you had in mind, and set me on the streets? You know I'm not going to play.'

'But you haven't heard my offer yet,' Silvan said coolly. 'I speak of a most generous pension – say, one hundred escudos a month? A number of your fellow countrymen already enjoy such sums, I believe. Or do you set your sights higher? What think you of an estate on the balmy shore of the Mediterranean? Men can live like kings in Barbary – have you not heard?'

Marbeck swallowed; his mouth was very dry again. He fumbled for the cannikin and took a drink. 'I've heard enough about the Barbary Coast,' he said finally. 'The haunt of pirates and renegades, men who can never return home. It wouldn't suit me.'

'Then, where would suit you? Where in all Europe would you like to live? You and your lady, I should add. And your servants, of course.'

Silvan was smiling: Marbeck heard it in his voice. The man truly believed he could bribe him. What exactly had Moore told them, he wondered. But somehow he knew now that this was Juan Roble's man. Intelligence, drawn from Moore by torture, had been carried here from the Spanish Netherlands, via France. He frowned, and was glad they couldn't see his expression.

'I thank you, but I prefer England,' he murmured. 'We're the true power in Europe, after all. Even your new king, young and innocent as he is, is beginning to recognize that.'

147

'*My* king?' Silvan feigned surprise. 'I have neither king nor queen, sir. I'm a man for whom loyalties – and boundaries, too – have no meaning. Somewhat like you, I think.'

He sounded calm, but Marbeck's ear was attuned now. He had irked the man – and at once he strove to use it. 'You and I aren't alike at all,' he snapped. 'You think you can buy me as you buy an apple off a stall – or should I say *una manzana*? Just as your masters bought *Morera* – that's Mulberry, in my language. I fear his days are coming to an end, too.' He forced a snort of laughter. 'But, of course, you know that, or you wouldn't be trying to tempt me. I fear you've had a wasted evening.'

There was no answer, but Marbeck sensed a stirring. His breathing was somewhat laboured now, he realized. He put a hand to his chest and found his pulse racing. At the same time, a slight dizziness came over him. He cursed silently. The drink: it wasn't rose-water he had tasted.

'Are you feeling well?' Silvan's voice, somewhat harsh, floated out of the dark.

'Never better.' Savagely, Marbeck dug his nails into his palm. He knew he must fight to stay awake.

'I think otherwise,' the other said. 'But before you leave us, I'd urge you to think most carefully about what I've said. Will you do that?'

Marbeck breathed steadily, furious with himself for allowing this to happen. He snapped another question.

'Did you kill Ottone?'

But no answer came, and he knew he was losing

148

consciousness. He tried to stab his palm again, with no effect.

'You begin to bluster, Marbeck . . .' Silvan's voice seemed to come from far away. 'But take this offer with you. You know the windmills, in Finsbury Fields? There's a black stone at the foot of the westernmost one. You'll find a space beneath it, where you may leave a message. Think on my offer – it's a golden gateway. I think you know that.'

'Golden, is it?' Marbeck echoed, but his words were slurred. The room was fading . . . He tried to move, but his limbs wouldn't work. He stared, aware of shapes shifting in the gloom, then he sank into oblivion.

He awoke in daylight, opened his eyes and groaned as sunlight stabbed them. As he closed them again, someone spoke.

'Master Sands?'

'Hibbert?'

Blinking, he looked up into the face of his burly landlord. Street noises assailed him – hooves, a cart rattling past. He looked round: he was lying on the front step of the Dolphin.

'Zachary found you,' Hibbert said. 'You were like a dead man. You weren't drinking here last night, were you?'

'No.' His mouth felt furred, as if he had woken from a drunken stupor. 'I got waylaid,' he said, struggling to sit up. 'It was . . . a celebration.'

The landlord sighed and reached down to help him. Stiffly, Marbeck rose, leaning on him for support. Nausea threatened, then subsided. Finding he could stand, he straightened up.

149

'Your pardon, Master Hibbert. I'll go to my chamber.'

'I'll send the wench up with some water,' the other said, after a moment. 'Your clothes are in a poor state, sir.'

Marbeck looked down, saw his breeches were streaked with dust – and now events flooded back: the dark room, Silvan's voice in the blackness . . .

'I thank you,' was all he could say.

With a nod, the landlord turned and went inside. The moment he had gone, Marbeck sat down on the step again. This was more than carelessness, he told himself: it was stupidity. He had been followed – perhaps even watched as he sat with Augustine Grogan, then plucked off the street like some country gull. Then he had been turned about, his defences probed. And worst of all, he realized, Silvan had been right: what use was he now to Cecil, if his cover was known?

Sluggishly, he got to his feet again. The future looked grim. There was nothing for it but to write a report to Master Secretary and tell him every-thing. A coxcomb, Cecil had called him not long ago. He sighed. If the spymaster had been one for profanity, he would employ a stronger term this time. With a sigh, he went inside and climbed the stairs to his chamber.

Later that morning, however, he received a visitor. He was penning his despatch when the knock came. Opening the door, he was surprised to see Joseph Gifford.

'I'm in high dudgeon, Marbeck,' his fellow intelligencer said, entering without ceremony.

'And soon to be in disgrace, too. Would you care to get drunk and hear my tale of woe?'

'I'll hear your tale,' Marbeck said. 'But I'll forgo the drink just now.' He frowned: his friend looked tired and dispirited, which was unusual. He gestured him to a seat.

'I got back from Dover last night,' Gifford told him, sinking on to a stool. 'I looked in, but you weren't here. The matter is . . .' He shook his head. 'The nub of it is, all those weeks I spent dallying in the port appear to have been wasted. In short, I've allowed a papist agent to enter the country . . . right under my damned nose.'

'How do you know that?' Marbeck asked.

'We caught a terrified student – Magdalene man – about to get on a boat,' Gifford told him. 'The poor fool had turned papist and was bound for the seminary at Douai – but what matters is that he carried a despatch. It won't reach its destination now, but the news it carried was serious.'

'What was in it?'

'Well, now it seems there's a new gamester in the city,' Gifford replied. 'Odd thing: the message wasn't even in cipher. "Our brother arrived here safely a week ago", and so on. Plus some papist expressions of faith and loyalty to the cause, and so forth. And it was signed – with a big flourish on the M. Very Spanish—'

'You mean by Mulberry?' Marbeck broke in.

'So it would appear.'

'Then, we have a link. Question the student, and find out—'

'If only we could.' Gifford sighed. 'But the lad's so terrified, he's had some sort of a fit. He

151

won't speak – not even the threat of torture will work.'

In exasperation, Marbeck muttered an oath. 'Have you handed the letter to Cecil?' he asked.

'No, it's here.' Gifford tapped his chest. 'And I'm in no hurry to do so.' He shook his head. 'I let my quarry slip by me, and our master's going to want to know why.'

'Then, for once, you and I appear to be in similar straits,' Marbeck observed.

Gifford raised an eyebrow. 'I thought you looked somewhat under the weather. Shall we exchange news?'

They talked, without leaving Marbeck's chamber, and the morning turned into afternoon. Information and comment flew back and forth, until the picture became clear enough – and it wasn't encouraging. It seemed that Mulberry was still active in London, but there was a new force, too – a man who had already arrived by ship via Dover. His disguise, whatever it was, had been good enough to fool Gifford – and his name, Marbeck was now convinced, was Silvan. He felt certain that the man had replaced Gomez: a link between their spymaster overseas and Mulberry. And he now wondered if the other person in the room when Silvan questioned him had been Mulberry himself.

'And you couldn't place the man's accent?' Gifford asked, after pondering the matter.

Having pondered it himself, Marbeck voiced a theory. 'I think it was more like Italian than French,' he said. 'I believe he may be a Savoyard, though he's a man who left his home long ago.'

152

The words came back to him: *one without loyalties or boundaries . . .*

'What troubles me most is that we can't know how much Moore's told them – not just about you, but about any of us,' Gifford said. 'And to think this man's here – perhaps less than a mile away . . .' He uttered a curse. 'One chance is all I ask – the chance to run the whoreson devil through the heart.'

'If I don't get to him first,' Marbeck said. 'For I've a notion it was Silvan who killed Ottone.'

He had told Gifford of yesterday's events; now he expanded on the matter. 'It's clear that Ottone let his killer in after dark, when the fencing hall was empty,' he said. 'Why? Because he spoke Italian to him. Perhaps he claimed some kinship, or mutual acquaintance – it matters not. He was able to put Ottone off his guard, then slit his throat.'

'A skilled practitioner,' Gifford said dryly. 'And now he's recruiting, is he?' He thought for a moment. 'I think you may be right. Ottone was weak and posed a risk. If Silvan is under Juan Roble's orders, he was told to get rid of him.'

'He might decide to remove Mulberry, too,' Marbeck said, 'now that he suspects we're looking for him. If he hasn't killed him already . . .'

The two men fell silent, until finally Gifford looked up. 'So, what will you do?' he asked.

'The same as you, I expect.' Marbeck gave a shrug. 'Admit I've been a fool and throw myself on Master Secretary's mercy.' Then, seeing the frown that came over Gifford's face, he brightened suddenly. 'Unless . . .'

'Unless what?' Gifford muttered, in a suspicious tone.

'What if we wait a little while?'

'Wait for what?'

Slowly, Marbeck rose from his seat. He gazed through the window. Already the afternoon was waning. He looked out over the Spital Field, then turned abruptly.

'Cecil doesn't yet know of my encounter with Silvan,' he said. 'Any more than he knows you let the man into the country. But I've been offered a means of contacting him . . .'

Gifford frowned. 'Well, now,' he said. 'Surely you're not proposing to play a double game yourself?'

'Not quite – or not for long, anyway,' Marbeck replied, thinking fast. 'But the fellow knew enough about me to think he could rattle me.' He paused. 'They got that much out of Moore, at least. He knew about my family and my circumstances.' His mouth tightened. 'Silvan was bold enough to name a letter-drop – as if he was certain I'd change my mind eventually.'

'Overconfident, is he?' Gifford mused. 'You mean, if he thinks he's hooked you, we might play him instead?'

'It'll take a little thought,' Marbeck replied.

'Oh, but I'm ahead of you, sirrah!' Gifford's spirits were rising as he spoke. 'A windmill in Finsbury Fields?' He gave a snort. 'He may have thought it a good place, but we can set a watch. There are houses in Everades Well Street overlooking that very spot.'

154

'Hold fast.' Marbeck raised a hand. 'It might be a while before they look under that stone.'

'I doubt that,' Gifford said, smiling. 'If I judge a man like Silvan correctly, he's short on patience, and he needs results. Hence, if you went to that stone and slipped a letter underneath it – something containing intelligence which appears genuine—'

'We've opened the door,' Marbeck finished.

'And thereby we may redeem ourselves in Master Secretary's eyes, once we present him with a *fait accompli*.' Gifford's smile broadened. 'Now it merely remains for us to concoct a harmless piece of intelligence that will set Silvan's mouth watering.'

In some relief, they eyed each other. And, unbidden, a smile appeared on Marbeck's face, too.

Fourteen

That same evening, Marbeck moved out of the Dolphin. It had almost become home, which was unwise for someone like him; now that his whereabouts were known, it was also dangerous. By nightfall he had packed his belongings, telling Hibbert he was called away on urgent business. Since he had no funds to pay the man what he owed, he left Cobb in the stable as a guarantee of his return. Then, somewhat hurriedly, he and Gifford took themselves westward and found temporary lodgings at the White Bear in Red Cross Street, close to the Barbican. It was a crowded area, where both men could remain unnoticed. For now Marbeck remained John Sands, while Gifford used his Edward Porter alias. Once established in a cramped chamber on the inn's top floor, they set about constructing a piece of false intelligence.

'Short and terse, your letter should be,' Gifford said, sprawling on one of the narrow beds. 'You must sound regretful, but make it plain you've overcome your scruples. This titbit of news you're including is but a token of your good will – and a taste of what you might bring.'

'I know what to say,' Marbeck told him. 'Most important is the value of the intelligence. It should come as a surprise.'

'But they must believe it,' Gifford said. 'Well,

what's it to be? Shall we touch on the Low Countries, or Ireland?'

'Why not both?' Marbeck said, on impulse.

The other's brows knitted in concentration. 'Does anything spring to mind?'

Marbeck was on his feet, pacing the room. 'Suppose I say that we believe the new fleet – the one the Spanish are building in Lisbon – is destined for Ireland. And hence the Queen's Council means to forestall it?'

'What, get their fleet out first?' Gifford looked sceptical. 'We can't construct one out of thin air. Their spies would already have noted it.'

'Perhaps not, if it's small and has been put together quickly,' Marbeck countered. 'And if it's made up partly of Dutch vessels . . . Dunkirkers too, perhaps, who've been bribed to join in the fray.'

'You think they'd swallow that?' Gifford asked. But a smile was forming. Dunkirkers – the pirates who preyed on Channel shipping – were notorious: if the price were high enough, such men could be persuaded to follow any flag.

'We must add detail,' Marbeck said. 'Enough to make it stick. Give me a Dutch name, suitable for an admiral.'

'Van Zoren?' Gifford suggested.

'That should serve. I'll report that Admiral Van Zoren, with a fleet of thirty vessels – requisitioned merchantmen and others – is preparing to sail for Ireland. Cork, let's say. His orders are to anchor there and be ready to meet any Spanish force that might come to the aid of the Irish rebels.'

'I like it well,' Gifford said after a moment. 'But have a care. Even if Silvan believes you, he'll want corroboration – names of vessels, their masters and so forth.'

'I'll plead ignorance as to details,' Marbeck replied. 'But I can bluff about the guns they carry – I know a little about such matters.'

Gifford nodded approvingly, then a frown appeared. 'The question is, at what point do we take our story to Cecil?'

'When we're certain the door is really open. Which may take time.' Marbeck raised an eyebrow. 'Do you have money? I mean, enough to live on for a while?'

The other shrugged. 'For myself, I have enough – but I can't keep you as well.' He put on a thin smile. 'You'll have to call upon your friends.'

A look passed between them; then Marbeck sighed. 'In that case,' he said, 'can you lend me enough to hire a boat?'

Late at night, long after the city gates were shut, Marbeck left the White Bear and walked round the walls by Smithfield, Old Bailey and Fleet Street to Bridewell Dock. There he found a waterman who agreed to take him upriver as far as the village of Chelsea. Wrapped in a cloak, he clambered into the skiff and sat down in the stern. The air was heavy again, with a threat of rain; he hoped it would hold off for another hour. Luckily, the tide was in their favour, and the small craft was soon in midstream, the boatman bending to his oars. In minutes the city was behind them. But it was not until Westminster was passed, and the lights of Whitehall Palace a distant blur, that Marbeck relaxed and began to mull things over.

Thus far, matters had gone as planned. He had written his traitorous letter and was satisfied. Silvan would read the words of a disgruntled agent, who was prepared to betray the crown for a handsome reward. As proof of his intent, Marbeck offered a snippet of intelligence concerning an Anglo-Dutch flotilla, bound for Cork in Southern Ireland. A newly promoted admiral, Willem Van Zoren, would command it. That done, though the man knew his real name, he had nevertheless signed himself John Sands. As to where he might be found, he mentioned the name of a drawer at the Duck and Drake tavern in the Strand: a man named Thomas Rose, whose discretion he trusted. After that, it only remained to place the letter under the stone Silvan had described, by the windmill in Finsbury Fields. Gifford would perform that task under cover of darkness. He and Marbeck were of similar height; even if he were observed, they were confident of success.

So, the device was set in motion, and since for the moment Marbeck could do no more, he dismissed it. Midnight was drawing near, or would before he reached Chelsea. And now, at last, his thoughts turned to Lady Celia Scroop.

The fact was he was uncertain how he would be received. It was some time since he had seen her – back in the summer, before he'd gone to Flanders with Moore. She had been preoccupied, he remembered: rumours had reached her that her husband Sir Richard Scroop had a new mistress in the Low Countries. The knight was fourteen years older; Celia had been barely sixteen when they married. Now in her fortieth year, having borne him several children, of whom two had survived infancy, she had long since tired of him. Everyone knew Sir Richard was a blustering rake, who preferred the company of soldiers and whored as it suited him. Hence, his wife sometimes intimated to her closest friends, why should she not respond in the same coin? Though, the fact was, she did no such thing: Marbeck knew he had been her only lover. And though she had teased him often, he suspected that was still the case.

Now he held that thought, for he had little choice. This was more than a visit for the purposes of pleasure: he needed money, and could think of no one else who had as much of it to spare as did Lady Scroop. More, she was clever and discreet – which was why he despised himself for what he was about to do. It mattered little that the sum was needed in the Queen's service and would be repaid: he was coming to scrounge, if not to beg.

He lifted his head, hearing the call of an owl in between the plash of the boatman's oars. Mercifully, the man was not garrulous like most of his kind, and their journey passed without discourse. London was distant now. In the faint glow of the boat's stern lantern he could see fields drifting by, on the Middlesex shore at his right. To his left, the Surrey shore was lost in darkness. Now and then he made out the ghostly shapes of cattle or sheep, and was reminded briefly of the banks of the Scorff, back in Brittany. But

160

when the lights of a certain landing stage appeared ahead, he forgot all else. Soon he was clambering on to the jetty, paying off the waterman and walking up a flight of stone steps. Beyond a clump of trees, Scroop House loomed.

The lady was up, of course; she seldom went to bed until the small hours, or rose before noon. Marbeck was recognized by servants and shown into a firelit chamber. There he found Lady Celia Scroop, playing at cards with a young woman-in-waiting. As he entered, she looked up and froze.

'By all that's holy . . .' She gazed at him, then with a sigh turned to her companion. 'Will you leave me, Alice?' she said. 'Here's John Sands, wafted in on the night breeze as always. Some legal business, is it, sir?'

Marbeck smiled and bowed low.

He woke with the dawn and listened, lying still. Beside him in the vast, curtained bed, Celia slept on silken pillows. She looked at peace, thick auburn hair half covering her face. At the foot of the bed her voluminous nightgown lay in a heap, along with petticoats and stockings of fine lawn. Marbeck yawned, then turned on his back and thought about the previous night. As he'd hoped, if not expected, there had been little conversation: an exchange of pleasantries that soon gave way to words of affection, then to fleshly delights. To his relief, her feelings towards him appeared unchanged; when he finally slept, he was drained of all feeling and strength, like a man who has been close to death.

'Your lips move . . . what do you whisper?'

He turned; she was awake and watching him.

'Did I so?' He smiled. 'I forget . . .'

'No – you merely refuse to reveal it.' She gave a yawn and shifted her body to face his. 'Must it always be so with us?'

He drew his hand from under the coverlet and brushed the hair from her face. 'Why . . . are you discontent?'

'Perhaps I am.' But she returned his smile.

'You're lonely,' he said after a moment. 'I saw it last night, as you sat at cards. Do your children not lighten your days?'

Her smile faded. 'Henry's sixteen and at Oxford – perhaps you've forgotten he went up for the Michaelmas term. And Beatrix prefers exercising her pony to all else. So, since you ask, sir – somewhat late, I might add – no, my children do not provide much comfort.'

'I ask pardon.' He began stroking her cheek. 'Should I have come to you sooner? I've thought of it often enough.'

'Then, what stopped you?' Celia asked. But before he could answer, she laid a finger on his lips. 'Nay – spin me no tales, Marbeck. I ask not where you've been, nor what you've done. I learned that lesson long ago.'

He was silent, but his caresses continued.

'Yet now I wonder why you're really here,' she added. 'To ask what I've heard at Court? I regret to say I haven't been there, not since the Queen returned from her Summer Progress. I seem to have lost my appetite for tittle-tattle.'

'I came for several reasons,' he said finally. 'One is to ask you to loan me fifty crowns.'

Her eyes narrowed, but she made no reply.

'It will be repaid with interest,' he added. 'If there were another way, I wouldn't be so importunate – or so insolent. You're the only person I can trust to keep it secret.'

A sigh escaped her lips. 'By the saints, Marbeck,' was all she said.

Still he caressed her. 'None would blame you for refusing,' he said. 'Nor even for having me thrown off your landing-steps into the river. But I have to ask.'

Suddenly, she caught his hand and held it. 'And what if I ask something of you in return?'

He raised an eyebrow. 'You know I'll do what's in my power.'

'Though somehow you always avoid spelling out what that means,' Celia said. Then: 'I hear things about you, Marbeck.'

He waited.

'Lady Bacon – Sir Francis's mother – was a friend,' she went on. 'I haven't seen her in years. But it's an open secret what services her other son has performed for the Crown. Anthony is another who's never married, who spends much time abroad.' She sighed. 'You play the Great Game, too. And in the time we've known each other, I've seen it change you. I believe it devours you. One day, there'll be nothing left.'

He frowned slightly. 'Where does this lead?' he wondered. 'Would you wish me to stay in London, to be called at your pleasure?'

She shook her head. 'Not that.'

'Then what?'

But already his thoughts ran ahead. He gazed

163

at her face, bereft of last night's paste and paint, and for the first time noticed the lines about her eyes. She was tired, he saw: tired perhaps of being the dutiful wife to a man like Sir Richard.

'If I were widowed, what then?'

He blinked. 'What . . . surely you don't wish to take me as a husband?'

At that she gave a yelp of laughter. 'I never thought of it,' she said. 'You haven't a penny, nor a title, nor even the prospect of one. Neither can men like you be honoured, hence—'

'Then tell me, for I grow weary of this.'

He spoke sharply, but she was unfazed. She knew Marbeck better than most – better than he liked; and at what followed, he was the one taken aback.

'Could you arrange it?'

He feigned not to understand, but she saw through it.

'You have the means, do you not?' Celia spoke very quietly. 'Or, at the least, you know men who do. I hear the Low Countries is a cauldron . . . a quagmire, where sickness accounts for more deaths than the war. A man may die a thousand ways.'

'You truly ask this of me?'

She hesitated. 'If I did, would you carry out my desire?'

'What, become an assassin – kill Sir Richard?' They gazed at each other. Then a suspicion dawned. 'Or do you merely test my feelings?' he added.

She was still holding his hand. Now she released it – and, catching him unawares, thrust it down

164

suddenly, below his waist. 'How strong are those feelings, truly?' she demanded.

He caught his breath.

'How strong?' she repeated harshly. 'You dally with me like a whore, then disappear again as if whisked off the face of the earth. How do I know who you are with betimes – or what taint you may carry?'

'You said long ago, you'd not ask these things,' Marbeck answered, his voice taut.

'Then, perhaps I've grown weary,' she threw back. 'Like Her Gracious Majesty, for all her wit and gaiety, her paint and finery. You know what's underneath it all, as well as I: a wrinkled, bald old woman, who stares at death.'

But it was Marbeck who laughed then. 'The Queen is sixty-seven years old! You're a maid by comparison—'

'I speak not only of age, Marbeck!' With an impatient sigh, Celia withdrew her hand. 'A body growing old is one matter – what about the end of all that we've known? The end of the Tudors?'

He stared at her. 'Well, that will come,' he said, after a moment. 'Elizabeth is the last. But it's plain enough who will succeed, even if few want to admit it. We'll have a king – he may be a Scot, but he's a king already and knows what to expect.'

'No – you fail to understand.' She sighed. 'I speak of this new century, and the new England to come – one to which you may find yourself unsuited.'

'I?' He gave her a puzzled look.

'You, and those like you.'

'How is that?' he asked, not liking the notion.

'I answer to Whitehall – to the Council. Whether Queen's or King's, makes no difference. The state needs men to serve—'

'Yet James Stuart, if he does become king, has little stomach for the war with Spain – just like their new king,' she said, in a gentler tone. 'He's a parsimonious man, they say, and wars are costly. Master Secretary Cecil understands that. Let the hotheads – Essex and his friends – pursue their warmongering ways; Crookback Robert merely counts the cost. And if James becomes king, he may choose to forget what's past and make peace with the Spanish, the first chance he gets.'

'He may do so – but what of it?' Marbeck countered. 'Do you think England lacks enemies? There's always another war beyond the horizon—'

'And you will attach yourself to it – just like my husband.'

Her voice was flat. Taken aback, he made no answer.

'Well . . . so it has always been, and so it remains.' Celia let out a long breath and finally put a hand to his cheek. 'I'm a fool to expect anything else,' she added. 'You're too restless to do otherwise . . . as you're unfit for marriage. Perhaps I did test you, though I had no strategy. Nor do I look to the future, as a rule. I find it arrives quickly enough.'

They were both silent for a while. Then, catching sight of the marks on his arm, she frowned. 'I would have asked you yesternight,' she said. 'Are those burns?'

He nodded, not wanting to elaborate.

'Well . . . mayhap we've said enough,' she

166

murmured. 'Go now to the chamber where you're supposed to have slept, and I'll send a servant. Ask what you will of him. Then, when you've refreshed yourself, take your leave. If anyone should ask . . .' She broke off and gave a wan smile. 'But none will, for they know what's passed.'

There was nothing to say. Marbeck hesitated, then brought his mouth close to hers. She accepted his kiss; then she lifted a hand and pointed.

'There's a little chest inlaid with tortoiseshell, on the table by the wall. The key is in the left drawer. You'll find gold crowns therein – take what you will. That's what you have always done, is it not?'

Then, before he could speak, she turned away and drew up the coverlet.

Fifteen

In mid-morning Marbeck returned to the White Bear, to find that he was not the only one who had spent the night elsewhere. There was no sign of Gifford; nor, to his chagrin, was there any word from the man for the rest of the day. Moreover, rain had arrived in the night and did not let up for some hours. By late afternoon, having made a few purchases in the sodden streets, Marbeck's patience was gone. Buckling on his sword, he was preparing to go out when the door flew open and his fellow intelligencer stalked in.

'So you've returned,' Gifford observed. 'I hope you had a pleasant night – or at least a profitable one. For my part, I was busy with matters of state.'

'Of course you were,' Marbeck retorted. 'Perish the thought that you might have run into one of your drabs and made a night of it – and a day of it too, come to that.'

'You wrong me, sir.' With a smile, the other threw himself on to a bed, which creaked alarmingly. 'I did spend time with an acquaintance, but to our purpose. In short, I was at a house in Everades Well Street that overlooks the windmill where I laid our missive last night. It's a perfect vantage point.'

'That's why you appear so smug,' Marbeck

168

said. He produced a newly bought purse, weighing it in his hand. 'I've obtained funding – more than enough.'

'Hard-won, was it?' Gifford put his hands behind his head and regarded him. Receiving no answer, he added: 'Well, you can buy me a supper in return for the one I bought you in Dover. I'm a hungry man.'

'We'll go to the Duck and Drake,' Marbeck said. 'If Tom Rose is to serve as my go-between, he'll expect payment.'

The old tavern on the Strand was busy when the two entered. Pushing through the throng of customers, they found the grey-headed drawer beside a barrel, working the spigot. At sight of Marbeck, a frown appeared.

'I wondered when you'd show your face. I'd be glad of a warning in future if you're planning to use me as a letter-drop.' He glanced at Gifford, who grinned.

'Remember me, Rose?'

'By the Christ . . . why are you here?'

Thomas Rose, a Crown pursuivant of old, surveyed both of them without warmth. He was one of those men who had lost his place as a result of pure ill luck: in his case, a sword wound that had lamed him badly. Though he still acted as a messenger on occasions, he was an embittered man. But his irritation lessened when Marbeck produced a half-angel.

'Use you as a letter-drop?' he echoed. 'Why, has someone been asking for me?'

With a practised movement, Rose took the coin and stowed it away. 'I'll bring you a mug presently,' he said, lowering his voice. 'If you can find somewhere to sit.'

'We'll have a supper, too,' Gifford told him, and received a grunt in reply.

They squeezed on to a bench by the window. Private talk being impossible, they both ate hurriedly and in silence. Thomas Rose served them, letting them know he had words for their ears only. Finally, they got up, caught his eye and made their way to the rear door, which led out to a walled yard. There, amid a clutter of kegs and barrels, they received the news. Neither of them had expected it to come the very day after Marbeck's letter was delivered.

'It was but an hour ago,' Rose told them, wiping his hands on his dirty apron. ''Twas a simple message, for the man known as Sands: your friend sends his thanks for the gift of stockfish. You're to look again soon, at the place you know.'

'That was all?' Gifford enquired.

Rose merely shrugged.

'My thanks,' Marbeck said. 'There may be further discourse between me and the other party, if you're willing.' But when the drawer nodded and turned to go, he stayed him. 'Wait,' he added. 'I want to know who delivered the message – can you describe the man?'

Rose raised his eyebrows. 'Well now, there's an odd thing,' he said. ''Twas in the shape and garb of a man right enough, but I saw through the disguise: it was a woman.'

The other two looked sharply at him.

'You're certain of that?' Gifford said, frowning.

'Eh? Who do you think you speak to?' Without

warning, Rose's temper flared. 'I was serving Sir Francis Walsingham near twenty years back, when you were a snot-nosed boy!' he retorted. 'You think I can't tell a pair of dugs when they're under my nose? She'd strapped herself about, put a thick jerkin and breeches on, but there was a woman's body under it all.' He glared at Gifford. 'If you want I'll swear it, you damned popinjay!'

Becoming angry in turn, Gifford would have replied, but seeing the look on Marbeck's face he kept silent. Marbeck's thoughts were racing: he was in the dark room facing Silvan, with a whiff of sulphur from a primed pistol . . . and a notion sprang up.

'Very well,' he said to Rose. 'I'll come by again, see you're rewarded.'

The drawer was breathing hard, his eyes filled with cold rage. Finally, he turned, dragging his weak leg, and went inside.

'Well, that's a turnabout,' Gifford said, letting out a breath. 'So it wasn't Silvan, or Mulberry . . .' He eyed Marbeck. 'Unless Mulberry's—'

'I think it was her,' Marbeck said at once. 'As it was her sitting with Silvan while he questioned me, holding the pistol and keeping silent. She had to, or she would reveal herself.' He cursed under his breath. 'So much for Master Secretary's suspicions as to the traitor in his service.'

Gifford stared at him. 'So you've been on the wrong track,' he said at last. 'Chasing cocks, when your quarry was a hen all along.'

Marbeck merely looked away.

* * *

171

That night in their chamber, the two men fell into heated argument. There was no disagreement as to the plan they had adopted: that had produced results, far sooner than either of them expected. What divided them was which course of action to take next.

'I say we seek an audience with Cecil, this very night,' Gifford said for the third time. 'We've opened the door. He will want to decide how to ensnare Silvan and his little circle.'

'He will,' Marbeck allowed. 'But it's too soon. Silvan's no fool. We can't know yet whether he believes my tale about Van Zoren and his fleet – he's testing me still.'

'Then drop another message, and let others keep watch on the whoreson windmill,' Gifford said tiredly. 'I'm spent. I was hours sugaring Mistress Mason, for the loan of her back room—'

'*Mistress* Mason, is it?' Marbeck said dryly.

'She's a woman past sixty years, who dwells with her husband!' Gifford snapped. 'A pox on you and your suspicions, Marbeck. You can do your own letter-carrying from now on. After all, this is your mission, is it not?'

'It was,' Marbeck replied. 'But you were happy to attach yourself to it as I recall, to get on the right side of Cecil again. It wasn't I who let Silvan into England—'

'Nor I who got drunk and got himself picked up off the street like a fool,' Gifford broke in. 'Moreover, it was you who sat only yards away from Mulberry, without realizing she was a woman!'

Marbeck had no answer to that. The dispute

172

had begun with both men sitting on their beds; now they were standing, railing at each other. Fortunately, the din from the taproom below was enough to drown their words.

'See now . . . can we not look at it afresh?' Gifford stifled a yawn. 'Even if we waited until tomorrow, then found another letter under the stone, what would it avail us? Whether Silvan asks for further intelligence or not, we need to move swiftly. One of them will have to collect the messages, so—'

'And I want to know who that is,' Marbeck broke in. 'We can dog them, using disguise.'

'No.' Gifford shook his head firmly. 'I'll not play at shadows, trudging through London streets. Master Secretary can set someone to watch the place, then they can follow whomever they wish.'

'He could,' Marbeck said. 'But I still say we haven't enough to satisfy him.' He gave a sigh. 'May we not strike a bargain? Give it two days. Then, if we're no further towards finding Mulberry – let alone Silvan – I'll go to Prout and spill everything. Moreover, I'll make it clear this was my scheme and you were an unwilling party. What say you?'

Gifford sighed too, and flopped down on his bed. 'Two days,' he said finally. 'We go to the Mason house, say we're constables lying in wait for a thief. You go to the stone tonight, collect a message if there is one, then leave another in reply. Thereafter, we'll watch the spot like hawks. But whichever of us spies the carrier – man or woman – you can trail them.'

Relieved, Marbeck nodded. 'I'll pen the letter,

173

but I'll give no further intelligence. Instead, I'll ask for a payment, as proof of Silvan's intent.'

'Very well.' Gifford nodded in turn. 'Now, if it's all the same to you, I'm taking a nap.'

By the following morning, all had been done as agreed.

Both intelligencers had spent an uncomfortable night, in a small chamber at the rear of the house of Gilbert Mason and his wife. Being simple folk, the couple accepted the explanation given them, even if both were alarmed at the thought of their home being used to watch for a thief. A modest payment for their trouble helped smooth matters, however. Left to their devices, Marbeck and Gifford settled down to keep watch on the westernmost windmill in Finsbury Fields, some hundred yards away.

Late at night Marbeck had walked up to the windmill, which was silent and deserted, and, with the aid of a blazing torch, had found the black stone. It was smooth and flat, and lifted easily. As he'd hoped, there was a scrap of parchment beneath, folded tightly. Back in the house, he and Gifford pored over it by candlelight. Its contents were short:

I wish to know more of Van Zoren's ships: from where do they sail, and when? What gunnery is carried, and how many troops?

To those questions Marbeck would give no answer. Instead, he wrote a terse reply, saying he needed time to obtain further intelligence. Meanwhile, he demanded a payment of ten crowns. Having set this down, he went back to the windmill, lifted the stone and placed the letter beneath. His fear was that the ink might run if left too long in the damp ground. But judging by the speed Silvan had thus far shown, that seemed unlikely.

The morning came, overcast but dry, and the two men resigned themselves to what was now a routine task of surveillance. Neither was a stranger to such work, and they soon fell into a pattern. To sustain them, they had bottle-ale, very weak, and rye bread. Thus provisioned, they would each watch for four hours in turn, allowing the other to go out when necessary. They said little; there was nothing to discuss. By mid-morning, their world had narrowed to a view through a rain-washed window, northwards across Finsbury Fields. There stood four wooden wind-mills on the rise beside Holywell, their sails turning slowly in the breeze. In particular, each man's gaze was fixed on a spot to the right of the westernmost mill, close by its base. Whoever passed by there was scrutinized, very carefully. The Fields were rarely empty. This open space north of the overcrowded city was a favoured spot, used for many purposes. Men exercised their hunting dogs, practised their archery, or simply strolled. In fine weather, women laid washed sheets on the grass. Children played, lovers walked hand in hand, old folk stood and gossiped. By noon both Marbeck and Gifford were bleary-eyed from staring. At last, having finished another stint, Gifford broke the silence.

'You realize two days could pass with us still in this room, and nothing to show for it,' he grunted. 'Indeed, how can we be sure Silvan's courier didn't sneak up in the night?'

'There was enough moon to see by.' Marbeck, who had taken most of the night watch, half turned from his stool by the window. 'I'm satisfied no one's been there.'

'I hope you're right.' His companion stretched, yawned and rubbed at his beard. 'By the Christ, I need a wash and a change of clothing.'

'Then go and pamper yourself,' Marbeck told him, turning away. He had been eying a group of men practising with longbows, shooting at a straw target close to the windmills. It being past midday, they were gathering their arrows and preparing to return to the city. He watched them amble away, taking the path towards Moorgate.

'What about digging into your hoard?' Gifford said. 'Now I think of it, you haven't repaid me the sum I loaned you for boat-hire.'

With a sigh, Marbeck fumbled for his purse . . . then paused. The group with longbows had moved off and were almost out of his vision. But another archer had appeared, seemingly from nowhere. As Marbeck watched, the man stopped some distance away from the spot they surveyed. Casually, he bent his bow, strung it, then appeared to test its strength.

'What is it?' Noticing his demeanour, Gifford came and crouched beside him.

'Does that fellow look like a bowman to you?' Marbeck enquired.

Gifford narrowed his tired eyes and peered out across the Fields. The man had taken an arrow

176

from the quiver on his back and was fitting it to the string. They watched him take aim, then shoot . . . and, as one, they stiffened.

'He's no more an archer than I'm a Bankside whore,' Gifford said. 'So why do you wait?'

But already Marbeck was on his feet. In a moment he was at the door, then sprinting downstairs, startling Mistress Mason in the hallway. He hurried past her, out of the house and into Everades Well Street, where he broke into a trot. The house was at the end of the row; in seconds he had rounded it and, slowing to a walk, entered the Fields – just in time to see the lone archer stooping to retrieve an arrow from the grass. As Marbeck moved towards him, he saw the figure lift the black stone quickly, take what was beneath and drop it back into place. Whereupon, he turned and began to walk off in a northerly direction, crossing the ditch into Bunhill Fields.

Head down, Marbeck followed. There were houses bordering the Fields on the west, up to the turning into Old Street. Allowing his quarry to draw ahead, Marbeck held back until he saw him reach the corner and disappear. Then he too walked smartly up to it. When he rounded it, the archer, longbow slung across his back, was twenty yards ahead. Thereafter, falling into a steady pace, Marbeck began to trail him.

It was straightforward at first. Confident he had not been seen, Marbeck nevertheless kept a good distance behind his mark. There were people about, and it wasn't difficult to conceal himself. But quite soon he began to wonder if the man was leading him by a roundabout route, which could mean two things: either he knew he was followed, or he thought it likely and was taking precautions.

The suspicion grew soon after the fellow turned left, out of Old Street into Whitecross Street. Since this ran parallel to the Fields and back down to Everades Well Street, it meant that quarry and pursuer would have described a loop. Fully alert, Marbeck followed, walking between the tenements of this sprawling suburb and eventually crossing the end of Well Street. Here his mark took a right turn into Beech Lane, which led into the Barbican. They were now in Cripplegate Ward, close to St Giles, and the streets were becoming busy. If they kept to this course, following the road into Long Lane, they would soon be at West Smithfield, which was always crowded. It would be easy for the message-carrier to lose his pursuer; Marbeck quickened his pace, shortening the distance between them.

With the crowd thickening, he followed his man across Aldersgate Street into Long Lane. The din of the market was ahead, the stench of animal dung in his nostrils. Horses, sheep and cattle would be milling about . . . and as passers-by got in his way, he was obliged to close up the gap again. But he kept his gaze focussed on the point of the longbow, jigging up and down above people's heads. Then quite soon they were in Smithfield, with the noise and press of folk on all sides.

Doggedly, Marbeck weaved his way through the throng, peering between bodies. He passed horse dealers engaged in fierce bargaining, farmers and drovers in from the country, housewives and servants with laden baskets. At one point he feared he had lost his target, then, with relief, caught sight of him again, heading in the direction of Saint Bartholomew's. Hurrying now, he closed the gap once again, dodging a porter with a load on his back and slithering on the foul cobblestones. He eased his way to the southern end of Smithfield, passing Hosier Lane on his right. But he kept his eye on the bobbing tip of the longbow. For a while it was hidden, then it reappeared . . . then, suddenly, it was gone.

Breathing fast, Marbeck pushed his way forward. The market din was behind him now, though the street was still crowded. He was at Pie Corner, with Cock Lane at his right and St Sepulchre's ahead. Swiftly, he scanned the streets in three directions . . . then froze.

Someone was approaching him, carrying a longbow – the same one, he knew, that he had been eying ever since he'd left Finsbury Fields. But this was not the person he had trailed: it was a barefoot boy in poor clothes, holding the bow before him – and he was smiling.

'Here, master!' the urchin piped as he drew close. 'I was told to give 'ee this – someone back there said you wanted it, and you should have it. Said you'd pay me three pennies!'

'Someone?' Spirits sinking, Marbeck looked into the child's dirty face. 'Was it man or woman?'

But the boy merely held out his hand. Inaudibly, Marbeck cursed. With apparent ease, Silvan's letter-bearer had given him the slip.

Worse, it meant that his role as a traitor to the Crown was over as soon as it had begun, and his plan was in ruins.

With a sigh, he reached for his purse, while the child grinned from ear to ear.

Sixteen

It was past midnight before Marbeck and Gifford were admitted to Sir Robert Cecil's private chamber at Burleigh House, led by a grim-faced Nicholas Prout. In silence, the two intelligencers filed in, to stand like guilty schoolboys. There was a moment while Prout hovered near the door, but seeing that his presence was not required he soon left. Master Secretary then eyed both men coolly, before inviting them to explain themselves. Whereupon, as he and Marbeck had agreed, Gifford spoke up at once, giving an eloquent account of recent events. It didn't take long, and though delivered with the best polish he could put upon it, the implications were not lost on the spymaster. Finally, when Gifford had said all there was to say, he fell silent. Stiff as posts, two of the Crown's best intelligencers waited.

'Good,' Master Secretary said at last.

'Good?' Gifford blurted. 'You . . . you approve of our strategy, sir?'

'It was bold and inventive,' came the reply. 'If somewhat precipitate . . . but, then, that was always your way.' He threw Marbeck a wry look. 'The situation obliged you to act swiftly. And, as you say, you opened up a way to our new friend Silvan.'

'Only to close it again,' Marbeck said, concealing his relief. 'I was sluggish in pursuit

181

of the courier . . . now that I fear I've shown my true hand, they'll drop me like a stone.'

'Well, what's done is done.' Cecil was seated behind his table, propped on cushions. He thought for a moment, then looked up. 'We might even build upon it,' he said.

Though startled by the turn of events, Gifford recovered quickly. 'Indeed, sir,' he agreed. 'Perhaps if you were to draw up a new list of intelligencers currently about London, we may question them and—'

Cecil cut him off sharply. 'That would take too long. Besides, this talk of a woman running messages throws everything into question. I have no female agents – that's a French practice.'

'Perhaps a Spanish one, too?' Marbeck ventured.

Master Secretary was frowning. 'If it was anyone else but Rose, I'd have been sceptical,' he said. 'But he has the eyes of a goshawk. I trust the man's judgement – as I do yours, Marbeck. Though it's a leap of imagination, to assume the person who was alongside Silvan when he had you at his mercy was the same woman – let alone that she is Mulberry.'

'Yet I believe it's so, sir,' Marbeck replied. 'I think a new circle has been formed – a regrouping, after Gomez was taken. They got rid of Ottone too, to clear the way . . .' He broke off, as a look of irritation appeared on Cecil's face.

'That was a loss I could have done without,' he murmured. 'Coming on top of the capture of Moore – who, it seems, is being racked in the Spanish Netherlands, for whatever intelligence he can give . . .' He looked away. 'If

182

there were a way to put an end to his suffering, I'd like to know of it.'

Marbeck caught Gifford's eye. Master Secretary could be ruthless, and the true meaning of his words was not lost on either of them: to stop Moore's mouth, he would have ordered his death in an instant.

'How may I serve, sir?' Gifford asked. 'I would ask that—'

'Enough of your flannel.' Cecil's voice was icy. 'I have a notion what to do next, and there may well be a part you can play. But the plain fact is Silvan's only here because you failed to keep a close enough watch at Dover.'

Silence ensued. Gifford lowered his gaze, whereupon Master Secretary eyed Marbeck. 'The false fleet bound for Ireland was a good device,' he said. 'Yet it will be only a short time before it's exposed for the pack of lies that it is. If Silvan's half the man I think he is, he's already seeking verification – and trying to get a despatch to his master, perhaps.'

'Gifford intercepted one message at Dover from Mulberry,' Marbeck began, but the spymaster looked up sharply.

'You mean the one taken off the papist student?' He moved a few papers and picked one up. 'But this isn't signed by Mulberry.'

Gifford blinked. 'Forgive me, sir, I thought—'

'Do you mean to say you haven't examined it thoroughly?' Cecil demanded. 'This word isn't *Morera*. It's the name of another fruit – *Membrillo*. That means a quince, in case you wonder,' he added icily.

There was a moment as both men took in the information. 'Then, there's another of them?' Gifford blurted.

Inwardly, Marbeck cursed. 'So Silvan's circle is already wider than we thought,' he said.

Gifford swallowed audibly. 'Well, then, we must step up the search on all ships leaving the ports,' he stammered. 'Strengthen the watch—'

'No – that would also take too long,' Cecil objected.

In silence, the other two waited.

'A projection,' their master added, after a moment. 'It's the only way to flush them out. We must outfox the foxes.'

'How so?' Marbeck asked.

'By making further use of your device while we may,' came the reply. 'In short, let every intelligencer about London hear of a fleet that's been put together rapidly, much as you've described. We'll even keep the name of your admiral – Van Zoren. We can come up with the names of other commanders, too – along with those of some of our vessels currently under repair, or decommissioned.'

Seeing Master Secretary rather animated – a rare event – Gifford spoke up. 'I have a few Dutch names I could add,' he said with relief. 'Sea captains who truly exist.'

'Yet surely the matter will not stand there?' Marbeck raised an eyebrow at Cecil. 'Do you mean to make it known that this flotilla is to anticipate the Spanish fleet bound for Ireland? In which case, we've shown that we already know its purpose.' He hesitated. 'It's a risky strategy, sir.'

'Perhaps,' Cecil allowed. 'But the Spaniards

184

wouldn't be surprised that we've already guessed what the new fleet's for. Their intelligencers are not idle, and they assume ours aren't either. Besides, I'm counting on a swift response from Mulberry. He – or she – will be eager to cast doubt my way. While every loyal agent will make haste to apprise me of this new intelligence, I think Mulberry's despatch will read somewhat differently.'

The other two saw it now. All Master Secretary would have to do, once word of the bogus fleet had been leaked, was to sift the reports that came to him. Any one that sat oddly with the rest would almost certainly be from the traitor.

'I wish I'd thought of such,' Marbeck said.

Cecil merely frowned at him. 'You may wish all you like, Marbeck,' he snapped. 'For your part, this is your chance to make amends for your recent laxity. The same goes for you, Gifford,' he added. 'When the time comes, I'll call on you both to apprehend Mulberry – alive. Following that, you may find yourselves alongside Sangers at the Marshalsea, when he draws every grain of truth from the traitor – and, if she is indeed a woman, I pity her already.'

Two days then passed. And by the end of the second, the tempers of both Marbeck and Gifford were close to breaking point.

'It could all come to nothing,' Gifford muttered. It was evening, and his tone was murderous. 'Like your feeble attempt to trail the false bowman. Once he – or she – sensed you were in pursuit, our whole strategy was doomed.'

Marbeck refused to answer.

'And you didn't even get close enough to see if it *was* a woman in man's attire,' Gifford scoffed. 'Whoever she is, she had the better of you from the outset!'

Still Marbeck declined to rise to the bait. He had more faith in Cecil's plan than Gifford did. And having expected the worst, he now had some hope of success. 'Silvan's people may have won a throw,' he said finally. 'But the game still runs.'

With a grunt, the other turned away and picked up a bottle of ale. They were back in their chamber at the White Bear, where they could be reached quickly. The projection had been put in hand – with some speed, it seemed – but neither Marbeck nor Gifford would know what followed until Prout came to find them.

'There are whores a-plenty but a stone's throw from here,' Gifford said, raising an earlier suggestion. 'What say I find a couple and bring them up here, to pass the time?'

Marbeck's response, however, was flat. 'Do what you will,' he said. 'But do it elsewhere. I'll be glad to have the chamber to myself.'

As he had already done a dozen times, he was thinking over Gifford's words: had the archer indeed been a woman in disguise – the same one who had carried the message to Rose at the Duck and Drake? He only wished he had got closer.

'By the Christ, this whole business is a rat's nest,' Gifford said, almost to himself. 'Why don't they just round up every papist in London? We need to shake a few trees, see what falls out.'

'Cherries?' Marbeck said. 'Quinces, perhaps?'

'I take back what I once said,' the other muttered. 'Your true bent is not for serious play-acting, but for comedy.'

But even he fell silent, bored with his own banter. Dusk came, and both men prepared for yet another night of waiting. Neither had much appetite, and since the food at the White Bear left much to be desired, they didn't bother to order a supper. Each lay on his bed, in private rumination. They lit no candle, allowing the room to grow dark, and finally both drifted into slumber. For Marbeck, it was a sleep shot through with vivid dreams, culminating in a vision of Lady Celia Scroop, stark naked. He was reaching out for her, when she spoke in a voice that wasn't her own . . .

'Marbeck! Wake up, damn you!'

He awoke with a start, to find someone shaking him by the shoulder.

'There's movement at last,' Gifford said, bending over him. 'Prout's waiting outside – get ready.'

Marbeck roused himself hurriedly. Gifford had lit a candle; by its flame, he saw him buckling on his scabbard.

'What news is there?' Marbeck asked as he dressed.

'I'm not certain,' the other replied. 'He said he'll tell us on the way.'

'On the way to where?'

'I know not – will you cease questioning me?'

No further words passed. Both men were relieved to be of use after the tedium of the past days. In a few minutes, alert and armed, they made their

187

way out of the inn into the murky light of early dawn. There in the street stood Nicholas Prout, hatted and muffled against the chill. With him was a well-armed pursuivant, the same man who had stood beside Marbeck in the fencing hall and looked upon the body of Giacomo Ottone.

'At last.' The messenger eyed the two with his customary air of disapproval. 'May we proceed now?' He set off up Red Cross Street, the others following.

'Where are we going?' Marbeck asked. 'And what's the—'

Prout raised a gloved hand. 'I'll convey my master's orders,' he said stolidly, 'if you'll hold your peace. Can you do that?'

Reining in their impatience, Marbeck and Gifford exchanged looks. But they fell into step, allowing Prout to lead the way along the street. The soldier brought up the rear.

'Very well.' Having marshalled his facts, the messenger began to relay them. 'I've no need to go over the projection, have I, that you spoke of with Master Secretary? But I'll say one thing: I never knew such a flurry of despatches, not since the Armada – or even the Queen of Scots business. Anyhow, it's brought a result in the end, that's put Sir Robert in a poor humour.' He sighed. 'Loyalty comes cheap nowadays, is all I can say.'

They had turned into the Barbican and were tramping westwards. Dawn had barely broken, but already people were about. 'Will you get to the nub of it, Prout?' Gifford said, his patience exhausted. 'Whom do we seek?'

188

'I am coming to it,' Prout retorted. 'Will you let me get there in my own time?'

They were at the crossing with Aldersgate Street, whereupon something struck Marbeck so forcibly he almost stopped in his tracks.

'What's wrong?' Prout slowed down, frowning at him.

'Nothing . . . Tell us, if you please.' Marbeck began walking again, but his thoughts whirled. They were retracing the route he had taken three days back, when he followed the bogus archer from Finsbury Fields to West Smithfield . . . A suspicion had formed, but he kept it to himself.

'As I said—' Prout drew a breath – 'reports have come in thick and fast. Not all the ones Master Secretary wanted, but enough for him to take a decision. One stood out like a jewel in a dunghill, it seems. Tried to tell him rumours about the new Spanish fleet are all lies. According to this report, which the sender claims to come from a new source, the fleet's not bound for Ireland, but is a new Armada. It's supposed to come sailing into the Channel as before – and it's only forty ships.' He grimaced. 'He must think Master Secretary's a fool to swallow that. There was other stuff too, but it's by the by . . .'

The messenger trailed off, but Gifford would wait no longer. 'The traitor, Prout!' He put a hand on the other's sleeve. 'In God's name, who is the subject of your warrant?'

There was a moment in which Marbeck expected a rebuke from the messenger. Instead, the man met Gifford's eye.

'The report came from number nineteen,' he

189

said. 'That's where we're bound – he lives by St John's. Ex-soldier, by the name of—'

'Saxby.'

Marbeck spoke the name before him, prompting sharp looks from the others. There, in Long Lane, the little group stopped.

'Saxby – the one without a leg?' Disbelief was on Gifford's face. 'That's absurd!'

Prout glared at him. 'Do you doubt Master Secretary's judgement?'

'Well, mayhap I do . . .' Gifford began. But he looked at Marbeck, a frown on his face. 'You questioned him, didn't you?' he went on. 'You said you'd sounded him out . . .'

'I did,' Marbeck said, not really listening. 'But I may have questioned the wrong Saxby.'

The others were silent. The soldier stood aside, impatient with the delay. But Prout was frowning at Marbeck.

'What say you?' he demanded. 'Speak now, for I've to serve a warrant on Thomas Saxby, then take him to the Marshalsea. Do you know some reason I shouldn't?'

Slowly, Marbeck shook his head. The truth, he saw, had lain just beyond his vision all along. He pictured the grim hovel where the ex-gunner lived, and the spirited woman who had stood by him. He saw Saxby's haggard face, in the Red Bull in St John's Street, as he told how his wife had nursed him back from near-death, shared his hardship . . . and he remembered the look in the woman's eyes, as she took the coin he had given, to aid her in her poverty.

'No . . . there's no reason not to go there,' he

said to Prout. 'Master Secretary's right: nineteen is the false agent. Only nineteen isn't one person, but two – one who runs errands and carries messages, because the other cannot. She's the one disguises herself as a man.' He faced Gifford. 'Mulberry's a man and wife – and her name is Anne.'

Seventeen

Dawn had broken by the time the four men marched down the narrow, refuse-strewn street in Clerkenwell where Marbeck had walked a month before. This time, however, people stepped aside in alarm at sight of the heavily armed group. Thomas Saxby was known to possess firearms, and both Prout and his guard carried pistols. Their orders were to capture the man alive, Marbeck and Gifford to assist if required. But now that it seemed both Saxby and his wife should be arrested, everything had changed.

There had been heated words back in Long Lane, but the dispute was short. Once Marbeck had spelled it out, it made sense even to Nicholas Prout. Saxby's lameness was beyond doubt – if he was a double-dealer, he must have had help. Marbeck almost believed he could picture Anne sitting in the gloom when Silvan had tried to persuade him to turn traitor. How long had it been since such an offer was made to the embittered ex-soldier – and to his wife, too? It now looked as if the false physician Gomez had recruited them. In spite of himself, Marbeck had to admire the Portuguese. He had been tortured unto death, yet had not revealed the identity of his double agent in London. Now Silvan was their master. A grim resolve formed in Marbeck's mind. Once the Saxbys were taken, surely a path could be laid to the other?

Now, at Prout's order, the group halted. The messenger glanced at Marbeck, who pointed to the last house in the row. He and Gifford loosened their swords. The other man readied his short pistol.

'There's no light,' Gifford said. 'They're still abed.'

'We'll break the door in,' Prout said. 'We take Saxby; you two follow and take the woman. Can you accomplish that?'

'Most amusing,' Gifford muttered, but was ignored.

'If he tries to fight, aim to wound,' Prout told his man. 'Disarm him at all costs.' He threw a questioning look at Marbeck.

'There are stairs at the rear, as I recall,' Marbeck said. 'But he sleeps on a pallet on the ground floor. He had an old wheel-lock, though it wasn't primed.' He shrugged. 'Yet, with all that's happened lately, they may be on their guard.'

'Why do we wait?' Gifford jerked his head towards the tumbledown dwelling. 'By the look of that door, one good push will cave it in.'

With a grunt, Prout gestured them to take their places on either side of the doorway. No sooner had they done so than he clapped his guard on the shoulder, but the man needed no prompting. In a moment he had thrown his body against the timbers, which gave way at once. He and Prout hurried in, the messenger shouting as he went.

'Thomas Saxby, I arrest you in the Queen's name! Show yourself!'

But the answer was as immediate as it was unexpected: a deafening roar. Close behind Prout,

193

Marbeck ducked instinctively. There had been a red flash, and the air was now filled with powder-smoke. He was aware of a grunt and a body crashing to the floor: the guard had been shot.

'Get back, or I'll fire, too!'

It was a woman's voice. Prout fell forward, stumbling over his pursuivant, while it was all Marbeck and Gifford could do to avoid falling over him in turn. They blundered into the house, scattering to left and right.

'Throw down your weapon! One warning is all I'll give!' Prout cried. He was on his knees, coughing in the smoke. Peering through it, Marbeck saw Saxby's bed where he remembered it, but it was empty. He had barely time to register the sight of someone crouching in the corner – then came another pistol-shot, and this time Prout fell. But even as he did so, the messenger fired his own weapon. The result was a cry – and the figure in the corner collapsed.

'Prout . . . are you hit? Speak, damn you!'

It was Gifford. Turning, Marbeck saw him bending over the wounded man. Beside them, the guard lay groaning.

'I can fadge for myself – attend to your duty!'

Gifford's face showed relief: Prout was not badly hurt – but immediately his gaze swept past Marbeck's shoulder.

'Look out!'

Marbeck snapped round, almost too late. He saw the dagger and weaved aside. But the blade jabbed his torso, slashing his padded doublet. There was a stab of pain in his side. He staggered, but managed to grab the arm of his assailant. At the same time he looked up into a narrow face: a woman's face, contorted with hatred.

'You whoreson javel!' Anne Saxby cried. 'I'll spike you!'

But Marbeck held her, tightening his grip. Falling to a sitting position, he used both hands to force her wrist backwards until she dropped the poniard. And though she fought him, she was slender and had little strength. Soon she sank to the floor, panting with the effort.

'Jesu, what a coil . . .'

Gifford appeared, to seize Anne from behind. She struggled, but knew she had lost. In a moment she had been yanked to her feet, her arms pinioned. Only then did Marbeck get up, breathing hard. There was a wetness on his left side; he glanced down, saw the stain.

'Is it bad?' Gifford asked.

He shook his head. The two eyed each other, then looked to their prisoner. She was slumped, head bowed.

'She fired the second shot,' Marbeck said.

'I know.' Gifford nodded towards the corner. Now that the powder-smoke was clearing, the crumpled figure of Thomas Saxby could be seen, wearing the same old jerkin that Marbeck remembered. He lay half on his side, his ruined leg stuck out at an angle. Beside him was the pistol with which he had shot the guard, before Anne had fired at Prout. Prout's answering shot, however, had found Saxby and not his wife.

'I'll hold her,' Gifford said. 'You'd better see . . .' He broke off. There was a murmur of pain: Saxby was alive. And at once Anne's head flew up.

'Tom!' she screamed.

Marbeck stepped across the room and got down on one knee beside the ex-soldier. The man's eyes were open, though he remained still. A welter of gore was spreading outwards from his body, pooling on the floor.

'You . . .?' His face drawn with pain, Saxby narrowed his eyes. 'I know you, do I not?'

Without answering, Marbeck lifted the man's wrist and felt his pulse. Then he looked down at the terrible wound and finally leaned back. His expression was enough.

'So . . . I'm to perish at home?' Saxby let out a sigh. 'Then, I thank Christ it's here, and not in some Irish swamp.'

Marbeck made no answer.

'Please – let me go to him!'

He looked round, to see Anne straining against Gifford's grip. 'I beg you!' she cried. 'He should die in my arms . . . for the love of Jesus!'

'Let her be with him.'

It was Prout who spoke. Marbeck and Gifford turned quickly to see the messenger on his feet. He was stooping, one arm hanging uselessly. Blood ran from it and dripped to the floor.

'We've made enough of a farrago already,' he breathed. 'And any man should be allowed to make his peace.'

Gifford hesitated, but Marbeck shifted his gaze to Anne. 'We'll sit him up,' he said.

There was a moment before Gifford unwillingly released his prisoner. Anne darted forward and fell to her knees beside her husband. Between them, she and Marbeck raised the man's limp body and turned it, so that he could rest with his back to the wall. He winced with pain, but made no further sound. There he sat, his face ash-grey, blood seeping through his jerkin.

'Gifford and I can question him,' Marbeck said. 'We'll wait to the end, then make full report.'

'So be it,' Prout murmured. He looked to his guard, who was also bleeding profusely. 'I'll get him to a surgeon,' he added in a dull voice. He looked like a spent old man.

'Not on your own, you can't,' Gifford said. 'Yet, if he can stand, we may move him between us. But two of us should be here,' he added, with a nod towards Anne. 'I'll bind her hands—'

'Whose warrant is this, Gifford?'

Prout's voice was savage. Gifford blinked at the expression on the man's face. But Marbeck recognized the look: the same one he had seen that night in Gracious Street, outside Ottone's fencing hall.

'Let Prout look to it,' he said.

He turned back to Anne, who sat beside her husband, holding his hand. Tears stained her cheeks, but she was silent. Behind him Marbeck heard Prout and Gifford lifting the wounded guard up, but he didn't look round. There were murmured voices, and, further off, the noise of people gathered in the street. Then Prout and his man were gone, and Gifford was back.

'What in God's name made you turn, Saxby?'

Marbeck looked up, saw no sympathy in Gifford's gaze. His fellow intelligencer gazed sternly upon the pair of unlikely traitors and shook his head. 'What did they offer you – gold?'

There was no answer. Anne refused to look at her captors, but kept her eyes on her husband. Despite everything, Marbeck sensed love flowing between these two ragged people. Yet, like Gifford, he knew he had a task to perform. With an effort, he got to his feet, to see that his companion had found a stool and was placing it behind him.

'You should get to a surgeon, too,' he muttered.

'Soon.' Marbeck sat down, throwing him a glance which conveyed enough: the wounded man had only minutes to live. Gifford took a step forward.

'There's no sense in holding back now, is there, Saxby?' he said in a flat tone. 'We can do no more harm to you . . . but we can to your wife. You should think upon that.'

Saxby gave a start. 'You would sweat her, in my place?' There was fear in the man's eyes – though not for himself. He peered up at Gifford.

'I wouldn't, but there's one who would, and smile while he did it,' Gifford answered. 'Name of Sangers . . . you'll know who he is.'

There was a gasp from Anne. Her eyes flickered towards Marbeck, who remained impassive. A current of understanding passed between him and Gifford: like it or not, this was an interrogation. Gifford had already chosen to play the hammer role; Marbeck would be the anvil.

'Was it Gomez who came to you?' he asked Saxby. 'The man you swore you hadn't heard of?' Receiving no answer, he added: 'No matter, let's say it was him. So – was it merely money he offered?'

'Of course it wasn't. D'you think you can buy a man like Tom as easily as that?'

Anne was overcome with fury. Hatred shot from her eyes, as she turned them on Marbeck. And she would have said more, had not a word from her husband stayed her. Swiftly, she turned back to him, squeezing his hand.

'Let me talk,' he said weakly.

There was a brief silence, before Anne sagged. Racked with sobs, she began shaking her head from side to side.

'Nay, forbear to weep,' Saxby murmured. 'There's things to be said.' He eyed Marbeck. 'I want your word she won't be punished for my sake.'

'You know I can't give that,' Marbeck told him.

'Then, the devil take you!' The man's breathing was laboured now, but a fierce light burned in his eyes. 'For you'll get naught but my contempt.'

'Your words may help, though,' Marbeck added, his gaze steady. 'And I would hear them anyway. When did they recruit you? After you got back from Ireland?'

There was a moment, then a grim smile appeared on Saxby's face. 'Nay, they'd no need to do that . . . My mind was altered long before I was shipped back from there.'

Without warning, Gifford dropped to his heels beside Marbeck, making the wounded man start. 'Do you mean you converted to the Roman faith?' he snapped.

'Nor that, even,' Saxby answered, his voice low. 'You may blame the Queen's commanders in Ireland if you like . . . for they did Spain's work for themselves.' He closed his eyes: his life was ebbing away. Impatiently, Gifford leaned forward.

'Then, what say you?' he demanded. 'Was it the plight of the Irish people that moved you? The burning of their fields, the starvation . . .'

'In heaven's name, why can't you leave him to die?'

Anne faced Gifford, her voice torn with grief. 'I can tell you as much as he,' she cried. 'More, even. You think I haven't heard all there is to hear about Ireland? Women and children burned alive in their huts – treated worse than dogs! The English soldiers are become animals over there. Tom was all fired up for Queen and country too, when he went – but 'twas a different man who came back!'

She fell silent and turned to her husband. Thomas Saxby's face was taut, but he was smiling at her.

'She's painted the picture well enough.' He sighed and turned his gaze upon Marbeck. 'I remember you now,' he added. 'You bought me a mug in the Red Bull, only you'd come to rack me for a turncoat . . . but I gave a good account, did I not?'

Marbeck said nothing.

'Well, I lied to you,' Saxby went on. 'Just a little. I wasn't always with Chichester's force. I was with Sir Henry Harrington's, too – you know what happened to him?'

Gifford frowned. 'Harrington's army was beaten by the Irish last year, at Wicklow . . .'

'Aye – and you know what our Queen's commanders did, to pay him out for that?'

From somewhere Saxby had found a shred of energy: the last gasp of a dying soldier. Angrily, he eyed both men, fixing at last on Marbeck. 'The Earl of Essex – damn his heart – took it as an affront to his command,' he muttered. 'Called our men cowards. He executed every tenth man as punishment – officers, too. How is that for English justice?'

'So – you saw your comrades slain, by our own men?' Marbeck asked calmly.

'Not just comrades: his own brother!'

Both Marbeck and Gifford showed surprise, as again Saxby's wife turned her fury on them. Eyes blazing, she spat the words out. 'Tom would have died in his place – his brother was but a lad of seventeen! He begged them to spare Samuel and take him instead, but they wouldn't listen. He had to stand with the others and watch him perish! Do you wonder that he hates Elizabeth, and all those who do her bidding?'

Gifford drew a sharp breath. 'By the Christ – do you tell us all this was but a matter of revenge?' he said harshly. 'Because Essex is a vain fool, you turn against your own country – to work for Spain, our sworn enemy?'

'The boy was all the family I had,' Saxby breathed. 'They showed no mercy . . . Soldiers are but tools to them, to be used and thrown aside. I lost my loyalty back there in the bog, along with my leg . . . Do you tell me you'd have done any different?'

To that Gifford made no answer. Instead, with a swift glance at Marbeck, he straightened up.

201

'I've heard all I want to,' he said. 'I'll wait outside.'

But even as he moved away, Saxby appeared to forget him. The man's eyes were glazed, his breathing shallow.

'He's near the end,' Marbeck said to Anne. 'I'll leave you, too.' He paused. 'Do you wish me to fetch a parson?'

But the woman barely heard him. Shakily, she raised a hand and laid it against her husband's face. Marbeck got up stiffly and took a step, whereupon a jolt of pain checked him. He glanced down, saw the dark stain that had soaked his doublet and his breeches, as far as the thigh. He looked to the doorway, where his companion stood.

'You must attend to that,' Gifford said.

Weakly, Marbeck nodded.

'I'll finish up here,' the other added. 'Then I'll take her to the Marshalsea. They can get all they need from her now.'

Marbeck nodded again.

'Surely you're not going to peg out too, sirrah?' Gifford made an attempt at a smile. 'Master Secretary would be most displeased to lose another man – especially so soon.'

'I don't believe so,' Marbeck said at last. 'I've a score to settle yet, with the one who runs these people.' He indicated the dying man and his wife. 'It may have been she who pointed a pistol at my head that night, but Silvan's voice was one I shan't forget. I mean to see it silenced, one way or another.'

There was a cry of anguish. Both of them

202

looked towards the corner. Anne was leaning forward, peering into her husband's face, but even from a distance they could see it was over. Saxby's eyes were closed, his body lifeless. His wife lay her head upon his bloodstained chest and wept quietly.

'Let her alone for a while,' Marbeck said.

Gifford sighed and looked away.

Eighteen

Three days later, on a bright morning that carried the chill of approaching winter, Marbeck crossed London Bridge and made his way to the Marshalsea prison.

He walked stiffly through the crowds, with his sword on the right; he was bandaged, to cover the stitches made on his left side by a barber-surgeon. The wound was raw but it was clean, and he was recovering. Yet his mouth was tight; what lay ahead was something he did not relish at all.

Once he and Gifford had made a full report to Sir Robert Cecil, the spymaster had wasted no time. He was displeased by the outcome of the raid on the Saxby house, and by the death of the false agent now known to be Mulberry. There was some relief in the knowledge that both Nicholas Prout and the other man would recover from their wounds. But, in the light of what had emerged, his orders were clear: every scrap of knowledge must be extracted from Anne Saxby, by any means necessary. Marbeck and Gifford were to conduct the interrogation, with Richard Sangers in attendance.

He reached the gates, showed his written pass to the turnkey and entered the prison as he had done a month earlier. This time he was directed not to Sangers but to a small cell with a barred window. The room was bare save for some straw – and an iron ring set high in the wall, with a set of manacles attached. Here, Gifford was awaiting him.

'How is the wound?' he asked.

'It's healing.'

They fell silent. Even Gifford, he thought, viewed the task before them with distaste. The pair had not seen each other for the past two days, since Gifford had left the White Bear and found lodgings elsewhere. Marbeck had used the chamber to rest, though he too would remove himself soon.

'Where's Sangers?' he asked.

'Collecting the woman. She's been put in with others. One of them's a prison louse, but it seems she was wise to that ploy. She hasn't spoken a word since she was captured.'

That came as little surprise to Marbeck. He had formed an opinion of Anne Saxby as a woman of shrewdness and courage, which made what would happen here all the more terrible. Restlessly, he took a few paces about the room, while Gifford stood by the door, looking tense. From nearby a jumble of sounds reached them: shouts, harsh laughter, the clang of a tin jug. The prison was damp and chill, and the reek, as ever, was all but unbearable.

'Have you no paper and ink?' Gifford muttered. 'If there's matter to set down, I mean . . .'

He broke off. From the passage outside came a squeal of hinges, and at the sound of the voice that followed both men stiffened. Gifford stepped back, both he and Marbeck facing the doorway, to see Sangers enter in his rough leather apron. With him, barefoot and shivering in only a shift, was Anne Saxby. Beside the interrogator she looked like a waif.

'See, what did I tell ye?' With a broad grin, the fellow turned to his prisoner. 'These men are come to have a talk with you. You'll like that, eh?'

She looked sharply at them both, before recognition dawned. But she said nothing, lowering her head and offering no resistance as Sangers pushed her against the wall. But no sooner had he chained her than the woman's ordeal began – for only by standing on tiptoe could she reach the floor. There she hung by her arms, her body stretched to its full extent; it was clear to any man she would not endure this for long.

Satisfied with his work, Sangers stood back and turned to the intelligencers. 'Ask what you will, masters,' he said with a sniff. 'I've the means to get everything you need.' He patted his belt, from which hung several implements. 'If you need me to step things up . . .'

'We'll call on you.'

Gifford didn't trouble to conceal his disdain for the man. He caught the eye of Marbeck, who moved close to the prisoner.

'You need to tell us all, Anne,' he said. 'This man enjoys meting out pain – he needs no persuasion. Do you see?'

She was breathing fast, her chest rising. He saw the dark patches under her eyes and knew she had slept little. Nor had she been fed, by the look of her. Her lips were cracked, her cheeks pinched. But she managed a quick nod.

206

'I've no cause to lie now,' she said, in little more than a whisper. 'I tried to speak to him, but he wouldn't listen.'

She meant Sangers. Without looking round, Marbeck nodded. 'It was you, sitting in the dark that night with Silvan, was it not?' he said, after a moment.

But she looked at him uncomprehendingly, whereupon Gifford stepped forward at once. 'Don't try to dissemble!' he snapped. 'You had no scruples shooting a messenger of the Crown. You stabbed this man, too – you aimed for his heart!'

She caught her breath. 'Please – I know not what you speak of,' she said to Marbeck. 'I never saw you again, after you came to see Tom – until the day he was killed . . .' She hesitated. 'Save for the time you followed me, from the Fields.'

Gifford gave a snort and would have spoken again, but Marbeck stayed him. For some reason, he believed the woman, whereupon a new thought sprang up.

'Then, if it wasn't you, who was it? Membrillo, perhaps?'

Mournfully, she shook her head. 'I don't know that name,' she said. 'Please believe me.'

'Did your knave of a husband teach you how to handle firearms?' Gifford broke in.

'He did.'

Her voice was taut. Whatever energy the woman had possessed since the debacle that had resulted in Thomas Saxby's death, it was now ebbing away.

'Speak up!' Gifford ordered. 'Are you too

207

dull-witted to judge your position? Before you leave this cell, you'll spill everything you know, and wish there were more you could tell. The Queen's loyal servants have no mercy for traitors!'

A look of anguish came over Anne's face. Marbeck expected tears, but instead she shook her head weakly. 'I'm not a traitor . . . not like you think.'

Gifford opened his mouth, but Marbeck stayed him again. 'Then, go back to the start and tell us,' he said. 'But leave nothing out, or I will be overruled. Do you understand me?'

She understood well enough. Her gaze went to Gifford, then to Sangers, who stood only feet away, his enjoyment of her plight obvious to all. Finally, she met Marbeck's eye again.

'They used me badly,' she muttered. 'Tom never knew. He would have killed them if he'd known . . . if he could have done.'

'They?' Marbeck raised his eyebrows.

'The Portuguese . . . Gomez . . .' She faltered, as if the memory pained her. 'It began with him, after Tom came home and lay sick. Tom was like a child; he couldn't walk or do aught for himself. But they knew already how his mind was turned. They knew even before he left Ireland. There are priests that spy for the Spanish.'

By the wall, Sangers grunted his contempt. But now that the testimony was flowing, Marbeck and Gifford relaxed slightly.

'How did Gomez make himself known?' Marbeck asked.

'He came to our house . . .' Anne was tiring, the pain of stretching already taking its toll. But

208

when she looked into his face, she saw no pity. 'He knew where to find us,' she went on. 'He came as a physician, to attend upon Tom. He even had some skills . . . and he gave us money. No one else helped us. I was grateful, even when I found out what he wanted.'

'And what was that?' Gifford asked.

'When Tom could walk, he had to go to his old captain, beg him to find him work as a prison informer,' Anne answered. 'He would befriend those they think traitors and uncover their secrets. He would claim he was a papist – they gave him a crucifix, to keep under his shirt. His lameness was good cover, they said.' The words caught in her throat. 'What else could he do?'

'But when he went to work for the Crown, he was really working for Gomez.' Gifford's voice was flat. 'So he passed a few titbits to his masters, but more intelligence flowed the other way – to your friend the Portuguese.'

After a moment, Anne gave a nod.

'And Gomez gave Tom a name to use – Mulberry?'

She nodded again, quickly. 'He said it was a kind of jest. That we were the fruits of our masters' toil.'

'Who was Gomez's master?' Marbeck asked casually.

'I never asked, and he never said. I didn't dare—' She broke off suddenly, but Marbeck saw.

'He could make you do anything, couldn't he?'

She met his eye – and for the first time, there was terror in her gaze. Gifford saw it, too – and when she made no answer, he spoke up. 'So you would run errands, serve any way you could,' he said. 'Even serve Gomez. Isn't that so?'

Her expression was answer enough.

'Well now . . .' Gifford put on one of his thin smiles. 'At last, we have a picture. She has no one to protect her, so wicked Gomez does what he pleases with her. And after he's used her, she's too frightened – or too ashamed – to tell her husband.' He eyed Marbeck. 'Plucks at the heart, does it not?'

'When did the next part begin?' Marbeck asked, ignoring him. 'I speak of the putting out of false reports . . . Did Gomez write them?'

'I can't read well, but Tom could,' Anne said hoarsely. 'Gomez told him what to say, and Tom would write it out using cipher and such.'

'Even to the very last?' Gifford enquired. 'The story of the Spanish fleet that will become a new Armada?'

'I think that was Silvan's work,' Marbeck said. 'We'll come to him soon.'

There was a moment, then a moan of pain escaped Anne's lips. She stretched her feet, striving desperately to touch the floor. Sangers snickered.

'Please set me down,' she gasped. 'I'll tell all, though there's little more . . .'

'Pray, tell us from there,' Gifford murmured.

'How you must have feared, after Gomez was caught,' Marbeck went on, as if he hadn't heard. 'I wonder you and Tom didn't try to flee the country.'

'Quite so,' Gifford said conversationally. 'If I was Saxby, I'd have soiled my breeches.'

'We went invisible!' Anne cried. 'We never left

210

the house – we watched the street. Then after you came poking about—' she jerked her head at Marbeck – 'we knew it wouldn't be long. Tom told me to get a second pistol. We were ready to die . . .'

'Well, one of you did,' Gifford observed dryly. Over by the wall, Sangers guffawed.

'And then Silvan appeared,' Marbeck said quickly. 'Having slipped in past those who were supposed to watch out for him.'

Gifford bristled, but said nothing.

'He came to us – mayhap three weeks after Gomez was taken,' Anne panted. 'He goes as a priest sometimes, or a merchant. He can be anyone he chooses . . .'

'But disguise isn't your forte, is it?' Gifford put in, in a tone of mock sympathy. 'Was that Silvan's idea? The drawer at the Duck and Drake saw through it. And as for trying to pass yourself off as a bowman . . .' He gave a snort of derision.

But Anne wasn't listening. Instead, she threw an imploring look at Marbeck. 'Please get me down,' she begged. 'You know I'll not lie—'

'Who is Membrillo?' Marbeck broke in. 'Do you know the name?'

'I do not – I swear it!' she cried, and now tears welled. She closed her eyes, her face contorted with pain.

'So Silvan killed Ottone, the fencing master – didn't he?'

'I know naught of that either – I swear!' She let out a sob. 'Silvan has his own orders, that he brought with him . . .'

211

Marbeck threw a glance at Gifford. Then, on impulse, he said: 'He's worse even than Gomez, isn't he?'

Her reply was an anguished wail. 'He said he'd have to kill Tom – he was too much of a risk!' Anne cried. 'He said he'd come to clean out the stables, start afresh . . . Then, when I begged him, he said he might spare me. He could use a mare, he said, that was willing . . . How could I not do as he said?'

Weeping, she hung her head. Marbeck drew a breath.

'You work fast, friend . . . I'll say that much.' He turned sharply to find Sangers eyeing him. 'I'd likely have took more than an hour to get all of that,' he added, rubbing his beard. 'She owes you, right enough.' A sly grin formed. 'I could arrange for you to collect, if you like – for a price.'

'Take her down,' Marbeck snapped.

The interrogator's grin vanished. 'Eh?'

'I said, take her down,' Marbeck ordered. 'I've heard all I need to.' Deliberately, he faced Gifford, who caught the look in his eye and gave a sigh.

'You heard him,' Gifford said, turning to Sangers. 'She's told us all she can.'

'Well, what of it?' the other retorted. 'She's a traitor – a papist's whore. She should hang all day and all night.'

'This is our warrant, Sangers.' Marbeck took a step towards the man. 'Master Secretary may have further use for her – do you not see?'

Sangers frowned. 'No one's said aught to me of that,' he muttered.

'I'm saying it,' Marbeck told him. 'And you

should mind your place . . .' He matched the man's frown. 'It wasn't so long ago that you let this woman's master perish, when he might have told more – have you forgotten that?'

Already, Sangers's bull neck was swelling. 'I've not forgotten,' he muttered. 'Nor have I forgot you, Sands – a snooper who thinks he's a gentleman.' He glared from Marbeck to Gifford, and back. 'It's not wise to wrangle with me,' he added. 'Master Secretary needs me more than he cares to admit – mayhap more than he needs men like you.' But he flinched as Marbeck laid a hand on his sword hilt.

'For the last time, unchain her and take her down,' he said.

A tense moment followed as Sangers's gaze wandered towards Gifford. He too had his hand on his sword hilt.

'As my friend told you, this is our warrant, Sangers,' he said coolly.

The interrogator opened his mouth – but there came a scream of pain that startled even him. At once Marbeck turned away and went to Anne. He bent stiffly, grasping her legs.

'Stop, you fool – you'll tear your wound open!'

In a moment Gifford was beside him, swearing under his breath. Between them they lifted her body, taking her weight. As they did so, a look passed between them. Anne, of course, was their only route to Silvan. Marbeck glanced up, saw her eyes were closed. She had fainted.

'Get over here, Sangers!' Gifford shouted. 'Unchain her and help us lay her down. Do as I say!'

213

The interrogator was still glaring. But at last he sniffed and reached for the key at his belt.

Marbeck sighed: this particular ordeal was over. What came next, he knew, would depend upon the wretched woman whose limp body he and Gifford now held. But somehow he was determined to lay a trap for the smooth-voiced spymaster who had been the cause of two deaths, and come close to causing his own.

And he had an idea that, even after this, Anne would help.

Nineteen

There was a low tavern in Thames Street, which Marbeck had used for various purposes in the past. Four days after her ordeal, Anne Saxby was removed from the Marshalsea prison by night, taken across the river and hurried up the inn stairs to a tiny chamber. There, by candlelight, her future was spelled out for her in the starkest terms: the one concession that Marbeck had been able to win from Sir Robert Cecil.

'Be under no illusions,' he told her. 'Your life depends upon your helping me. If you fail, the worst that's likely to befall me is a drubbing from my master. Whereas you will be taken back to the prison, there to remain until you are executed. Are you clear upon that?'

'I expected little else,' came the reply.

She was sitting on a low bed, in borrowed clothes. Marbeck was the only other present, though a guard was posted outside. Anne was still in pain from the torture she had been subjected to, but she was recovering, bodily at least. Her mind, however, had suffered hurts that would never heal. Bleakly, she faced her former captor, who now seemed to have become her guardian.

'First, tell me of Silvan,' Marbeck said. 'My fear is that he will flee from England. Indeed, some might say it's likely he's gone already. What do you say?'

215

'He's here yet,' she answered, after a moment. 'He won't leave until he knows what's become of me.'

Her answer came as a relief. Marbeck took a few paces about the chamber. It was two days since he had endured a short but gruelling encounter with Master Secretary, in which his own position had been set out in terms as stark as those he had put to Anne. His orders were to put an end to the whole untidy business, by any means necessary. The responsibility was now his alone, Gifford having been sent elsewhere. Then, Marbeck preferred it that way. He had a score to settle with the man who called himself Silvan – one that had become somewhat personal.

'But he will know you've been taken.' He turned to face Anne. 'As he knows your husband's dead – it's the talk of Clerkenwell.'

She looked away. 'He will know . . . as he is aware you tried to betray him. After you followed me from Finsbury Fields. He was very angry. You can't know what he's like, at such times.'

'I think I can,' Marbeck said. 'But did he really think I would turn traitor – that I could be bought so easily?'

She gave a shrug. 'I know not what he thinks. He tells me little.'

Suddenly, Marbeck thought of Moore's testimony. Perhaps his fellow intelligencer had kept his wits to the end, after all. If he'd told his Spanish interrogators that Marbeck was ripe for turning, that would explain a great deal . . . He almost smiled. Moore was one of the best: even at the last, he had led them astray. The least Marbeck could do now was avenge him.

'How do you make contact with Silvan?' he asked.

'At the riverside,' Anne answered. 'By the Three Cranes in the Vintry. I pass there and put a mark upon a certain doorpost with chalk. Then I wait near the tavern – sometimes an hour, sometimes a whole day – and he finds me.'

Marbeck considered. 'Do you think he has eyes and ears in the prison? Will he know you're gone from there?'

She shook her head. 'I know not.'

'Do you still swear you don't know who Membrillo is?' he asked, watching her closely.

'I do,' Anne said. 'He never uttered that name to me.'

'Was it Silvan who ordered you to dress as a bowman? It was a foolish notion.'

She sighed. 'Nay . . . it was Tom. He hated Silvan from the start, as he hated me taking risks for him. He would have gone himself, save that he stood out so. But Tom never believed you would turn. It was he told me to see if I was followed – and how to lose you, in the market.'

'He was right,' Marbeck said shortly.

But his mind was busy. The Vintry was the wharf where cargoes of wine were landed, winched from Thames lighters by the cranes on the quayside. The ghost of a plan was forming . . . and all at once he saw the likely means by which Silvan had entered the country.

'He goes as a wine merchant, does he?'

'That and other things,' Anne said, after a moment. 'He speaks many languages. He can be a Frenchman, if he wishes.'

'If he knows you were taken, he'll assume you were questioned,' Marbeck broke in. 'Hence, if you were to place your chalk-mark on that post now, he would suspect a trap.'

Having no answer to that, she gave a shrug. Marbeck turned away, thinking fast. He knew that three vessels had left London for the Continent in the past week, but he doubted Silvan had been on any of them. Searches had been stepped up in recent days. Yet he knew the man would be planning his escape. Haste, it seemed, was now essential.

'I'll have to take a risk,' he said finally. 'Could you convince Silvan you've been released from the prison, without telling all? If I gave you a tale, could you spin it?'

Anne shook her head. 'I couldn't lie to him – he's too clever.'

Marbeck frowned. Suddenly, a solution sprang up. 'What if you'd passed word to someone else?' he asked. 'Someone who was about to be freed? Might the chalk-mark make him think you'd sent him a message?'

'It might,' Anne admitted. 'Yet he trusts no one. At sight of a stranger, he would be wary . . .'

'That's not your concern,' Marbeck told her. But having thought of someone who suited his purpose, he relaxed. 'I have to go out now,' he added. 'You should rest . . . Do you have all you need?'

She nodded listlessly. But when he started for

218

the door, she looked up. 'What am I to do, then?' she asked. 'Act as bait, until he comes for me?'

Without answering, Marbeck left her.

The someone he had thought of was Augustine Grogan. And that same night, late though the hour was, the player found himself being collared in his usual haunt – the French Lily – by a suspiciously cheerful Marbeck.

'You surprise me, Sands,' he murmured. 'When we last spoke, you couldn't wait to send me away, as I recall.' His eyes narrowed. 'I wonder what occasions this bonhomie?'

'Well might you wonder,' Marbeck said. 'But let me buy you a cup of Charbon's best, and I'll reveal all.'

The other needed little persuasion. Within minutes the two of them were seated in a booth, where Marbeck wasted no time in outlining his proposal. Grogan was intrigued.

'You wish me to act as a decoy?' he blurted. Seeing Marbeck's expression, he clamped a hand over his mouth. 'Your pardon . . . I take it a degree of discretion is required in this matter?'

'A very great degree,' Marbeck answered, speaking low. 'In short, the man I want you to fool would slit your throat if he suspected you.'

The other blanched. 'I like this less and less.'

'How would you like a purse with ten crowns in it?'

A moment passed, then: 'What should I do? Or, shall I ask, what role is it you wish me to play?'

'The sort you've played since you were around

219

twelve years of age, I would guess,' Marbeck said.

At that Grogan sighed. 'I should have known.'

'I've even chosen a name for you,' Marbeck went on. 'Madge Mullins. You've just been released from prison.'

A frown appeared. 'I hope you're not implying I should perform services of a physical nature,' the player said with a frown. Marbeck shook his head.

'You're there to convey a message, and then direct the man in question to a place nearby. After that your part is ended. But we will rehearse it, to the last point. So – are you my hireling, or are you not?'

The player hesitated, though it was a theatrical pause. With raised eyebrows, Marbeck waited.

'Forgive my poor memory,' Grogan said at last. 'Did you mention twenty crowns?'

'I thought I said ten,' Marbeck replied. 'But it might have been fifteen . . . Will that serve?'

The other picked up his mug and raised it in mock salute.

By mid-morning of the following day the scheme had been set in motion. It was not without difficulties, one of which was the role Marbeck had chosen for himself. Silvan knew him, so his disguise had to be convincing; he, on the other hand, had not yet set eyes on Silvan. Having obtained a description from Anne, however, he believed he could identify the man. He was not overly tall, she said, but he was muscular. He wore his hair curled and his beard trimmed to a point. At the quays he dressed as a prosperous merchant, in a feathered hat and silk-lined cloak. And he wore a sword with a distinctive hilt, its tip fashioned into the likeness of an eagle's head. This touch of vanity pleased Marbeck; it might even be Silvan's undoing.

Now, at last, he was ready. Amid the noise and bustle of the Vintry quay, he took a place near the corner of Three Cranes Lane, close to the tavern entrance. The day was fair, with a breeze off the river, from where the cries of watermen echoed. On the wharf, men were busy, handling casks of wine and loading them on to carts. The cranes were at work, their pulleys squealing as barrels were hoisted up from a lighter moored below. Few people paid any attention to the shambling figure of a beggar swathed in rags, who appeared from somewhere and sat down against a wall, setting his wooden bowl at his feet.

Marbeck had employed many disguises in his time, and this was not one he relished. But discomfort he could bear, along with the smell of the moth-eaten clothes he had picked up. Nor did he fear recognition, for his face was grimed with dirt and partly hidden by a torn, wide-brimmed hat. What made him uneasy was the prospect of being confronted by a constable and arrested for vagrancy, or sent on his way. There had been no time to arrange a forged licence. He knew a long wait was likely; indeed, his plan might not even bear fruit at all. Yet he had no choice but to settle to his task.

A short time after his arrival, the second player in the plot appeared: Augustine Grogan. Nobody, however, would have recognized him; Marbeck was satisfied on that score. For his role as Madge Mullins, a woman of the streets, Grogan had excelled himself. Under an old gown of red taffeta, fluffed out with layers of petticoats, he wore a padded bodice. His hair was concealed beneath a thick horsehair wig, his face whitened, cheeks rouged and lips painted with vermilion. He had been a boy actor, playing female roles by the score then and since, and even at close quarters could convince most people. How long he would be able to fool a man like Silvan, however, remained to be seen.

Now, as instructed by Marbeck, he approached the doorway of a warehouse near the end of the quay. From the corner of his eye, Marbeck watched him take a piece of chalk from his gown and make a sign on the doorpost: a rough fleur-de-lis. Then, with a practised gait, he moved to a position a few yards away from Marbeck. Between them was the entrance to the Three Cranes Tavern, where Anne had once awaited her spymaster – and where she waited now, in a back chamber, with an armed guard at the ready. And then the waiting began.

It was a long morning. For his part, Marbeck had an easy time. A few coins were dropped into his bowl, but no one challenged him, nor did any official appear. He grew stiff and longed to stretch himself, but had to keep his place. His growing fear was that, as the hours dragged by, Grogan would lose his nerve. At first the player had enjoyed himself. Flirtatious behaviour came naturally to him, as did ripostes to the lewd remarks he attracted. When propositioned, he would claim he was awaiting a customer. Since he was within earshot, every word reached Marbeck . . . but after a while he detected a strain in the man's voice. Though neither looked at the other, an understanding grew between them: Grogan could not keep up his role indefinitely. Indeed, Marbeck knew that only the promise of a handsome payment was keeping him there at all.

As noon came and went, with no sign of anyone who looked like Silvan, even Marbeck became restive. The tavern had grown noisy, and customers wandered in and out, threatening at times to kick his bowl away, or even to kick him. Then, when he was on the point of getting to his feet and taking a walk, something landed in the bowl with a clack. He saw a small pebble, and his eyes flew up towards Grogan. The player stood poised, one hand twisting a strand of his wig, but he caught Marbeck's eye, before looking pointedly away. Marbeck followed his gaze to the door-post with its mark . . . and froze.

Someone was standing there, apparently in idle conversation with another man. He was exactly as Anne had described him – down to the blue velvet cloak with its silk lining – but it was the sword that gave him away. Even from a distance, Marbeck caught a glimpse of the silver hilt with its beaked point. Now he watched Silvan clap his acquaintance on the shoulder and turn away. As he did so, his eyes went to the chalk-mark, though he gave no sign of noticing it. In fact, stifling a yawn, which only Marbeck and Grogan would have known was forced, he promptly walked away and rounded a corner.

Marbeck glanced aside and saw Grogan looking uneasy, but when he turned again, it was all he could do not to flinch. From another corner, Silvan suddenly reappeared and strolled towards the player . . . and the moment he spoke Marbeck knew for certain he had found his man.

'Do I know you, mistress?' Silvan stopped, eyes upon Grogan, who quickly summoned a smile: he was on.

'I think not, sir – but we can soon remedy it,' Grogan answered coquettishly. Then, as the other waited, he lowered his voice. 'My name's Madge – mayhap you know my friend, mistress Anne?'

'Anne?' Silvan raised an eyebrow. 'The name means nothing.' He used a French accent, that of a fluent native speaker.

'No . . . nor should it, master,' Grogan said quickly. 'Only she and I were at close quarters . . . in a confined place, you might say. Poor Anne was in bad straits; she feared to die there. I was the one she trusted with her tale.'

He was smiling, but Marbeck, listening with face averted, cursed silently. Grogan had spoken too soon, and he sensed that Silvan was suspicious.

'And what tale was that?' Silvan enquired in a bored tone. 'Not that it matters . . . I had a mind to pass a moment with you, but I'm a busy man. My cargo won't wait.'

'Your cargo?' Grogan appeared to be thinking fast. 'I believe Anne told me of such. You import fine wines, don't you, sir? From Bordeaux – and Savoy, even?'

'Do I?' Silvan replied. 'What else did your friend Anne tell you?'

There was a pause, then Grogan took a breath and delivered his crucial speech. 'She told me to make that mark on the post yonder,' he said, his voice falling almost to a whisper. 'And then to await you with her message – the one she entrusted to me, where we both were confined. 'Twas in the Marshalsea, a few days past. I faced a whipping – but she faced death.'

'So Anne is dead?'

The words came sharply, though Silvan kept his smile. Any casual observer would have seen a man of business dallying with a trull, as if trying to decide whether she was worth his trouble. Before answering, Grogan glanced both ways, a little too like a player for Marbeck's liking.

'Nay, sir . . . she lives,' he murmured. 'And she awaits you, not far away—'

Then he yelped. Without warning, Silvan had grabbed his false bosom and squeezed it. 'As I thought,' he said flatly. 'You're not Madge, any more than I'm Queen Elizabeth. Is there anything more you would like to tell me? But have a care – for if it's another lie, I will know. And your reward will be a poniard in the cods – do you see?'

Grogan went rigid. From his seat by the wall, Marbeck cursed the weakness of his plan. Silvan had seen through the disguise in a moment. He was readying himself to spring, when the player spoke up.

'All right! Sweet Jesu, don't hurt me!' he begged, dropping his performance in an instant. 'I'm a player. I got taken by the watch for stealing. I was facing a branding, or worse – but I swear I was in the prison with Anne. Her husband was killed in a fight in Clerkenwell . . .'

'Stop there.'

The command brooked no refusal. Grogan fell silent. He was shaking, and it was no act: even he knew a killer when faced with one. Tense as a wand, Marbeck waited.

'Now, answer my questions, and you live,' Silvan breathed. 'Lie, and I'll slit your gizzard. First, I ask again: is Anne dead?'

'No – she's alive, and she's near. I spoke the truth!' Grogan protested.

'How did she get out?'

'We bribed a turnkey . . .'

'With what? No, it matters not.' Deliberately, Silvan put a hand to Grogan's face and, still smiling, brushed his cheek. Even from yards away, Marbeck heard him gulp.

'You said she gave you a message for me?'

'Only what I've told,' Grogan answered. 'I was to direct you to her . . . she wouldn't trust me with more than—'

'Was she questioned?' Silvan asked abruptly.

'I know not,' Grogan said. 'She was in fear of it – but she's unharmed, if that's what you mean.'

'So . . .' Silvan glanced round, and Marbeck tensed further. His face was shaded by his hat, but he knew the man had looked down at him. There was a moment, then:

'So, you can take me to her?'

226

'There's no need for that,' Grogan said hurriedly. 'She's here, in the Three Cranes – the back room.'

'And you will take me.'

It was an order, not a question. Grogan hesitated, then forced a nod, whereupon Silvan linked arms with him, smiling broadly, and guided him to the inn doorway.

On the threshold he paused, glanced down and fumbled in his cloak. A coin appeared, which he tossed into Marbeck's bowl. Then he was gone.

Twenty

Marbeck counted to five, then got to his feet.

The back room of the Three Cranes was normally used for dicing and gaming, but early that morning he had hired it exclusively. It suited him, because there was a rear entrance. Once Silvan and Grogan had gone inside the inn, he slipped down a side alley and entered the room, which was bare of furniture apart from a few stools. It was also in semi-darkness, because he had curtained the windows. He was elated, though uneasy at Grogan's involvement. Grogan was no longer supposed to be part of the plan.

As he entered, Anne got up from the corner. The guard, one of Prout's best men, was almost hidden in another corner. He too rose, but Marbeck raised a hand.

'Stand ready,' he said.

The man melted back into the shadows. Marbeck motioned Anne to sit, then stationed himself behind the door. Moving swiftly, he threw off his hat and ragged coat and picked up the sword he had secreted. Then he flattened himself against the wall and waited.

But nothing happened. Seconds became a minute . . . Across the room, he heard the guard stir. Noise came through the wall, that of the Three Cranes on a busy afternoon. Marbeck stooped to look through the keyhole, peering along a passage, but could see nothing. He pressed himself to the panelling again. Another minute had passed, and all at once he feared the worst. Did Silvan suspect a trap, after all? Had he seen through not only Grogan's disguise, but his, too? Then suddenly the latch clicked, the door opened, and a figure in hat and cloak walked in. Immediately, Marbeck's sword point was at his back.

'Be still,' he ordered.

The man halted. With a squeal of hinges, the door swung to behind him. Marbeck walked out from the wall, sword levelled. From the corner, he heard the guard move. He rounded the cloaked figure . . . then froze.

'It's me.' Grogan's whitened face stared at him from under the hat brim. He was shaking like a leaf.

Marbeck whirled round – too late. The door flew inwards, cracking him on the forehead. He staggered back, while at the same time Grogan was shoved forward. Then mayhem broke out.

There was a scream – from Anne, he thought. There was a shout, too – from the guard, no doubt. Then came a clash of weapons, more cries, and bodies were swaying about in the gloom. In a daze Marbeck raised his sword – and when a shape loomed over him, he lunged. He felt the point strike home – there was a fearful shriek, and the figure collapsed.

He lurched across the room. There was a grunt, and someone fell to the floor in front of him.

'Anne!' he shouted.

Figures flitted across his field of vision, then

stopped. There was a brief silence, which was broken by an anguished cry from behind. Marbeck's heart gave a jolt.

'Help me . . .'

It was Grogan. In dismay, Marbeck snapped round, knowing at once what he had done. As he did so, he realized that the other on the floor was the guard, who lay still.

'Your friend needs help, I think.'

There was the voice in the dark again: Silvan's. But as Marbeck raised his sword, something swung at him, thudding into his shoulder. Pain shot through him. He reeled and fell to the floor, squinting up at his assailant: it was Anne.

She dropped the stool and stepped back. As she did so, the rear door opened, flooding the room with daylight to reveal Silvan, minus his hat and cloak. His sword was in one hand, while with the other he took Anne's arm . . . and he was smiling.

'You are a disappointment, *signor*.' He looked down at Marbeck. 'You and I could have done much together.'

Then he was outside, and Anne with him.

His shoulder throbbing, Marbeck staggered to his feet. There was a noise at the other door, and a face poked round: that of the landlord of the Three Cranes.

'What's the coil here . . .?' he began. Then he gasped.

Walking heavily, Marbeck came forward and knelt beside Grogan. The player was shivering, while his heart's blood pumped from the wound: the fatal wound that Marbeck himself had inflicted.

'I was good, wasn't I?' Grogan gazed at him, his eyes very bright. 'My Madge Mullins, I mean . . . and my extempore, too.'

Slowly, Marbeck nodded.

'I always tried to give my best,' the player added. He shuddered, and his eyes closed.

'You were superb, my friend – as always,' Marbeck said. Then he fell silent. He was talking to a dead man.

Bleakly, he looked up at the landlord. 'Will you call a constable?' he said. 'Tell him two players were practising their swordplay and suffered an accident . . .' He broke off. There was a groan, and he looked round to see the guard stirring.

'Accident?' The landlord stared at the scene of carnage. 'And what of him?' he demanded.

Dazed, the guard sat up. His and Marbeck's eyes met, whereupon the other gave a brief nod. His hand was bloody where Silvan's sword had slashed it, but otherwise he had suffered nothing worse than being knocked unconscious.

'He was our umpire,' Marbeck said.

Outside on the Vintry wharf, he leaned against a wall to collect himself. People looked askance at him: a beggar, holding a sword. They would think he had stolen it. He shook his head and, with the noise of the quayside in his ears, indulged in a moment of self-excoriation. To say that he had failed would be inadequate. He had underestimated his opponent, who had escaped with ease. More, in the confusion he had killed the man he'd hired to help him, and lost his hostage into the bargain.

Silvan and Anne could have gone in any direction. The great city seemed to roar defiantly at Marbeck's back, with its myriad streets and alleys. Before him stretched the river, swollen and sluggish at high tide, dotted with craft of all kinds. Over on the Southwark shore he could see the theatres: the Swan, the Rose and the Globe, flags fluttering to denote a performance about to begin. Now there was one less player to strut their stages, he thought grimly.

'Oi, you – what are you doing?'

He turned to see a heavy-set man in a russet coat staring at him. There was a billet stuck in his belt. As Marbeck looked, the fellow started towards him.

'That's two laws you've broke,' he announced. 'A sturdy beggar with no permit, and carrying a sword. Where'd you filch it from?'

'It's mine.' Just then Marbeck hadn't the energy to lie.

'And I'm the Lord Treasurer,' the constable jeered. 'Hold still while I take it off you.'

'Truly, I wouldn't advise that,' Marbeck said.

His tone checked the man. Here was a dirty vagrant, speaking like a gentleman. A frown appeared.

'Who are you?'

'Name's Sands,' Marbeck said automatically. His gaze shifted back to the river. Then he gave a start. A skiff had entered his vision, from somewhere to his left. The waterman was heaving at the oars, taking his boat into midstream . . . He stared at the two passengers seated in the stern, and his pulse leaped.

232

'I have to go,' he said. And before the constable could reply, he darted past with a speed that caught the man by surprise. But as he went, he called out. 'You're needed in the tavern – hurry.' Then he was running along the quay, and down the Three Cranes Stairs.

There were two watermen waiting. One was young and lean, eager for trade; the other was a grizzled Thames veteran, his shoulders thick and bowed from a lifetime of toil. Marbeck took one look and went to the older man's boat.

'There's a shilling to get me across,' he breathed, dragging a coin from his jerkin. 'Another if you can catch that fellow – do you see?'

The waterman stared. But he took the coin, then followed Marbeck's outstretched arm to pick out a boat bobbing in midstream, the heads of a man and a woman visible.

'Best get in, then,' he said.

Marbeck stepped into the skiff and sat down. He still carried his sword, but the boatman ignored it. In a moment he had put an oar to the stairs and shoved his little craft out. It turned with the current, then shot forward as he plied both oars; at last, the chase had begun.

As the spray hit his face, Marbeck found hope surging through him. Now, too, his reasoning kicked in. It was no great surprise that Silvan had taken to the water. He might intend to go down-river, and take passage to Dover from Deptford. Or perhaps he had a bolthole on Bankside – that would make sense. Whatever the reasons, Marbeck was on his heels.

It took a very few minutes to reach the middle

233

of the stream. The grey-headed boatman uttered not a word, but every now and again he looked round, eyeing the other craft. They were gaining, Marbeck was certain of it. He also grew aware of more small boats clustering on the opposite shore. People were spilling out, flocking to the theatres. His mouth tightened: he could lose Silvan in the crowd.

'Pull to your larboard,' he said. 'Forget the other boat; just get me ashore.'

The waterman looked up. 'They'll be packed together like eels,' he said. 'Better I take you to the Falcon Stairs.'

'No, go the shortest way.' Marbeck peered forward, gripping his sword hilt, keeping his eye on Silvan's boat. He could make out faces now, but to his satisfaction neither of the two occupants looked behind. He guessed they did not expect to be followed, but he couldn't be certain. On impulse, he leaned over the boat's side and scooped up a handful of water. Tearing off his ragged jerkin and shirt, he used them to clean his face and hands. The boatman glanced up to see his passenger now stripped to the waist.

'Your coat,' Marbeck said, fumbling in the jerkin. 'How much will you take for it?'

Without pausing at his task, the old waterman eyed him. 'On the run, are you?' he muttered.

'In a way. But the money isn't stolen, I swear it. I'll offer you four crowns.'

The other blinked. 'You must need it bad.'

'I do,' Marbeck said. He found the coins, counted them out and laid them on his palm. 'What do you say?'

234

After a moment the man nodded. And within minutes, somewhat better attired, Marbeck was stepping ashore on Bankside with the great wooden theatres towering above and people surging about him.

Sword in hand, he walked parallel to the river. He had lost sight of Silvan and Anne, but now, to his relief, he saw them again: they too had alighted and were walking away from the shore. Soon they had rounded a corner and disappeared, but he kept his eye on the spot. The Globe, the splendid new theatre built the previous year by the Lord Chamberlain's Men, was at his left; he heard the roar of the packed crowd. The Rose Theatre – older, smaller, but just as noisy – was ahead. It was the Swan that was still filling up, he realized; that was some distance upriver, with people streaming towards it. Picking up pace, Marbeck strode along Bankside, threading his way through them. He passed alehouses, bowling dens and low dwellings. Then he reached the corner where Silvan and Anne had turned, and halted. There was no sign of them in the narrow street, nor in the open space ahead. The way led to fields, and to ponds: the Pike Gardens. The ground here was marshy and criss-crossed with drainage ditches. He tensed: it was a likely place for an ambush.

He took a breath and started down the lane. There were few people here, though they threw him some wary looks. Eyes ahead, Marbeck walked to the end of the short street, where he slowed . . . then stopped dead.

The point of a sword had appeared, an inch from his nose.

'So you followed,' Silvan said softly. 'That was quick work. I may revise my opinion of you, after all.'

Very slowly, Marbeck turned his head. The man stood beside the wall of a rough-timbered house, thatch sagging above his head. Anne was nowhere in sight.

'Drop your sword, please,' Silvan added, stepping out to face him.

But Marbeck remained motionless. Now, at last, he was able to view his opponent at close quarters. He was a handsome man, he realized, with the face of a native of southern France rather than of Italy. His dark eyes regarded Marbeck coolly.

'Come, you know this is not the time to fight.' His voice had acquired an edge; the sword trembled slightly.

'I asked you before,' Marbeck said. 'Did you kill Ottone?'

The other gave a sigh of irritation. 'Let fall your weapon,' he snapped. 'Or it ends now.'

Marbeck's eyes flicked aside briefly. There was no one in sight, and from Bankside the noise of the theatre crowd had diminished. Ahead of him was a meadow, its only occupant a cow munching grass.

'You mean, we should fence here?' Marbeck asked.

'I mean no such thing!' Silvan snapped. Marbeck remained motionless, assessing his position.

'I meant to give you one more chance to consider the offer I made,' the other went on. 'Let's leave

236

aside your tiresome attempt to entrap me since.' He gave a snort. 'Is your master Cecil so short of ideas, or was the failure your own?'

'Well, we found Mulberry,' Marbeck said gently. 'That's *Morera* to you – or *La Mora*, perhaps. And now I'm at close quarters with his – or I should say *her* – master.'

Silvan bristled. 'Perhaps I was mistaken,' he said flatly. 'I heard you were a man of taste, and of vision – one who hopes for better things than have come to you.'

'Did your people get that from Moore?' Marbeck asked with interest. 'If so, he lied.'

'Drop the sword,' Silvan hissed. 'Or I'll pierce you.'

Marbeck appeared to waver. Finally, he sighed and let his sword fall to the ground.

'This way.' Silvan stepped back, jerking his head towards the house. Eyes peeled for any movement, he kept his sword levelled. With a shrug, Marbeck complied.

'Through the gate,' Silvan added, close behind him.

Marbeck found himself at the rear of the small house, which looked derelict. There was a garden, badly neglected, with fruit trees. He lifted the latch of a wicket gate and walked in. Silvan's sword was at his back.

'Go inside.'

The house door was ajar, approached by an overgrown path. As Marbeck neared the threshold, he sensed someone within. Anne was there, he was certain. He slowed, then stopped. The spot wasn't ideal, but . . .

'What is it?' Silvan demanded, then caught his breath. In that split second Marbeck had dropped to his heels. It was a Ballard trick: with a single movement, he rolled aside, grasping Silvan's leg as he did so. The man lurched, his sword arm flailing. As he fell, he swept the weapon downwards, scraping Marbeck's arm, but the blow was weak. The blade sliced through his new-bought coat. But no sooner had Silvan hit the ground than he found his wrist pinned down by Marbeck's knee.

'Now *you* drop it,' Marbeck breathed.

Twenty-One

The two men locked eyes; there was little doubt that this fight had barely begun.

'Let go your sword,' Marbeck repeated.

Silvan hesitated, then his left hand flew to his belt. Even as Marbeck grabbed it, a poniard appeared, and suddenly both men were locked in a struggle for the weapon. In the process, Marbeck's weight shifted – which was the momentum Silvan needed. His sword hand broke free, though, since he was on his back, the position was awkward, and he took too long to strike. Risking a wound from the poniard, Marbeck seized Silvan's arm in both hands – as he had done on a Spanish ship in the Blavet – but even as he bent it, the man's other hand came up. He glimpsed the dagger point flashing towards him and jerked his head aside. Then came a dreadful crunch, as Silvan's elbow was broken. With a cry of agony, he went limp.

Panting, sweat running down his face, Marbeck seized the man's sword by its ornate hilt, pulled it from his grasp and threw it away. Though white with shock, Silvan fought back. Grunting with pain, he jabbed a knee into Marbeck's side. Marbeck winced, but put his strength into forcing his opponent's dagger hand down. He was gaining ground, he thought – until he made a slip. It was an old trick: Silvan allowed Marbeck to force his wrist flat, then used his own weight against him. The next moment he had been toppled aside into the grass, and his opponent was struggling to rise.

On their knees, the two faced each other. Silvan's right arm hung at a bizarre angle, while his face was a mask of pain and rage. But Marbeck still gripped his left hand with the poniard – and, as if at a signal, they began to strain against each other, tiring quickly as they fought for mastery of it. Silvan was the weaker now, however, and he knew it. For the first time an expression appeared – not of fear, but of uncertainty. Then all at once he fell backwards. In a second Marbeck had wrenched the poniard from his fingers and put it to his neck.

'Be still,' he panted.

A hiss of pain escaped Silvan's lips. His eyes darted aside, to his shattered arm. Then he spoke.

'Let me die, or let me live – choose now!'

For a moment Marbeck was seized by an impulse to do the first. The heat of combat had cooled in him, to be replaced by a cold fury. Here was the cause of his misfortunes, at his mercy, and there were no witnesses . . .

A sound startled him, only feet away. He looked up sharply, to the doorway of the house. Anne stood there, gazing down at them. She was holding a small pistol.

'Kill him,' she said quietly. She lifted the gun and pointed it.

But Marbeck shook his head.

'Then, get out of the way.' Anne's voice rose.

From the grass where he lay, Silvan let out a groan.

'Is this why you helped him escape?' Marbeck said, forcing her to meet his eye. 'So you could get him alone? Is that what you intended?'

'Stand up and move away,' Anne ordered.

'I cannot.' Suddenly, Marbeck was calm, and his calmness unsettled her. Though she was shaking – whether with fear or anger or both, he was unsure – she wavered.

'I do it for Tom,' she muttered. 'And for the things this devil made me do.'

'You could hang,' Marbeck said. 'Do you think he's worth that?'

She shrugged, to show she no longer cared.

Slowly, he got to one knee, keeping Silvan's dagger pressed against the man's neck. 'He's my prisoner, Anne,' he said. 'My masters want him alive. They need to question him.'

She hesitated. Marbeck turned and put his face close to Silvan's. 'Who's Membrillo?' he demanded.

There was no answer.

'It was him beside you that night, when you had me at your mercy, wasn't it?' he persisted. 'He held the pistol.'

Through his pain, Silvan managed a harsh laugh. 'You cannot kill us all,' he breathed. 'Others will come – every year, a new harvest—'

'Who is he?' Marbeck shouted, and he jabbed the point of the poniard, drawing a little blood. Silvan flinched. Then, from the corner of his eye, Marbeck caught a movement from Anne, and for a second his attention shifted – which was a

241

mistake. Silvan's left hand shot up and seized his wrist, shoving the dagger point aside. Crying out, with the last of his strength, he forced the point upwards. Marbeck veered away – but as he did so there was a deafening explosion. Half blinded by the flash, he fell over.

A long moment followed. His ears ringing, Marbeck got to his knees and stared downwards at Silvan's body. There was a gaping wound in the man's head, from which blood and brains had welled. The eyes were open, but they were lifeless.

He looked up, but Anne would not meet his eye. Without expression, she dropped the pistol.

'Why did you not shoot me?' Marbeck asked finally.

She made no reply. Stiffly and painfully, he stood up.

'Now I have to take you back,' he said. 'There are things they'll want from you; you're still a source of intelligence.'

'I would shoot you, too,' Anne said abruptly. 'If I had the means.'

'Well, you stabbed me once,' Marbeck replied. 'And now I'm torn again.' He looked down at the blood seeping through his doublet. He was hurting in several places, but he was alive. He drew a long breath.

'You said my life depended on me helping you,' Anne said. 'Are you a man who keeps his word?'

He nodded. 'I am. Though they'll hold you for a while yet, until they've got all they need. I speak not of close questioning. You endured it once; they'll know they only need to threaten it.'

She gave a long sigh. A breeze had got up, blowing in from the river. Absently, she surveyed the overgrown garden.

'We wanted damson trees,' she said, almost to herself. 'Me and Tom . . . we were promised a house with an orchard, in Barbary.'

Marbeck gazed at her. All at once something fell into place. His mind flew back to Silvan's tempting of him, in the darkened room: the promise of riches, if he turned traitor. All along it had troubled him – how Silvan knew where to find him that night – and suddenly he saw it: the French Lily.

Someone, for reasons of his own, had tipped off Silvan, and suddenly he saw the stern face of Charbon, peering down at him.

He faced Anne again, saw her staring at him. 'Did Silvan ever send you on an errand to the French Lily?' he asked. 'In Mark Lane?'

'The Frenchman's place?' she nodded. 'Two or three times . . . but 'twas only about wine. Consignments and such . . .'

She trailed off, for Marbeck was no longer listening. Her face blank, she watched him turn away and go to pick up the pistol.

After conveying Anne Saxby back to the Marshalsea – a procedure she submitted to in silence – he crossed the river again. First, he found a barber-surgeon and had his wound newly sewn. Then he returned to the White Bear, where he washed, attired himself in his own clothes and rested with a jug of Rhenish wine for comfort. By evening he had gathered himself and knew what to do; but it would require help, which presented a difficulty. Gifford was the man he wanted just now, but that wasn't to be. Nor could he go to Prout; in fact, none of the Crown's servants were available to him. He would have to make a full report to Sir Robert Cecil first, which would take time. But at last he saw a solution. If it was unorthodox, just now he had little choice. So, at twilight he left the inn and walked to the Strand, where he entered the Duck and Drake and found Thomas Rose.

'What do you want of me now?' the grizzled drawer asked sourly.

'I had a mind to take you on a search,' Marbeck said. 'Like in the old days. If you're interested, that is.'

'A search – for what?'

'The usual matter – seditious books and papers.'

'Are you mocking me?' Rose grunted. But when he caught Marbeck's expression, he gave a start.

'I need someone discreet, and I need him quick,' Marbeck told him. 'It's not a warrant – just a notion I have, to sound out a man who might not be what he seems. Will you hazard it with me, or no?'

Rose frowned at him, standing by the barrels. The inn was not yet crowded, but men were calling their orders. At that moment the hostess appeared, her hands full of empty mugs. 'What are you about, Tom?' she demanded. 'You're paid to serve, not to gossip. Move yourself!'

Her eyes went to Marbeck, who turned away.

But he threw Rose a look . . . and suddenly the man made his decision.

'I've got to go, mistress,' he said. 'There's bad news – someone's sick.'

She peered at him suspiciously. 'Who's that, then?'

'No one you know.' Calmly, Rose took off his apron, but there was a light in his eye that Marbeck hadn't seen in years. And when the hostess opened her mouth to protest, he held up his hand. 'There's no sense wrangling with me. I'm going, and that's that.'

'Is it indeed?' She breathed in hard. 'And how long will you be gone – can you answer that?'

'Nay, I can't,' Rose told her. And with that he thrust his apron at her and followed Marbeck to the door.

Outside, dusk was gathering. But when Marbeck told where they were going, the older man's face fell. 'That's a mighty long walk for a sluggard like me. And we'd need to hurry – they'll be closing Ludgate soon.'

'We'll take a boat,' Marbeck said. And he set off at a pace, with the other hurrying to keep up. Fortunately, it was not a great distance to the Ivy Stairs, where skiffs were waiting, their stern lanterns lit. In minutes the two were seated together, heading downstream on the current, and in a low voice Marbeck told his companion of his plans.

'Charbon?' Rose showed surprise. 'But he's a Huguenot . . . he hates papists. As would anyone who went through what he did, on Bartholomew's day.'

245

'So he's always maintained,' Marbeck said. 'But has anyone ever questioned him about it? Supposing it was a cover, all along?'

Rose thought for a moment. 'Then, I'd say it's been a mighty good one,' he muttered. 'What set you on to the man?'

'Just a notion,' Marbeck replied, not wanting to add details. 'A feeling I've had . . .' He frowned. 'You're unarmed – I should have thought of it.'

'I've a dagger,' Rose said, indicating his belt. Noting Marbeck's sword, he added: 'And from what I remember, you're no slouch with that.'

The boat lurched just then, as another passed too close, heading upriver. Their waterman shouted a curse at his fellow, then bent to his oars again. Marbeck lowered his head.

'When we get to the French Lily, we'll enter separately,' he said. 'I've an idea the cellar's the place to look. I'll move towards the door and wait for you.'

'If there's anything Charbon doesn't want us to see, the cellar will be locked,' Rose said. 'We'll have to spin him a tale, or there'll be trouble.'

'I've no time for tales. If I have to force him to open it, I will,' Marbeck replied. He didn't add that, provided his suspicions were right, Charbon knew who he was and what he did, in which case trouble was likely enough. In fact, he wondered how long the man had known – that was a troubling thought, too.

'What, in a tavern full of people?' Rose was saying. 'The fellow might have friends he can call on.'

'He might, but I doubt he'll want them to hear what I have to say,' Marbeck said. 'So you'll have to trust me.'

'You and this feeling you've had,' the other replied, with a wry look. 'I hope your nose hasn't failed you, now that I've gone and walked out of the Duck.'

'And, yet, when was the last time you had any excitement?' Marbeck asked, raising his brows. 'Let alone a chance to serve the Queen's Council in a proper manner. Doesn't it stir your vitals a little?'

Rose eyed him; slowly, a grim smile appeared. 'Mayhap it does, a little,' he admitted.

They stepped ashore at Billingsgate, having shot the arches rather than alight above the Bridge, which would have meant a walk from the Old Swan Stairs. Soon they had made their way by Thames Street and Hart Lane into Tower Street, where they halted. They were at the corner of Mark Lane, with the French Lily a stone's throw away. Here, after some last-minute conferring, Marbeck left Rose and walked to the inn, entering once again to the strains of a lute. The place was filling up, the drawer busy serving tables. With a casual air, Marbeck threaded his way across the large room, one eye on a door in the corner which he knew led to the cellar. But before he could reach it, a familiar figure barred his way.

'Monsieur Sands?' Charbon regarded him coolly. 'You have returned – what a pleasure.'

'Monsieur Charbon.' Marbeck matched his

247

stare. 'I wish I could return the compliment. Last time we met, as I recall, we didn't get the chance to talk.'

The other looked puzzled. 'Last time we spoke, sir, I fear you had taken too much drink,' he said. 'You and the player Grogan – you were harsh with me, I recall. Nevertheless, you are welcome. What is your pleasure?'

'Grogan's dead,' Marbeck said, watching him carefully. 'Have you not heard?'

A frown creased the other's brow. 'No, I have not.'

'He died trying to help me,' Marbeck went on. 'But I can say that the man we were chasing has paid with his own life. He too was known to you, I think.' And when the other looked blank, he added: 'His name was Silvan.'

Charbon was silent.

'You heard me, I think,' Marbeck persisted. He took a step forward, until the two of them were barely inches apart. 'Your friend from Savoy is dead.'

'My friend?' The man's frown had deepened, but he appeared calm. 'I don't understand you, Sands.'

'I think you do,' Marbeck said. 'As I think you know my real name, and that I serve the Queen's Council.' Before the other could speak, he added: 'It was you who knocked me out that night in the street and called Silvan. As it was you in the dark, pointing a pistol at me. You didn't speak, because you knew I would recognize your voice.'

Charbon's gaze shifted, as if he was looking

248

for assistance. Marbeck put a hand on his arm. 'There's no one to help you now,' he said mildly. 'And if anyone here knew who you really are, they'd come to my aid in a trice.'

The landlord's bushy moustache was twitching. Finally, he spoke, very low. 'What do you want?'

'I want to look in your cellar,' Marbeck said. 'I think it may hold treasonable matter.'

A pause, then: 'By what warrant do you demand it?'

'I have none,' Marbeck said. Then he glanced aside and was relieved to see Thomas Rose moving towards them, dragging his weak leg. He faced his suspect again.

'You may know this man,' he said. 'What you don't know is that he's a Crown servant, too – or was once. Now, will you open up your cellar, or do we have to force you?'

There was a moment while Rose came puffing up to stand at Marbeck's side. He said nothing, merely fixed Charbon with a hard stare. For some reason, the man relaxed.

'Force me?' he echoed. 'But there is no need. The cellar is not locked – pray, look for yourselves.' And he stood aside, gesturing to the doorway. Immediately, Rose went towards it, grasped the latch. The door opened.

'Search there, if you wish,' Charbon said in a harsh voice. 'Then, when you're finished, you can leave. Henceforth, you are not welcome at this inn. Now, I have work—'

'No – that won't do.'

Marbeck spoke sharply. He glanced at Rose,

who stepped back, not needing any instruction. Charbon was between them. The man's chest rose, but he was trapped.

'That's right,' Marbeck said. 'You're coming down with us.'

'I have an inn to keep,' Charbon persisted.

But Marbeck merely gave him a push that brooked no argument. In a tight group, the three of them descended the cellar stairs, Rose bringing up the rear. At the foot of the steps was a lantern. The old pursuivant found his tinderbox, struck a flame and lit it, whereupon he and Marbeck looked about. Charbon stood by the wall, from where he watched the other two without expression.

But it soon became clear that the search would be useless. The room was small and low-ceilinged, and held nothing but barrels of beer and wine. Rose knocked on all of them, and on the walls, too – without result. Marbeck then took the lantern and peered into every corner. Finally, he turned to see Rose shaking his head.

'Well – are you finished now?'

They looked, and saw Charbon wearing a disdainful expression.

'If you're done, *messieurs*, I will go back upstairs,' he said coldly. 'I would offer you refreshment after your labours, but – I repeat – I do not want you at the French Lily. So, with your permission . . .'

He moved to the stairs, but at once Marbeck was at his side. 'No, I'm not finished,' he said. 'And I won't be until I've been over every inch of this house – whether you've barred me or not, Charbon.'

250

Then, leaning so close that the man flinched, he added: 'Or should I call you *Membrillo*?'

The other's sharp intake of breath was all the confirmation he needed. The next moment Charbon found himself being shoved up the stairs, with the other two on his heels.

Twenty-Two

The three men emerged from the cellar doorway into the noise and bustle of the tavern, only to find that their activities had not gone unnoticed. There stood Charbon's drawer, a big man in a stained apron, looking puzzled.

'What goes on, Gaston?' he enquired, looking uneasily from his master to the others. 'Is there trouble?'

'No trouble,' Marbeck said. 'The landlord's helping us search for something.' He turned deliberately. 'Is that not so?'

Charbon hesitated, and for a moment Marbeck thought he would try to bolt. Casually, he took a sideways step to forestall such action. Rose was behind them, and then the Frenchman twitched, as if at a spasm of pain.

'Yes . . . all is well, Peter,' he said quickly, with a nod to the drawer. 'Monsieur Sands and I will go to the upper chambers now. It's business. You may go back to work.'

He indicated the stairway, which was close by. After a moment the drawer shrugged and moved away. Marbeck glanced round and understood: Rose's fist was pressed tightly to Charbon's back. There was no sign of the tailor's bodkin Marbeck had given him out in the street, but he knew it was there.

'Upstairs it is, then,' he said.

They climbed to the upper storey, where there were bedchambers for hire. Once out of sight of the crowd, however, Charbon turned on Rose.

'You 'ave no right for this!' he spat. 'I will—'

'You'll do nothing,' Marbeck said. 'Except stand where we can see you – and if you try to run, I'll use this.'

He placed a hand on his sword hilt, whereupon the man's face twitched. 'This is all a foolish nonsense,' he said, wetting his lips. 'You confuse me with another, I think . . .'

But he broke off, as Marbeck merely pushed him through the open doorway of the first room. It was empty save for a bed and a chamber pot. Rose followed them in, found a candle in a holder and lit it. He peered about and knocked on walls for a while, then shook his head. So they moved across the landing to a second room, Charbon sent in first again. This chamber, at the front of the inn, was grander, with a curtained four-poster, stools and a table. There was also a chest, but it contained only linen. Rose rummaged about in it, then slammed the lid.

'Rest yourself,' Marbeck suggested. 'Keep your eye on this one, while I look about.'

With a nod, Rose went to a stool and eased himself down. But he never took his eyes off Charbon, who stood stiffly aside. Marbeck began to search the room, more urgently now. Since the fruitless visit to the cellar, he was less certain of his theory, yet he persevered: peering under the bed, lifting the mattress and coverlet, standing on a stool to look above the tester. It was all to no avail, however. Finally, he stood in the middle

253

of the room and gazed down at the floorboards. But when he glanced at Charbon, he saw a look of contempt on the man's face.

'Lift the boards, if you must,' he said. 'Do as you will – you'll find nothing. Why do you not listen to me?'

Marbeck caught Rose's eye; even the old pursuivant, veteran of many searches, appeared to be wavering. Half-heartedly, he lifted a hand and knocked on the wall beside him, then gave a shrug.

'Well, we've hardly begun yet,' Marbeck said, with a show of confidence. 'There's a yard, isn't there? And a stable.'

'Indeed.' Charbon nodded. 'Look there, too – dig around in the horse-dung. It seems you 'ave naught better to do.'

Without expression, Marbeck crossed the room to the single window. The jutty projected for several feet over the lane, almost meeting that of the house opposite. He looked out into the darkness that had fallen, heard voices from the street below. He thought fast – where to look now? Idly, he banged the wall below the window, in three places . . . then paused. The first two knocks had produced a hollow sound; the last one, a muffled thud. He span round – and at last Charbon made his move.

With sudden energy, the man darted forward and pushed Rose over. The stool crashed to the floor, sending the old pursuivant sprawling. But as Charbon lunged for the door, he found Marbeck was quicker. With a rasp, his sword flew out. The other lurched, then stopped in his tracks with the point at his chest.

'Kneel!' Marbeck ordered, his voice cold as steel.

The other looked up and saw his expression. With a curse that was almost a groan, he dropped to his knees.

'By the Christ, why don't you prick the bastard?' Like an ungainly spider, Rose was struggling to his feet. Breathing hard, he bore down on Charbon, but Marbeck stayed him.

'I'll watch this one,' he said. 'Why don't you do what you're best at – what you used to do?' He nodded towards the window. 'Your dagger should serve.'

Rose eyed him, then gave a nod. Drawing his poniard from its sheath, he went to the window and began prodding the wall beneath it. Soon he found a crack and forced the point in. With an effort, he prised out an oak pale, along with a shower of plaster dust. Then, stooping, he put his hands to the opening and wrenched. With a great noise of splintering staves, part of the panel came away – whereupon Rose gave a cry of triumph, and fell back on his rump.

'Found!' he shouted. 'Will you look at this?'

Keeping his sword levelled at Charbon, Marbeck looked – and breathed out in relief. In the dim light he saw papers, tied up in neat bundles.

'Would you care to tell us what those are?' he asked Charbon. The man looked balefully up at him, but refused to answer.

'Shall I hazard a guess?' Marbeck went on. 'Gifts from friends in Douai or Paris – or even Rome, perhaps? Treatises that speak of that

255

joyous day when England is returned to the true faith. Do I hit the mark?'

'I think you do, Master Sands.' Rose was on hands and knees with the candle, peering into the recess. 'I don't read well, but I'll wager the top one's in Latin . . . *Papa loquitur*.' He rummaged about, then dragged a bundle towards him. 'Now see this: *The Abomination of Luther: to all servants of the true faith*.' He grimaced. 'That'll make fine reading.'

'It will,' Marbeck agreed, his eyes still on Charbon. 'Especially for those who've been looking for such cargo. Indeed, I think one of them intercepted a letter from you – Membrillo.' He rolled the word round his tongue. 'You it was, I think, who reported the safe arrival of *our brother*, was it not? I speak of Silvan – who received a ball in the head but a short while ago.' He paused. 'A sort of justice in that, wouldn't you say?'

Charbon was shaking now. His chest rose and fell, his eyes going from Rose to the stack of forbidden pamphlets, and back to Marbeck.

'The papers came in hidden in wine casks, didn't they?' Marbeck went on. 'To be unloaded at the Vintry, in full view of anyone. Wrapped in tarred leather, were they?'

Suddenly, Charbon spoke. 'You will have your judgement too, one day,' he said bitterly. 'As will all of you heretics, when that she-viper Elizabeth is dead, and a man rules in her place – a man born of Mary Stuart, a lady of the true religion.'

'But King James is a Protestant down to his soles,' Marbeck replied calmly. 'Or so I hear.'

256

He shook his head. 'You're a bold one, Charbon, I'll admit that. A clearing house for secret matter – right under the shadow of the Tower. Who'd have guessed it was here all along?'

'Well, you did,' Rose said from the window.

He got up, dusting off his hands, and threw Charbon a withering look. 'But now you have him. And in time he'll tell all he knows. How this stuff was distributed, and who it was destined for.' He eyed Marbeck. 'You haven't lost your nose, after all,' he added. 'I hope you get thanks for it . . . It's more than I ever did.'

'Perhaps I can remedy that,' Marbeck said. 'Once I've made my report.'

The older man shrugged. 'Just put in a good word for me at the Duck, will you? I wouldn't want to lose my place.'

The next day, tiring of the White Bear, Marbeck threw caution aside and moved back to the Dolphin. Hibbert seemed glad to see him, and not merely because Marbeck still owed him money for Cobb's stabling. He paid the man a little on account, promising the remainder soon. That, he hoped, would follow after he had seen Sir Robert Cecil. This time he would not forget to ask for payment.

Once installed in his old chamber overlooking the Spital Field, he set himself to writing a detailed report: of the death of Silvan, whose body still lay in a house on Bankside, and the subsequent discovery of a cache of Catholic propaganda at the French Lily. There was no hiding the fact that Silvan had been killed before

257

he could be questioned, in particular about the spymaster Juan Roble. But now, with Charbon's capture, new intelligence would be gained. Marbeck drew some satisfaction from that, though he had one uneasy thought: that Master Secretary might decide to send him to Paris again – whereas he had other plans, which did not involve taking ship to anywhere.

Returning to the Dolphin was a rash decision, he knew, but he had ceased to care. Silvan and Charbon, the enemies who had known his true identity and where he lodged, were finished: one dead, the other a prisoner. Whereas Anne . . . He thought hard about Anne. He intended to ask Cecil whether some sort of reward could be got for her. And he was especially remorseful about the death of Augustine Grogan. He meant to find out if the man had any family, and, if so, to ask for a pension to be paid them.

He was pondering the matter two nights later when someone knocked. Half dressed and half asleep, Marbeck listened until the knock was repeated, then got up and answered the door. Without speaking, Nicholas Prout entered the room. His arm was in a sling, and he looked a tired man.

'Does it mend well?' Marbeck enquired.

'They dug a ball out, the size of a pigeon's egg,' Prout replied gloomily. 'Thanks to my prayers, though, there's no infection.'

Marbeck gestured to his table, where a jug stood. 'I'd offer you a drink of good Rhenish,' he said, 'if I didn't think you'd turn your nose up at it.'

258

'Well, I've a mind to be contrary,' Prout said. 'So I'll say yes.'

Without comment, Marbeck went to the table, poured two cups and carried them over. Prout took a long pull from his. In silence, the two eyed each other.

'It's been a farrago, all this,' the messenger said at last.

Marbeck gave a shrug.

'I asked Master Secretary for a pension for Mistress Ottone,' Prout added. 'But not only does he refuse to reward traitors, he says he won't reward traitors' wives either.'

'Is that what you came to tell me?'

'Not only that.' Prout's eyes scanned the room. 'Mind if I seat myself?' At Marbeck's nod, he took the stool by the window. Marbeck sat on the bed facing him.

'Grogan, the player . . .' Prout frowned. 'Seems his father's a gentleman, out in Suffolk. He's now a very angry gentleman.'

Marbeck looked away.

'I know how it happened,' Prout said. 'You shouldn't bear the guilt alone. Though Sir Robert doesn't see it that way.'

'What of the woman?' Marbeck asked suddenly.

'She's confined,' was all Prout would say.

They drank in silence for a while.

'You did good work, ferreting out Charbon,' he added. 'There were enough seditious books in that hiding place to fill a cart. Papal tracts, reports from the seminary in Douai – a bale of popery and wickedness.'

259

'I take it Master Secretary's had my report,' Marbeck said.

'He has, and that was my chief reason for coming,' Prout replied. 'You're ordered to Whitehall, tomorrow morning.'

'My chance to make amends, perhaps?' Marbeck said wryly.

'You and I both, Marbeck,' came the reply. 'There's a lot to do, now the Queen's short of intelligencers all of a sudden.'

From somewhere, Marbeck's anger rose. He thought of his talk with Lady Celia, in her bed at Chelsea. Fixing the other man with a look as bleak as his own, he said: 'Tell me – how long do you think this will last?'

'What do you speak of?' Prout asked, not understanding.

'This cat-and-mouse game with Spain. The toing and froing.' He sighed. 'They capture one of our men; we unmask one of theirs. They put out a false rumour; we counter with another. Then we each kill one of the other's, only for someone to take his place . . .' He broke off and took a gulp of wine. 'And all the while, commanding them from the shadows are those we never get close to. Men who spend their agents' lives as gamesters spend halfpennies.'

'This isn't like you, Marbeck,' Prout remarked after a moment. 'I always thought you're a man who enjoys the game, as you call it. More than most, anyway.'

'Well, I could do with a holiday,' Marbeck found himself saying. Then he laughed at his own words. 'By the Christ, now listen to me.'

260

Prout tilted his cup and drained it. 'I'll leave you to take some rest,' he said, and got to his feet.

'Have you had any tidings of Moore?' Marbeck asked him.

'Dead, we think,' the messenger replied. 'The Spaniards had him in their fortress at Brussels, but there's been no further word.' He frowned. 'If you've got notions of revenge, I'd allay those,' he added. 'They blur your vision.'

'That's true enough,' Marbeck said, and saw him to the door. Outside, Prout checked himself.

'I shouldn't tell you this, but Gifford's going back there. To the Low Countries, I mean.'

Marbeck gave a wry smile. 'That should please him . . . I hope it pleases a certain Dutch doxy.'

Prout gave a snort of disgust and left.

In the morning Marbeck was conducted to Sir Robert Cecil's privy chamber by Henry Weeks. Outside the door, however, he startled the clerk by producing a slip of paper.

'There's a list of costs I've incurred, these past months,' he said. 'Among them is a loan made by a friend – someone of noble birth. It should be repaid with interest.'

'I'll need authorization from Sir Robert,' Weeks said pompously.

He sniffed, sneezed and opened the door. Whitehall Palace, draughty at the best of times, was especially cold and damp this morning. And Master Secretary, it seemed, was also nursing a cold. He sat behind his table wrapped in a heavy cloak, a scarf about his neck. A fire burned in the grate.

'I've read your report,' he murmured, in a voice clogged with phlegm. 'Finding the cache of papist matter was neatly done – that's a route we needed to close off.'

Marbeck nodded politely.

'And yet Silvan's doings have cost us dearly,' Cecil went on. He fingered the papers before him, then looked up. 'Is there anything further you wish to add?'

'No, sir,' Marbeck replied. 'Save to ask for reparation, for the families of those who've died—'

'That's not within your compass,' Cecil broke in. 'You must leave such matters to my discretion.'

'And to ask for some time,' Marbeck persisted. 'To visit relations, perhaps . . .'

'Indeed?' Cecil raised his brows. 'From what I've heard, your father has all but disowned you – or is it you who've disowned him?'

Marbeck stiffened, but made no reply.

'In any case, I can't spare you,' the spymaster went on. 'We are depleted, thanks to this Mulberry pickle. I want you to find some new men – people we can trust.'

'What incentive can I offer them?' Marbeck asked, glimpsing an opportunity. 'For, if I might refer to my own case, I've been hard pressed for money these past months.'

Master Secretary sneezed and dismissed the matter impatiently. 'Draw up an account and submit it to Weeks. I'll approve remuneration.'

Without expression, Marbeck inclined his head.

262

'Where would you like me to start, with recruiting?' he enquired.

'I leave that to you,' came the terse reply. 'But look not to former soldiers – especially those newly returned from Ireland.'

There was no irony in his tone, but Marbeck sensed his irritation. 'Touching on that matter, sir,' he said after a moment, 'I had a mind to speak to you of Mistress Saxby.'

At once Cecil's brows knitted. 'What of her?'

'You recall our talk, some days ago. When she's freed, I would like to help her in some manner if—'

'Freed?' Cecil echoed. 'She will never be.'

'You recall our talk, some days ago,' Marbeck repeated carefully.

'That was a matter of expediency,' Master Secretary said. 'I'm surprised you would question it – especially in view of subsequent events.'

In dismay, Marbeck watched as the man turned aside, sneezed again, then plucked a handkerchief from his sleeve. 'We strike no bargains with traitors,' he added.

'Then . . . she will be executed?'

'Of course – she's committed treason.'

'The matter is, I gave her my promise,' Marbeck said, speaking quickly. 'She risked her life to—'

'This sounds like impertinence, Marbeck.' Cecil regarded him stonily.

'Forgive me, Sir Robert—' Marbeck drew a breath – 'but I was given to understand that—'

'Then you *mis*understood,' Cecil snapped.

Anger threatened Marbeck's composure, but he

knew further protest was useless. With an effort, he lowered his gaze.

'Find two or three loyal men and sound them out to the very bottom.' Deliberately, Master Secretary returned to his earlier subject. 'The Universities remain a fertile field, but I leave details to you. Indeed, you may regard this as a form of promotion,' he added. 'Later, I might authorize you to assign missions to those new intelligencers, who will report back to you. I haven't time to do everything.' He paused. 'And I may need to send you to Scotland soon. You can take ship for Leith. I hear it's even colder and wetter than London. Now, if there's nothing further?'

Without waiting, Cecil picked up his bell and rang it vigorously.

In silence Marbeck turned and walked to the door. Not until he was outside did he realize that the name of Juan Roble had not been mentioned. But somehow that no longer mattered. Drawing a deep breath, he walked out of Whitehall Palace, and kept walking until he found himself by the riverside, where he stopped.

There were many sorts of double-dealer, he thought; and his master was merely another.

Twenty-Three

It rained that afternoon, an icy rain from the east, but Marbeck barely noticed. Carrying a pack, he entered the Dolphin stables, to find Zachary in the harness-room, dozing by a small fire.

'Master Sands . . .' The old man shook himself awake. 'Your pardon . . . You'll be wanting to take Cobb out.'

'I will,' Marbeck said. 'But first here's something for you, along with my thanks for caring for him.'

Zachary blinked at the gold angel. 'You're kind, sir,' he said, taking the coin. 'But 'tis no burden to mind a horse like Cobb. He was well exercised, I should add. Out on the road to Newington and beyond.'

'So I understand,' Marbeck said. 'Pray, keep your seat. I'll saddle him and be gone.'

'Business again?' the ostler enquired.

'No – a matter of pleasure.'

A short while later he led his mount out of the inn stable towards the busy crossing of Houndsditch and Bishopsgate Street. He was pondering whether to go north by Shoreditch and turn west through the fields, or to ride through the city, when someone hailed him. He turned, and was surprised to see Gifford hurrying towards him in a new hat and cloak.

'I'd a mind to spend my last evening with

265

you,' his fellow intelligencer said. 'Even to buy you a supper . . . but I see you're engaged elsewhere.'

'I am,' Marbeck said. 'I'm riding west.'

'To Chelsea?' Gifford raised an eyebrow. 'Better to go by the river, surely?'

'I've had enough of boats just now,' Marbeck replied. 'And of remaining where I can easily be found,' he added.

'I sniff the odour of dissent,' Gifford said. 'Not that I blame you, for I'm weary of Master Secretary myself. They say the Earl of Essex is plotting some sort of rebellion from his lair. Perhaps that'll keep our little crookback busy for a while.'

'And I hear you're bound for the Low Countries,' Marbeck said. 'Flushing, perhaps?'

'You may wager that I'll go there, sooner or later,' Gifford said in a casual tone. He frowned slightly. 'I won't enquire as to your welfare. I heard part of the tale from Prout – I can imagine the rest.'

'No doubt you can,' Marbeck said. He gripped Cobb's rein; with the din of passing traffic, the horse was becoming fretful. Gifford put a hand out and stroked his neck.

'A splendid beast,' he murmured. Suddenly, a thought struck him. 'I almost forgot: I have other news. It seems Sir Richard Scroop was caught with his force near Breda – got into a fearful tussle with the Spanish, I hear.'

Marbeck stared. 'You mean . . .'

'I do. He's dead – shot through the neck, they say.'

They stood still, surrounded by noise. A cart rumbled by, plodding out of Bishopsgate.

'Is this widely known?' Marbeck asked.

Gifford shook his head. 'Not yet. The news came in on the tide, I believe. Though word will be taken soon, to his widow.' He paused. 'Then, perhaps you'll wish to forestall the Crown's messenger?'

Their eyes met, and a wry smile appeared on Gifford's handsome features. '*Ecce Aurora*, eh?' he murmured. 'Or if not the dawn, then the promise of it?'

Then he stepped back, as Marbeck gripped the pommel of his saddle and swung himself up on to Cobb's back. The horse jerked, causing his master to tighten the rein.

'We'll take that supper when you return,' he said, leaning down. 'In the meantime, be mindful of the danger in Flushing.'

'Do you speak of the Spanish threat?' Gifford enquired. 'Or of other matters?'

'Both,' was his reply.

Putting heels to the horse's flanks, Marbeck shook the reins. At once Cobb sprang forward into the crowd. People fell back in alarm, calling to the rider to have a care.

But Gifford laughed, and watched him disappear through the great stone gateway into the city.

267